JOY RHOADES

Joy Rhoades was born in a small town in the bush in Queensland, Australia, with an early memory of flat country and a broad sky. At 13, Joy left for Brisbane, first for school and then to study law at university. After graduating, she worked all over the world as a lawyer. It was in New York that she completed a master's degree in Creative Writing

JOY RHOADES

The Woolgrower's Companion

VINTAGE

1 3 5 7 9 10 8 6 4 2

Vintage
20 Vauxhall Bridge Road,
London SW1V 2SA

Vintage is part of the Penguin Random House group of companies
whose addresses can be found at global.penguinrandomhouse.com

Penguin
Random House
UK

First published in Vintage in 2018
First published in hardback by Chatto & Windus in 2017

First published in Australia by Bantam in 2017

penguin.co.uk/vintage

A CIP catalogue record for this book is available from the British Library

ISBN 9781784705022

Printed and bound by Clays Ltd, St Ives plc

Penguin Random House is committed to a sustainable future
for our business, our readers and our planet. This book is made
from Forest Stewardship Council® certified paper.

For my family

PART I

CHAPTER 1

A lone sheep, until it no longer has strength to stand, will seek to return to its flock.

THE WOOLGROWER'S COMPANION, 1906

**Longhope Railway Station, New South Wales
10 January 1945**

The train carrying the prisoners of war was overdue. Kate sheltered in the shade of the station shed, wary, and watchful of her father, who stood along the tracks with the other graziers. Beyond them, pepperina trees flanked the road. The train tracks ran on across the valley bed with its handful of myalls and eucalypt gums, climbed up into the low hills at the edge of the tablelands and disappeared in a glint of summer heat on the southern horizon.

With her gloved hand Kate brushed away a fly. A drop of sweat ran between her shoulder blades and caught at the waist of her good frock, the wool crepe prickly and damp. Her father had asked Kate to come with him today and she'd worn her pink striped dress when he'd asked, her pearls too: it was easier to do as he said. But she felt like a barber's pole in the dress.

Down the tracks, her father, Ralph Stimson, stood ramrod straight, his grey hair short and neat. He wasn't concerned about the prisoners – glad to get them, even. But Kate was worried. To take in soldiers? Men who'd fought Australians in North Africa, fought her husband, Jack? To her, these POWs were still the enemy, even if Italy had changed sides.

She scratched at the nape of her neck. Kate had her plait up to come into town, pinned in place under her hat but keen to escape. Her wayward hair always reminded her of her mother. At fifteen, Kate had cried in her arms, cried that she was stick-like with a head of No. 8 fencing wire. Her mother had hugged her. 'But you *are* pretty,' she'd said. 'Just in a different way. And anyway being fair-haired and curvy doesn't get the washing in.'

A pair of black cockatoos watched from a branch of a dead pepperina tree. Kate felt the sweat gathering in her nylons between her legs and shifted her feet apart a little. It made no difference. She moved deeper into the shade and glanced again at her father. She loved him dearly but he was volatile – excitable, her mother had called it. He should be all right for the moment, though, as he stood with his men, Ed Storch and Keith Grimes. Grimes was their manager. In his fifties, he was about the same age as her father, and they were both returned servicemen from the First War. But Grimes looked younger, not yet grey and without her father's weariness. And Grimes was taller and broader, with heavy eyebrows and a firm mouth. The other man, Ed, Kate liked. At twenty-one he was younger than Kate by two years. He had arms the size of tree trunks, but with his gammy foot he wasn't fit for service. You'd never know about the foot once he was on a horse, though. He'd been their head stockman since the war started. He was dark, with olive skin that went black in the sun, and Grimes reckoned he must be part Aboriginal. But her father liked Ed, and respected him, so Grimes kept quiet.

Ed waved at her and pointed towards the horizon. A shape expanded from a dot into an engine and carriages, smoke and dust trailing behind. Soon she felt the first vibrations in the ground under her feet. As the tremors welled, the din merged into a swell of steam and power. The train's engine, an outsize bottle-green drum, pulled two passenger carriages and a long, long line of empty cattle wagons, ready for stock to feed the troops.

The vibrations, the funnel of the train and its black smoke brought it back to her, the time a bit less than two years before when Kate had been there at the station to farewell Jack. Met and wed and then he was gone, all in just five months. Her mother wanted to see Kate settled before she died, and Kate was glad to do that for her. She loved Jack too, of course, and wondered what he was doing right at that moment, whether he was out in the heat of the afternoon. Probably shouting orders at new soldiers, cranky to be in Sydney training men instead of fighting.

A blast of the train whistle jolted her, and steel shrieked against steel amid fumes and heat. Coughing lungfuls of thick air, she put her hands over her ears as the train screeched to a stop. Through the smoke and steam, she saw an Army staff car coming in from the main road.

The smoke drifted away to show weary soldiers standing guard on the end platforms of the first carriage. Garrison battalion, to guard the POWs. The windows of both carriages, heavy with soot, had been fixed shut but for a slit of two inches at the top. The carriage next to the graziers looked empty except for a small shape moving along inside. But the first carriage, the one stopped close to Kate, was full, the inside a solid block of plum colour. She'd read that the bright colour was chosen to make it easy for the public to spot an escaping prisoner of war. Magenta, the *Tablelands Clarion* had called it.

'*Bella*,' Kate heard from the carriage. '*Eh! Ciao, bella!*'

The meaning was clear and she ducked behind the shed.

'*Aw, bella!*'

5

Her face hot, Kate had a narrow view through the gap between the shed and the tank – of a soldier on the dirt by the carriage – but with luck the POWs couldn't see her.

Key in hand, the soldier waved his clipboard for attention. 'Afternoon, all. I'm Corporal Boyle.'

Oil, the locals had christened him. He checked his clipboard and then called into the crowd, 'Amiens!' He pronounced it properly, the *s* silent. Kate's father had named their property for the First War battle in France, where he'd lost so many friends.

'Ami – bloody – en!' Oil yelled again.

'Yes,' Keith Grimes replied, curt. The big man went through the crowd, in his uniform of sorts: riding boots, moleskin trousers and blue shirt. Shotgun in arms, Grimes stopped in front of the corporal, his face set. Grimes had been a POW of the Germans in the First War, one of the few Australians to have that honour. He had no time for enemy of any kind.

Ed limped over to stand behind Grimes, moving his bad foot up to the good.

'Where you going, Twinkle Toes?' Oil said to him.

'That'll do, thank you, Corporal.' A captain had come out of the staff car and through the crowd. He was older, with a handsome face ruddy from the sun. He climbed the ladder to the carriage-end platform, the khaki cloth of his uniform jacket taut across his back.

'Afternoon, gents. I'm Captain James Rook, head of the new POW Control Centre. A few words. First, we expect you will find these men willing and inexpensive.'

A voice floated from the back of the crowd: 'They're costing us Australian jobs.' Frank Jamieson, the editor of the *Tablelands Clarion*. He was at the back of the crowd, his unlit pipe in his mouth as always. Jack's crude description of him popped into her head: *Big temper, small dick*.

Jamieson moved his pipe about like a horse with an

uncomfortable bit. 'We should ship them home now. Before the Eye-ties switch sides again,' he shouted.

Kate sympathised. His son Doug was in a POW camp in Singapore, a prisoner of the Japanese.

'Your paper's reported it, Mr Jamieson. Italy might've joined the Allies but all Italian POWs *remain* prisoners. We are putting them to work, here and in other districts, to relieve the labour shortage in essential industry.'

Jamieson shook his head. 'They'll stay after the war too.'

'All POWs will be shipped back to Italy when the war's over.' The captain kept his eyes on Jamieson, and the editor said nothing more.

'Most of these men were conscripts – they're gentle and easily led. You've been issued the Army phrase book for talking to them, yes? And you might find the words "*Hai capito?*" handy. They mean "Do you understand?"' He repeated the words for the crowd. '"*Hai. Capito.*" You should expect a lot of handwaving too. Normal with these blokes when they talk. All right?' Speech over, the captain dropped to the ground from the first rung of the ladder. 'Get on with it, Corporal. Get em outta there. That carriage must be hotter'n Hades.' He moved a few feet along the tracks.

Up on the narrow platform, the corporal unlocked and slid open the door. 'Orright, you blokes. Step lively when I say your name. Canali,' he called into the carriage, his eyes on his clipboard. 'Luca Canali. Get your boots out here.'

A man appeared, compact and neat in the plum-coloured POW uniform. But he was most foreign-looking, with a very dark complexion, black, black hair cut close to his head, and a five-o'clock shadow under a substantial nose. Kate had seen foreigners before, of course: Chinese vegetable growers and Indian hawkers. She knew Aborigines too, lots of them – their stockmen and Daisy, their half-caste house help, the other little ones at the Domestic Training Home. But this man was different. Young, in his mid-twenties perhaps, the only evidence of his long journey was the sweat ringing the armpits of his uniform and the battered portmanteau he gripped in one hand.

He set the case down next to him on the transom, and moved straight to attention, eyes front. He seemed to rest on the balls of his feet, ready, sinew and force. More soldier than prisoner, he didn't seem 'gentle' or 'easily led'. Then with shock Kate realised that he was looking at her. She pulled back, embarrassed.

'Off the train, Canali,' the corporal called. '*Hai capito?*'

Unhurriedly, the POW climbed down the ladder. Grimes moved forward at the same time, shotgun in arms. Still facing the train, the POW lifted his case down. He turned and looked into the muzzle of Grimes's shotgun, pointing at his chest from three feet away.

Half a head or more shorter than the man with the gun on him, the POW didn't flinch. He stood, locked still, his eyes on Grimes, though his knuckles were white on the suitcase handle.

The captain moved towards the two men, carefully, purposefully. 'You can put the shotgun away.'

Grimes stayed where he was, the muzzle aimed at the POW's chest until the captain stepped between them. He reached for the muzzle and steered it dirt-wards. 'You'll put it away,' he said again.

Grimes resisted. Then with a grunt, he stepped back.

'Carry on, Corporal.' The captain stayed next to the POW.

'Bottinella. Private Vittorio Bottinella,' Oil called.

A second prisoner appeared on the carriage-end platform, clutching a grey duffel bag against his bright uniform. This man had a thick beard but was swarthy and skinny like the first.

'Righto, Blackbeard. On the dirt,' the corporal said.

The man hesitated, looking at Grimes. The captain waved him along with a frown and the POW dropped his bag over the side, climbing down after it. When he turned towards the crowd, his head was drooped and he clasped shaking hands together.

The officer reached up for the clipboard. 'Mr Stimson? Ralph Stimson of Amiens?' he said to Grimes.

As her father went forwards, Kate shuddered. That first man would surely come to Amiens.

'You got these two, Mr Stimson.' The captain flipped over a page on the clipboard, and pulled a thin file from under the list. He opened it. 'Basic information. Canali's a sergeant, twenty-four. Bottinella, the one with the beard, is a private. He's twenty-one. He arrived here in '41 from a camp in India. The Canali chap's only been in Australia since last year.'

'Any English?' Kate's father asked. He frowned, knocking one boot against the other to shift some manure.

The captain looked again at the file. 'You're in luck. Canali – no beard – he's got some. Guard at the Hay Camp taught him, apparently. Not the other fellow.'

'They ride?'

'Yes, according to this.'

'Orright,' Kate heard her father say. 'These blokes'll come in handy. Amiens carries eight stockmen plus a manager usually. Now I'm down to four men and I'm counting two Abos in that. Better than a poke in the eye with a burnt stick.'

She hoped there'd be nothing worse from him today, with so many people about. But her father took the file he was offered, and walked away towards their truck. Grimes motioned for the POWs to move along as well. He cradled his shotgun in his arms, ready enough.

When Kate could no longer see the Amiens men through the gap, she followed but round behind the crowd. She hoped her father remembered they were collecting a boy, too, off the train: a distant relative of Grimes's from Wollongong.

The calling of the POWs went on and another pair of grim, skinny men jumped down onto the dirt by the train.

At the second carriage, Ed Storch pulled himself halfway up the ladder, hopping his good leg up one rung at a time. He yelled, 'Harry Grimes! You about?'

A boy of ten or so appeared, mostly hidden by an old suitcase, with a scruff of fair hair visible above and skinny legs below. He lowered the suitcase, and Kate could see he needed to wipe his nose.

She wanted to think his frown was a squint against the sun. This boy's mother had died when he was born, and his father was killed at Tobruk. The grandmother was too ill to look after him, which left only Grimes. Grimes might have his hands full, and he had no experience, no wife or kids of his own.

The suitcase slipped from the boy's hands and landed on his foot. 'Bugger,' he said.

Kate's father raised his eyebrows and looked across at Grimes, but the manager had not heard; his eyes were on the POWs. The boy shoved the suitcase off the edge of the carriage platform and it hit the dirt next to Ed with a hollow thud.

'Hullo, Harry. I'm Ralph Stimson from Amiens. That's your uncle over there. Great-uncle, is it?'

Grimes nodded a greeting but the boy kept his eyes down. Kate's father went off towards the Amiens car and truck. Ed followed, then the POWs, with Grimes behind.

Kate went over to the boy. 'Hullo, Harry. Shall we go?'

The boy scuffed at a near-dead tuft of buffel grass. 'Who are you then?'

'I'm Kate – Mrs – Dowd. I live on Amiens, too.'

'So?'

He reminded Kate of a baby magpie, never still; peck you soon as look at you. She watched the POWs and the others walking towards the truck.

'Thirsty, eh,' Harry said.

'What's that?' She was distracted. 'There's a water bag at the truck.'

Above them, the cockatoo pair wheeled off, black dots on the cloudless sky, but they turned south. East would have been better, east towards the coast. Black cockatoos headed for the shelter of the seaboard before a big wet. They needed rain, as the drought was in its fifth year.

The suitcase banged against the boy's leg as they walked. Kate was surprised to see Addison, the local bank johnny, speaking to her father at the truck.

'I will be clear. You must —' Addison stopped. 'Mrs Dowd,' he said. He looked back at her father. 'We'll take this up again, Ralph.'

They watched Addison get into his car.

'What's wrong, Dad?'

'Nothin. Addison's a drongo.'

Grimes usually drove, but today Ed got behind the wheel, as Grimes stood guard in the truck tray with his back against the cab, the prisoners at his feet. Up close, the two POWs looked sullen and dusty, the younger one with a piece of grass caught in his beard. Canali, the other one, wiped at the sweat on his brow with the back of his hand and stole another glance at Kate.

'Let's get going, Ed,' Kate said, trying to ignore the POW.

CHAPTER 2

As to Australia's proud place as keeper of so much of the world's sheep, it may safely be said to spring from the arrival, in 1796, of the first Merino to these shores.

THE WOOLGROWER'S COMPANION, 1906

Kate was glad to be with her father and Harry in the safety of their Hudson. She kept her eyes on the side mirror, watching the Amiens truck as they went through Longhope, past the houses, the pubs and the churches, the stock and station agents and the sapphire buyers. They crossed the dry creek bed that wound through the town like a snake, and then her father turned the vehicle onto the main road running west. 'Now, off to Amiens,' he said, settling into the driver's seat. The drive home was nineteen miles, at least an hour, of mostly straight dirt road, at this time of day directly into the western sun.

'Harry, you'll have the time of your life on Amiens.' Her father was not much of a talker, but for some odd reason he seemed to have taken a shine to the boy. Harry was lost in the bench seat, eyes on the bush spinning by.

'Four-hundred-odd head of cattle, seven thousand or so sheep. Merinos, all of em. Best wool in the world.'

'Why's that, then?'

'Merino's the finest. Makes the best cloth. And it's all

12

Merino in this district. And us? We've got a lot of country. Fourteen thousand acres.'

'A helluva lot,' Harry said.

Her father laughed. 'A good bit of dirt, as they say in the bush. Weren't always, of course. I built her up from a soldier settler block after the First War to the biggest in the district.'

The boy nodded.

In the driver's seat Stimson smiled. 'You know, an Abo fella – a stockman – he said to me once, "We don't own the land, boss." Well, of course Abos don't own land. But you know what he said then, this old bloke? "The land owns us. The land owns us." I think that fella might have been onto something. Amiens? It owns me. Have to look after it.'

In the mirror, Kate saw Harry's head drop back, resting in the corner between the bench seat and the car door. The drive would put him to sleep, no doubt, after nine long hours on the train from Sydney. The miles went by, Kate's eyes shifting between her father, the side mirror with the Amiens truck behind them, and the horizon. POWs or no POWs, she liked this time of day, the late afternoon turning the leaves and trunks of the gums pink. These colours leaked into the sky, soft pinks and reds creeping up into the clouds from the horizon as the sun dipped. But with a pink sky, there'd be no rain the next day.

Red sky at night, shepherd's delight. She'd grown up with the saying but always found it odd. It must have been an English shepherd, a shepherd with too much rain rather than too little. A red sky here made no one happy.

'Here we are.' Her father turned the big Hudson off the main road. He slowed the vehicle to a crawl to cross the stock grid, and they shuddered over it, coming to a stop just beyond. 'It's land like this, Harry,' her father said of Amiens, 'land, or somethin y'can hold in y'hand. Not money in the bank. A bank'll take your money and pull the rug out soon as look at you.'

13

Her father put the vehicle into gear. 'An there's a lot t'be proud of. Forty-odd-thousand reasons.'

'*Dad!*' Kate looked back. Fortunately, Harry was asleep. 'Dad, please don't mention money to Harry.'

He shrugged.

Kate looked out to her right at the dam. At least that was a constant. She loved the dam, even in a drought and even with its history; it had been built when her father had cut off the creeks from the neighbours below. Tonight its surface was graveyard-still in the dusk light, broken only by the bare trunks of drowned trees. As much dried mud as water now, it still ran at least a hundred yards across, and they were so lucky to have that water.

She looked up the hill to the line of bunya pines, the tall evergreen conifers hiding much of the squat homestead. As the car came out of the gully, a lorikeet shot up from the track ahead and then the dogs were upon them, barking and leaping.

Her father brought them to a stop outside the double gates. 'This is the homestead, Harry,' he said.

'He's asleep, Dad.'

Her father ignored her. 'She's got a beaut garden, even in this dry. And a bowerbird. Kate'll show ya.'

Out of the car, her father stretched and rubbed the base of his neck. Kate leaned over to the backseat to nudge the sleeping Harry awake. The pup, Rusty, jumped up and put his head and paws in Kate's open window for a pat. Ed thought Rusty wasn't the full quid but Kate had a soft spot for the pup. She got out and Harry unwound from the car slowly, like a possum from a hole in a tree.

'What's that then?' he said, pointing to a fenced area away beyond the homestead.

'It's private,' Kate said. 'It's my mother's grave.'

He looked again, appraisingly. 'Big enough for all of yez, eh.'

She was taken aback, until she remembered he'd lost his own mum.

'What about that?' Harry pointed again.

'The meat house. For hanging the carcasses.'

'You mean a stiff?'

Kate laughed. 'No, a sheep carcass. Or a bullock. For eating.'

Rusty and the other dogs, Puck and Gunner, lost interest in the men in the truck and came back. Rusty took a sniff at Harry's privates, and the boy backed away and the pup chased, thinking he was on for a game. Harry was stuck up against the car, the dogs hemming him in.

'They're just being friendly,' Kate said. 'The pup, the one with the patch on his ear and his eye, that's Rusty. Puck's the big one, the blue heeler with the piece out of his tail. The third one's Gunner.'

Harry stayed put up against the car, his back arched away from the dogs.

'They won't hurt you, truly. Let's get you over to your uncle. C'mon.'

Harry frowned but followed her across to the truck, trailed by the dogs. There Kate nodded a hullo at the two men, Johnno and Spinks – Amiens' only remaining stockmen – who'd appeared from the yards. They'd worked on Amiens since the war, when the white stockmen had all joined up. Aboriginal men could not enlist, officially anyhow. But that was the silver lining for the graziers. Grimes had them working out in the paddocks or cutting feed and fixing fences, though Kate suspected they preferred to be in the bush by themselves and away from Grimes. She knew she would.

'That a uniform?' Harry asked.

Kate laughed. Both lanky, the men were in identical get-ups, ration-issue clothes bought with Amiens' coupons – the same straight brown dungarees, big-buckled belts, white shirts rolled up to their elbows, and ten-gallon hats.

She glanced across at the POWs. The bearded one, Bottinella, had climbed down from the truck. Canali hadn't moved, was standing in the back of the tray, looking about with his odd pale eyes.

Harry was staring at the two stockmen. 'I never seen boongs up close before.'

'You shouldn't say that. Boongs, I mean. It's not nice. Aren't there lots of Aborigines in Wollongong anyhow?'

'Nuh,' he said, his eyes on the stockmen. 'They cleaned em out years ago.'

Johnno saw Harry staring and came over slowly. 'You orright, mate?'

'This is Harry,' Kate said. 'This is John Banning – but everyone calls him Johnno – and Billy Spinks.'

Johnno smiled, a missing front tooth smile.

'You lost y'tooth,' Harry said.

Johnno's hand went to his mouth and worry creased the stockman's face. 'Spinksy hit me agin this mornin, eh.'

'I decked im. I got a short fuse, like ole Grimesy.' Spinks loomed over the boy and Harry shrank back.

'Cut it out, Billy. Y'scarin im,' Johnno said. Billy grinned and the pair of them faded back to the truck.

'Johnno's always stirring for a laugh,' Kate said. 'Your uncle'll be finished soon, and then he'll take you to the manager's cottage. You want to come with me, for now?'

He followed her across the house paddock and through the white wooden gates. A black chook picked its way up the inside of the house fence. Kate went past it, round the circular drive in front of the homestead and up the short verandah staircase at the side, near the big veggie garden. She had to step over the black–and–white cat lying across the middle rung.

Harry stopped at the cat.

'That's the house cat, Peng. Peng for penguin because she's black and white.'

'Fat cat. She preggers?'

'No, no. Just round.'

'You got kids?' Harry asked.

'What? No.'

'But y'hitched?'

She nodded, feeling the familiar pang of failure. It had only been a few months though, that she and Jack had been together as a married couple, just while his hand wound healed, before he got classed as fit again. He'd taken to her and to the district like a duck to water. Met, courted, married, gone off to fight again, all too fast. But no baby.

Daisy, the Aboriginal domestic, appeared in the kitchen doorway. She was sweet and gangly with a big head, a skinny body and long legs, hidden today in a shapeless brown dress, government issue, a remnant of the Home.

'Boss want tea, Missus?'

'Yes. Please. Oh, and Daisy – this is Harry Grimes.'

The girl nodded a hullo but she didn't look at the boy. Harry ignored her too.

'Daisy? I'd stay out of sight for a bit, away from those men. You know?' Kate said.

The girl nodded, frowning, and went back into the kitchen.

'She a half-caste? Where she come from?' Harry asked.

'The Domestic Training Home in town. But she lives here now.'

'When she see her mum and dad?'

Kate paused. 'She doesn't. She's from Broken Hill, way out west. But she goes to the Mission once a month on a Sunday. For church.'

'To make up for it? That's piss-poor.'

Kate's father came in through the gate. 'Cuppa tea, Kate? Bet young Harry'd like a bikkie too.' He didn't wait for her answer and went up the steps.

17

Bikkies for Harry, no less. Kate wondered whether she would have to look after this odd little boy.

Outside, Grimes was shifting the POWs. 'Move out,' he called. Ed went first and the bearded POW followed along the track towards the single men's quarters, a chook hurrying out of their way. The other POW took his time but there was efficiency in the way he moved; nothing was without forethought.

'Come on then, Harry. Let's get this tea,' Kate said.

'*Gorn!*' Grimes shouted and Kate looked back, surprised that Grimes would use a command for the dogs on a POW. But it was for Rusty. The pup was chasing sheep, a wether, in the paddock just beyond the house, just for the fun.

'Git im!' Grimes shouted again and whistled up the other dogs. They went after the pup and cut him out and away from the sheep. With no dog behind it, the wether slowed to a stop, its fleece brown with dust after months without rain.

Rusty was lucky it had not been a ram he picked on; a ram would have a go at a dog. Kate made a note in her head to tell her father that Rusty might be a chaser. Then she thought better of it – she didn't want to trouble him. But Rusty had better learn.

~

A half hour later, Kate, her father and even Harry were seated in the wicker chairs on the house's eastern verandah, having tea. A blue shirt appeared over the rise from the single men's quarters: Mr Grimes. When he got close and saw Harry sitting up with his boss, his brows set with disapproval. Kate agreed. There was a strict hierarchy in the bush, and the children of the stockmen, even of the manager, did not take tea with the grazier's family.

With Grimes just below them on the mostly dead lawn, Kate poured the tea, offering him a cup by convention. He, in turn, shook his head.

'We'll take the Italians out first thing tomorrow so they get the lay of the land,' her father said, a booted foot jiggling as he spoke. 'Get em into the routine – checkin fences, cuttin feed for the sheep and for the cattle, too.'

Grimes said nothing, his eyes on the boy in the verandah chair above him.

'Got em settled in at the quarters?' Her father stirred two spoons of sugar into his tea and reached for one of Daisy's scones, spread with a little precious butter and some jam.

'Yeah. Ed's camped out up there to keep an eye on em, with a shotgun. But I tell you, I reckon —' Grimes stopped and frowned at Harry as he licked the butter and jam off his scone.

Kate was distracted by her father, who was scratching hard at his groin. '*Dad*,' she urged, a half-whisper, and he stopped.

Grimes either hadn't seen it or chose not to. 'Anyhow, I reckon we need a few more blokes up there tonight. In case they go on the run.'

Her father laughed. 'Where they gunna hide? Here?' He waved a hand out across the property, its miles of bare paddocks.

'That first fella? Canali? Don't turn y'back on im. An they might come after *us*, if you get my drift.' Grimes looked at Kate. 'She should know how to use your revolver, boss.'

'I'm tellin ya. Not dangerous.' Her father was starting to get annoyed. He stood up, brushing the crumbs off his hands at the edge of the verandah.

Grimes changed tack. 'Another thing, boss. I need the cheque for the men's pay.'

'What?' Her father was distracted, still annoyed.

'It's Friday. Payday.'

'I'll get the cheque-book,' Kate said. She ran to the kitchen, got the cheque-book then put it down, open, in front of her father. She held out a pen. 'I can write it if you like,' she said, reaching for the book. She'd seen him do it. 'I make it out to *Cash*, don't I?' She went ahead, finding the amount of the previous week's pay on the stub and writing the figure well clear of the *Amiens Pastoral Company* signature line. He signed and she handed the cheque down to Grimes on the lawn below. He slipped it into the breast pocket of his shirt.

'Orright. See ya at first light, then. C'mon, Harry.' Grimes put his hat on and went.

The boy stood up but stayed put, with one small hand on the armrest of the wicker chair.

'C'mon.' Grimes's tone was brusque from the gate. Harry grabbed an extra scone on his way and ran to follow his uncle's march across the flat. He caught up and fell in, and blew raspberries in time, one for each step marched, until Grimes gave him a filthy look and Harry stopped.

Inside Kate could hear Daisy in the kitchen, the clang of a saucepan. She tried to think of a way to ask her father about Addison and the bank. But they sat, silent, in the dusk. A flash of green and blue caught Kate's eye over the drive. A rainbow lorikeet swooped across from the big Californian pine to join two others in the black-branched wattle by the side gate. On the fence line with the stringybark paddock something moved. A rabbit, foraging.

'Bit prickly,' Kate said to her father. 'The boy Harry, I mean.'

'Mebbe.' Her father rubbed his hand backwards and forwards over the salt and pepper stubble of his short back and sides. 'He's had a bad trot. Which reminds me,' he said. He got up and went along the verandah and into the office, boots and all. Boots came off at the door in the bush; it was universal in homesteads in case dirt or spiders or ticks were onboard. But her father was forgetting now, sometimes.

She could hear him shifting things about in the office. 'What are you looking for, Dad?' He reappeared carrying her old draughts box and a dusty jigsaw puzzle, a map of Australia. 'You want to play?'

He grinned, blowing dust off the top of the draughts box.

'You used to let me win, Dad.' She smiled. 'All the time.'

'Well, they're not for you. For Harry. He can do the puzzle on the end o' the kitchen table.'

She tried not to be annoyed, about the kitchen table or about Harry. They sat in silence for a time, with the soft backdrop of Daisy moving about in the kitchen. Kate needed to get on with it.

'What did Mr Addison want today?'

'What?' Her father studied the draughts on the board.

'Mr Addison. From the bank.'

'Nothin. Had his facts wrong.' He stood up and went inside, boots on, leaving the games.

Kate stood too and hurled the dregs of her tea onto the lawn, aiming for one of the yellow clumps. By now, the sky had turned a deep pink as the last of the sun slipped behind the blue-black of Mount Perseverance, right on the edge of Amiens. *Red sky at night, shepherd's delight.* Pommie bastard shepherds, her father would say. She stacked the cups and saucers onto the tray and went in. She needed to find the keys. They never locked the homestead doors, but she would now.

CHAPTER 3

While boldness in a ram may portend vigour in its offspring, belligerence means danger for all.

THE WOOLGROWER'S COMPANION, 1906

Just before half past six the next morning, Kate and her father sat at the kitchen table eating their way through a wordless breakfast, the *plip-plop* of Daisy's shoes against the lino the only sound in the house.

'You wan another chop, Missus?'

Kate shook her head, her mouth full.

'Daisy's the one who should have the damn chop. Skin and bone.'

Kate looked hard at her father. Embarrassed, Daisy turned away to the sink. She was only fourteen. But she was skinny, as skinny as the POWs – that was the truth, no matter how much Kate encouraged her to eat. She hoped the girl wasn't still pining for her family.

'You too, Janice,' her father said. 'You're skin and bone.'

'What's that, Dad?'

'Like when we got married. You were skinny then too.'

'I'm Kate, Dad.'

'What?' he said, looking at her.

'It's me, Kate,' she said, worried. 'Not Mum.'

22

He shook his head and went back to his chops.

Kate stared at him.

'Mornin, boss.' Grimes tapped on the frame of the gauze door. As he came in, Daisy disappeared into the laundry.

Grimes had the Amiens pay ledger tucked under one arm and he put it on the end of the kitchen table.

Her father kept eating. 'They saddled up?'

Grimes started to laugh, scratching an eyebrow. 'Here's the bloody thing,' he said. 'The dagos. They can't ride.'

Kate wondered if her father would pull Grimes up over the slur but he did not.

'The captain fella said they could,' he said, mildly.

'I swear. The young'un – Bottinella? I sent im out to catch the horses about an hour ago. But he doesn't know a horse's arse from its fetlock. Sorry, miss.'

Kate nodded. She reminded herself that with her father more and more unreliable, she was lucky they had Grimes.

'Can't ride, eh?'

'Nope. Not a flamin clue.'

Her father frowned. 'You better teach em.'

'Not sure y'can learn these buggers.' Grimes went out, letting the door bang behind him. Peng shot away into the corridor as the blue of Grimes's shirt disappeared off towards the yards.

Her father stood. 'I'll be off then. Back for lunch,' he said. He blew his nose on his napkin and rolled the fabric into the silver-plate ring. Kate retrieved it and put it aside for the dirty clothes. He pulled his boots on at the back door and was gone.

Kate spotted her father's forgotten hat on the bench. And mixing her up for her mother? She frowned, picked up the hat and went through the hall onto the back verandah. The hat was old but still in one piece, the rabbit felt soft in her hand, with a broad brim and a hole at the top of its pinch crown. He wore it so much he looked undressed without it. But now he was hatless, already halfway to the yards.

'Cooee!' Kate tried again: 'Cooooee!'

But he didn't hear her.

She went back to the kitchen with the hat. 'You know, Daisy, you need to be careful of the POWs. They might try to do a line for you. You'd have to go back to the Home if anything happened.'

Daisy nodded over the washing, unsmiling. Kate returned to her toast, glad the girl understood. By all accounts, the Home was strict. It probably had to be, with dozens of girls, all half-castes like Daisy. They had to be fed and clothed, taught please and thank you, and stopped from speaking their own languages.

Kate put the tin basin inside the sink and ran a little water into it for the washing up. Before the war, she had never washed up, as they'd had more house help. Now Daisy was all they could get so the two of them did everything between them.

As she scrubbed the chop pan, Kate thought about what Addison, the bank manager, might have meant. With her father off at the yards, she was tempted to go into the office to see what she could find in the way of bank statements. Then again, Addison was a drongo, as her father put it. She put the pan on the sink to dry, wiped her hands and collected the broom from the cupboard.

On the verandah, she started in the corner nearest the kitchen, sweeping her way backwards and forwards, past the beans in the veggie garden, heaping the leaves and dust into a neat pile up against the house wall, always with one eye on the office door, fighting the temptation to look. A gust of wind threw leaves hard against the corrugated iron of the homestead roof and blew her pile of swept leaves about as well. She cursed it and started again.

She saw the dogs shoot off down towards the gully. It was

mail day. Kate left the broom in the V of the verandah's Isabella grape vine and went in. In the kitchen, Daisy was making scones on the marble end of the table. It still sometimes caught Kate by surprise to see Daisy preparing food, and she was careful not to tell anyone the girl cooked for them. Aboriginal girls weren't ever to touch the food, for fear of contamination. But Kate had decided when Daisy arrived that was silly. And no one had got sick either.

Daisy was dividing the scone dough, cutting delicate circles with a floury upturned glass.

'Hold still,' Kate said and wiped flour from Daisy's cheek with a tea towel. 'You're good at scones, Daisy.'

'Me mum's recipe.'

'She a good cook?'

In the awkwardness that followed, Daisy nodded quickly, her eyes on the dough.

Kate turned away, mad with herself. She shouldn't be talking about family with Daisy. The matron at the Home had warned her against it.

Peng was curled up on the seat, unworried by the barking. 'Siddown, Rusty,' a man called. The barking stopped, and Daisy disappeared with the egg basket, escaping to the chook run.

'G'day, Mrs D.' Mick Maguire filled the kitchen doorway. A whisker over six foot, and round too, although his girth was partly hidden today by the Amiens weekly bread order. He also had a rolled up *Tablelands Clarion* and the week's post. 'There's a letter in there for yez, Mrs D, from that handsome man o' yours. On top.' Maguire winked at Kate. She pounced and put the letter from Jack in her apron pocket, desperate to open it, just not in front of Mr Maguire.

'Cup of tea?' she asked.

'Wouldn't say no. Got your POWs, I hear?'

Kate took Daisy's scones out of the stove. But there was

only a little sugar in the bowl and, rationing or no rationing, Mick had a sweet tooth.

'Back in a jiffy,' she said, holding the sugar bowl. She picked up the post and pushed open the hall door.

'Few bills in there, eh.' The mailman's voice followed her.

She stopped, looking at the letters in her hand. She never looked at the post.

Kate pulled the rubber band off the bundle and flicked through the envelopes. There were nine, all addressed either to her father or to *Amiens Pastoral Company*. Four were stamped *Overdue*; one from Mr Babbin, their stock and station agent; one from *The Pastoralist*, the periodical that her father liked, although less so of late; the third from Darcy's, the engineering shop in town; and the last from Nettiford's, the haberdasher-cum-general shop in Longhope. Kate held these four, two in each hand, and stared at them. It didn't make sense. Her father was scrupulous about paying bills on time.

'Jack still at Kogarah?' Maguire called. 'In Sydney, isn't it?'

'Yes.' She got the sugar and went back to the kitchen. 'As soon as his hand healed, and he managed to get it working again, the Army posted him to train new recruits. He's been at Kogarah since, chafing at the bit to get back to the fighting.'

'Good thing he's safe here, eh. You seen that plane stuff in the paper? The Japs is usin planes as bombs again, crazy pilots blowin emselves up in the Philippines.' Maguire put his mug down and pulled the rubber band off the rolled-up *Tablelands Clarion*.

'Heaven help us,' Kate said.

'It'll take years, they reckon. To beat em.'

That's what she had heard too. 'I'll take a quick look at Jack's letter.'

'You do that.'

Kate pushed open the verandah door to step outside. His letter was just one page, the usual. A letter from him at all was rare as hens' teeth: he was busy with his work. This one was not too much blacked out by the censors. And it had only taken a month to arrive.

Dear Kate,
*   I hope you and the Boss are well, and that Longhope is holding up in the drought.*

Funny that he mentioned the district, rather than Amiens. Jack had taken to the locals; made some mates. He was different from her father, who didn't give a hoot what people thought.

*   Kogarah is still full of conscripted blokes. Wheelbarrows, they call them, because they have to be pushed. We train ▮▮▮▮ of them a month now, more troops for the Islands and even maybe Japan one day.*
*   I've had a gutful of playing soldiers, teaching these blokes. It was my bloody luck I didn't get back to the fighting in '42, as soon as my hand got better. But not long to wait now. I'm trying to swing a posting back to the fighting. I hear I ▮▮▮▮ or maybe even ▮▮▮▮ later this year, up into ▮▮.*

Kate went cold. Jack might be overseas already.

*   The tucker is still bad, and the Yanks' rations are better than ours. Once in a blue moon I'm off and I get a lift into the centre of Sydney for a good feed. We got the news that General Rommel is dead. Cheers here, I can tell you.*
*   Love,*
*   Jack*

He was never one for flowery words, but Kate was glad to hear from him. She hoped he was still training wheelbarrows, not back in the islands on the front. She reread the few lines then folded the letter, put it in her apron pocket and went back into the kitchen.

Maguire took two scones, one with each hand, and put them on his plate. 'How your POWs gettin on, then?'

'Good.' He was a bit of a gossip so she was careful not to say much.

'They funny buggers? I hear they're funny buggers. Little blokes.'

Kate said nothing.

'Out in the run, are they? Your Eye-ties?'

'No. At the yards.'

'Yards, eh?'

'I'll walk you out,' she said; he was angling to see the POWs. She set the tea things in the basin and gave him her weekly letter to Jack to post. Then she went for her hat on its peg at the gauze door. She liked the hat. It had been a hand-me-down from her mother.

'You seen them bills in your post?'

Kate paused, looking at her hat in her hand, and she took her time in turning back. If they *were* short of money, it would not help to have Maguire know that. 'Dad's been here since the First War. I'm sure we're all right. But with a place as big as ours, people will always talk, don't you think?' She smiled at him and put her hat on.

She walked so fast across the lawn towards the wooden gate and his truck, he had to move to catch her. Out the back of the house, Daisy was at the clothes line, wrestling with a white sheet in the breeze. Above her, two rainbow lorikeets, a flash of bright green and blue and yellow, swooped across, screeching from the bottom of the garden to the jacaranda tree. Daisy stopped, her hands on the sheet, her eyes following them. She loved the lorikeets.

'See ya, Daisy,' Maguire called. She delivered a half-wave, bumping the sheet on the line with her hand, then disappeared into the washing.

'She's shy, your Dais. She ever smile?'

'She's better than she was when we first got her. Took her a while to settle in here after the Home.' In fact, it was Ed who could make Daisy laugh out loud. She suspected the stockman had a crush on Daisy, but she certainly wouldn't tell gossipy Maguire that.

After Kate got Maguire into his truck and watched it retreat down the hill towards the creek crossing, she collected her father's hat and headed for the yards.

Once over the rise, she could see the men, with Harry, and all eyes were on the ring. Grimes had the bearded POW in there with Mustard, one of their young stock horses.

'You forgot your hat, Dad.' Kate gave it to her father and turned back towards the house.

'You should stick around.'

Kate stopped, uncomfortable; the only woman among these men. Next to her, Ed had his stock whip as always, coiled and hooked onto his belt. Buffalo Bill, Grimes called him, as most used whips only for cattle work, not sheep. But Kate knew Ed was always prepared, in case he came across a cranky scrubber in the wrong paddock, or a ram that wouldn't back off.

In the ring, Grimes held the stock horse's bit but Mustard shook her head unhappily. Not their quietest, she was an odd choice for a teaching mount. The bearded POW, his shirt half untucked now, hung his head but kept a wary eye on Mustard. Kate noticed a scar on his arm that she hadn't seen at the station: a long scar. Eight or so inches and up to half an inch wide in places, it ran from below his elbow to the back of his bicep. It was purple and white – a wound that had healed badly. He looked scared, and Mustard would know that. 'Dogs and horses smell fear,' her father always used to say.

The bearded POW opened his mouth and took a breath. He grabbed the pommel of the saddle with his right hand and hitched his foot up, trying to get his boot into the stirrup. He failed and dropped the foot to the dirt again. Mustard flicked her tail and pulled up with her head, once and then again.

'Bottinella!' Grimes yelled. 'Reins. Pommel. Stirrup.' He pointed out each item as he went through the list, the reins still hooked round his arm. 'Up. Orright?' His voice was loud, as if the man was hard of hearing.

Bottinella looked blank.

'Get outta the bloody way and I'll show ya,' Grimes said. 'Watch me. Reins. Pommel. Stirrup. Up.' In one fluid move, he mounted Mustard. The horse seemed relieved to have someone on her who knew what he was doing. When she made for the yard gates, the manager pulled her round.

Grimes dismounted and held the reins out to the POW. 'You have another go,' he said, still loud. He held the bridle strap to keep Mustard where she was.

The POW got the reins crossed right on this go, yet still too loose.

'The reins gotta be taut, bit to pommel. Not like this!' Grimes yelled, flapping them.

The POW's face was still blank. He managed on the next try to get his left foot into the stirrup but the horse moved off round Grimes. The POW hopped along on his right foot to keep up with her.

'Git up, for Chrissake,' Grimes called.

Kate's father raised his eyebrows, and Ed grinned.

With one final push the POW flung his right leg up and got a foot almost over the horse's back. He hung there like a saddlebag, his head and body against Mustard's flank, and the horse moved about sharply.

Ed chortled, and even Kate's father smiled.

'Sit down, you idiot.' Grimes pulled the POW off Mustard and dropped him on the dirt as the horse backed away. The man didn't move for a bit, and Kate felt sorry for him.

'I reckon we try the other dago, boss,' Grimes said.

Kate didn't want to see this. Dislike the Italian as she did, he'd rubbed Grimes up the wrong way at the station, refusing to be cowed, and that was a mistake. This would be his first lesson. 'Dad, I'll go back to the house now,' she said.

'We'll be here for a bit, I reckon,' her father replied.

Grimes handed the reins to Canali, who looked at them curiously.

'Reins. Pommel. Stirrup. Up!' Grimes yelled, pointing.

As Kate left, Grimes's voice followed her. She was about halfway home when she heard shouting and hoof-beats, fast and deliberate, with Rusty barking up a row. Was somebody hurt? She ran back to the yards, now alive with dust and movement.

In that dust Grimes dodged the horse and rider that came at him. Canali was mustering Grimes like a calf, forcing him back into the centre when he tried to run or to break for the yard rails. The POW was angry, pushing the horse to muster a man. Grimes would be hurt. Her father and Ed shouted, waving at Canali. He rode straight at the manager again. Kate was sure she would see Grimes brought down, yet at the last moment the Italian wheeled the horse away.

'Cut it out!' Her father's voice came through the dust and the noise. But the POW rode on, and Grimes was trapped in the ring. He knew he was being toyed with; he was red in the face, angrier than Kate had ever seen him.

Her father waved Ed into the ring, and the stockman climbed between the rails, good foot first. With a big arm, he unfurled his whip and cracked it once. At the bang, the horse pulled up its head. Still the rider urged Mustard on, trapping Grimes in the centre. Ed cracked his whip again, getting closer to the horse. Mustard pulled up, only to be pushed on, a white lather of sweat across her flanks. But on the next whip crack, Mustard baulked and the man brought the horse up. They stopped, mount and rider breathing hard.

Grimes leapt up at the POW, grabbed his shirt and an arm and hauled him off onto the ground, giving him a kick to the ribs as he hit the dirt. The POW took hold of Grimes's sleeve and brought him down too.

'You blokes! Cut it out!' Kate's father yelled.

The bearded POW, worried, paced to and fro beside the rails, calling, 'Luca!'

Harry stood atop the second rail, watching.

Ed led Mustard to the far side of the ring, out of the way of the men on the ground, moving her in circles around him, murmuring to her. Astride the POW, Grimes landed one punch on Canali's mouth, then a second closer to his nose.

'*Cut it out!*' her father shouted for the third time and got into the ring himself. He went to the men and took hold of his manager's arm, stopping the blows. Breathing heavily, Grimes dropped his arm and released the POW's shirt. Canali fell back onto the dirt, his chest heaving. Grimes got up, dust coating his face, his eyebrows and his shirt. He moved to lean on the rails. The POW started to get up too but stopped on his knees, one arm on his chest where he'd taken a boot.

'Jesus. Bittuva show, eh?' Ed laughed nervously. But Johnno and Spinks were quiet, watching Grimes. Kate's father exhaled, shaking his head, unhappy.

'Quick learner, that second bloke,' Ed said to Grimes.

'I'll job ya.' Grimes took a step towards him, and Ed slipped behind Mustard, grinning. Ed had gumption.

Grimes climbed out through the rails and went off towards the manager's cottage. Harry followed close behind, casting glances back at the POW, still in the dirt. Canali pushed himself up, bringing a hand to touch the blood on his mouth. He looked at Kate, and grinned, arrogant even with a mouthful of bloody teeth. When she frowned, he spat blood onto the dirt and she walked away, knowing he watched her.

CHAPTER 4

A ewe deprived of good pastures during her pregnancy, whether by a poor season or otherwise, an inferior mother makes. She cares less for her smaller offspring, which in turn suckles less and succumbs in greater numbers than their more fortunate brethren, the offspring of well-nourished ewes.

THE WOOLGROWER'S COMPANION, 1906

Back at the homestead, Kate put her hat up on its hook. She washed her hands with as little water as she could manage and got the post from the hall table.

'Give me a shout if you hear Dad, will you? I'll be in the office.'

'Orright, Missus,' Daisy said.

The office was cool and dark after the sunshine of the garden. Papers were scattered across the divan, on his desk chair and even on the floor under the desk. A box of pay packet envelopes lay tipped over on the desk itself. Her father tolerated only a rare tidy of the office and that was overdue. Kate put the envelopes back in the box and then the box on the shelf where it belonged.

At least the bookcases were pretty tidy. The farm journals, the working diaries her father used to write up day in and day out, were lined up in chronological order, one volume for every year since 1918, when her father took up the first blocks of Amiens.

At the desk, the first thing that caught her eye was the file sitting on top of all the papers. Typed lettering ran across the cover: *Rural Employment Scheme: POWs assigned to* – with the word *AMIENS* written in ink after that. It was the file Captain Rook had given her father at the station. She set it to one side, then cleared a space among the papers and arranged the day's post with the envelopes marked *Overdue* on top. She gingerly tried the flaps on the letters, but each was sealed.

She looked through the other correspondence on the desk: livestock reports, Wool Board newsletters, and copies of *The Pastoralist*. And bills: from Babbin, from Darcy's, and one from Nettiford's. None was marked *Overdue* but even the most recent was more than a year old.

Kate pulled on the handle of the first desk drawer. Locked; every drawer was locked. She sat back, staring at the desk. Taking the post with her, Kate went to the kitchen to help Daisy with the lunch.

She and her father sat down together to a plate of tinned bully beef and lettuce from the garden. Her mother had hated the tinned meat – only working men ate it. Kate didn't much like it either, but her father loved it.

'Is Grimes all right?' Kate asked, nudging the letters with her fingers. She'd kept an envelope marked *Overdue* on the top.

But her father reached over the post for the pickles. 'Yeah. The story'll be round the district in a day. That'll get his goat.'

'That POW, Canali, can ride.'

'Grimes gave him a hiding in return; boys will be boys. Ed tells me he was a stable-hand before the war.' He took a mouthful but did not stop speaking. 'A tad older'n you. He'll be useful. He's got some English. But the other fella with the beard? Bottinella. A basket case from the war.'

She took a breath. 'About the post, Dad.'

'Ya not poured your tea?'

'No. I wanted to talk to you about these.' Kate touched the envelopes in front of him.

'Well?'

'They're bills,' she said softly.

'Bills? Yes. And?'

She forced herself on. 'They don't seem to have been paid.'

'You have an interest now in business, Kate? In the books? Have ya? What would y'mother say about that, eh?'

She couldn't bring herself to speak.

He drank the last of his tea in one gulp and stood, yawning. 'Think I'll have forty winks.'

At the door he turned back to her. 'The money, the banking. Ya want t'have nothin t'do with the bank fellas. Mongrels, all of em. Steal ya blind. Best stick to the housework. Do that for me, will ya? Leave business to your father.'

She was so angry she couldn't look at him.

'Oh, and another thing. You could do with some help in the vegetable garden. I told the rider fella, Canali, to give you a hand.'

'Oh, please, Dad. No,' Kate protested.

'The other fella's got no English. No, Canali'll work in the afternoons with you when they come in from the run. Startin Monday.'

'But he's better in the yards. Working with the stock. At least give me the other one. Bottinella?'

'You runnin things, Kate?' he said. 'You'll do as I tell ya. Canali worked the gardens at the camp at Hay, apparently. No, you're having Canali.'

She heard his tread on the wooden floorboards of the house, along the hall to the office at the back, where he now took an afternoon rest.

Daisy appeared in the dining room to clear up. Kate started

to pour herself some tea but stopped. The pot was cold. 'Make yez ot water, Missus?' the girl asked.

Kate shook her head. She banged the lunch things onto the tray and followed Daisy into the kitchen.

~

The following Monday afternoon, as Kate sat, pulling on her boots to work in the garden, she considered what was ahead. The POW would start work in the veggie beds this afternoon, and she was dreading it. She had the first boot on when she heard barking and hoof beats, and she hopped out and across the verandah. Rusty was in the paddock, running behind the stock horses, barking, nipping, giving them curry.

'Rusty,' she called, but the dog chased on, cutting Mustard out from the other horses.

Her hands cupped round her mouth, Kate shouted again. 'Rusty!'

He stopped.

'Come here!' she shouted.

He cast a longing glance at the horses but turned back. It took him only a minute or so to cover the distance. Kate pulled the other boot on and went out the gate, grabbing the dog waddy as she went. The waddy, a rolled-up newspaper held together with rubber bands, was for meting out punishment, but more for noise than pain. Rusty sidled the last yard in, dropping at her feet in submission. He knew, all right.

'Bad dog, Rusty.' She hit his haunches once with a *thwack*. His punishment had, he slunk away down the fence line. He had to stop chasing stock. If her father knew, the pup would be put down.

Still dreading Canali's arrival, she started her usual circuit to enjoy it in peace. She went first to look for the bowerbird. A small brown ground-dweller, they were canny enough to avoid snakes and the claws of the house cats and the shed cats alike.

36

The current bower was tucked in between the base of the California pine and the fence. A tiny avenue only six inches long, it was two walls of short sticks set vertically against each other like a long teepee, the uprights intertwined here and there for strength and beauty. Gathered round one opening was the bowerbird's careful collection, ordered by category, shells here, gum nuts there, bits of glass beyond them and then shiny rocks at the far end. This bowerbird liked the drive's white pebbles too, and his collection was laid out in a neat fan from one end of the bower avenue of sticks. 'It's an ad,' her father had explained when she was small. 'With his work, the male bird is saying "See, ladies? See what I can do?"' But where was he? Kate waited.

From behind the corner fence post came the little bower-bird, with a pebble in his beak. He stopped, wary when he saw Kate. He was tiny, no more than four inches high from beak to feet, fully grown, including his outsize stick legs. And he was pretty, his grey and white feathers perfect for blending into the mess of the bush floor. He darted in, dropped the shiny pebble by the bower and scuttled away to eye Kate from behind the pine.

She left him in peace and walked in the shade, past one surviving zinnia with a single white flower, self-seeded. Across the front of the house, Kate enjoyed the mock orange, its perfume heavy and sweet in the still heat of the afternoon. A walk through the wisteria arbour brought her to the corner of the house yard with the fruit trees, quince and apricot, eleven of them now, one lost to the drought.

Her track took her past the lean-to of tools, and the lawn at the back of the house. From time to time she'd considered putting another bed in here, for more potatoes, cabbages and other veggies. She'd never quite found the time to ask the men to do it. With the drought, she couldn't ask; the soil would be like cement.

Her circuit done, she took her kneeler mat from its hook under the tank stand upright and checked it for spiders and centipedes. Then, on the strip of yellowing lawn that separated the beds from the fence line, she knelt down to weed. She was happiest with weeds dead, Mayne's curse especially. Oh, she knew from endless childhood Sundays at church that officially everything on God's earth had a place and deserved God's love. But she didn't hold much with that view. In a country where every day was a prayer for moisture, where life was threatened by centipedes and spiders and snakes, where the sun could fry eggs on bitumen, that original gentle version of Christianity, the one the English had brought with them when they came, didn't fit well.

Kate now practised her faith from afar – she hadn't been to church since her mother died two years before – with unspoken amendments, giving thanks where she could and forgiving where she should. Weeds were on the wrong side of that divide and deserved to die.

A movement on the other side of the fence caught her eye. Rusty sidled towards her, getting closer to the ground as he approached, fawning his apology. When he was within three feet of her he lay down and rolled over, arching and hunching his back to push himself along the ground.

'You goose,' Kate grinned, patting the dog's belly, 'stop mucking around, or I'll have to let Grimes have his way.'

'*Signora*, you worry for me?' The POW Canali was just outside the fence, a swollen smile under his odd pale-green eyes.

'Hardly.' She went back to her weeding, embarrassed, her heart pounding.

But the man squatted beside Rusty and rubbed his ears. The pup nudged at the POW's shirt, and his nose left a wet mark. His uniform was neat, even after most of a day's work.

Kate stood up, cross. 'You're here to work, aren't you?'

He came through the gate and stopped near her, his hands on his hips. His fingernails were stained black with sump oil from the engines. Grimes had him doing all the dirty work.

He looked about appraisingly, as if she wasn't there. Kate threw her gardening gloves on the lawn and walked round the corner of the house to the lean-to at the back. When he caught up, she pulled a pick from the neat row of tools and held it out to him.

He didn't move.

'This is a pick.'

'Peek,' he said, nodding. When he took the tool from her, she felt the quick brush of their hands sending heat to the tips of her ears. Why did he rattle her?

'C'mon.' She strode back the way she had come, gathering her wits, then stopped in the middle of the dead lawn behind the house. 'We need a bed here.'

'Bed?' He leaned the pick handle against his thigh and put his palms together against his cheek, miming sleep.

'A *garden* bed. Here.' She pointed down at the hard dirt under their feet.

'*Sì*. Big?'

'Big,' she said and left him. That'd teach him his place. Then it struck her she sounded just like her mother.

There was only a little noise from the back of the house so he must have got on with it. A dusty white chook wandered by looking for grubs as Kate tugged and pulled at her weeds, breaking roots off. She was still annoyed with the POW twenty minutes later, when a girl's voice rang across the paddock to her.

'Hulloooooo!'

It was Meg Yorke, on horseback, coming from the lane that ran along the southern side of the house paddocks. The lane saved a few gates if you came overland from the east, as Meg did a bit, for a cup of tea and the gossip you couldn't risk on the party telephone line. Her family's property, Blairvale, was a couple of miles along the main road – fortunately not on Four Mile Creek, which her father had dammed, so the families were still friendly.

Meg looped the reins of her horse round the top rail, and pulled a magazine out of the saddlebag. She vaulted over the fence, magazine rolled up in her hand. She managed to look comely, even in blouse, joddies and riding boots, flashing Kate her gap-toothed smile from a head of fair curls. Just seventeen, with an hourglass figure, she was, according to Jack, going to be a handful.

'Cup of tea?' Kate said.

'Is the Pope a Catholic?'

'You'd better cut that out. We've got POWs. They're —'

'Tykes. The whole country is.'

Kate pulled off her gloves and went ahead, inside. She was glad the POW was on the far side of the house and would not see Meg. It'd be like bees to a honey-pot.

'Brought you a pressie from the hospital. The *Weekly*.' She dropped the *Women's Weekly* on the table.

'How is the hospital?' Kate asked.

'Busy. But I love it.'

'You're better than me. I wasn't good at nursing.'

Meg leaned over and tapped her arm. 'Don't do yourself down. You took such care of your mum, all those months. And she appreciated that more than anything, I reckon.'

Kate said nothing; it was so painful to think of.

She put the kettle on. 'We've got two. POWs, I mean.'

'We didn't put in for any, y'know. Dad won't have them. Not with Robbo still a prisoner in Singapore.'

'I can understand that.'

Meg pushed a wayward curl behind her ear and leaned over the jigsaw puzzle, a map of Australia, spread as threatened across one end of the kitchen table. 'You doing this?'

Kate rolled her eyes. 'Dad got it out for Harry. The little boy our manager has taken in. His great-nephew, I think.'

She scooped tea leaves in, one heaped spoonful for each of them and one extra 'for the pot'.

'According to Elizabeth Fleming, their POWs are built like Greek gods. Only Elizabeth's would be anything more than just plain gorgeous.' Meg laughed. 'I hear they all are, you know. Even got the odd girl knocked up.'

'No,' Kate said, disbelieving. She was glad Daisy wasn't hearing this.

'Yeah – down south. Stands to reason. The war's got everything topsy-turvy. Our boys are all away and there's a nice handsome chappy on your doorstep.'

'Never. People wouldn't.'

Meg laughed, her tooth gap clear. 'Anyhow, I've come to chivvy you into the CWA tennis one Saturday arvo.'

Kate frowned. The ladies of the Country Women's Association were lovely. That wasn't the problem.

'I know what it is. You don't like to leave your dad. How is he?'

Kate trusted Meg. They'd grown up together, and Meg was like a sister to her. 'The nightmares are always with him. He wakes up shouting, thinks he's in the trenches.'

'So better or worse, you reckon?'

Kate took a breath. 'You remember I told you he went downhill after Mum died. I was very worried for those months. Then he seemed to get better. But now?' She shrugged. 'He's getting bad again. He even thought I *was* Mum the other day.'

'Crikey. You've got a lot on your plate.' Meg fiddled with the jigsaw, holding up a piece marked *Yeppoon*.

'Maybe. How are your oldies anyway?'

Meg shrugged, trying to find a home for the piece. 'They're getting along. But there's no word from Robbo. Or poor old Doug Jamieson either. The Army's bloody useless. Still, maybe the Japs don't tell them anything.'

Kate put the teapot on the table and turned it three times to send the leaves to the outside.

Meg pressed the Yeppoon piece into its spot on the central Queensland coast. 'I worry about Robbo. I never say this to Mum or Dad, but he's a softy. I don't know if he'll cope.' She sat. 'I wish it were me up there.'

A knock at the gauze door interrupted them. Kate turned in her chair, ready to have some straight words with Canali. Instead, it was the one with the beard, Bottinella, and today he held a hand up against his jaw, as if he had a bad tooth.

'Miss,' he said, through the gauze. 'Luca?'

Kate got up and went to the door. 'Round the back.' The smell of him wafted across, ripe, as if he hadn't found the shower yet.

Meg had come to stand behind Kate. Kate knew that, because the man's eyes had moved and were not on her. He dropped his hand from his jaw.

'He's round the back,' Kate said again. But the man stared at Meg.

'How do you do. I'm Meg Yorke.' She smoothed her curls with a hand.

Kate could hear she was smiling.

'*Sì*,' Bottinella said, smiling back. '*Ciao bella.*'

'It is hot, isn't it? Is he saying it's hot?' Meg asked Kate, who frowned.

'Round. There,' Kate said again and stuck her hand out of the door to show him.

The Italian backed away, nodding and grinning.

'My goodness. Greek gods, indeed. Short Greek gods.' Meg sat herself on the table, tapping a piece of the jigsaw against her lips.

Kate started to answer when Harry appeared at the back door with Rusty at his feet. She got up again. Her kitchen was like Central Station.

'No dogs in the house paddock,' Kate said. Rusty stopped but didn't retreat. '*Gorn!*' she called and the pup ran back across the lawn and leapt at the fence, scrambling over. She waited to make sure he didn't have a go at Meg's horse, tied up at the fence.

'Come in then,' she said, holding the door for the boy. 'Harry, this is Meg Yorke, a neighbour.'

'You up from Sydney?' Meg asked.

'Wollongong.' Harry sat down at the table and looked at Kate expectantly. He took a swipe at Peng with his foot.

'Don't do that, please. Where's your uncle, Harry?' Kate asked.

'Dunno. Out on the run, eh.' He wasn't interested and scratched at his spikey hair. He watched as Peng delicately positioned herself by her milk bowl and lapped. 'Can I've some milk?'

'All right,' Kate replied.

'Would you like a bikkie?' Meg asked.

'Yep.'

'Yes please, Miss Yorke,' Kate corrected. 'Can you wash your hands, please, Harry?'

Daisy materialised and put a biscuit onto a plate for him, as the boy stretched to wash his hands in the sink. Tap running, he leaned in and tipped his head on the side to get a drink of water.

Daisy held out the hand towel to him. He wiped his hands, then his mouth.

'Please don't wipe your mouth on the hand towel,' Kate said.

'She gets after you, Harry, eh?' Meg said.

'What do you do for a crust?' Harry asked. Kate couldn't help but smile.

'I'm a VA. A Voluntary Aide. It means nursing aide. I help at the hospital, nurse the soldiers sent here to convalesce. To get better, I mean.'

'Why'd they send em here to the middle of nowhere?'

'I'll ignore that,' Meg said. 'The Army's gotta send the wounded fellas where there's empty hospital beds. So they go all sorts of places. Like Kate's husband, Jack. He came with his bung hand, to get it better. He was only here five minutes when Kate married the poor fella.'

Kate rolled her eyes.

'What about you? You going to school at Frenchman's Creek?'

Kate gave her a look. The boy was working in the paddocks with his uncle – Grimes had said no to school. And that nagged at Kate's conscience.

'Nuh. Not allowed,' the boy said, peeved. 'I wanna go, eh. M'uncle says I can't, but.'

'Hullo, all. Young Meg too, today, eh?' Kate's father was up the steps and into the kitchen like a man with a winning ticket in his pocket. 'Now, young Harry, what's that y'uncle says you can't do?'

'I can't go t'school.'

Her father gave Kate a look and went back out the door onto the verandah. Harry followed him, a biscuit in each hand, and the door banged after him. Kate frowned. Her father hated loud noises.

'Ya wanna see the bowerbird, boss? I seen im near them big gates,' Harry said.

'Why don't I beat the pants off you at draughts instead, eh?' Kate's father said.

Harry went to the wall of the homestead, peering into a hollow. He pointed at the slot, about two inches across. 'What's this then?'

Kate's father laughed. 'An auger hole.'

'Don't push on it,' Kate warned from inside. 'It's stopped up, and you'll pop out the plaster in here if you're not careful.'

Meg went out to see.

'What's it for then?' Harry swivelled his head round to look down it.

'The muzzle of a shotgun,' her father said.

'Yeah?'

From inside, Kate called, 'Dad . . .' It was too late.

Her father was off. 'It's an old homestead, ya see. Been here long before me. The early settlers had a lotta trouble with the Abos. In point o' fact, I hear the blacks were winnin for a while round here. Them auger holes were to see em off, when they had to. Hole's t'put a rifle through, from inside the house.'

'For shootin?' Harry said, eyes wide. 'But the Abos buggered off by theirselves.'

Her father laughed. 'Nuh. They had some encouragement. Quite a bit, they say, from the first settlers.'

Kate looked behind her into the laundry, hoping Daisy was not hearing this.

'And some o' those families are still about. The first settlers. The "good families", as Janice used to call em.' He snorted a laugh. 'They look down on us, Harry, cos I was a soldier settler, here only since the First War.'

Kate wanted her father quiet on this before Daisy appeared. She called to them. 'Harry, can you tidy those draughts up now?'

But her father went on. 'I used to say to Janice, "I didn't shoot Abos. That makes me beneath the blokes whose grandfathers did?"' He shook his head in disgust. Kate thought it but said nothing: some parts of the district had been set aside for the Aborigines by the government, but their land was taken back at the end of the First War and turned over to soldier settlers like her father.

'And we're bigger'n all them other properties now anyhow.'

Meg came back inside and left them to their game. She spoke softly to Kate. 'Sorry about that school thingy. But it's a bit tough, if he wants to go?'

Kate waggled her head. Harry *should* go to school, but she'd avoided telling her father that Grimes had said no, worried it might set him off.

Daisy reappeared, put on an apron and began peeling potatoes in the sink for dinner.

'I better shuffle off,' Meg said at the door. A man's deepthroated laugh reached them.

'Your POWs still at it? It's knock-off time, isn't it?' Meg went out and Kate followed.

'You should go,' Kate said, shooing Meg towards the fence.

'Yes, I should,' Meg said, deadpan. She walked with Kate round the back of the house towards the voices.

As they came round the tank stand, Kate stopped. Meg pulled up behind her, grabbing her arm in delight. Canali and Bottinella were shirtless, their bodies slick with sweat, as they dug. They were skinny but fit, sinewed like wood-chop champions. Kate's eyes went to Canali. His skin was darker than his companion's, much darker, with terrible scars, long crooked lines across his chest, incongruously pale on his skin.

Canali saw the women and said something to his bearded mate. The younger man stopped digging and straightened up, his hands on the shovel in front of him. '*Buona sera, Signora Dowd. Signorina.*' He smiled at Meg.

'It's him. The Greek god,' Meg whispered.

'Mr Botta . . . Bottinella,' Kate said, flustered. 'That's enough for today.' She retreated, pulling Meg with her.

'Enough?' she heard Canali say. 'Enough for you, *Signora*?'

Kate didn't turn but she almost smiled. He rattled her, this POW. And he knew it.

CHAPTER 5

A sheepdog drives only on command of its master. So a pup which
chases stock for its own amusement, and will not be broken of the
urge, must be culled and a fresh start made.

THE WOOLGROWER'S COMPANION, 1906

Kate woke early the next morning, the verandah door
windows bright with the light glow of sunrise. The sun
would come on soon. She'd seen the creek break its banks
once, when she was a little girl, and that's how she thought
of dawn. It lapped at the edges of the horizon, then broke,
flooding the sky.

She enjoyed the solitude of her room but she missed Jack,
missed his company. This had been their room for the few
months after they married, before he got his hand working
and he was called up again. Jack was a great mimic; he could
do an excellent Mr Grimes, moving his eyebrows as if they
had a life of their own. She'd loved those mornings with him,
lying in his arms in the squeaky bed, trying not to laugh too
loud, with her father's room next door.

It was very early. She reached out to pick up the *Women's*
Weekly Meg had brought her. Kate never bought it any more
as it reminded her too much of her mum. Her mother used to
read it every week, cover to cover, at least once and sometimes

47

twice, to be sure that the Stimsons did what all 'good families' across Australia were doing.

Her mother had had ambitions for Kate. The *Weekly* was her compass. Kate was grateful, though; one of the reasons she was accepted by the district's good families was because she was seen to have been brought up properly. *Brung up proper*, her father used to say, to annoy her mother. But they both knew, she and her father, that it was one's station at birth, along with money and manners from then on, that made a person 'worthy' to these old families. So the Flemings and their ilk might embrace Kate, yet never Ralph Stimson or his wife. Her father wouldn't say that to her mother, though. He was not cruel.

Which made her think of him. She dropped the magazine on the floor. Things were too quiet this morning. She couldn't hear him moving about. He and the men were leaving at first light to cut trees to feed the sheep, but her father might have overslept. He'd had a bad night, and she'd been up to him several times, when he woke, shouting, shouting about the trenches.

She pulled on her clothes, pushed her unbrushed hair into a ponytail (too knotty even for the usual quick plait) and went to her father's door. She tapped, welcomed by the faint smell of chops and toast from the kitchen at the end of the hall.

'Dad. You up? I think brekkie's ready.' When she heard movement inside, she went on to the kitchen.

'Mornin, Missus,' Daisy said, from the stove. Daisy was not much of a smiler, but maybe she missed her family. Elizabeth Fleming maintained all Aborigines were sullen, that it was in their blood. Elizabeth was a hard nut.

'You got four this morning, Daisy?' Kate asked, eyeing the eggs on the kitchen bench.

'Maybe they clucky. And, Missus, nextta nothin in tha water hole, eh.'

Kate sighed. Damn drought. The chook run was just up from the creek bed, near what was a fairly constant water hole in good seasons.

Daisy cracked one of the eggs into the pan. Kate sat down, just as she saw Grimes's blue shirt in the upper square of the gauze door.

'Mornin, Mrs D. We're ready when the boss is. Ed's got them POWs in the truck.'

'I'll check on Dad. Come in, Mr Grimes. Daisy will get you a cup of tea.' If she needed to curry favour with Grimes, she'd better start doing it.

Grimes hesitated. Daisy set a metal mug of tea on the table for him.

'Dad.' Kate tapped on the door of her father's room. 'Grimes is here.'

Nothing. She tapped again. 'Grimes is here, Dad.'

Silence.

'To cut feed. Remember?'

'I'm not coming,' she heard through the door.

'Are you sick, Dad?'

When he didn't answer, Kate didn't know what to do. She stood for a moment longer then went back to the kitchen. Grimes was perched on the edge of one of the kitchen chairs. He jumped to his feet as she came in.

'I think you should go ahead without him,' Kate said. 'He's sick.'

'He's crook?'

But her father appeared in the doorway, unshaved and unkempt, and started to yell, 'Grimes! Get outta here!' He wore only pyjama bottoms and his bathrobe, and the robe was not tied off; a pale torso with a matt of grey chest hair was visible between the gown's lapels, its cord ends dragging on the floor after him.

Daisy backed away, putting her hands in front of her.

Grimes got up, his eyes and mouth wide. 'Boss, Mrs D said —'

'You dumb bastard,' her father said, flicking his arm at his manager. 'Get your arse out of here!'

'Dad!'

He barrelled past the table as Grimes got out the door and across the dead lawn, off towards Ed and the POWs in the truck.

Daisy disappeared too, and Kate and her father were alone in the kitchen, the room silent apart from her father's heavy breaths, laboured after his yelling. But then he turned on the wireless and sat down at the table. Her father slid Kate's empty tea cup across in front of him and poured, as the voice of the announcer filled the air:

'...*Australian yarn to be made up into clothing and blankets for our Australian soldiers and their American comrades who are here to defend our ...*'

'It was the Americans, y'know. In the First War. On the sideline till the end, then rode in like bloody heroes.'

Kate swallowed, rocked by his volatility. 'What was wrong, Dad?'

'Wrong? Grimes in the homestead? Drinkin tea like he owned the place?' He shifted his eyes to the wireless and yawned widely.

'What about today? You going out with the men?'

'He's a lazy bugger, Grimes. Ed's the worker.' He stood up. 'Think I'll have forty winks.'

'Are you all right, Dad?'

But he'd gone, his dressing gown cords still trailing behind him like the reins of a loose horse.

Kate sat down at the kitchen table and stared at the tea in front of her. Before today, her father had never misbehaved for anyone but Kate. He'd never been indecent. In front of Grimes, of all people. Grimes prided himself on knowing his place and he kept everyone in theirs, from the POWs to the Aboriginal stockmen. And he'd be off in a flash if he suspected there was something amiss with her father or if he thought he might not get paid.

After the house had been still for some time, Daisy returned and went about her business, washing up the dishes.

'Sorry,' Kate said. 'About that.'

Daisy looked away, expressionless.

Later that morning, Kate was sweeping the verandah when her father emerged again, dressed for work, the usual moleskin trousers, kangaroo-skin belt, his RM riding boots.

'Morning,' he said, looking at his watch. 'Didya forget to wake me up?'

'No. You don't remember, Dad?'

'Remember what?'

'You were up, Dad. In the kitchen. You said no. They had to go without you.'

He shrugged and looked off towards the Box Ridge paddock.

'You sure you're all right, Dad?'

'Right as rain. See ya later then.'

'Your hat,' she said, softly.

Kate watched him walk off towards the meat house and the stables. A hot breeze rattled the bunya pines along the house fence and Kate tried not to think of that as an omen.

~

The following day was quiet and weirdly normal. Kate got to the end of it with relief, and made some tea. She thought about her father as she watched the steam rise off her mug. He'd been his usual self all day and even appeared for a game of draughts when Harry (and, as always, Rusty) turned up at four. She'd not seen Grimes and was glad of it. She didn't know what she was going to say to him if he asked about

51

her father. What if Grimes twigged and then left?

When she heard the truck in the gully, she went inside, not wanting to be caught sitting down with a mug in her idle hands. It was about time to put the meat in the oven, anyway.

In the kitchen, Kate got the leg of mutton out of the kero fridge and dropped it into a baking dish. She was putting a good sprinkle of salt over the top when the truck came to a stop by the house. Damn, she'd have to speak to Grimes. And she must stop swearing, even to herself.

Grimes got out of the driver's seat and, with two loaves of bread in his arms, came towards the house fence, leaving the POWs and Johnno and Spinks in the tray of the truck. Ed was nowhere to be seen; he must have decided Grimes could handle the POWs. Kate left her apron on and went out to meet him. She was conscious of the Italians watching her.

At the fence, Kate took the bread from Grimes. 'Thanks. No newspaper?'

'Jamieson's got a problem with his press.'

Kate had turned to go back to the house when Grimes said, 'The boss orright, is he?'

'Yes.'

He frowned, scratching an eyebrow. 'I needa word with im about Rusty.'

'I'll see if he's about,' she said and went back up the steps and into the kitchen.

She knocked on the office door, and pushed it open a little. 'Dad?'

The room was quite dark, the curtains drawn. She opened the door all the way and was taken aback. Her father was sleeping on the floor on his swag. Curled up like a child, he had his elbows tucked in close to his waist, hands coiled under his chin, and his feet were hidden under the stained canvas ground sheet.

'Dad, Grimes wants to speak to you.' Kate heard him breathing normally, not the regular rhythm of real sleep. By his feet was a worn book, *The Woolgrower's Companion*. Its leather cover, once bright blue, was spotted with age and use.

'Dad?' She heard herself sounding nervous. Nothing. She pulled the door closed behind her and stood in the quiet stillness of the hall. She wasn't ready to tell Grimes to put Rusty down. Her father would, if he knew. She just couldn't do it. Yet.

Grimes had one hand on the top of the fence, the other on his hip, waiting. He was watching the POWs in the back of the truck.

'Dad's on the phone,' Kate said, at the fence. 'But he gave me a message for you.'

'A message.' Grimes weighed that up.

'Yes,' she said, swallowing. 'He said to keep at it. To keep training Rusty. Stop him chasing sheep.' Kate's voice sounded artificial, like a ten-year-old pretending to be the teacher.

'Did he now?'

The POWs and the stockmen in the back of the truck were listening, and she was conscious of Canali watching her closely. She felt he knew she was lying. Ridiculous.

Grimes turned to go then stopped. 'One more thing. We've got a ram, Basil, in the house paddock. Keep an eye out. Ed reckons he might have a go at you. Only a young'un, but he's feelin his oats.' He put his hat on, and Kate went back to the house.

From the kitchen, she heard the truck start up and pull away. The brakes screeched, and a curse of complaints went up from the men in the tray. Grimes was standing on the driver's door running board, looking down the hill to the crossing.

'*Gorn!*' he shouted.

Kate followed his eyes. Rusty was chasing wethers about a hundred yards away, towards the gully and into the dry creek bed.

'*Gorn!*'

This time the pup stopped still, panting, tongue out, and looked back at Grimes.

'Come ere!' Grimes yelled.

But Rusty must have known he was in for a hiding as he sloped off into the gully and disappeared.

CHAPTER 6

The Merino thrives in hostilities of climate in which other cud-chewers are known to perish.

THE WOOLGROWER'S COMPANION, 1906

Grimes brought them to a stop in the dirt in front of the Frenchman's Creek school, the corrugated iron roof shimmering in the heat of the afternoon sun. Kate was to speak to the teacher about Harry. Grimes had eventually agreed, to her great relief, although it'd taken a while. Her father finally just told him to do it.

'Did you want to come in with me, Mr Grimes? To talk about your nephew?'

He folded his arms across his chest. 'Y'don't need schoolin to know how t'hold a shovel.'

Kate was starting to feel quite sorry for Harry Grimes.

The building was not a thing of beauty. Still, it did the job, providing shelter to the twelve children, aged between five and eleven, who attended under the stern eye of the formidable Mrs Pommer. School was over for the day, and it was a large, be-hatted Mrs P who stood in the corner of the horse paddock next to the school, a pony and four children about her. The children who lived on farms outside Frenchman's Creek rode to school. When they got there, they had to unsaddle their pony and let it loose in the horse paddock for the day, before catching it to ride home again.

Kate waved a hullo. The teacher was known as 'Mrs P' to the parents but as 'Bomber' to the children. Today she was holding the reins of a black pony, one boy already on it, while a second, a bay, was being saddled by a child behind her.

The school building seemed unchanged since Kate had left twelve years before to go to high school in Longhope. *FRENCHMAN'S CREEK SCHOOL 1913* was painted in white across the narrow end of the rectangular building, itself a dull brown with windows along both sides. Even the two thunder boxes – the outhouses, Mrs P called them – were the same.

'Hullo, dear.' Mrs Pommer smiled. 'Do come along, Mullinses. And Matthew, you know better. Bits and bridle all ready before the saddle goes on.' She shook her head.

Kate knew them. They lived on the Longhope Road and their father worked on Tindervale for the Rileys. Matthew, Mark and Jean, from memory.

'Jean – why don't you get up with Mark? You'll set a record in the Empire Games for the slowest mount.'

The boy on the pony laughed and the little girl started to cry.

'You're a big sook, Jeannie,' Matthew said.

'Manners, please, Matthew.'

'C'mon, Jeannie,' Matthew called again. From atop the mounting stump, Jean scrambled onto the pony's back, at the front. Almost before she was onboard, the pony moved off, the boys each with his arms around the waist of the child in front; Jean, incongruously, with the reins.

'See you tomorrow,' called Mrs Pommer. 'Now, Kate. How are you? Would you like a cup of tea?'

'Mr Grimes is waiting, so I must be quick,' Kate said, with a glance across at the truck.

'It's Mr Grimes's boy, isn't it? He'll come here?' The women walked towards the school building.

'Sort of. He's a relative of Mr Grimes, a great-nephew. And yes please. Dad would like him to come to Frenchman's Creek.'

'How old is he?'

'Eleven.'

'No other family? Siblings?'

Kate shook her head.

'What sort of boy is he? First impressions?' They'd reached the school gate. 'An only child can be quite mature. Beyond their years.'

Kate smiled. 'I don't think that's Harry. Not yet, anyway.'

Mrs Pommer smiled then. 'All right. I'll see for my —' The older woman stopped mid-sentence and stared out into the bush on the far side of the horse paddock. She yelled suddenly. '*Gorn!* You get along!' At her shout, a dog barked from the house on the other side of the school.

'That's our Rollo barking,' Mrs Pommer said. 'He knows when that darky kid's about.'

'Who is it? Why's he not living on the Mission?'

'It's the boy the McGees adopted.'

'Oh.' Kate had heard the story. A childless couple, Scottish, not long in Australia, had managed to adopt a little half-caste boy. Presbyterian, they were apparently.

'Soft in the head is that McGee,' Mrs Pommer said. 'And it'll all end in tears, I tell you. You know, the boy hangs about the school after hours. I've caught him looking in the windows.'

'Why does he do that?'

'His mother, for some reason, tells him he can learn like white children. And they adopted him – they've got the papers and everything – so Sergeant Thompson can't pick him up.'

'Wingnut?'

Mrs Pommer frowned. 'Yes.'

Kate smiled. The name was on account of the sergeant's

large ears, evident only when he removed his cap. 'Where does the McGee boy go to school?'

'Well, he's not coming at the moment. Mrs McGee says the children here picked on him and she won't send him. I think that's why he sneaks over after school, to see where we're up to. Easier with him not here, to be honest. Some families complained.'

'What about the Mission school? Too far?'

'Too far. So she – Mrs McGee – is teaching him herself, filling his head with nonsense.' From across the street, the dog picked up with another round of barking.

'But now. This young Harry. Eight-thirty sharp Monday morning? You'll remember the timetable.'

'He'll be here.' And he'd be quite chuffed too. That thought made her oddly happy; he'd wormed his way in, had young Harry. She walked back to the truck with one eye on the bush for the boy.

~

In town, while Grimes went into the bank to cash the wages cheque, Kate popped into Nettiford's, the haberdashery, for some tea towels. The bell jangled, loud in the cool silence of the shop. Kate's eyes took a moment to adjust to the dark.

'Mrs Dowd.' Mrs Nettiford's voice was as cool as the shop and Kate wondered about that unpaid bill in the post. Surely that was a mistake.

'Kate, dear!' Elizabeth Fleming appeared from the other side of the shop.

The 'dear' part was a bit much. They were hardly more than a couple of years apart in age. And Elizabeth had always been too snooty to chat to Kate's mother. 'How are things on Avondale?' Kate asked.

'Not bad. Dry, though. Busy. In the yards.' Elizabeth held a bright tablecloth, running her fingers over the bumpy surface.

'You're working in the yards?' Kate asked.

'Not really. The POWs help our men with the heavy work now, and anything else, we do.'

'Is it hard?'

'Only wrestling the rams!' Elizabeth laughed. 'Seriously. To get the upper hand with the young rams, I tip them over and sit on them.'

'You sit astride?' Kate couldn't picture the prim and proper Elizabeth on a ram.

'No, no. If they have a go at you – you know, charge you – then you twist them on their back and sit on them. They'll leave you alone for a bit. Only works while they're quite small, mind.'

'Did you want anything today, Mrs Dowd?' Mrs Nettiford was almost moving her on.

'Here,' Elizabeth interrupted, 'you should take a few of these tablecloths. They're new. It's called seersucker. You don't iron them, you see.'

'Daisy – our domestic – spends hours starching tablecloths.'

'She from the Home?'

'Yes,' Kate said. 'Been with us a couple of months. Got her in November.'

'Cheap as chips, aren't they?' Elizabeth said. 'We have a new one too, so there are tears every morning. I remind her that this is her only chance to better herself, away from the black part of her family. She should be grateful, if anything. What's yours like?'

'Daisy? She's a sweetie. A half-caste, too. Her dad is a drover, apparently. She was going to the Mission school at Broken Hill before the Board shifted her here.'

'The Board gets them far away from their own district,' Elizabeth explained. 'Away from the bad influence of their parents and so on.'

'So, you takin anythin, Mrs Dowd?' Mrs Nettiford asked.

'No. Thanks. I must be on my way,' Kate said. 'Best wishes to John, Elizabeth.'

Outside in the sunlight, Kate was annoyed with Mrs Nettiford. Well, more fool her. Kate could always order by post up from Sydney.

'Mrs Dowd!'

Kate turned towards the voice, a man's voice, from along the street. It was Mr Addison from the bank. Kate had always found him a bit snake-like, with heavy-lidded eyes behind thick glasses.

'I'm sorry,' he said, glancing to see who was about. 'I wanted to catch you. To speak to you without your father. I'm sorry, I tell you.'

'Sorry? What for?'

'About Amiens. It's a great shame.'

Kate stared at him. Beyond, Grimes waved at her from the Amiens truck. Time to go.

Addison followed her gaze. 'I could give you a lift home, Mrs Dowd. I have a meeting in Wingadee this afternoon, anyway, and we could talk. Tell you how sorry I am.'

'Mrs D.' Grimes's tone was impatient. But Kate needed to know what Addison was rabbiting on about. When she told Grimes she'd accept Mr Addison's lift, he left for home.

As Kate pulled her door shut, Addison reversed out, his cigarette smoke swirling about the car. She wound her window all the way down.

On the Wingadee road, Addison soon overtook the Amiens truck. Grimes did not wave.

As a blur of eucalyptus streamed by, Kate inhaled to ask Addison what he meant. 'You're sorry about Amiens, Mr Addison?'

'The Amiens debts. The overdue interest.'

'Overdue? You're mistaken,' Kate said evenly. 'My father always pays his bills.'

'Incorrect. You're overdue in the most serious way.' He drew on the cigarette and blew the smoke over his shoulder out the window.

'Dad will not be happy you're saying these things.'

Addison brought the car to such a sudden stop off the bitumen, the wheels skidded in the dirt and Kate put a hand up against the wooden dashboard. 'You don't know,' he said.

'Know?' She fought to stay calm. She would wonder later if it was at this moment that her old life ended.

Dust floated past the vehicle, sliced by the black myalls that lined the road. Addison flicked ash through his open window, let the clutch out and steered the car back onto the road.

'You should know.' He looked straight ahead and spoke slowly. 'Your father hasn't paid any interest since December '42. The annual payment was made that year. But not in '43, nor in '44.'

'Nothing would be overdue.' Kate repeated what she knew, what she used to hear over and over from her father when she was growing up.

Addison shook his head. 'Your father mortgaged Amiens – mortgaged it heavily – to buy Binchey's, in '39.'

'I know he had to mortgage then. Even so, he always pays on time.'

'He did pay the annual interest that first year, in December '39 – after the wool cheque, you know – and on time again for three years, in December '40, '41 and '42. Then he stopped. Nothing since.'

'That can't be right.'

He went on as if he had not heard her. 'You might have survived that, but there's worse. Even with the mortgage, he still had an overdraft – a big one – available. My predecessor at the bank made the mistake of leaving the overdraft available for him. Until '43 it was largely undrawn, so your father was all right, you know, still able to make a go of it, and paying the interest on the mortgage each year. But in early '43 – before I arrived in the district, coincidentally – he drew down most of the overdraft in one go.'

'Drew down? What does that mean?'

'He borrowed. He withdrew almost all he was entitled to borrow under the overdraft.'

'What for?'

'I hoped you might know. He won't discuss it with me. But an overdraft is a *temporary* accommodation. Not two years.'

'This was early '43?' Kate's voice was soft.

'Yes. March, from memory. Did he buy anything? A ram? Anything?'

Kate shook her head. But she remembered the time. She'd nursed her mother through much of '42. 'My mother passed away that January. January '43.' Her father had grieved so deeply, she'd worried for his mind.

'I'm sorry, Mrs Dowd. But he's missed two annual interest payments. He owes a great deal of money. Our head office in Sydney is insisting that if a payment is not made shortly, we must begin proceedings to enforce the mortgage.'

'Enforce?'

'If there is no payment very soon, Amiens will be sold.'

'But Amiens is not for sale. We're not selling it.'

He shook his head. 'The *bank* will sell it.'

'But we don't owe any money.'

'On the contrary! It's a great deal of money. And if a borrower doesn't pay his debts, the bank can sell the property mortgaged against that debt. You understand that, don't you? You should, you're a director of the Amiens Pastoral Company. And a signatory on the cheque account.'

She didn't tell him but her mother hadn't believed in ladies working in the paddocks or 'doing the books'. So Kate knew less than most about the business side of things, just what she'd heard and picked up on the sly. But she knew people who'd gone bust, like the Bincheys and the Drummonds. Then again they were poor graziers or they borrowed too much, on places that ran short of water in a drought.

Addison turned off the main road into Amiens. 'I'm telling you this —' he stopped mid-sentence as his voice shook over the grid '— so you can arrange for somewhere to go, when the place is sold.'

'*Go?*' she said, incredulous.

'I'm telling you, we will serve notice to take possession. You should make arrangements to get off the place before the 31st of March.'

'I beg your pardon?'

'If nothing is paid this quarter, then we'll enforce at the first opportunity, or early the next quarter. So you need to be long gone by the 31st of March.'

'Oh.' Kate's mouth shaped the word but no sound came.

'At the very most you have eight weeks, Mrs Dowd. That's not a lot of time given the packing and the shift you need to do. Take your personal possessions only, no farm equipment, of course. That belongs to the bank. No feathering your nest.'

'How much do we owe?'

Addison inhaled. 'Mrs Dowd! I couldn't possibly disclose that to you.'

'But you're telling me everything else? Please. I must know.'

'Certainly not. Client confidentiality must be respected.' Tell her some things but not the most important bit? He was a drongo. Her father was right about that. Kate kept her eyes straight ahead. 'If. If we do owe all this money, what can I do?'

'You'd need money, Mrs Dowd. A great deal. If you have a pot of gold in your garden, I suggest you sell it quickly.' He laughed. 'Frankly, it's too late to do anything. The land is falling in value every month the drought goes on, so the bank's position worsens. You simply need to make plans about where you'll go. There's a tiny bit left on your overdraft for food and wages for a short time. What's left should cover some frugal moving expenses too but we will foreclose, so you must plan now.'

She wanted to reject everything he had said but she was very worried. The car jolted to a stop, and Kate was surprised to find they'd arrived at the homestead gates. She got out slowly, the Amiens dogs barking and jumping around her.

'You must make your plans fast,' Addison said again and she swung the heavy car door closed. She could not imagine living away from Amiens, from the gully and the dam and house. She watched the car go, a trail of dust behind it. He took the gully too fast and Kate got a small amount of pleasure as his car bottomed out with a bang.

'Gotcha!' Harry came running along the verandah from the direction of the kitchen and jumped off onto the lawn next to Kate. 'Aw. I thought y'was Daisy. I'm it, see.'

'What?' Kate asked. She rubbed her sunburned forearm, thinking of what Addison had said about selling Amiens.

'I thought you was Daisy. Hidey-go-seek,' Harry said. 'I never bloody hear her, but.'

'Harry,' Kate said automatically. 'No swearing.' She liked Harry and Daisy to play together now and then. There were no other children on Amiens.

'She won't be inside. That's fer sure,' Harry said.

Her father appeared in the office door. 'Cuppa tea, Kate?'

'All right.' But what she really wanted was to ask him about the money. 'Daisy, can you come out? Wherever you are?'

Victorious, Daisy appeared from the wisteria arbour and, with a big grin, took herself off to the kitchen. Even through the fog of her worry, it struck Kate that Daisy was pretty, prettier all the time. Her mother used to say of Aboriginal women, 'They're attractive only to a certain sort of man.' But it seemed to Kate that men were men. Daisy would be beautiful one day.

Harry came up onto the verandah and spun the wicker chair with one hand, and it fell over with a loud bang.

'Harry! Ya bloody drongo,' her father shouted, startled by the noise. 'A dolt could of guessed the arbour. Hide in plain bloody sight. That's the trick.'

Kate shook her head. Her father was unpredictable. Harry stomped off, offended, towards the manager's cottage. She followed her father inside in case he was difficult with Daisy. She'd try him after dinner and hope he was approachable by then. He had to tell her what he'd done with the money.

CHAPTER 7

In an excellent season, as the fleece grows long and full upon his flock, a woolgrower might well revise his ambitions (and indebtedness) upwards. However, he should postpone grand plans. 'Spend not before the clip is in,' might fairly be said to be the woolgrower's equivalent of not counting one's chickens.

THE WOOLGROWER'S COMPANION, 1906

A few hours later, after their meal, Kate followed her father onto the cool of the verandah. She usually enjoyed this time of day, the noise of the cicadas and the galahs and the bats in the air. Not tonight. Her father sat, socked but bootless, with a book in his hands, at what had become a permanent draughts table, the pieces set out in front of him. Kate sat opposite him, her hands clenched in her lap, and tried to get up some gumption to talk about the debt.

She waited until the washing-up noise from the kitchen had finished, to be sure Daisy had gone to her room, the sleep-out off the back verandah. Her father was reading *Gunfight at the Corral*, a penny dreadful he'd got from somewhere.

'Dad. I need to talk to you.'

'Righto.' He didn't look up.

She leaned forward over the pieces on the board. 'I spoke to Mr Addison.'

'Man's a drongo. Never trust a bank johnny.'

'He says —' she started.

Her father cut her off when he held up a hand. 'Listen!' Alert, he dropped the book to his lap, and sat very still.

'He says we've stopped paying the mortgage. That we owe the bank money. A lot of money.'

'Shush.' Her father shook his head, his eyes on the trees. 'That's a whip bird.'

Kate waited. There was a long bird call, broken into longer and longer pieces, with a sharp crack-like whistle at the end.

'There it is,' he said. 'Ya hear it?' Her father went back to his book.

'Addison says you – we – we owe money, Dad.'

Frowning, her father lowered the book and looked at Kate. 'He says they'll sell us up. That we'll have to leave Amiens.'

'Bullshit.'

Kate inhaled. He never swore at her. 'But is it true? Did we forget to pay the bank when the wool cheques came in?'

When his face hardened, she glanced away, afraid she'd lose her nerve. 'Mr – Mr Addison says. He says it's the overdraft.'

She heard the wicker of his chair squeak as he shifted in his seat. 'Did you buy something, Dad? With the overdraft money?'

'Jesus.' Her father stood up so suddenly he overturned the draughts board, sending the pieces flying across the verandah. Kate gasped, and her eyes went to the black and white checkers rolling across the timber floorboards. She dropped down on her knees to pick up the pieces.

'Money's safer with us than in the bloody bank!'

Checkers cupped in her hands, she looked up at him. 'Where's the overdraft money? They'll take the place if we don't pay it back.'

'Let em try.' He shook the book at her then threw it hard. It hit the homestead wall with a bang and he stalked into the house.

Kate sat back on the floor, looking at the checkers in her hands. With shaking fingers, she gathered the others, laying them onto the board. She picked up her father's book but it tore in two, its spine split.

~

Later, when her father had turned in, Kate had calmed down and she took the time to think. She made a mug of tea, and got herself into her room, passing a curled up Peng in the hall. On her bed, cross-legged, with the tea in her hands, Kate went over what Addison had said. She had to find some money.

Kate knew they had £5 hidden in the storeroom. It had been there for years. Her father had started to squirrel other things away in recent years too – mostly supplies, like nails, inner tubes, and tins of sump oil – and he sometimes forgot he'd bought them, or where they were. But the £5 was different. That money was for dire circumstances. And if Addison was right, £5 would be a drop in the bucket.

What could she do? She felt her mother's absence keenly, as she had every day in the two years since she'd passed away. But now her old insistence that Kate not learn about the running of the place was making things very difficult for her. She cursed her own ignorance.

What *could* she do? She must write to Jack. Shameful as it was, maybe he could ask his family if they could borrow some money. She'd never met them but had the impression they were well off. She felt a pang. Here she was, wanting him to ask his people for money, while he was away, transferred to the fighting in the islands for all she knew. She suspected, Jack being Jack, he would not want to ask them for money.

But maybe her father had not *spent* the overdraft money, given how much he hated banks? Maybe he'd taken that overdraft money out and hidden it? She'd search for it, that was for sure, in case her father had it planted somewhere on Amiens.

68

What else had Addison said? 'If you have a pot of gold?' She had her little engagement ring and her wedding ring. The engagement ring had been her mother's, a tiny green sapphire, much loved by Kate. She had no other jewellery except her pearls.

The pearls. They were a single strand, graduating from a tiny orb near the clasp to the size of a large pea in the middle, a gift to Kate on her eighteenth birthday. Her parents had brought the pearls back from Sydney, maybe to take their minds off her mother's health. As Kate unwrapped them, her mother had said, 'Rub them across your teeth.'

'Against my teeth?'

'You'll feel roughness. If they glide smoothly, they're not real pearls.'

Kate had tried it and wrinkled her nose. They felt sandy.

'See? Real,' her mother said.

'Easier than draggin a bloody ram across y'teeth,' her father had complained.

'He's whinging about the cost,' her mother had explained. 'They weren't as much as Minute Man anyway, Ralph.'

Kate smiled bleakly at the memory, wondering what their prize ram had cost. She went to her wardrobe to get the pearls. Behind her jumpers, she found the box, its carved wood ridged under her fingers. She took it down and felt about on the shelf in case her father had stashed money there. She got nothing but dusty fingers.

The jewellery box was dark-brown polished wood, carved with leaves and flowers and held shut by a small brass clasp shaped like a snail. When she opened the lid, a faint smell of sandalwood escaped.

The box held only a necklace of glass beads, her baby charm bracelet, and the chamois case of her pearls, tied off with cord, the name *McGintey's Jewellers* printed in black Edwardian script on the case. Her parents had spoken of meeting Mr McGintey himself, of his kindness in helping them choose these pearls.

Kate undid the drawstring and tipped the pearls onto the bedspread. They were pretty, with a soft creamy luminescence. She hoped they were valuable as well. But how would she sell them? She couldn't in Longhope without letting the whole town know they were in trouble.

Mr McGintey. That was it. She would go to Sydney, where she'd never been, to see the jeweller. To sell her pearls. Although another memento of her mother would be lost, Kate had no choice. If they were worth half a good ram, that was something. If only it were possible to see Jack too, find a way to get out to the suburb of Kogarah, from central Sydney. But the Army was strict – no visits, and leave rare, and only if requested long in advance.

~

The kitchen was empty. Sunday was Daisy's morning off and Kate was glad she was alone. She hadn't slept well and she'd woken before dawn, worried about her trip to Sydney.

A dog barked and through the kitchen's gauze door she could see Rusty looking at her from the other side of the fence.

'Morning,' she said. The dog whined a little. It was funny; the other two, Gunner and Puck, stayed away from the house paddock. They were more interested in work.

Rusty barked again.

'No tucker now. Bottinella'll feed you tonight.'

Ed had organised this. Ed had Bottinella feeding the chooks too, and he'd probably feed the poddy lambs come lambing. It was all he was good for. Young as he was, Ed already had a knack for seeing who did what best. He even got along with Grimes.

Rusty rolled over, begging for his belly to be rubbed.

'Not now.' She shook her head at the dog. She didn't want to be caught in her jarmies and dressing gown traipsing across what was left of the lawn. Something on the step outside caught her eye. It was a tin bucket, a bucket piled with sweet-smelling passionfruit, smooth green orbs against the metal's grey. Kate glanced about for any sign of the giver. Only the dog moved, watching her in the hope that she might relent and come out to pat him.

Kate held the gauze door open with her foot and leaned down, her nostrils filling with the scent of the ripe fruit. Clutching her dressing gown closed with one hand, she picked up the bucket. The only passionfruit vines were on the fences at the single men's quarters.

It must have been Canali. Conflicted, Kate stifled a flush of pleasure at the thought of him leaving these for her. But she put her face close to the fruit, letting the aroma fill her head with its sweetness.

~

Harry appeared in the kitchen the next day, after school, his white-blond hair as wiry as ever, his shirt untucked, and his shorts in need of a wash. Kate had her joddies on, though, ready for the garden later, and she was up on a chair, searching the top cupboards.

'Whatcha lookin for?' Harry said, dropping himself on a chair at the end of the table.

'I'm just cleaning.' But she got down. 'How was the first day of school?'

He said nothing.

'What's for homework?'

'Readin.' He reached into his school case (her old school case) and tossed a thin book along the table. *Our Kings and Queens* was printed below the stern face of Elizabeth I.

'That old battle-axe got beat with the ugly stick, eh.'

Kate hoped Harry was talking about Elizabeth I, not Bomber.

'Why don't you read to me?'

'Nuh. Where's your pop?' he asked, looking out along the verandah to the draughts board.

'I don't think he'll want to play today.'

Harry was disappointed. 'Where's Daisy? She's not bad at draughts, eh. Her pop learned her. She used t'beat him, she reckons,' he said.

'Daisy's working. And *taught*. Her pop – father – *taught* her. Not learned.'

He scraped his chair as he reached forward for a biscuit. Kate worried Harry's noise would annoy her father.

'I have to go to Sydney. But you'll do your homework while I'm gone, won't you?'

Harry groaned so loudly Kate thought it wise to get him outside. 'Want to go and see Minute Man? He's in the ram paddock.'

'Orright. Grimesy's gettin im in t'morra mornin, y'know. Old Minute Man. Into the yards. See his condition ahead of joinin.'

They walked together across the house paddock, Gunner and Rusty doing reconnaissance circles about them, glad of the run. On the other side of the fence, a big roo bounded off in a smooth movement, each jump a couple of yards in length, the tip of his long tail held high. Kate's father reckoned hopping was more efficient than running on all fours; that it took less feed.

'We better keep an eye out for that young ram, Basil,' Kate warned Harry. Basil was in the house paddock, and he kept himself far away from the house. Which was good. 'Jack was tree'd by a ram once. He's quick on his feet. Got up the trunk just before the ram got him!'

'He a townie?'

Kate smiled as they walked. Harry clearly no longer considered *himself* a townie. 'He was. He's a Perth boy.'

'So where'd he learn stock work?' Harry asked.

'He never liked the city. Left when he was sixteen for South Australia. Became a jackaroo.'

'Y'know what I heard, but?' Harry said.

'What's that?'

'He's a bit of a bastard, your Jack.'

'Harry! No swearing.' She suspected Grimes had told Harry that. He and Jack rubbed each other up the wrong way. Jack rubbed a lot of people up the wrong way. She loved him, but he was prickly.

'I heard other stuff too. 'Bout y'pop.'

'Don't listen to gossip, Harry.'

''E dammed the creek, eh, your dad. Stopped it up. And them graziers went bust cos of it.'

Kate looked off towards the woolshed.

'Your pop bought em up then, real cheap, those bits of dirt. Got a lotta good country for nothin, he did.'

'You shouldn't believe all you hear,' Kate said, her eyes still on the woolshed. But Harry had bits of the story right. The dam accounted for her father's reputation. A neighbour, Mr Garrier, another soldier settler like her father, went down the drain in '23 and had to walk off his place. Her father had quick-sticks put in a bid for Garrier's block. In the middle of a drought, he got it for a song.

As soon as the transfer of Garrier's block had come through, her father hired a couple of local men to dam the creek. That pretty much cut off reliable water from the Drummonds on Bellwood, and below them the Bincheys who'd been on Ferngrove for donkey's years. The Drummonds and the Bincheys got up in arms over the dam and there was even talk of solicitors. Luckily, nothing came of it. Then Mr Drummond went under in the '29 drought. Old Mr Binchey lasted longer.

He lost his place in '39. But the district laid all the blame with her father. He didn't care; by then, he had the dam for all his places.

In the next paddock, Minute Man came up the hill towards them.

'He's big, eh?' Harry said. Close to two hundred and fifty pounds, the ram had two thick cowls of wool that hung from his neck, draped down across his front legs.

Harry climbed up on the gate with the ram thirty feet or so beyond on the other side of the fence, watching them. 'Why's he called Minute Man?'

Was he taking the mickey out of her? 'He gets the job done quickly.'

'What job?'

She turned to explain, and he was grinning at her.

Rusty went under the fence and into the paddock towards the ram. Gunner, smarter, stayed put with them.

'Rusty's a dumb bastard,' Harry said, smiling. He loved the pup.

'Yes. No swearing.'

Minute Man moved from a slow amble to trot towards the dog in its paddock. Rusty didn't retreat even when the ram picked up speed, the cowls of wool about his neck flopping with each stride. About four feet from Rusty, the ram pulled up, stomped his feet and put his head down to challenge the dog. At this, Rusty backed away enough to turn and run to scramble over the gate. Harry laughed.

His paddock cleared, Minute Man moved towards Kate and Harry. Up close, the short hair on his muzzle was pale against the dirty grey of his fleece. His wrinkly horns curled round his ears, then turned out.

Harry stretched his hand over the fence, and Minute Man came right up to him. The ram lifted his head, and the boy scratched his chin and then his ears.

'C'mon,' Kate said. 'I have to get back to my jobs.'

He followed reluctantly, and they walked across the open expanse of the paddock towards the house.

'Crikey. It's Baaa–sil.'

'No swearing, and don't muck about.'

'Not kiddin.'

The young ram Basil was coming at them across the house paddock, only forty or so yards out. At four months, he was only half the size of Minute Man. His horns were big enough, though, and she and Harry were too far from the fence or the trees to make a run for it.

The ram broke into a gallop. Kate moved in front of Harry. 'Stay behind me, all right?' The ram pulled up twenty feet out and dropped his head to charge. What had Elizabeth Fleming said? Sit on them?

'Walk when I do, Harry.' She heard her voice quaver but she went straight at the ram. When he lowered his head further to charge, that gave her a chance to cover the last feet at a run. She got into his blind spot, grabbed his head, one hand on the top, the other under the muzzle, then twisted hard towards his tail. The ram dropped his head to save his neck and then Kate pushed on his hind saddle. She gasped in surprise when his back legs went down. She kept his head twisted as he fell, then dropped herself on top of him with all her weight. There she sat, Basil under her, stuck, thrashing his legs.

'Crikey! You're a bloody shearer!'

'Cut it out, Harry,' she said. 'No swearing.' But he couldn't help himself and whooped and cheered. Gunner re-appeared, barking, now he was not needed, darting in and out. Coward. 'Harry. Get to the fence. Take Gunner.'

The boy dragged the dog off by the collar. He hooted from the safety of the other side of the fence. Kate wished he'd be quiet. Someone approached behind her. Thank goodness. Basil heard it too and struggled more, thrashing his legs until he threw her off.

'*Va via!*' Canali shouted, clapping his hands at the ram. He shouted again, waving his arms, warding off the animal, who moved away.

Canali offered Kate his hand and she reached to take it, then thought better of it, and she scrambled to her feet on her own.

'*Signora* chase his sheep?' he muttered, shaking his head.

Kate smiled, dusted off her jodhpurs. 'Basil chased me.'

'*Sì*,' Canali said, with a shrug. What ram wouldn't? he seemed to say.

Kate laughed and he smiled back, pleased he'd made her laugh. With Harry ahead of them, they walked back towards the homestead gate in silence. She said nothing about the passionfruit, too shy to thank him, and still shaken.

Inside the garden, with a quick smile for her, he took the shovel from the bed, to clear its trench. She was near the steps when he spoke to her.

'She is beautiful,' he said, conversationally. 'Very beautiful.'

'What's that?' Kate coloured.

It was his turn to be embarrassed. 'No, no. This.' He waved an arm about.

Amiens. He meant Amiens.

'Beautiful but not the water,' he said.

'Yes,' she said. 'But we have the dam.'

He shifted dirt from the trench. '*Signora*. You no afraid me.' It was a plea.

'I'm not afraid,' Kate said quickly. Too quickly.

'Good. This is good,' he said. It occurred to Kate he was so different from the other POW, who seemed to struggle with everything. Canali was interesting. And in the Greek god box.

But with something like panic, Kate turned and went to the house at a clip. She was a married woman.

~

In the kitchen, Daisy set a big mug of tea in front of Kate.

Harry jumped around the table, yelling, wrestling a make-believe ram. 'She twisted is head and she got im in the guts!'

'Not true, Harry. And not so loud,' Kate said, shaken, holding onto her mug for comfort. But the noise brought her father out of his office. Kate hoped he was all right.

'You shoulda seen it, boss. She grabbed im in the privates.'

'Not true,' Kate repeated.

'Where's the draughts board, Kate? What have y'done with it?'

'Outside, Dad. On the table. Where it lives.' Then they were gone, onto the verandah to play.

Kate sat, comforted by the quick *plip-plop* of Daisy moving about the kitchen, the snippets of the Kate-wrestles-ram story floating in from Harry on the verandah.

'Y'orright, Missus?' Daisy asked, looking hard at Kate. 'Ya real white.'

Daisy cracked a smile. Kate laughed and it struck her that, for a few minutes, she'd forgotten about the bank.

~

That night, once her father was safely in bed, Kate fetched paper to write to Jack. To tell him everything. She scratched out more than she kept from her first attempt.

Dear Jack

I hope you're well. ~~I have very bad news.~~ I'm sorry I have very bad news. ~~They're selling us up.~~ The bank manager Addison says Amiens is going to be sold up. He says Dad ~~has not paid~~ borrowed a lot of money and has not paid it back. He hasn't paid interest since '42. ~~The overdraft money is missing too.~~ Dad's also spent the overdraft but ~~what?~~ we don't know what he bought.

~~So~~ I am going to see if I can sell my pearls. I've made an

appointment with McGintey's, the jeweller in Sydney. I know I can't see you. I'm sad about that.

~~What else can I do?~~ Please tell me what else you think we might do to get some money. ~~There's nothing else that we can sell.~~

~~What about your family?~~ Could you please ask your family for ~~money~~ help? I am ashamed to ask this. I would be so grateful. I'm so sorry to worry you. I miss you.

Love from

Kate

Reading the letter over again, it still sounded terrible, but it wasn't going to get better so she wrote it out neatly, hoping, somehow, he'd find some money.

CHAPTER 8

In any arena of the woolgrower's purview, dispense at once of any who would mistreat stock.

THE WOOLGROWER'S COMPANION, 1906

Kate willed the days of that week to go faster. What she could not do, though, in all that time, was tell her father she was going to Sydney. On the Tuesday afternoon, the day before she was to leave, she got up the courage. She was struggling to lift her suitcase off the high shelf in the laundry when her father came in behind her.

'Let me get it.' They switched places. He slid it down and set it on the floor beside her. 'What's the case for?'

Kate inhaled. 'The christening. Remember, Dad? For Janette's baby.'

'Christening? Janette?'

Kate felt her heart pounding, weasel that she was. 'Janette Tonkin from school. She was a Woods. Her father was the magistrate in Longhope before they got transferred to Sydney.' Kate had chosen Janette as she'd long been out of the district. 'The christening's in Sydney. I go tomorrow, back on Saturday. Remember?' Kate picked up the suitcase. Her father took the handle and carried it for her.

'Boy or girl?'

'Boy. It's a boy.' Kate moved between her wardrobe and the suitcase, packing anything that came to hand, willing her father to go.

'Doesn't matter anyhow what it is. So long as it's healthy. That's what your mum used to say. You'll have em, y'know, Katie. Babies. You mark my words.'

She stopped packing.

'You'll be a good mum too. I used t'say that t'Janice.'

Kate couldn't look at him. A sudden tear slid down her nose onto the jumbled suitcase full of clothes. He left and she heard the gauze door bang as he went out.

Be sensible, she told herself. Think about the pearls, not babies. Think about Sydney. She had never taken a trip by herself, let alone one to Sydney to sell something. When you were selling sheep, you had to look prosperous. So she started again, and this time she packed her best things.

Now, something to read. Kate tapped on the office door, just in case. Inside, there were papers on the floor, letters on the desk and books on the divan. The shelves themselves were still pretty tidy, and her mother's gardening books filled much of the top. Her mother loved to garden and had taught Kate. It was a ladylike pursuit. At the end of the top shelf, a glass bottle sat in its usual place. Full of small black seeds, it was labelled *White Wisteria 1941* in her mother's neat handwriting. Each year, it was Kate's job to collect the tiny seeds thrown out of the pods so her mother could dry them. As a little girl, she had often asked, 'Why do we keep the seeds for a year? We have the plant.'

'Our vine may die, dear, and a white wisteria is rare,' her mum would say.

Kate pushed the bottle of seeds to the back of the shelf. Lying flat next to it was the dog-eared copy of *The Woolgrower's Companion* – she might as well take that to read on the train. She also took the Army folder. She wanted to know more about the POWs.

~

As it got heavy, Kate swapped the bucket and her shovel from one arm to the other. She was carrying a bucket of chicken and mutton scraps down to the creek where she would bury them. The dogs might choke on them, so the bones had to be buried far from the house to stop them digging them up.

When Kate skittered down the bank into the dry creek bed, she was surprised to find Canali there, already digging a hole. He stopped, watchful, resting his arms, almost black from the sun, on the long handle of the shovel. Beyond the hole was a filthy tarpaulin, dark with what looked like oil.

'What are you doing?' Kate asked.

He shrugged, frowning. He wanted her gone. That was a good thing; they were right to be wary of each other.

'I dig.' He motioned with his head to the lump under the tarp.

'What's that?'

'This dog Rusty. Is dead.'

'Dead?'

'*Sì.*'

So Grimes had told Canali to do it. Poor Rusty. And poor Harry. And ruddy Grimes, who'd gone ahead without her say-so. 'Can . . . Can you bury these bones too please?'

She put the bucket of bones on the ground. Close up, she saw it wasn't oil on the tarp, but near-dry blood. The tarp was thick with it, and she backed off. In her hurry, she got a foot tangled in the rope and she stumbled, pulling the tarp away, uncovering the carcass.

Rusty was almost unrecognisable: a pulp of sinew, muscle, blood and fur, his head all but gone, only the collar intact with a piece of rope still attached. His one white ear was there, black with blood, parts of the skull visible, sheared back, crushed. Not even a bullet or shotgun pellets could have done this. He'd been hit, beaten.

Kate got herself upright, moving, and gasped at Canali. 'Did you . . . Did you . . . ?'

'*Signora!*' Canali reached out to her and Kate recoiled. She backed away, stumbling as she went and bile rose in her throat. She got to the bank, falling as the compacted sand collapsed under her. She pulled herself up, got over the top of the bank and ran to the house.

Kate got through the gate into the homestead garden as bile filled her throat and she threw up, vomiting until there was nothing left. She panted and straightened up to find Peng eyeing her from the verandah.

Daisy appeared at the kitchen door. 'Whatcha doin, Missus? You sick?' When she came out with a basin and a rag, Kate shook her head. Instead she unlooped the end of the garden hose off its holder, turned it on and pulled the hose with her to the closest patch of lawn. She pointed the stream of brown water across her mouth and chin, then shut her eyes and splashed it across to wash the rest of her face. A black chook wandered in to peck at the vomit specks at Kate's feet, and she shooed it away.

Daisy followed Kate into the kitchen. Her hands shaking, Kate started to put water in the kettle for a cup of tea. The girl took it from her. 'You crook, Missus?'

Kate sat. 'No. Down the creek, I . . . I saw.'

'What down the creek?'

'Rusty.'

'Rusty crook?' Daisy said, starting to take off her apron.

'No. No.' Kate put a hand on the girl's arm, white on black. 'He's. He's.' She shook her head and swallowed. 'Canali, he . . . he killed him.' And Kate started to cry, for Rusty. And for Canali. For what he was.

'Put im down?'

Kate shook her head, hot tears on cheeks. 'He beat Rusty, Dais, beat him to death.' She put her hands over her mouth to stop herself crying.

Daisy frowned and shook her head. She patted Kate's back and went to put tea leaves in the pot. Under the table, Peng rubbed herself against Kate's legs.

Kate saw it clearly. Canali had to go. If he could do what he did to Rusty, he was dangerous. And it would put an end to whatever she'd felt for him. Grimes would probably be pleased to have a reason to get rid of him, too.

'Cuppa tea?' Her father appeared from the office.

Daisy got another cup and poured both. Kate could not have done so; her hands were still shaking. She swallowed hard. 'Dad, we need to get rid of Canali,' she said, her voice uneven.

'What's that?' He ratted through the tins, looking for a bikkie.

'He ... he ... When he put down Rusty, he beat him.'

Her father looked up. 'Why'd he do that?'

'Rusty was chasing sheep.'

'He had to go then, eh.'

'But he *beat* him, Dad.'

Her father picked up his tea. 'The poor bugger's a soldier, Kate.' He went back to the office.

She was shocked. It was unlike her father to condone cruelty. She would tell Grimes, on the quiet, as soon as he came in from the paddocks at dusk. If he agreed that the POW had to go, she'd tell her father it was Grimes's suggestion.

~

Harry didn't turn up for his usual cordial and bikkie after school. As the afternoon lengthened, she stayed near the kitchen, keeping an eye out for the truck and for Grimes or Harry. She started the potatoes, peeling them at the sink, dropping each into a pot of cold water on the drainer.

By half past six, Kate still had not seen the truck so she guessed they must have been out near the State Forest land and come in the other way, not by the homestead. She'd been saved having Canali in her garden. Still, their late finish in the paddocks meant she had no choice but to go over to the manager's cottage.

She went out the kitchen door into the dusk, and Gunner trotted with her as she walked. Concerned about snakes, hard to spot in this fading light, Kate walked along the vehicle track rather than the shortcut Harry had worn in the grass in the month he'd been on Amiens.

Gunner looped about her without jumping. 'How are you, old fella?' She bet he knew Rusty was dead.

The front door of the cottage was open and a light was on at the back. Next door, at the single men's quarters, the garden beds were weeded and the passionfruit vine on the fence had been trimmed. Kate shivered, hoping she didn't see Canali.

As she got closer, she heard a wireless or chatter or something. Maybe Harry was home. She stopped outside the gate with the dog and called, 'Mr Grimes?' Inside, a chair squeaked, followed by soft footfalls on the wooden boards. Bootless, Grimes came to the end of the hallway. His pipe in his mouth, he was still in his blue work shirt. He motioned her inside the gate and she stood at the bottom of the three steps leading to the enclosed porch.

'What's the trouble, Mrs D?'

'It's about Rusty.' She swallowed and dropped her voice. 'And Canali.'

'Yeah?' Grimes didn't move from the doorway, and in the shadow of the sleep-out awning, it was hard to see his face. But his pipe bowl glowed, and he blew the smoke away from her. Beyond him, a narrow bed was pushed up against the sleep-out wall, blankets awry, Harry's school case open on the floor next to it.

'Where's Harry?'

'He'll be back when he's hungry. What's got your goat, Mrs D?'

'Rusty's dead,' she said.

'The dog hadda go.'

'But Canali beat him to death.'

'Yeah?' Grimes said. She couldn't see his face. He sounded amused.

'I think we have to get Canali off the place. Dad won't stand for cruelty.'

'Now you hold on, Mrs D. Your father wants Canali off?'

Kate swallowed. 'I haven't had a chance to tell him yet. But he's sure to want Canali gone.'

In the silence, Kate knew he saw her lie.

'Don't worry your head about Canali, Mrs D. I got me eye on im.'

'But I go tomorrow to Sydney. I don't want to leave Dad and Daisy alone.' She regretted mentioning her father, as if he needed protecting. She half wondered if Grimes didn't suspect.

She tried again. 'We have to get rid of him. Ask Captain Rook to replace him.'

'They won't do that too easy. Gotta be somethin serious, like knockin up a sheila – no offence – before they'll take a POW off a place. Canali's a trouble-maker f'sure, but I'm all over im, Mrs D.' He went back along the hall.

She'd been dismissed. With Gunner circling, she started back towards the house along Harry's path, too cross to worry about a snake in the dark, and looking all the while for any sign of Harry. There was none.

When Kate got back to the homestead, her father was sitting at the kitchen table wearing a pyjama shirt with his work trousers.

'Been for a walk?'

Kate shook her head.

'I'm hungry,' he said, getting up. She heard him in the bath-room, getting washed up for some tucker.

Daisy came in from the laundry, and Kate leaned against the

kitchen bench, trying to decide if she could still go to Sydney. Addison had said he would foreclose at the end of March, in just seven weeks' time. With only two trains a week and at least a week for a cheque to clear, she had no choice. She had to go to Sydney on the train. She looked at Daisy, straining the water off the potatoes at the sink. 'Dais, will you promise me something?'

The girl looked up at her, surprised.

'You need to mind out, Daisy. For that POW. Don't talk to him.'

'That beard fella?'

'No. The other one. Canali. Don't let him inside the fence. You understand?'

The girl looked away, nodding slowly. 'Orright, Missus.'

Kate hoped her father was still well enough to protect Daisy if he had to.

CHAPTER 9

Things foreign strike fear in sheep, slowing rumination and damaging lambing rates. But above all, it is the shifting to a new pasture – the transportation to a new territory – that will have the gravest effect.

THE WOOLGROWER'S COMPANION, 1906

Her alarm clock woke Kate just before dawn and the kooka-burras laughed in the trees around the homestead. She wished she felt like them. It was Wednesday, train day.

Hearing Daisy in the kitchen, she got up, put on a dressing gown and tried to pull a brush through her hair. Even squeaky clean, it was as brown as the dirt outside and thick and stiff, with an occasional wisp of a curl at her hairline. Nut-brown, her mother had called her hair colour. Jack had laughed. 'Mouse-brown, not nut-brown,' he'd said. 'Mouse-brown Hausfrau.' Kate didn't like that, whatever it meant. Mouse-brown or not, today it was knottier than usual, the ends a tangled scraggle that took time to unlock. After the trip, maybe she should cut it – follow all those government posters calling for working girls to have short hair for safety.

Kate dressed, pulling on her good pink-and-white stripy frock, with some clean but tired bone-coloured shoes over a pair of her precious nylons. She caught sight of an unfamiliar figure in the long mirror of her wardrobe. She was more angular than curvaceous, with that wiry, nut-brown hair. But she did have her mother's nice cheekbones and hazel eyes. She scrubbed up well; that was the best that could be said.

The kitchen was empty but for Daisy's bustle and the smell of frying chops.

'Dad not up yet?' Kate asked, pouring herself some tea.

'I heard im go inna th'office, Missus.'

Kate ate her breakfast quickly, grabbed another sip of tea and went to find her father. The office door was closed. 'Dad.' She tapped and pushed the door open a little.

Inside, the air was musty from having been shut up. He was curled up on the divan, facing away from her. At least he wasn't on the swag on the floor. She pushed the door wide open for light and air.

He rolled over and yawned. 'You off, Katie?' He swung his socked feet over the side of the bed and sat up, rubbing a hand across a prickly chin of salt-and-pepper grey. 'What time's your train?'

'Half-past seven. Will you be all right?'

'Right as rain,' he said. 'Right as rain. You're a worrier like y'mother. Ya shouldn't, you know. Nothin in it. Worryin. When are you back?'

'On the Saturday train. Harry's still going to come after school, though. Don't forget, will you?'

'Oh I reckon young Harry and I'll rat about to find him a bikkie at smoko.'

'Daisy'll be here. Don't let him eat them all at once. And Harry can ride Ben while I'm away.'

'Harry ride your Ben? Y'got a soft spot now for the boy, Kate?'

'Not at all. Ben needs the exercise.'

He smiled. 'Give my best to Janette.'

'What?'

'Janette. The christening.'

'Yes. Yes, I will.'

'Safe trip.' He stood and kissed her on the cheek. There was no hug; he did not go in for hugs.

Kate heard the truck come to a stop outside. 'That's Mr Grimes, Dad. I better go. Be careful, won't you?'

'What?'

'Daisy'll lock up at night. All right? Just for me.' She squeezed his hand and left, closing the door behind her.

Grimes met her outside the kitchen door and took her small belted suitcase. Kate walked behind him across the dead lawn. She was conscious of Canali watching her from the tray of the truck. Hatless, his face set, he leaned with straight arms on the rail above the cabin. Only the top of Bottinella's head was visible, as he sat in the tray.

She tugged at the truck's passenger door but it wouldn't give. Grimes, inside, pushed it open for her.

'Are you taking the POWs in too?' Kate asked him.

'Army dentist fella's in town this week. Bottinella reckons e's still got a bad tooth.'

Grimes steered the vehicle out to the main road. Their dust trail clung in the air after them, tracking the truck like a thirsty dog.

Kate spoke carefully. 'Canali isn't to come into the homestead garden while I'm away. Dad said.'

'Yeah?' Grimes glanced across, and Kate looked straight ahead.

'Yes. Did Harry come back?'

'When he got hungry, like I said.'

The train was already at the station, two passenger cars and more than a dozen cattle wagons, full of stock, being transported to feed the troops. Kate was jealous of the cattle owners, the graziers on properties out west, properties big enough to get the contracts to supply the Army.

Grimes brought the vehicle to a stop under one of the

three surviving pepperina trees and Kate inhaled. She gathered her things and pulled at the door handle but couldn't move it. Then Canali was out, his pale-green eyes and dark face only inches from hers through the open window. He was so close she could smell him and she shrank back in fear. But his smell stayed with her, sweat and soap and charcoal ash. He yanked the door open and held it for her. Kate didn't look at him. She clutched her things and walked straight past, angry with herself for feeling his attraction even while she knew what he'd done to Rusty.

'*Arrivederci, Signora.*'

She kept walking, through the smoke and steam of the engine and the braying of its thirsty cattle. She had to get Canali off the place. For everyone's sake, even her own.

Onboard, she felt relief. When the train drew away, she watched the Longhope station shed grow smaller and smaller until it disappeared into the dirt of the horizon.

~

The corridor ran the length of one side of the empty train carriage. Each of its wooden pull-up windows was dropped open for the heat. Dust motes, almost as thick as the smoke they'd come out of, whirled about in shafts of broken sunlight. Off the corridor to the left were small cubicles holding bench seats facing each other across a narrow space.

The seat numbers were painted in gold on the wood panelling. She found her seat, 8B. After brushing the film of red dust off the brown leather of the bench seats, she sat, and got out her father's 1941 journal from her bag. At random, she started to read.

22 February. Up at 96 degrees today early on. We had 10 points in the house paddock late. May use Minute Man on the maiden ewes. Need to consider next year if we'd use him again on their offspring. MM's progeny supposed to grow pretty quick, so worth the inbreeding problems? The weaners in Donnybrook couldn't find the trough. Grimes shifted them from the south-east corner up towards the windmill.

Kate flipped forwards in the journal.

2 October. 85 degrees. No rain. Boys cleared up the woolshed ahead of shearing next month. Finnegan crew booked for the 9th. Ordered the wool bale bags from Babbin, on the shearing overdraft. Bought in 100 lambs from Riley to replace them lost. Janice saw Dr King. Killed a snake in the chook pen.

October '41 must have been when her mother first got sick. She sighed, for her mum and also because she'd not found what she was looking for, the price her father paid for Minute Man. Frustrated, she switched the journal for the Army POW file.

According to the first form, Bottinella was twenty-three and married. He had been a clerk, then conscripted at seventeen in a village in Lombardy. *North Italy* was written in ink in brackets next to the typed *Lombardy*. He'd been a mess hand in the Army. But he didn't last long, as he was captured six months later in North Africa, in January '41. It looked like he'd had time in a POW camp in Egypt, then was shipped out to Sydney in May the same year. She could see he'd been in the POW camp at Hay since, for almost four years. Whatever had happened to him, Bottinella was skittish; that was for sure.

She turned with a frown to the next form, headed *Sergeant Luca Canali*. He was twenty-four and, like Bottinella, from Lombardy. He'd been conscripted in '39, and then captured in El Alamein in November '42. El Alamein was a big victory for the Allies in North Africa, Jack had told her.

She ran a finger down the page and then stopped. Tobruk.

He'd been with the Axis forces through their siege of Tobruk in '41. So it could have been him. Canali could have shot Jack's hand. Kate knew it probably wasn't. Then again the time and the place were right, and she'd seen what he'd done to the poor dog. *Bastard* is what Jack would have said, and worse.

She read on. After capture at El Alamein, Canali was shipped to India. From the form, he claimed he was tortured there as a suspected Fascist. It looked like he'd even lodged a complaint with the Red Cross. Then he'd been shipped out to Sydney a year ago. The box marked English was ticked, with a handwritten note: *Some. Taught by a guard at Hay POW Camp.* She scanned the carbon copy again. There was little to hint at Canali's violence. And nothing to hint at a wife.

With the rocking of the train and the heat, she was drowsy and she dozed. When she woke, she turned to the journal this time.

Her father had bought Minute Man sometime in early '41. And joining was always in April. Odds on, they'd bought the ram a month or so before that, to settle him in. Kate went back to the February entries in the journal.

1 February. 89 degrees. 12 points. Drafted the weaners from the ewes. Marking tomorrow.

She scanned the entries, day after day, the life of the property rolling before her. Finally, she found it.

14 February. Babbin delivered MM today. Flighty but time to settle him in yet. Told Babbin at 80 guineas the ram better sire only twins and triplets and nothing else and every one with superfine, as well.

'Half a ram,' her father had said, complaining about the cost of the pearls. Now at least she knew what the pearls were worth new. They must have cost about forty guineas, that extravagance explained only by the uninterrupted run of good seasons that preceded the purchase.

Forty guineas. If only she had five hundred sets of new pearls, she could pay back the mortgage. And Mr McGintey would never give her all of the forty, as the pearls were second-hand now. Still, at least she'd have *something* to give to Addison.

She dropped her head back against the seat, rocked by the gentle swaying of the train. Outside, the plains of the tablelands were gone, replaced by steep hills and narrow valleys with thickly set timber and an occasional tree fern, living remnants of the ancient origins of the land. She rifled around in her bag to find her sandwiches. Daisy had them wrapped in grease-proof paper inside a paper bag. Kate lifted one side of bread off the mutton and sniffed. The butter had melted in the heat. Despite the soon-stale bread and runny butter, the mutton was still good, earthy and moist with a shake of salt on it.

Kate shifted to *The Woolgrower's Companion*, but found it hard to concentrate on breeding and joining, so tried composing sentences in her head for Mr McGintey. She dozed again, but in the late afternoon dusk, as the train approached the outskirts of Sydney, Kate was wide awake, watching as dots of houses here and there became huddles and the huddles joined up, until all she could see were buildings, no matter where she looked. She couldn't believe it and kept her nose to the window as the streets and suburbs went on and on, and even as the train slowed into Central Station.

Nervous, she spilled all her things on the carriage floor. Scrambling to pick them up, she worried the train might leave with her still on it. But she was also afraid to get out onto a platform teeming with people, more people than she'd ever seen, even at the annual agricultural show in Armidale.

Above the crowd, over the platform, was a huge poster, thirty feet high or more. A young woman was drawn in front of a bright Australian flag, billowing red, white and blue behind her. She wore a factory apron, her short, neat hair peeking out from under a scarf, her hand clenched into a fist. *Change over to a Victory Job! Contact your National Service Office Now!*

Only Kate seemed to notice. Everyone was going somewhere – Army people in their khakis; older men – civilians – in suits; Air Force bods; the AAMWS ladies in khaki; and VAs in their sky-blue uniforms. A soldier was making his way through the crowd when he stopped and dropped his duffel bag, his face split into a wide smile to greet the young lady smiling back at him. He scooped her into his arms, lifting her off her feet, kissing her so hard Kate looked away, embarrassed. The girl's laughter floated across to her, and Kate envied them.

CHAPTER 10

When a drought is visited upon a district, the prudent woolgrower shall not stand by whilst his flock suffers distress but rather shall set his plan early, revisit it often and act quickly throughout, until the coming of rain brings blessed relief to man and beast.

THE WOOLGROWER'S COMPANION, 1906

After an hour in the queue at Central Station, Kate got in a taxi. She didn't mind the long wait, relieved to be away from all the people.

The elderly cab driver scrutinised her in the rear-view mirror. 'Where y'goin, love?'

'Potts Point. The Country Women's Association Hostel.'

'Righty-ho.' He steered the big black Ford into the stream of traffic, mostly civilian, with an occasional Army staff car or truck. The footpaths were full of people. Where did they all live?

'What can I get for yez?'

'Pardon?' She looked at his eyes in the mirror appraising her.

'Potatoes. Even peas, if you goin posh. Anythin y'like, if ya got the money. Nylons, even. On the quiet, of course.'

'No, thank you,' Kate said.

'This is Elizabeth Street. Streets signs all gone, of course, for the Japs. Where y'up from?'

'Longhope.'

'Where's that?'

'The Tablelands. North of Armidale.'

'In the sticks, eh? Near Woop Woop. First time ere? I'll take y'down Crown Street. Bedda view, eh.'

They went over a rise, and there it was, the harbour, a stretch of bright blue water between tall buildings. She'd seen the sea once before, when she was eight. Her parents had taken her on a rare trip, to Port Macquarie, and she remembered the salt foam of strong waves that sucked her off her feet.

'It's so blue,' she said. 'And big.'

'She's big, orright. Finest natural harbour in the world, the guide books say. But them Yanks'll tell ya New York Harbor's twenty times the size.' He shook his head.

Kate half-listened, agog at the height of the buildings and the magic of the water. Across the other side, yellow sandstone cliffs and green bushland hugged bottle-blue coves and white sand beaches.

'The bridge,' she cried. Its broad steel spans stretched from west of Circular Quay all the way to Kirribilli on the north shore.

'Ah, the coat hanger. She's somethin – twelve hundred yards across.' He pulled up in front of what looked like an office building. 'And here we are, love.' It was very big, with five or so storeys. A sign with the CWA emblem hung above the wide steps and double doors through which a river of young women in the VA uniform ebbed and flowed.

He drove off, leaving her all alone on the busy footpath with her suitcase and bag at her feet.

~

The next morning, even after some tea and toast, Kate was weary. A saggy bed, a noisy city and her nerves had made for a sleepless night. Sydney was a city of servicemen carousing, men going to pubs, in pubs, leaving pubs. Then came the rubbish trucks, with bottles smashing and the clang of empty kegs. Kate missed Amiens and its gentle noise, the kookaburra chorus, and the rabble and squawk of the galahs. She thought of Daisy and her father, hoping they were all right.

She found her bus, and was relieved, about a half hour later, to get off at the Double Bay stop. It looked very smart. At one end, the street was all large houses, each set back from the road, their arched verandahs and mowed lawns shaded by neat palms. On the other side of her, expensive-looking shops competed for the residents' money. She was conscious of the worn gloves in her hands. There were no less than two jewellers there, one with a sign that read: *H.K.J. McGintey & Sons. Fine Jewellery and Chattels*, in gold script on shiny black paint.

She gathered her wits and looked in the windows. Her mother had told her years before that McGintey's sold *only* these beautiful things, no colanders or tea towels, tablecloths or wooden spoons. Now the proof was in front of her, and Kate grew more nervous.

Mr McGintey turned out to be little and round with glasses on a serious face. He greeted her with an odd sideways dip of his head. When it happened a second time, Kate knew; he had palsy. At the back of the shop, Mr McGintey made his way up a staircase. Kate followed, her eyes on his polished shoes. His office was lined with the same wood panelling as the beautiful shop windows. There was even a grandfather clock by the door; Kate had only seen them in books.

A large mahogany partner's desk sat in front of two enormous windows, each drinking in the blues and greens of Sydney Harbour. The desk was empty, except for a silver-framed photo of a serious young man with very dark hair, in Army uniform. The man almost had a bit of Canali about him. Kate looked away. Beside the photo was a dark-blue fountain pen standing in its own holder, a small silver bell and a little silver tray of metal tweezers. She clasped her shabby hands in her lap and looked across the desk.

Mr Harold Kenneth John McGintey was a much smaller man than his name had suggested. Kate had some difficulty seeing much of him at all behind the big desk. He reminded her of an elderly wombat, low to the ground and slow moving.

She had come up with and discarded many openings on the train, and she still had no words for him. But Mr McGintey was unperturbed by the mute young woman.

They sat in silence until Mr McGintey reached for the small bell located in the corner of his desk. He rang it efficiently, restored it to its place and waited. A discreet tap at the door preceded the arrival of a biggish lady, bearing tea on a tray.

The lady might have been big but she was swish. She wore a lovely twinset, mulberry-coloured, and her hair was pulled tightly into a long-ways bun at the back of her head. She smiled at Kate, and with pale hands she put the teapot and a tea strainer, along with two fine china teacups – the same pretty blue pattern as in the show case downstairs – in front of Mr McGintey. An exotic, aromatic scent filled the air and Kate savoured it. Was it the lady's perfume?

'Some tea, Mrs Dowd?' Mr McGintey asked with a nod, his head twisting sideways a little.

It was the *tea*. Kate smiled a yes. That tea could smell so sweet!

The tea was delicious, a wonderful and curious flavour, familiar but unusual, like honey from a hive near stringybark gums.

They drank in silence but Kate's concern built with each sip. What if she could not bring herself to say anything? She cleared her throat to speak. Mr McGintey must have seen the terror on her face, for he smiled in encouragement. Still she couldn't say anything.

'More tea, Mrs Dowd?' The teapot was in mid-air, lid rattling gently.

'No. Thank you, Mr McGintey.'

He withdrew his watch from a waistcoat pocket and wound it carefully.

'You have jewellery to sell, Mrs Dowd?'

'Yes,' she said, relieved that he'd guessed.

'Please show me.' He reached into a desk drawer and brought forth first a jeweller's monocle, wrapped in a soft cloth, and then a small square velvet-lined tray. Kate's hands shook as she passed the soft chamois case over to him, conscious of her hands, her wrists tanned to the colour of tea.

He dropped the strand of pearls onto the tray.

'My parents bought them here. At McGintey's.'

He nodded, neither in agreement nor denial, just an acknowledgement that she had spoken. She watched as he examined them, carefully working his way, pearl by pearl, along the strand from one end to the other. From time to time, he cleared his throat.

Nervous, Kate tried to sit still. The ticking of the grand-father clock was loud behind them.

'I can offer you fifteen guineas, Mrs Dowd,' he said, looking up at her. The monocle remained in his right eye so he took on the appearance of a demonic wombat now, its face domi-nated and distorted by the monster eye.

'Fifteen, Mr McGintey?'

'Yes,' he said and began putting the pearls back in their case.

'But my parents paid more than forty for them new.'

He shrugged. 'These are second-hand. We could give you a cheque now. Or you could try the Cross, of course, if you need the money more . . .' he searched for the right word and looked up from the pearl case to her eyes '. . . more urgently.'

'The Cross?'

He nudged the tray towards her. 'Kings Cross, Mrs Dowd. The pawnbrokers there. You could always go to a pawnbroker.'

Kate thought about drab Kings Cross and what she had seen of it from the bus on the way that morning. And she knew she could not expect much from anyone for the pearls.

'Fifteen will do.'

He took out a small book with a dark-green cover marked *INVOICES* and began to write, his hand a spidery record of their bargain. 'Nothing else to sell, Mrs Dowd?'

'No.'

He smiled then as he wrote, animated for the first time. 'I was rather hoping you'd brought the sapphire.'

'Sapphire?'

'The one your father bought for you. If you didn't want to sell it, we could cut it for you.' But when she said nothing, he looked up from the invoice book. His eyes widened in alarm. 'You didn't know? I should not have said anything.'

Kate forced a laugh. 'He's dropped big hints about a sapphire. So it's true?'

Mr McGintey exhaled, his face relaxing. 'Yes. He wanted a rough stone, a yellow, on the big side and of exceptional quality. But it had to be uncut. Quite unusual.'

'Why's that?' She forced another smile.

'Customers want certainty, Mrs Dowd. They want the secrets of their stones unlocked. I suggested he buy a cut stone as they're easier to come by at that size. But he insisted uncut would be better for you. Safer, he said.'

Kate felt a sob rise in her throat. She didn't understand why on earth her father would buy a stone, but she did understand that he wanted to look after her.

Mr McGintey tore the invoice from the book. She forced another smile, still trying hard not to cry at her father's concern for her, no matter how muddled his efforts. 'How . . . how big is the sapphire?'

'Just over thirty carats, roughly.'

'What was it worth?'

He laughed nervously. 'Well, I couldn't tell you what he paid.'

'It's important, Mr McGintey, that I know.' She surprised herself.

His face grew serious. 'About £6,000.'

Kate gasped. Was this the overdraft money? A small farm could be had for less than that.

'He paid cash, you know, Mrs Dowd. Quite took us by surprise. We'd not seen that amount before.'

'And second-hand, Mr McGintey? What would the stone be worth? About the same as new? It's never been . . . worn, as it were.'

He looked at her with new respect. 'That's right. They don't fluctuate too much in value, uncut stones.'

'What does it look like?' There were sapphire mines around Longhope, so she'd seen a few. 'Like the one in my ring?'

'No, no, my dear.' The old man laughed. 'It's bigger, about the size of a hen's egg, I recall, and rough, of course. Uncut. Here, I'll show you.' He shuffled to the cabinet at the side of the room and used a key on a chain from his pocket to open it.

'Sapphires,' he said, tipping the contents of another soft chamois bag onto the tray between them. Seven stones tumbled across the velvet, rough with jagged edges and unusual colours, some dark greens and dark blues, and even one of a pale honey colour. They varied; the smallest, a blue, was grape-like, and the biggest, a green one, the size of a small bird's egg.

'These are washed, of course. Rinsed to get the dirt off.' Mr McGintey picked through the stones with his tweezers.

'Here you are,' he said, holding up the honey-coloured stone. 'This is a yellow, the same colour as your father bought. This one's smaller, of course. And yellows are among the rarest.'

He passed the tweezers to her, and Kate peered at the gem. It looked just like a smoky pebble or smoothed broken glass. It was about the size of a sheep's eye and on one edge it was smooth, like a piece of quartz rolled over and over for an age in a running creek.

Kate held the sapphire up. Shafts of deep yellow light ran through it, the colour of sunlight. When she set it back down, it became a pebble like the others.

She stared at the stone. 'It could be anywhere,' she said.

'I beg your pardon, Mrs Dowd?'

'Anywhere,' she repeated, unconcerned with the odd look the old man gave her. 'It could be anywhere on Amiens.'

CHAPTER 11

A ewe separated from its lamb in the yards or elsewhere shall seek tirelessly to return to it.

THE WOOLGROWER'S COMPANION, 1906

Friday in Sydney dragged for Kate, as she killed time waiting for the train home on Saturday, made all the worse knowing that Jack was only a matter of miles away at the Army camp at Kogarah. But he might as well have been on Mars: no leave, that was clear. With all these hours to fill, in the end she'd taken herself off on foot to the Royal Botanic Gardens, and had spent the day there, trying to looking at roses and shrubs, thinking how much her mother would have enjoyed it. But her thoughts returned again and again to Amiens, Canali and the sapphire.

By the time the train pulled into Longhope station on the Saturday afternoon, Kate was itching to get off, ready well before it would come to a stop under its dirty blanket of smoke and steam. She was anxious about what might have happened while she was away, keen to ask her father about the sapphire.

First things first. Something had to be done about Canali. She pushed at a bobby pin escaping from her hair, then searched her handbag for the war bonds flyer a VA had pressed on her at the CWA hostel. Folding the flyer to have the writing on the inside, she put it on top of her handbag and scanned outside for Grimes's distinctive blue shirt. It looked like he'd come to collect her alone, thankfully.

She got down into the remains of steam and smoke, and Grimes nodded a greeting at her from under his eyebrows.

'All well at Amiens?' she asked as they walked towards the truck.

'I reckon. Not seen mucha y'father. An he gimme no cheque this week.'

'For the pay?' That wasn't good. 'No problem with Canali?'

'No. The pay's the ruddy thing. The men are spittin chips.'

Kate opened her mouth and shut it. Payday was the day before, Friday. The men would have had no drinking money last night, and that would be all round the district by now. Grimes must know about her father. She buried the thought.

'I'll get the money.' As she climbed into the truck, she prayed there was still enough in the bank. The pearl cheque would take days to clear and they needed the wages now. In the confines of the car, she noticed that the smell of pipe smoke hung about him.

'I'd like to drop in to the POW Control Centre on the way, please.'

He looked across at her, curious. She rifled in her handbag and then flashed the folded paper at him. 'Captain Rook wanted Dad to sign some form, and I forgot before I left.'

Grimes grunted. She was relieved when he turned off the main road towards the Control Centre. It was housed in what had been the Longhope Amateur Dramatics Society Hall but was now given over to the Army for the Rural Employment Scheme. Grimes stopped the truck inside the yard, in front of the hall, a corrugated iron shed. Kate went in between the two large rolling doors open across the front, towards the voices from the office box at the back of the shed.

She tapped on the half-open door and went in. The second

he saw her, Captain Rook was on his feet, a smile across his ruddy face. 'Mrs Dowd,' he said, stubbing his cigarette into a dirty ashtray on the desk. A little ceiling fan turned, squeaking on each revolution, shifting what seemed like hot air about. Maybe she was just nervous.

Corporal Oil was slower to get up, taking the opportunity to check her out. Behind him was a large colour poster of a Japanese soldier stepping across a map into the brown empty north of Australia.

'What can we do for you, Mrs Dowd?' the captain asked, still smiling. He motioned for Kate to sit down, pulling out the only spare chair, the one next to Oil.

'It's about our POW, Canali. He has to be replaced,' she said.

Oil raised his ginger eyebrows. He leaned back in his chair, hands clasped behind his head. He was so close to Kate she could smell him. Sweat and stale cigarette smoke.

'Canali giving you trouble?' Captain Rook swung round in his chair and pulled open the filing cabinet behind him. Its top was crammed with papers.

'He killed one of our work dogs. Beat it to death.'

'Not a dog lover then?' Oil said.

'The dog had to be put down. It's *how* he did it.'

The captain frowned and shifted the ashtray. 'Is he the gun rider chappy? The bloke that gave your manager curry on the first day?'

'That's him.'

'How's your father find him otherwise? And the manager – Grimes, is it? What do they think of this fella?'

Kate knew what he was asking; why was she raising this, and not her father or Grimes? When she said nothing, he changed tack. 'Does he do his work? Is he cooperative?'

'He's . . . he's opinionated.'

'Opinionated,' Oil repeated, nodding slowly.

'I want him off. He's slow too. Mr Grimes says he's a bludger.'

The captain stood up and pulled a small book with a bright green cover off the top of the filing cabinet. 'Problem is,' he said, flipping through the book, 'it doesn't sound like he breached a regulation.'

'But you must have to take him off, if we ask?'

'Aw, we can take im off orright. Can take im off today. But we can't put nothin back,' Oil said.

Captain Rook frowned. 'The corporal's right. Until he breaks one of the rules of assignment —'

'Or *commits a crime*,' Oil added, officious.

'— you'd be down a man. You'd be in the queue with the rest of the district for the next allotment of POWs. If there is one.'

The ceiling fan squeaked in the stuffy silence of the office. Kate knew they could not cope on Amiens without Canali. Not now, with her father unwell.

'I say, Mrs Dowd,' Captain Rook began slowly, 'I say we keep an eye on him. You, and us too here at the CC. If there's a problem, a reg breach, we'll get him off the place. If you want.'

Kate looked away, angry she had no choices. She got up.

'I got some mail for your bods that I'll give you too.' Captain Rook extracted two letters from the mass on top of the cabinet.

Oil got up as well, shaking his head. 'A man that'll beat an animal to death? Got a nasty streak.'

The captain came out from behind his desk. 'You watch him, all right?'

Kate nodded, grateful for the captain's kindness. But she was stuck with Canali.

~

'You still got y'form,' Grimes pointed out as she got into the truck with the war bonds flyer in her hand.

'What? Oh, he said he didn't need it after all.' She pushed

the flyer down into her handbag as the truck moved off. 'He did give me some mail for the POWs, though. If you can deliver them when we get home.' The POWs' letters sat on her lap. The one on top was for Canali. She eyed it on the quiet. It was a small envelope on thin paper, greyish in colour, and the name and the return address on the top were written in a clear, firm hand. Another Canali: a Giuseppe. His father? It was postmarked July 1944. It had taken eight months to reach him.

They were nearing the Amiens homestead when Grimes spoke. 'Give the old man a message, will you? Need to buy feed. Grain. Joinin's next month and there's no feed on the ground in Riflebutt.'

This worried Kate a bit, because when her father was well, he'd complain that Grimes was good at spending other people's money. Kate did know that they built up the ewes before joining, to get them into good condition. That increased the number to fall pregnant. But when? Was it too soon to start buying grain?

'Let the old man know. We'll do the rams too. The rest'll keep on with the branches we cuttin'.'

'I'll ask him now, and get you the cheque for the wages.'

Grimes frowned as she got out of the truck. She knew why. This grain business wasn't a request: it was a statement. He didn't like her putting the brakes on him.

Inside, there was no sign of Daisy. Kate grabbed the cheque-book from the drawer en route to the office. She tapped and went in, having to step over a pile of books. Her father was lying on the divan, a lump, an old blanket pulled up above his ears.

'Hullo, Dad.' He shifted a little, under the blanket, and she patted him. Was he cold in the middle of summer? Three dirty plates sat on the desk. Poor Daisy probably hadn't been able to get in here.

'Sydney was all right, Dad, but Mr Grimes wants to talk to you about buying grain ahead of joining.' Kate opened the cheque-book on the desk and leaned over to write out the cheque. 'Also, do we need to buy grain now for the ewes and the rams?'

That did it. The blanket dropped away as he sat up awkwardly, with hair awry, and his shirt crumpled.

'You all right, Dad? Did you hurt yourself?'

'What you say? Grain?' he asked.

'Yes, Mr Grimes says we need to buy grain now.'

'Have Janice talk to him,' he said and lay back down again.

She leaned down to kiss his cheek, the stubble scratching her face. A sour smell reached her and she wondered if he'd had a bath while she was away. That worried Kate. Now was not the time to ask him about the sapphire. She turned to go, then she remembered the wages cheque.

'Dad, I need you to sign for the pay.' She put the cheque-book beside his head on the divan, inches from his eyes.

He grunted and, still lying down, he took the pen and tried to sign.

'You'll have to sit up, Dad.'

He did sit up, as carefully as before, and signed in wobbly scrawl. Kate decided it would have to do as he lay down again and pulled the blanket up over his head. She stacked the dirty plates and took them back to the kitchen, stepping over the books at the door, careful to keep the plates away from her good dress and the cheque. Grimes would have to take it to the bank on Monday. She'd go with him to see Mr Addison and deposit the other cheque, for the pearls.

Kate delivered the cheque to Grimes, and told him, to no comment, that her father would think about the grain.

Back inside, she unpacked, put her dirty clothes in the laundry and tidied more books off the floor in the sitting room, all the while keeping an eye out for the sapphire. She was in the kitchen, making a cup of tea, when she heard someone in the laundry.

'Daisy? That you? I'm back.'

Daisy was scrubbing something in the tub.

'You all right, Daisy?'

Still with her back to her, the girl nodded.

'Do you want a drink of water?' Kate asked. Daisy shook her head.

'I brought you something from Sydney. You want to see it?'

More scrubbing.

'I'll get it. Come into the kitchen.' Kate went to her bedroom to get the presents, one for Daisy and one for Harry, hoping Daisy might be in the kitchen by the time she got back. Still there was no Daisy.

'Look,' Kate called out, 'I hope you like it.' She set the brown-paper packages on the kitchen table, however there was no movement from the laundry, and no sign anywhere of Harry either. Kate shook her head, starting to feel like she was the only sane person left on Amiens. She took a hand towel and one of the packages and went into the laundry. Daisy was still at the tub.

'Come on,' Kate said, holding out the towel in one hand and the package in the other. 'Dry your hands. That can wait.'

The girl turned, keeping her eyes down. She took the towel to dry her hands, and Kate realised that Daisy was crying. When she rubbed her arm, Kate noticed dark welts on the girl's skin, bruises round her wrists.

She took Daisy's arms in alarm. 'What happened?'

Daisy pulled them away, her head down. She started to cry again.

'Who did this? Canali?'

Daisy shook her head and wiped her nose. 'Can't tell, Missus.' Her voice was thick with tears. Kate led her into the kitchen.

109

Why would she not say? Could it have been Grimes? Or Ed? Kate could hardly believe him capable of it. 'Tell me who it was.'

Daisy shook her head again. Kate felt sure it was Ed she was protecting.

She patted the girl on the shoulder awkwardly. 'C'mon, Dais.'

Her tears continued to fall, the drips making neat dark circles on the brown paper. She sat there, her fingers on the package. After a bit she started to open it, unwrapping the paper from a small spoon. Its handle was extra-large, in the shape of a shield, and drawn on it was Sydney Harbour Bridge.

Harry appeared on the other side of the gauze door and came in, school case in one hand, something little and wooden in the other. Even in the midst of her worry about Daisy, Kate was surprised to find she'd missed him. 'Hullo, Harry. You all right?'

He shrugged, not looking at her.

She'd not seen him since Rusty died. 'What you got there?' she asked, reaching for his hand.

'Nothin.' He held whatever it was against his shirt so she couldn't see all of it. It looked like a carved animal, a couple of inches high, in red gum wood.

'Sydney's big. And the new Harbour Bridge is too. Enormous,' Kate said.

'I seen it already.'

'I *have* seen it already,' Kate said. 'Really?'

'You callin me a liar?'

Not Harry as well. Kate was glad she rarely went away. Everyone seemed to go off the rails.

Harry put the wooden thing on the table and walked it along with his fingers. A dog, a carved dog, just like Rusty.

'That's good. Did you make it?'

'Nuh.'

'Bottinella do it?'

'Nuh.'

'I brought you a present too,' Kate said.

'Is it one o' them?' Harry pointed to the spoon.

'Yes.'

Harry frowned, took the still-wrapped package and went out. Daisy left too with her spoon in one hand.

Kate sat down in the quiet kitchen, her head full, full of worry about her father, about Canali, the bank. Harry.

Turning her worries over and over produced no answers. She wanted to be by herself, away from people, get out of the house for a bit. Visit the chooks – that's what she'd do. She'd look for eggs and even hunt around in the chook run for the sapphire.

CHAPTER 12

Droughts are perhaps the harshest of times for a man wanting to make an honest living as a woolgrower.

THE WOOLGROWER'S COMPANION, 1906

Kate picked her way along the track up the little hill that separated the house and the chook run. The run was a fenced enclosure, with eight feet of chicken wire (six above ground, two below for the snakes and the foxes) and one gate. The four wooden laying boxes inside were made from truck part boxes, each up on stilts again to keep out predators.

A black chook strutted towards Kate. 'No scraps. Sorry, old girl,' she said. The chook stalked off again. The gate that served as the entrance to the run was pulled back on itself, open for the day. Bottinella looked after the chooks now. He fed them the scraps every morning, let them out for the day and locked them up on dusk, to be safe from the goannas, foxes and dingoes. Kate checked for the snake waddy. It was where it should be, hanging on the fence by the open gate. About four feet long, it was made of No. 8 wire doubled over and twisted together.

She walked round the fence, looking for somewhere her father might have hidden the sapphire. Would he have wrapped it in something? Newspaper? She tried to remember the weight of the stones Mr McGintey had shown her, their feel in her hand.

Inside the run, she searched each of the four egg boxes. In the last box, she disturbed a clucky black-and-white hen and got one egg for her trouble, and that was all. No sapphire. She savoured the quietness there, just her and the chooks. And at least the chooks were predictable.

She made her way reluctantly back to the house, with the egg, watching where she put her feet as she walked. 'A snake never means to kill you,' her father used to say. 'He's just shirty when you step on him.'

In the kitchen, Daisy was peeling potatoes at the sink for the evening meal, a tune on the wireless the only sound in the quiet house. There were no tears, and Kate hoped Daisy was feeling better. She put the egg in the basket on the top of the kerosene fridge and got the post that had accumulated while she was away. She sat at the kitchen table, steeling herself for more bills. Kate half tuned in to the words on the wireless.

Yes nothin like a night in the air raid shelter,
Cards and tea and prayers and heat and fleas.

'Must be terrible to have to go down into those things,' Kate said, her eyes on the Babbin envelope in her hands.

'Ya gotta do that, Missus? Go unna tha ground?'

'I think so. If the siren goes off.'

'Better a hole in the ground than one in y'head.' Kate's father had appeared in the hall doorway. He was beltless and she suspected he could do with a change of shirt.

'Dad, you're up,' she said. She gathered the bills into a pile as casually as she could, covering them with her elbows. Daisy disappeared into the laundry.

'Them air raid shelters are probly dry. Dry. Think of that.' Her father looked away, shaking his head, and went back out the way he'd come. Kate hoped that was it. She listened for the door to the office as the wireless played on.

Nothin like a night in an air raid shelter . . .

Daisy came back, and Kate spread out the post again. Not only was there no letter from Jack but there were bills, one each from Nettiford's, Darcy's, and Babbin's. The Babbin's account was for £7-4-2d, all of it *90 days overdue*. The detail column said *Wool bales*. Kate couldn't believe it. Her father must not have paid their stock and station agent for the shearing supplies last November. And Babbin had not even docked her father's wool cheque after he arranged the sale. She shook her head, touched at Mr Babbin's belief that her father would pay. They needed Babbin's for pretty much everything – for shearing supplies and even to sell Amiens's wool.

'Yoo-hoo.' Meg's voice floated through the afternoon heat into the kitchen.

'Yoo-hoo, you too,' Kate called back. She could do with a dose of Meg. She put the bills into the junk drawer and pushed the gauze door open.

'You're pretty cheerful for a girl who just came back to the bush.' Meg slid down off her horse and tied the reins to the railing. 'Swim? We should get over to your dad's dam while there's still water in it. Get your cozzie.' Meg had already decided. A teenager going on twenty-five, as Jack said.

'I'm not sure there's enough water in the dam.' Kate held the door open for her. 'Is that lipstick?'

Meg grinned, the little gap between her front teeth smiling at Kate. 'My word, yes. Old Winston Churchill says lipstick is good for morale. Maybe he wears it himself?'

'Your lipstick will be wasted today. The POWs are out in the back paddocks.'

'Canali too?' Meg looked disappointed.

'Both of them, but Canali's a dark horse. Awful. I'll tell you.'

Meg came into the kitchen while Kate went into her room to ferret about in her chest of drawers for a cozzie, having a quick look – a new habit – for hidden bank notes or even the sapphire.

114

'Will we walk?' Kate called through the house.

'Fiva'll take us,' Meg's voice came back. 'How's Sydney then?'

'You know, big.' Kate took two worn towels from the linen cupboard.

Outside, Fiva was pulling clumps of dry grass into his mouth, and Kate stared, distracted.

'Everything all right?' Meg untied Fiva's reins.

'Not really. That POW Canali beat Rusty to death.'

'You sure? Can't see him doing that.' Meg led Fiva to the old wooden stump next to the fence.

'I'm telling you. He's terrible.' Kate pulled at a persistent knot in her hair, partway down her plait.

'You planning a nest in that?'

'I might cut it short,' Kate said.

'Whatever will Jack say?'

Kate grimaced. It was true he would be unhappy. She hung the two towels round her neck and pulled herself up behind the younger girl. The horse moved away, wanting to be off.

At the fence line, Kate slid off to get the gate. She unhooked the chain to let them through then climbed back on.

'How's your dad these days?' Meg asked.

'He's all right. A bit worse, maybe.' Kate looked away, embarrassed. 'He thinks I hide things from him now.'

'Ooof.'

Kate nodded. 'But he hides the stuff himself – for safe keeping, he says. Then forgets where.'

'Dead set?' Meg put her arm back and patted Kate's side. 'Is Amiens all right then? I mean, who's managing it? Are you?'

Kate waggled her head. 'Sort of. But I pretend Dad's running things.'

'You're not short of money, are you?' It was almost a whisper, even here in the middle of nowhere.

Kate wondered what Meg might have heard. 'Don't say

anything, will you? But I think we are. That's why I went to Sydney. To sell my pearls. I'll take the cheque in to Addison first thing Monday.'

'My poor Kate. You need a swim.' They slid off the horse and walked up the side of the gully and then across, out onto the dam wall. In front of and below them lay a stretch of water about the size of a cricket oval, with a boundary of cracked mud pieces. 'It might be deep enough right in the middle, I reckon,' Kate said.

The girls took off their old shirts, and Kate hooked the damp towels and their clothes onto the rain-gauge post. Above them in a high branch was a pair of black-and-red Banks cockatoos, watching.

Meg ran, first one way, then the other. She grabbed a small stone from the ground and threw it hard at the birds.

'*What* are you doing?' Kate asked.

'Trying to get em to fly east,' Meg said, coming back to Kate. 'The cockatoos.'

'I don't think that's how it works.'

Meg took her boots off and put the top of one upside down inside the other, to keep out ants and anything else that might bite. Then she turned towards the water and ran in, full pelt. Within two paces, her feet stuck in the mud and she belly-flopped into shallow brown water. Landing hard, she lifted her face out of the water, coughing and laughing.

Kate entered the water carefully, walking into it until she could lie, then she breast-stroked out to join her friend. She rolled over onto her back and let the water fill her ears, looking up. She loved to float, to be cut off from everything, even sound, nothing above her but a bright blue sky. A splash of water landed on her face and she rolled upright.

'Wish you had a tooth gap now, don't you?' Meg took another mouthful of water and spurted, hitting Kate's face again. 'Such a good sight. Even a little bit of water. When was it last full?'

'All the way? Years now.'

'It's dry all over. We're buying grain again this year, to build up the ewes for joining. The rams as well.'

So Grimes was right. They needed to buy grain now. But they owed Babbin money already. 'I'm sick of it all. The whole jolly thing,' Kate said.

Meg sniffed. 'Can you smell that?'

'Smoke?' Kate was all attention.

'I smell a martyr burning.'

Kate rolled her eyes.

'You must miss Jack,' Meg said.

Kate looked up at the sky. If she thought about it, she'd idolised him when they got married. She loved his noise and his jokes and his bluster, how he seemed to fill a room, a wonderful joyous thing in her family of quiet people. But now that he'd been away so long, she worried that they'd married too quickly, just because her mother had wanted it. Whether they were suited, even. It occurred to Kate that Jack rarely ever made her blush. That damn Canali did, though . . . Even now she knew what he was like.

'That's a lot of thinking for a yes–no answer.'

'What?' Kate swallowed. 'I do miss him. Jack, I mean. Yes.'

'You must miss the best bit. What's it like? Making love.'

'Cut it out, Meg!'

'No, true blue. What's it like?'

'Well. It's . . . it's a wife's duty, isn't it?'

'Pretty bloody pleasant duty,' Meg cackled, 'so I gathered from Robbo.'

It might be fun for the men but not for her. Kate remembered their wedding night. All that fuss over nothing, she'd thought.

'Sometimes . . . I feel like I don't know Jack,' Kate said.

'What?'

'Well, he wasn't here long. We courted for a bit. Then we

got married just before Mum died. We only had a few months as a married couple before he was posted to Kogarah.'

'Aw, you'll get on after the war. How does he like Kogarah, anyway?'

'Can't stand it. Says he's missing out on the fighting. But he's a good shot, and apparently even better at teaching recruits to shoot.'

'I envy them, you know. Sort of,' Meg said, on her back, her eyes on the sky above her.

'Envy who?'

'The boys in battle. Oh I know they might die, and that's a terrible, terrible thing. Still, they'll have a moment, one moment, when they'll be tested, see what they're made of. We'll just have kids and make scones and grow bloody roses,' she said in disgust.

'It's not one moment for us,' Kate said slowly. 'I mean, I think for girls, *every* moment is a test in its own way. We hold things together, especially now. In wartime.'

'You're right about the war. We're doing stuff we never got to before. It's why I love being a VA. It's a real job, even if it is with bedpans and bandages and even if they don't bloody pay us. But that'll be over when the war is, when the men come back, back to tell us what we can and can't do. Does Jack do that? Tell you what to do?'

'Well, not while he was working on his hand. But once he was passed fit by the Army, for those weeks before he left, he started to . . .'

She didn't enjoy taking orders from Jack. He'd never really worked the place, not for long anyhow. Even though he'd jackaroo'd for a time, he knew little about grazing, that was for sure. Kate knew more, despite her mother's best efforts to keep her away from working the paddocks. After the war, having to take orders from Jack might well annoy Grimes and Ed. And her.

'Any news of Robbo?' Kate asked, changing the subject.

'No.' Meg shook her head and frowned. 'I kid myself that's good – that if he'd been killed, they'd tell us. I just want to get back at the Japs, you know. Got my very own bloodthirsty need to hurt em.'

'But not the Italians?'

Meg shook her head, wet curls limp around her face. 'No. The Eye-ties are all right, I reckon. And they're having a rough trot too. Luca's little sister is somewhere over there, swimming and worrying just like I am, eh? Wondering if her brother's orright.'

'Luca?'

Meg smiled, embarrassed. 'Canali. He's got a brother too, come to think of it, and four older sisters. I reckon it's having all those big sisters that has made him such a sweetie.'

Kate said nothing.

'But the brother's missing. He's only sixteen or something. Or was.'

'So they know his brother's dead?'

'His dad thinks so, apparently. The brother was helping the partisans up there in the north, in the bit that's still German. They say he got caught but poor old Luca doesn't want to believe that, of course.'

'How do you know all this?'

'I always yarn with Luca. He's handsome with those green eyes, and that Roman nose, don't you reckon? And he's a bachelor! I asked im. How'd *he* get away, eh?'

'Meg! He's a POW, for heaven's sake.' Worry filled Kate's head. She'd spotted Meg stopping by the garden to talk to Canali often enough on her way out. But Meg's parents would never approve of her chatting with a POW, let alone her crush.

A crow picked his way towards their boots on the dam wall.

'You know they bombed a whole town in Germany? Dresden? It was in the paper,' Meg said. 'But serves em right. That's how I feel now.'

Kate reached out in the water to take Meg's hand. They floated on until the sun dropped behind the dam wall and the light turned orange in the late afternoon.

~

Kate walked from Riflebutt to save Meg the bother of carting her all the way home. Her wet plait banged against her back, keeping her shirt damp when the rest of it dried in the heat. The track ran along the fence line, and she kept to one of its two dirt corrugations, head down, on the lookout for snakes. She liked the walk, wanting a chance to think about what she should do. She'd better tell Grimes to buy the grain, so long as Babbin would overlook their unpaid account.

The sun was low. Canali might be in the garden by now and she'd have to see him. She hadn't spoken to him since she caught him burying Rusty.

Gunner came out to meet her, and she stopped to scratch behind his ears. He stayed by her side as she walked on. And, Murphy's law, Canali was in the garden all right, throwing a pick easily into the ground, dark circles of sweat visible even through the purple of his shirt.

He straightened up, watching her as she went past him across the dead lawn.

'*Signora.*'

She didn't look at him.

'*Per favore, Signora,*' he called again, moving towards her. Kate heard him. All she could see was Rusty wrapped in that bloody tarp. She got inside and shut the door.

120

CHAPTER 13

Any man who might usefully impart some kernel of knowledge is to be valued by the prudent woolgrower, no matter his guise.

THE WOOLGROWER'S COMPANION, 1906

It was one minute after opening time when Kate climbed the stone steps of the Longhope branch of the Rural Bank of New South Wales. There was general acceptance that the bank building was an eyesore, all squat modern lines and pallid stone. 'It's a bloody mausoleum, not a bank,' her father had said of it.

Before this day, she'd always gone there with her father, never alone, and she jumped when the heavy door swung shut behind her with a bang, loud in the dark and quiet stone interior. Her eyes took a second to adjust. Beyond the teller counters were four desks with four bank johnnies, each head down, pencil in hand. And beyond them, in her cat's-eye glasses, at a corner desk in front of a panelled office, sat the secretary to Addison, the bank manager. At twenty-six and without a suitor, Emma Wright was a career girl, according to the more charitable, and a spinster waiting for Mr Right, according to everyone else.

'Morning, Emma.' Kate had been a few years behind her at school, so they knew each other a bit. 'Can I pop in to see Mr Addison?'

Emma shook her head slowly. 'He's free, but he won't see anyone without an appointment. It lowers the tone.'

The door behind Emma opened and Addison's head appeared round it, like a glove puppet, with a wispy moustache above a trim vest, collar and tie. 'Mrs Dowd. What a pleasant surprise. Come in, come in.'

Addison closed the door behind them, and its seal was good. The Venetian blinds in the window rattled as the air and her courage were sucked out of the room.

'Arriving without an appointment is somewhat unorthodox, Mrs Dowd. But anything for you.' He joined his hands together on his desk and smiled at her. It wasn't pleasant.

'I need to cash the cheque for the Amiens wages. Please.' Kate was struck that the desk was bare. Not a paper or file anywhere. 'I forgot, you see. I took the cheque to Sydney by mistake.' She pulled the Amiens cheque out from her bag and pushed it across the bare desktop towards him.

'You've been to Sydney?' He smoothed out the corners of her cheque with his bony fingers.

'Yes, to sell something, Mr Addison. As you suggested.'

'I suggested?'

Kate put Mr McGintey's cheque on the desk. Addison didn't touch it but tapped his fingertips together. He got up and pulled open the office door, rattling the blinds again.

'The Amiens file, please, Miss Wright.' He waited, his hand on the doorknob, and then returned, putting a large file tied up with pink cotton ribbon in the middle of the desk between the cheques. He brushed the ends of his reddish moustache with both index fingers, cleared his throat and untied the ribbon.

He exhaled slowly, removed his glasses and placed them to the right of the file. Then he pushed himself out from his desk, leaned back in his chair and put his hands behind his head to stare up at the ceiling of the office, as if he were thinking.

'These are difficult times,' he said. 'I want to help but we must do things by the book.'

'I know we owe some money, Mr Addison. But today I am depositing more than I'm taking out for the wages. So the bank is better off, isn't it?'

He rose and came round the desk to sit in the spare visitor's chair. When he leaned forwards, he was within a foot of her and she had to fight hard not to recoil.

His voice was soft when he spoke. 'I said to you the other day that I am sorry about your circumstances. And I am sorry. I would not have gone to you, as a friend, to tell you to make arrangements to move if I were not.'

Kate could feel a 'but' approaching.

'But, Mrs Dowd, this cheque is tiny – minuscule – compared to what you owe. It changes little, I am sorry to say. The bank will proceed.'

'How much do we owe?'

'I really should speak only to your father about these matters, but under the circumstances, I shall be open with you. The interest alone is more than £1,000. The principal on the mortgage is £20,000, and the overdraft is a bit over £6,000.'

'So that's £27,000? But Amiens is worth more than that.'

'Not much more. Not enough more, if you follow me. The property, with the stock (also encumbered to us), is worth about £42,000. Give or take. So, we're concerned. Very concerned. The amount owing is now at the cut-off point.' He went back to his own chair, sat and closed the file.

'But if Amiens is still worth more than we owe you . . . ?'

He shook his head. 'We never allow a loan to approach so close to the value of the security. It puts the bank's capital at risk. We must take action very soon, Mrs Dowd.' He reached into a desk drawer, removed a metal letter opener and tapped it against his open palm.

Kate had an unhealthy urge to plunge it into his aorta. 'Does this cheque make any difference at all?' She leaned forwards, her hands on the desk between them.

He shrugged, his eyes on her hands. 'Oh, out of respect for the token payment, Sydney will probably give you a little more time. To pack.'

'So when would that be, Mr Addison? By when would we have to leave?'

'The end of June.'

It was still awful but more time than Kate had expected.

'Bank procedures require the interval, Mrs Dowd. If a borrower, after a long period in arrears, makes a payment, I must report that to headquarters and make a recommendation as to whether full repayment, or any substantial amount, is likely to be forthcoming. A decision is then taken by the next quarter, which is why your payment of this amount, even small as it is, means we cannot proceed with repossession steps before the end of June. But that's it, then, given there will be no more repayments. You know what my recommendation must be.'

She knew. But at least the pearl money had bought a reprieve. 'Until then, Mr Addison? Can I keep going? I need to pay the wages every week, you see.'

He reached across. His hand was cold on hers, and Kate steeled herself not to pull away.

'It must be difficult for a lady on her own to deal with these things.' Addison's voice was soft again. 'I want to help, Mrs Dowd, I do. And I will help you today. I shall instruct Emma to make this deposit and withdrawal for you. But just today.' Addison pushed the cheques across the desk to her and patted her hand before rising. 'We should meet regularly. To discuss your situation and progress. I want to hear how the packing is going.'

He walked round his desk but paused at the closed door, his hand on the handle. 'And we must get to know each other better.'

CHAPTER 14

*The 'bloat' is a most serious condition arising from failure to allow
the animal's system to acclimatise to the introduction of grains to its
fodder.*

THE WOOLGROWER'S COMPANION, 1906

With the office door closed behind her, Kate stood for a
second to register what she'd heard.

'You all right?' Emma asked from behind her cat's-eyes.

Kate nodded slowly.

'Sit here.' Emma took the cheques from Kate's hand and
shuffled her into a chair. 'Hot today,' she said, putting a glass of
water next to her. 'Have a sip. Do you good.'

Emma completed deposit and withdrawal forms with the
speed of practice. 'Here you go.' She put them in front of Kate
and held out a pen.

'You're a signatory too, you know,' she said as Kate signed.

'A what?'

'A signatory. You can sign cheques. If your father's . . . busy.'

Kate avoided her eyes. Emma probably knew all about
Amiens's debts.

'I'll be back in a jiffy. Get this deposited for you and the
cash as well.'

Kate took a sip from the glass. Town water.

Emma was back. 'Feeling better?' She dropped her voice. 'A lot of hot air in that office.'

Kate smiled slowly.

'Cheque's gone in. It'll clear in about ten days. Cash's in small denominations so you'll have enough change for the pay.'

Emma might well have been speaking French. Kate did know that she could trust her, though, and she had an idea. 'Would you come out to Amiens one day?'

Kate felt her mother turn in her grave. Graziers and their families – people on the land – didn't socialise with town people, except maybe the doctor. Everyone else was beneath them. But now it didn't matter; Kate and her father might not be long on the land, anyway.

'Will you? Come out for a cup of tea?'

Emma shot a glance at Addison's door. She nodded, a tiny shift of her head.

Back outside in the sunlight, Kate looked across from the bank steps at the Amiens vehicle, parked in the shade of the acacias. There was just Canali, spruce in his plum-coloured POW uniform, sitting on the end of the truck tray, swinging his feet as if he were at the Picnic Races. As much as she wanted him gone, he was still needed on Amiens. The only thing to do was avoid him, and make sure Daisy did the same.

Grimes wasn't yet back from his chores and Kate needed to buy the grain, or try to. She'd told the manager she'd go to the stock and station agent for it. She wanted to buy it herself, without him, in case they asked questions about the overdue account.

Two cars were parked outside Babbin's, which didn't bode well. That'd be two customers, plus Grumpy, the parts manager. Mr Babbin himself was in his office. She didn't want to have a conversation about the overdue account in front of other customers; the bush telegraph would get the news out by lunchtime. But she had no choice. She needed the grain.

One of the customers turned out to be lovely old Mr Riley. That was a stroke of luck: Mr Riley wouldn't say anything even if Grumpy made a row about the account. The other customer might be more of a problem. It was the younger Wilson boy, the wild one, off Tintara up north. A roll-your-own cigarette burning in one hand, he squatted beside a Franklin water pump, with an old tin on the floor next to him. It looked to be full of sapphires to barter, from the Wilsons' mining lease.

Kate waited at the counter but Grumpy didn't acknowledge her, just went about his business. He was her height, with braces over a round gut. He went into one of the rows of parts shelves behind him, pulled a long narrow box off the shelf and leaned it on his gut to sort through for a bearing. Then he banged the bearing down in front of Mr Riley, who turned it over carefully.

'Mrs Dowd. What can I do for you? Grain, maybe?' Grumpy asked, his palms on the counter.

She nodded.

'Bit of a problem with that for you,' he said, pleased. 'The boss'll want to know about it.'

Kate stood very still. Grumpy took a file from under the counter and went to Babbin's office. The Wilson boy stood up, arms folded, his rolly smoking in his fingers.

Through the glass panel in the office wall, Kate saw Grumpy speak to Mr Babbin, then point to her.

'Kate,' she heard. Babbin was out now, by the counter, folder in his hand, Grumpy behind him.

'Hullo. Is there a problem?' she asked, and wished she hadn't.

'Grumpy with a problem? Not our Grumpy,' Babbin joked.

Kate smiled uncertainly.

'Get one of the men to move your vehicle,' Babbin said.

'Vehicle?'

'For the grain. You need to get the truck moved so they can load it,' he said, handing the file to a frowning Grumpy.

'Yes,' Kate said quickly. 'Thank you,' she said on her way out. 'Thank you.'

~

On Amiens later that afternoon, Grimes backed the truck up against the shed for the men to unload the grain, the two POWs and Ed on deck. Kate stood watching, with Gunner at her feet. Up in the truck, Ed crayfished the first bag across the tray with those big arms and off onto Canali's shoulders. The POW walked the ten steps across the shed's cement floor, dropped his shoulder and swung the bag off. It landed with a bang as it hit the corrugated iron wall.

'Don't stack em up against the wall, y'drongo,' Grimes called. 'We don't want to cook it.'

Canali pulled the bag away. Bottinella, a cigarette set in his lips, took the next sack from Ed in the tray, carried it back across the shed and dropped it on top of the first, shifting it to line it up. Bottinella seemed all right today, not sad, and that was a blessing. Dust from the truck and the bags floated around Kate.

'We gotta start slow with the grain, otherwise they get the bloat,' Ed said to the POWs. 'Over a coupla weeks, eh.'

'You got that?' Grimes said to Bottinella and Canali loudly. 'Not too much of this stuff, orright? You'll kill em.' Canali translated as Grimes turned to Ed. 'Bring some of that bloody corrugated iron down. Put the grain on top so they don't tread it in the dirt.'

Harry appeared round the corner of the shed, his school case on his back. He came to stand beside Kate, and Gunner jumped at his hand for a pat. The boy ignored the dog at first. When Gunner was persistent, Harry took a swipe at him with his boot.

'Hey,' Kate warned, then looked hard at the bruising round Harry's right eye. 'Someone at school give you a black eye? Who did that? Was it that Bert Patterson?'

'Nobody did, eh.'

'Nobody did a good job.' Kate worried about how school was going.

'What's in the bags?' Harry asked.

'Grain. To feed up the ewes and the rams for joining.'

'Aw.'

'*Aw*,' Kate mimicked, pleased to see him. 'You want your smoko? Let's go to the house.'

In the kitchen, Harry slung his case hard against the floor by the stove. It fell with a bang and knocked the *Tablelands Clarion* off the bench.

'Hands, Harry,' she said.

He came to her at the sink, washed up, then wiped his wet hands on the towel. She grabbed it when he tried to wipe his face and nose as well. Then he plonked himself at the end of the table.

Daisy appeared and put a bikkie and some milk in front of him. She picked his school bag and the newspaper off the floor, and hung the bag on the doorknob.

'How's school?'

Harry ate.

'Mrs Pommer give you any homework?'

He shook his head.

Kate was tempted to go through his school bag but resisted. 'Will you read for me?'

'Got nothin t'read.'

'Reading's reading,' Kate said. 'Here you go.' She put the local paper down in front of him.

'*The – Tablelands – Clarion*,' he read out loud, then pushed it away.

'Ha-de-ha.' She pushed it back. 'Read one of the articles. Please.'

Much of the front page was taken up with a big map of Asia. Curving arrows marked *Allies*, all pointing towards the Philippines and Burma.

Harry looked across the front page, dropping biscuit crumbs from his mouth. '*Abor . . .*' he began, frowning.

Kate looked over his shoulder. 'Aborigines,' she said. Luckily Daisy was outside, in case it was bad.

'*Aborigines Moving Camp*,' Harry finished and smiled.

'Good. That's the headline. Now read the article.'

'*A resolution protestin against the pro—*'

'Proposal.'

'*Proposal to transfer Aborigines . . .*'

Kate read the next words. '*. . . from Baryulgil to Woodenbong . . .*' She tapped the paper for his turn.

'*Has. Been. Passed by . . .*' Harry said and took another bite of his biscuit.

'*. . . the district council of the Primary Producers' Union.*' Kate tapped the page again.

'*The. Local. President said. Once a blackfella was removed from his own dis—*'

Kate heard Daisy come into the laundry from outside. 'Let's stop there, Harry.'

'Nuh. I wanna read it. Listen. *Once a blackfella was removed from his district —*'

'Please stop,' Kate said.

Behind Harry, Daisy appeared in the doorway between the kitchen and the laundry, the wicker basket of white sheets in her arms.

'*Once a blackfella was removed from his district he seemed to pine away and so the race was dying out.*'

Daisy set the wicker basket on the bench and went out the way she'd come in.

Kate shook her head. 'I wish you'd stopped.' He didn't even know Daisy had been there.

'Daisy ain't from round here. She gunna die?'

'Who?' Kate wanted time to think about how to answer that.

'Dais. It says, *The race is dyin out*. She gunna die soon? She's only little, like me.'

Kate got up and rinsed his cup. 'No. They mean the race, not one person.'

He frowned, his chewing slow. 'Struth? All of em'll die? They mean that?'

She glanced into the laundry, glad that at least now it was empty.

Harry looked at her. 'Poor bloody Dais, eh.'

Kate frowned. 'Poor bloody Dais' was right. Her mind went to the bruises on the girl's wrists.

Harry shook his head slowly. 'Bert tole me they shot a whole lot round ere one time, way back. Abos. Thirty of em in one go.'

Kate opened her mouth and shut it again.

'Mile Creek or somethin?'

Kate swallowed. 'Myall Creek. It's thirty-five miles from here.'

'So they shot all them Abos?'

'It was a hundred years ago. That doesn't happen any more.'

'Old Grimesy tole Johnno one time, but.'

'Told him what?'

'Said he'd give im the Myall Creek treatment.'

Kate cursed Grimes. 'Perhaps it was a joke.'

'Johnno never laughed.'

Harry picked up the newspaper again. 'I reckon they wrong, but. Bout the dyin out. They ain't seen the Mission, eh? Abo kids everywhere. Big mobs of em.'

Kate shrugged. 'Well it's in the paper. It must be right.'

Harry's face moved into a smile, as if he had a secret. 'Nuh. They wrong.' He laughed, looking again at the paper. 'Dead wrong.'

He grabbed one strap of his school case and dragged it after him, out the door and across the dead lawn.

CHAPTER 15

For a successful muster, the seasoned woolgrower will secure an early start, before a flock divides to the four winds of the paddock.

THE WOOLGROWER'S COMPANION, 1906

Standing on a kitchen chair, Kate lifted down a bowl from the top of the cupboard. She saw something inside, wrapped in white tissue paper. She'd been searching for the sapphire since she got home from Sydney a few days before, room by room, cupboard by cupboard, trying not to imagine her father moving the stone from one hiding place to another as she searched. Wrapped, the thing – whatever it was – was about the size of a lemon. Trying not to get excited she pulled at the tissue paper with shaking fingers. But as she unwrapped she heard a tinkling sound and her hopes fell. It was an old coffee cup of fine china, tiny with blue and white flowers, the handle broken off and stored inside, probably by her mother years earlier. She repackaged it carefully, and put it back.

Kate was still standing on a kitchen chair, searching, when she looked down to find Daisy in the doorway to the laundry. 'Careful there, Missus. Mebbe I can find somethin?'

'No. It's nothing,' Kate said automatically.

'Yeah?' Daisy's brown eyes rested on the neat piles of cups and saucers that filled the kitchen table.

Kate laughed. 'All right. I'm just giving things a clean.'

'My job, eh, Missus.'

'No. I have to do it.'

Daisy looked away and went back to the laundry. Kate frowned but carried on. After the china cupboards, she did the grocery shelves, shaking each bottle and canister in case her father had dropped the stone inside. Nothing. She was shaking a metal canister of flour, holding it up to her ear, when she realised Daisy was again in the doorway.

'I know, Missus. Nothin, eh.' And she went back to the laundry.

That day's search produced only clean shelves in the kitchen. Mid-afternoon, Kate gave up and sat down with *The Woolgrower's Companion* instead. She wanted to read about joining. She'd better know more than she did; it was in less than six weeks.

She had to read the chapter over several times before it started to make much sense. They were using terms she'd heard before but never had to understand properly. She got a piece of scrap paper from the kitchen drawer and started a sort of glossary. *Merino impregnation rates*, *ewe cycles* and *ram ratios* went onto the list.

The gist of it all seemed to be what she already knew, that joining was trickier in drought years. That she could under-stand. But what to do? Have at least three goes is what they were saying; join through three ewe cycles. And have more rams per ewe than usual? She thought so but wasn't sure.

Her study of *The Woolgrower's Companion* meant that Kate didn't get into the garden until late, by which time the magpies had started their chorus ahead of the dusk and one or two swallows were about. Harry had been and gone with no talk of the newspaper article, thankfully.

Kate went to the far side of the garden away from where Canali was working and she kept a careful eye, shifting when he did, to keep the distance between them. He moved easily, yet there was more to it. *Coiled* is what kept jumping into her head. She was on her knees, weeding, when he appeared next to her. He was in an old shirt, the sleeves cut out, and shorts that were a cast off from Ed, probably, a pair of clippers in his hand.

'I cut her, *Signora*?' He held up the clippers and pointed at the Virginia creeper.

Her mother had loved the creeper, though it was long dead now in the drought. 'Yes. Pull it out. Watch out for snakes.'

'Snakes?'

'I haven't seen one about, but be careful.' Perhaps you'll get bitten, she thought uncharitably.

As she worked, she tried to ignore Canali and think about the worst, about what she must do if Amiens was sold up. Go to Jack's family in Perth? In a city? She didn't know them at all, and she'd be a burden. Kate had never actually met Jack's family – they hadn't been able to come all the way from Perth for their wedding, which had been arranged quickly because Kate's mother only had a few weeks to live. What could she do? Not governessing; it was a job for a single girl. She had no experience of bookkeeping, not even doing the Amiens books; she wouldn't know where to start. She could read and write well, yet she couldn't be a teacher without somehow finding the money to go to teacher training college. She seemed fit only to run the Amiens house.

A car came up out of the gully. Not an Army vehicle and not one she knew either. A grey Humber. As the vehicle got closer, she recognised the driver. It was Emma from the bank. Kate was glad her father was off at the yards.

~

They sat in the wicker chairs on the verandah. Kate had brought their tea and bikkies out from the kitchen, careful not to let Emma know the bikkies had been made by Daisy. Emma was a good egg but she wasn't unconventional.

'I'm so glad you came. Addison's got me more than worried. Why won't the bank just wait until we get the annual wool cheque in November? That'd be something.'

'It's the overdraft that has him worried. Oh, it's true Sydney's not keen to throw graziers off before the wool cheque comes in, and not in a drought and not with a war on. But you owe so much, such a big proportion of the value of the place, that the wool cheque won't be enough.'

'Dad managed for years. I don't understand why now we're under water.'

'If the overdraft was paid back somehow, you might just make a go of it, as your father did, before he drew down that big lump. But you'd need six thousand quid at least, and soon.'

'Six thousand pounds. That bloody sapphire,' Kate said.

'What?'

'Dad bought a sapphire for me. He thought it would be safer than cash in the bank.'

'And now?' Emma said.

'Now he doesn't remember where he hid it. And I can't find it.'

'Whatever you do, don't tell Addison. Not unless you find the sapphire.'

'I won't. But I need to cash another wages cheque on Friday. Will he let me?'

'I had a look before I came out,' Emma said. 'You should be all right if you stay within the overdraft limit. All right until the end of March.'

'Really?'

'You made a payment. Little as it was, the bank won't want to throw you off in this quarter.'

'But —'

'Oh I know. Adders gave you a fright on Monday. Probably hinted you'd have to beg every week for the wages. Fact is, he can't stop you drawing on the overdraft until the bank has made demand for the overdue interest.'

Kate was lost. 'But he has demanded it. He told me on Monday we had to pay everything back.'

'No. That's different. The bank has to give you an official letter telling you that you are behind on your payments. Only then can they eventually get you out, and lock your gates.'

Kate was glad she'd sold the pearls. 'Could I put the bank off again if I could find more money?'

'You might. You'd need quite a bit. The bank reviews accounts quarterly, you see. If you could find some money – a lot – and pay it first thing in April, you might hold them off for that quarter. You have anything else you can sell?'

Kate shook her head slowly. 'I sold my pearls already. There's nothing else that'll bring that sort of money. Except the damn sapphire, which we can't find. No one'll buy the sheep.'

'What about cattle? I hear some people close to Uralla sold to the Army.'

'We've got four hundred head. The Army only take big mobs, in the thousands, don't they?'

'That's no good then. There'd be bank formalities too, if you wanted to sell stock.'

'What about the car? The men can't do without the truck but we could manage without the car if we had to.'

'No, don't sell the car. You might need it to move your things anyway,' Emma said.

'Oh.'

'They'd only hold off if the overdraft was paid back. You might be right then until the wool cheque and beyond. But that overdraft is so much money. I know you won't want to consider it, but perhaps you should. What about selling the place itself? Would your father do that?'

'Sell Amiens?'

Emma shrugged. 'Some prefer it to being pushed off, is all I'm saying. You'd get next to nothing – the drought means land prices are depressed – but you'd probably cover your debts. And you'd save your pride.'

'Dad'll never sell. We'll just have to keep on, living week to week.'

'Who does your pay?'

'Dad signs the cheque. Grimes cashes it and puts the right money into the pay packets.'

'Does your Dad check the pay or do you?'

Kate paused. Her father used to check it. But he must have given that up when he made Grimes responsible. 'Neither of us do.'

Emma reached for another bikkie. 'Better to have two pairs of eyes on it. I'm sure Grimes is honest as the day is long. But all it needs is someone to take a potshot at him and say their pay's not right . . . You can always back him up if you've checked it.'

Kate leaned forwards and squeezed the girl's hand. 'Thank you. I don't know how to tell —'

'Don't then,' Emma said, pleased and embarrassed.

Kate wondered how Grimes would take her meddling. Not well, she guessed.

CHAPTER 16

As with men, one ram is not like the next. But no ram can be controlled, and the prudent woolgrower is wary always of the beast's potential for meanness.

THE WOOLGROWER'S COMPANION, 1906

That Friday morning, just after nine, Kate was drying up the dishes when she saw Grimes get out of the truck cab, with a tie on, dressed for town. She was ready for him, the cheque for the week's pay sitting on the kitchen bench.

At the fence, Grimes took the cheque without looking at her. 'Pay packets?'

'I have them. Thing is, Dad has asked that you and I do the pay together from now on. He says he doesn't want anyone to be able to give you a hard time. That it might be wrong, you know.'

Grimes looked at her. 'Y'know what to do?' The eyebrows went up.

'I think so.' She watched him walk back across the dead lawn, the shape of his pipe in his hip pocket. It was a fine line she had to walk with Grimes. She could not manage Amiens without him, yet she had to know what was going on.

Wanting to get straight onto the pay, she went to the office and tapped on the door.

'Dad?' she said, nudging the door open a little. A sharp smell escaped. Wee. Or piss, as Jack would say. Her father had to be reminded to shower these days, but still, never this. She pushed the door wide open. Apart from the smell and the mess of papers on the desk, the room was empty. He must be out in the shed, tinkering with something.

The smell made it hard to concentrate. She made herself count the pay packets out from the box then went looking for the ledger. It was missing from its shelf. She ran a finger along the book spines on the shelves. The ledger was longer and thinner than the journals, and she found it on its side, in amongst her mother's gardening books, jutting out a bit. As she pulled, something came with it. A key.

She got the desk drawers open in an instant. The one on the top right was full of envelopes, unopened envelopes. Bills. There were no more bills in any of the other drawers. Her father was methodical, in his own way. She bundled all the bills together and put them with the pay packets. She relocked the desk and returned the key to the bookcase.

Then she went in search of the smell. On her hands and knees, she looked under the desk (nothing, apart from a lot of dust) and finally, under the divan. There, against the wall, was an old tin, upright. She stretched out and tapped it with her finger. It had something in it.

With the divan pulled away from the wall, she lifted the tin out. It was wee, all right. Holding the tin out in front of her, she went onto the verandah, down the steps, past a curious Daisy and round behind to the old outhouse.

Back inside, after a hard soapy hand-wash, Kate took the ledger, the pay packet envelopes and a pen into her bedroom. She didn't want to risk her father finding her doing the pay. But first, she sat on her bed and opened the bills she'd found, sorting them by merchant. Their consistency was depressing, a slow steady increase in the amount owed and no payments against the accounts for months, right up until now. She marvelled that people kept supplying Amiens. Then again, they probably felt after more than two decades on the land, her father was good for it. At least there was no creditor she didn't already know about.

Kate swallowed hard and opened the ledger across her knees.

The last entry was from the week before. Under *9 February 1945*, in Mr Grimes's neat hand, was a list of names with their weekly wages. Keith Grimes at £6, as manager, Ed at £3, as head stockman. The POWs' names, Bottinella and Canali, were listed there too but with *Rural Employment Scheme – paid to Local Army Control Centre on account* noted where their weekly wages should have been.

Johnno and Bill Spinks were marked at £1 per week each, and *some rations in lieu* was written against their names. Kate knew £1 per week was much cheaper than the award rate, the rate paid to the white men who had left to join up. One saving, her father had noted with satisfaction at the time. He'd never paid Ed as an Aboriginal, though. Maybe because her father liked him. And even if Ed did have some Aboriginal blood, he could pass for white.

Next to Daisy's name were the words *full food and board*, and her wage entry carried the notation: *to AWB less pocket money*. By law, the state's Aboriginal Welfare Board received Daisy's wage as an apprentice. Kate's mother had doubted the Aboriginal girls ever saw any of that, even little that it was compared to their white domestics. Now that she was doing the wages, Kate could at least make sure Daisy actually got her pocket money.

She balanced the pay packets on top of the ledger and, with care, wrote them out, one man's name and his pay on each. Then she went back to searching for the sapphire.

In the kitchen, she used a chair to work her way through the last high cupboards. She heard Daisy in the laundry.

'You want this, Missus?' Daisy held a clean rag in one hand and a bucket of warm soapy water in the other. 'For doin nothin agin?'

Kate grinned. She got down. 'Look, it's Dad. He's hidden something, a tiny thing, the size of a chook egg. A sapphire. I have to find it.'

Daisy nodded slowly.

'Can you look in your room too, just in case? But don't say anything to him, will you?'

'To the boss? Nuh.' Daisy's face was sombre. She understood.

Kate worked her way through the rest of the cupboards.

Just before noon, the dogs started up and she heard the Amiens truck crawl out of the creek crossing. She jumped down from the chair, wiped her hands and went out.

Grimes came up the verandah steps with an envelope in his hand and some mail cradled against his blue shirt.

'Everything all right?' she asked, eyes on the envelope.

'Yep.' He scratched an eyebrow.

She gave silent thanks. 'Shall we do the pay here?' At the draughts table, Kate shifted the board onto the shelf underneath.

Grimes tossed the bank envelope onto the table, along with a bundle of letters. She wanted to look at the post but resisted that and opened the bank envelope instead, relieved to see cash.

Faint noises of cutlery reached them; Daisy setting the dining room table for lunch. Kate counted out the cash for each pay envelope. 'Can you check them?'

'Struth. How many pairs of hands you want in this soup, Mrs D?'

'It's so no one can argue you gave them the wrong thing.'

'Who's gunna argue? Not the ruddy Abos. They're lucky they gotta job.' He shook his head in disgust. 'An the sooner this war's over and we get the white stockmen back, the better.'

Kate said nothing, hoping he'd wear himself out.

'Or you reckon I'm fiddlin the books, Mrs D?'

'No, no. Not at all.' As Jack said, Grimes was a bastard but he was honest. Kate gave up on getting him to check her figures. She closed the ledger and held it out to Grimes.

'Why don't y'do that too, Mrs D?'

Kate took a breath. 'I'd like you to pay the men, please.'

There was a long moment, as they stood there, Kate willing her hands not to shake as she held the ledger towards him. Grimes might resent her involvement, yet for all sorts of reasons, Kate had to be involved. Emma was right.

'Do you give a cheque to the captain for the POWs each week, Mr Grimes?'

'The boss does that.'

I bet he doesn't, Kate thought. But at that moment, her father surprised them both, bowling onto the verandah from the kitchen.

'G'day, Keith. You got the pay? Good man.'

Now Grimes took the ledger. 'Yeah. I got it.'

Her father turned to Kate. 'Cuppa tea?'

'Lunch is in a few minutes, Dad.' She watched Grimes march across the remains of the lawn, then remembered the post and rifled through it. There were bills she'd need to go through, and a letter from Jack. Thank God. He was all right. She ripped it open and sat on the verandah steps, the stone warm through her trousers.

Dear Kate   *Kogarah, Sydney*

I got your letter. Must say I don't know what to tell you. Sorry it's turned out like this. But if Amiens is sold up, we'll move away. No point in staying in the district and not being able to look anyone in the eye, like those poor bloody Bincheys.

I've been thinking anyway that after the war there's easy money to be made up north. In East New Britain or Papua. Big plantations there, and I hear Burns Philp will be looking for plantation managers again. That's what we'll do. No one will know you so we can make a fresh start.

Things will sort themselves out when we get away. We will go. Your father's name is mud now in Longhope.

I'm still stuck training bloody new recruits, but I'm pushing for a transfer up north to the action. Nothing to say. Want to get back to ▮▮▮▮▮ *and help them finish the job.*

Love

Jack

PS There'll be no money coming from my people. Don't worry, though. We'll start again up north.

Bloody hell. She was glad he was still alive so she could kill him. She stood, screwed up the letter and jammed it in her pocket.

'Kate,' her father called from inside. 'Y'll be black as the ace of spades unless y'get a hat on. And Daisy's got lunch on the table anyhow.'

She went up the stairs, feeling the edges of the crumpled letter against her thigh. She was cross and getting crosser all the time. Jack wasn't a quitter; she'd seen how hard he'd worked to get his hand moving again. So why would he not fight for Amiens? Had he even tried to get the money? But he might be fighting at the front now, for all she knew, and here she was thinking about his family's money. And Kate could almost understand; she was ashamed enough just asking him. But a niggling thought would not go away: did he even ask them, or had he lied about their means and there was no help to be had?

~

Lunch was silent, Kate thinking about Jack's letter. Her father didn't seem to notice. When he finished his meal, he said, 'Get Grimes over to talk about joining, will ya?'

'What?'

'Get hold of Grimes. And Ed. Late tomorrow's orright.'

'What do you want to talk to them about?'

'Joinin. I want Ed in on it.'

'Are you sure, Dad?'

'Of course I'm bloody sure. Ed's better on joinin'n Grimes.'

'No, I meant . . .' she started, but he'd gone.

Kate looked at her father's back as he went towards the office, glad he was lucid, wondering how long it might last. She'd have another read of that chapter on joining, just in case. It might take her mind off Jack, too.

She got into the vegetable garden at about four, still mad with Jack, keen to take out her temper on some Mayne's curse or some onion weed. At least Canali had not yet appeared. She tried weeding but did not have the patience for it. She was too angry to lever the roots out whole, so she got a fork and dug around the base of the bean vines, pushing and working the soil so it might take what little water they had to spare.

'Good day.'

Kate jumped.

'Sorry, *Signora*.' Canali was four feet away, his gaze on her. They returned to their work but Kate was always aware of where he was in the garden.

Just before dusk, the truck rumbled to a stop at the fence. Grimes got down from the cab, carrying the pay ledger. Kate went the few steps across to meet him, conscious that Canali could hear their conversation.

'Everything went well?' she asked, taking the ledger from Grimes.

'No arguments today,' he said.

'Dad wants to see you and Ed about joining. Please. Tomorrow at dusk, all right?'

Grimes produced a nod.

'I didn't see Harry today,' Kate said.

''E took a cricket ball in the hand, close up.'

'Is he all right?'

'E's orright. Stuffs everything up, he does. Cricket balls, the job on the bloody pup, you name it.'

'What pup?'

'Rusty,' Grimes said. Then he started to smile, caught out.

'What? You made *Harry* put Rusty down?'

'Look, the boy had to do it, the job on the dog.'

Kate was open-mouthed.

Grimes snorted. 'On a place, ya do your own dirty work, Mrs D. It had turned into his bloody dog. So he hadda do it.'

'What happened?' Kate managed to get out.

'Harry got a shot off but hit the dog broadside. Rusty run his guts around the yard afore I could get im. I only had a hammer handy so I finished im with that.'

Kate's hands went to her mouth in horror and Grimes left. She saw only Harry trying to shoot the pup, Grimes striking Rusty.

Canali stood up from his work, watching her. She looked at him across the width of the garden bed, conscious of how she'd misjudged him. 'Why didn't you tell me about Rusty and Harry?' Kate asked, confused and angry at herself and Grimes.

'*Signora*, she listen?' He shook his head.

'I'm sorry.' Kate swallowed, wishing she'd known, wishing she had asked. She tried hard not to cry as she returned to clipping, her head full of how Rusty had died.

CHAPTER 17

An inexperienced woolgrower might apply his joining ratio willy-nilly but he must always take account of the age of ewes and ram. Experience on either side and, at best, on both, secures greater lambing rates.

THE WOOLGROWER'S COMPANION, 1906

Kate was at the back of the house picking the first beans from the far garden bed when the truck pulled up outside the fence. Her basin of beans in one arm, she went inside to get her father. She called to him from outside the closed office door. 'Dad, the men are here. To talk about joining.'

He said something or other through the door and she waited. 'Remember, Dad? You asked me to get them to come and talk to you?'

'Tell em to bugger off!'

That was clear as a bell. Kate went back outside. As she walked across the dead lawn, she willed herself to be civil to Grimes, no matter what he'd done to Harry and Rusty.

'Dad's in the middle of something,' she said to the two men on the other side of the fence. Ed looked past her towards the kitchen.

'He said you should talk to me, tell me.' Kate swallowed hard.

Grimes glanced off towards the horizon and shook his head.

'Talk t'ya about joinin?' Ed looked confused.

'Yes. When we'll start, how many cycles and the joining ratio. I'll tell Dad.'

Ed looked at her curiously. She could see Canali in the back of the truck and didn't want him to hear her talking joining and impregnation rates. Ed and Grimes were bad enough.

'Orright,' Ed said and Kate was grateful.

'When will you begin them?' she asked.

'I reckon in about three weeks, once they built up a bit on the grain. Do the usual joinin over eight weeks, to catch three of the ewes' cycles.'

That sounded right. She racked her brains for the other drought bits. 'What about the ram ratio?'

'One ram to a hundred,' Ed said.

'Shouldn't we go higher? Because of the drought?'

Ed considered that. 'We could, yeah. Good thought. We'll have young Basil as well as Minute Man and the others.'

'Can we count on Basil? Will he be old enough?'

Grimes gave a noiseless laugh. 'He'll work it out.'

Kate felt the heat of her skin as she blushed. A chook darted out from under the tank stand.

'Basil'll be orright,' Ed said. 'He be six months b'then. We'll put Minute Man with the maiden ewes, Basil with the others. But lamb losses will be higher this year, if the dry goes on, eh.'

'What can we expect, do you think?' Kate asked.

'Depends,' Ed said. 'If we don't get good rain by lambin in August, it'll be bad, I tell ya, Mrs D. The pasture'll be gone. The pigs and foxes'll be more'n hungry and the ewes'll be toey, too. The ewes walk away, see, from a lamb, even from both twins. To save theirselfs.'

'Then the buy-in'll cost,' Grimes said.

'You mean buying other stock to replace the ones that have died?'

When Grimes laughed, she tried not to get mad. 'Well?' she said.

'Yeah. That's it. Prices'll be high to buy in, even for them with the money.'

Kate glanced away. They were edging up to the overdraft limit, and after lambing they'd have shearing supplies and shearers' wages to come, even assuming she wasn't off the place by then. There'd be little money left to restock.

'I'll tell Dad.'

With that, Grimes headed to the truck and Ed followed.

'Oh Ed, one other thing?' Kate called after him.

'Yeah?' He came back to the fence, as Grimes climbed into the truck cab.

'I . . . want a word about Daisy.' Her voice was soft.

'Yeah?' He seemed annoyed.

'If anyone touches her, they'll be sacked. You understand?' Johnno and Spinks had wives. Ed must know Kate meant him.

'Sacked,' she said again. She couldn't be clearer.

He opened his mouth to speak and then shut it, his face grim.

A shout went up from the rise towards the ram paddock. It was Harry, waving his arms. 'Minute Man!' he shouted. 'Minute Man!'

They ran, all of them, Kate, Grimes and Canali from the truck, and Ed with his uneven gait. From the top of the house paddock, Kate could see Minute Man was down, his four legs in the air, Harry crouched next to him.

The ram was in a bad way. Minute Man's stomach was bloated on the left side and the right was taut like a drum. Green froth oozed out of his nostrils, and dung and grain lay around him.

Canali clamped the ram's muzzle as Ed ran his hands over his belly. Kate pulled Harry back and could feel he was shaking.

'Get some bakin soda and oil,' Grimes called to Kate. 'Bloody fast. Run and git it.'

'He's too far gone. Gotta cut im.' Ed stood up, unclipping the cover of the knife sheath at his belt.

'You'll kill im. You'll hit a kidney.' Grimes turned and yelled at Kate, 'Get the bakin soda, Mrs D!'

But Kate didn't move, her eyes fixed on the ram's head in Canali's hands. The panting and the oozing green froth had stopped. 'What do you reckon, Ed?' she asked.

'He'll be dead by the time y'back.'

'Then go ahead.'

'No ya bloody won't,' Grimes said.

'The ram's dying,' Kate said. 'Go ahead.'

'Jesus. He'll bloody kill im.' Grimes, his face red, stalked off to the truck, cursing.

With Canali's help, Ed shouldered the ram off his back onto his right side. Then he lowered his left knee onto his neck, pinning the creature against the ground. Ed spread the wool on the highest part of the ram's swollen belly, brought the knife up against the animal's skin then drove it into the tight, distended stomach. A soft *whoosh* of air brought a smell with it and Minute Man coughed and struggled. Ed held him down, knife in place, even as the ram thrashed its legs. Then, in one movement he pulled the knife out and stepped back. Minute Man scrambled to his feet. The ram staggered a few steps, stopping about ten feet out, eyeing them warily. He panted, his eyes glazed still.

'Will e be orright?' Harry said, distraught.

'We'll see.' Ed wiped the knife on a dead tussock and put it back in its sheath. Beyond the gully, a mob of dusty kangaroos moved off.

'I'll get Johnno down here now to clean up the grain,' Ed said as they walked back. 'Someone musta give im too much.'

Kate took Harry's hand and for once he did not pull it away. 'I did,' she said. 'If anyone asks, I did it.'

'You're the boss,' Ed said.

Kate didn't feel like the boss. She looked at Canali. 'Do you understand?'

He gave her his half grin and tapped his chest with a thumb. '*Sì. Capisco, Signora*. Understand.'

Kate decided that would do, even if his grin was a little too familiar. And at least he seemed to have forgiven her about Rusty. She just hoped Grimes wouldn't find out that it was Harry who fed the grain to Minute Man.

CHAPTER 18

Where an experienced woolgrower is able to negotiate a private sale
for stock, he should take care to strike a fair bargain. Notwithstanding,
the prudent woolgrower is best served by disclosing his terms to no
one else save his bank manager.

THE WOOLGROWER'S COMPANION, 1906

The following morning early, Harry ran up onto the verandah.
'Bloody Minute Man run me outta his paddock just now, eh.
E's orright!'

'Well, good. But you better get going. Mrs Pommer'll have
your guts for garters if you're late for school,' Kate said from
the kitchen.

'Gotta get me plants.'

'What plants?' she asked.

He went by her into the laundry and emerged moments
later with a fistful of eucalypt and myall leaves, their stalks
dripping onto the floor. He shook the water off, and tied them
carefully together with string.

'Botany t'day,' he said, putting the tied bundle in his hat and
his hat on his head. 'Daisy learned me the poisonous ones. Her
nan learned her. Before she come here, eh.'

'Taught, Harry, taught. And you can't eat leaves.'

'Not me, ya drongo. Stock. What's poison for sheep and cattle.'

Kate ignored the drongo part. She was glad he and Daisy were mates. It was good for both of them. She watched him run across the dead lawn, pulling his school case onto his back. He jumped over a black chook at the gate, then climbed onto the mounting stump and onto a tetchy Ben. The pony, with boy aboard, moved off slowly down the track towards the crossing, just as the phone rang.

'Mrs Dowd? Captain Rook. Could I see you this afternoon on Amiens? Around two?'

'Of course. Is —?'

He'd rung off before she could ask why. Kate wondered what could bring the good captain out. If he wanted something, what could she get in return? She was turning that over in her head, her hands round a tea towel and a wet dish, when she saw Grimes pull up in the truck. He'd come to dress her down over Minute Man, for sure.

She took her time to wipe her hands and go out, preparing herself. She didn't want to have a go at him over the dog and poor Harry.

Grimes took his hat off, not out of politeness, and folded his arms across his blue shirt. 'Listen here, Mrs D. First, you give the bloody ram too much grain. Damn near kill im.' His face grew pink, colour flooding the broken capillaries that stretched across his nose and between his eyebrows. 'And then ya tell young Ed to cut im when I say don't. Looks bad for me with the men, what you did.'

Kate eyed her feet.

'An no offence, but I don't work for a slip of a sheila. I work for ya father. Stay out of things, Mrs D. Ya don't run the place and ya can't run the place. Ya hear me?'

She stuck her fingernails into her palms to keep quiet. Grimes went back to the truck.

In the kitchen, Daisy watched her closely. 'You orright, Missus?'

Kate nodded, picking up her tea towel.

'Is e dark about the ram?' Daisy asked.

'Yes.'

'Ed saved im but, eh?' she said, proudly.

'He did.'

She gave a tiny shrug and rolled her eyes.

Kate turned away, surprised that Daisy would still have a crush on Ed after the bruises he'd left on her arm. How could she?

~

That afternoon, on the dot of two, Captain Rook arrived in an Army staff car. Kate was pleased he was Oil free. They sat down in the wicker chairs on the verandah. The captain took off his slouch hat and smoothed his hair. Then he grinned at her, conscious that she'd caught him grooming.

Kate set a cup on a saucer for him and poured his tea.

'The Yanks are bombing Tokyo and Yokohama,' the captain said. It was his small talk but still good to hear.

'So it might end soon?'

He shook his head. 'It's not over yet. It'll take some doing to get the Japs out of the Pacific islands. Your father fought in the First War, didn't he? How is he?'

She wondered how much he knew. 'It catches up with him sometimes.'

'Battle of Amiens, I take it?'

'And before that too, all on the Western Front.'

'He get hit?'

'No. He had the three years there and was never wounded. He doesn't talk about it.' She shrugged. 'He's suffered a bit since too. More lately.'

'Most blokes don't, y'know, talk about it. But if he's sick, he could see the local Bones. Dr King.'

'He won't go.'

'The doc might talk to you, though. He's a good man, King. A returned serviceman himself.'

She smiled. 'I know Dr King. He delivered me.' There was a brief pause, and Kate wondered when the captain would get to the point.

'Any more problems with Canali, Mrs Dowd?'

'No.'

'Good. Which reminds me, I got a couple of letters for your blokes.' He extracted two small envelopes from his inside pocket. They were stampless but postmarked *Croce Rossa*, the letters arched around the simple red cross. Kate imagined the families handing them over on the other side of the world, hoping they would get through.

'I need to ask you, Captain. I think we owe you their wages? The POWs, I mean? I've been looking at our pay ledger.'

'You do, yes.' He produced a leather-bound notebook. 'Going back, it looks like here. Four weeks at £1 each is what you should settle up. In due course.'

Kate felt her heart sink; more money. 'We'll do that.'

The captain cleared his throat. 'Mrs Dowd, I've come to ask a favour. We need to bring all the POWs in the district together for a talk. Could we do it on Amiens? Say a week Saturday? The 24th, in the afternoon?' He looked away from her to the horizon.

Kate was curious. 'You don't want to do this at the Control Centre in town?'

'There'd be no danger, of course, to you. You know yourself these men are generally solid types. They just want the war to be over so they can go home,' he said, sipping his tea. 'I only ask you because of your father's support for the Scheme. It would be the POWs, me and Corporal Boyle. No other Army staff.'

'I can ask my father,' Kate said. 'He'll want to know what you're going to talk about though.'

'Understandable,' the captain said. 'The thing is, it's delicate.'

'Delicate?'

'I'm not saying it's a military secret, but we'd not want it to get about. We've had a, er, a . . . fraternisation.'

'Was she . . . hurt?'

'Crikey, no,' he said, then appeared to regret it. 'The lady was . . .'

'Willing?'

'Yes.'

They sat in silence while Kate digested that. The bleating of hungry sheep filtered across as they walked the fence lines looking for food. She spoke slowly, thinking out loud. 'You want to warn all the POWs against fraternisation. No graziers will want to hold that meeting in case people might think this fraternisation happened on their place. But you believe I would agree to it?'

He looked into his tea cup, embarrassed. 'I knew you'd give me a fair hearing. You and your father,' the captain said, looking away as he cleared his throat again. A tuft of hair he'd forgotten to smooth sat up at the crown of his head, pushed there by his hatband and his sweat.

'You can have the meeting here, Captain. Of course. But I wonder if you can do me a favour in return.' She tried to breathe evenly, not give away her fear, as the idea took shape in her head.

'Such as?'

'Amiens has four hundred head of beef cattle. I would like to sell some – all – to the Army. For meat.'

He put his tea cup down. 'I can't do that.'

'Surely one good turn deserves another, Captain?'

'I can't do that, Mrs Dowd.' He was apologetic. 'That's Procurement, not Control Centre. And they'd never take so few anyhow.'

'It would mean everything to us. Will you try? Please?'

155

He opened his mouth to say something and then shut it again. He stood up and put his hat on. 'I'm sorry, Mrs Dowd. I'm grateful, you understand, but the cattle?' He shook his head.

Kate stood and watched him go across the lawn, pulling a packet of cigarettes out of his pocket as he went to the Army staff car. Once the vehicle dipped down into the gully, she put the tea things onto the tray but her hands were shaking. She'd failed.

~

Late that afternoon, she was relieved to get into the garden. Canali was already there, up on a ladder with his back to her, cutting dead vines away from the tank stand. He turned and waved his clippers at her and she smiled back. She was pulling on her gloves when she heard the phone ringing. It rarely rang. She ran into the kitchen, her plait banging against her back, and grabbed the black receiver off its cradle.

'Mrs Dowd. Captain Rook.' He didn't sound pleased. 'I will be able to do that, do what you asked. And we'll do the gathering as agreed, Saturday week.'

'Yes,' she exhaled. 'Yes. Thank you so much, Captain.' But he'd hung up.

She smiled as she put the heavy receiver in its cradle. Then she pulled her gloves on and walked back into the garden, greeting Canali with a wide smile.

He stopped clipping and looked at her. 'Orright, *Signora*?' He gave her his half-smile and she realised she liked it. The smile changed his face, opened it. She went back to work and thought about the cattle. She wanted to tell Emma. She couldn't ring. It was too risky; Addison might get to hear of it from the party line. Better to just get the cattle sold, get the cheque to Addison as early as she could in April, try to hold him off for that quarter. 'You think much, *Signora*.'

'I'm thinking about money. But at least I've sold our cattle.' She stopped, worried she'd said too much.

'Is difficult. This farm. All the farms.'

She had an odd sense she could trust him. 'We have problems, with the money and the farm.'

'Ah.'

'And Dad, he bought a sapphire.'

'S'fire? What is this?' He bent down and gathered the clippings in his arms, carrying them to drop them over the fence.

'It's a precious stone, like a diamond.'

'He buy for you?' He clipped again, carefully, methodically.

'Sort of. But he ... he borrowed money to buy it.'

'Ah,' he said again. 'Now you must sell her.'

'Yes. But we can't find it. He's lost it.'

He stopped and looked at her, clippers in hand. 'Lost her?'

She nodded. 'I search and search. It's small, about the size of a tiny egg. Yellowy. Smooth. But at least now I've sold the cattle.' She was repeating herself.

'Your *papà*. He know this? You sell this cattle?'

There were no flies on Canali; he knew her father might object. 'Not yet. I need the right time to tell Dad. In case he ...' She struggled to find the words.

'She is still good, the family. Good also the bad, the two. *Papà, mamme, bambini.*'

'You must miss your family.'

Canali nodded slowly. '*Sì. Mio papà* now alone. Not my brother ... He ... He is gone perhaps.' He looked away.

'I'm sorry. But you'll go home, as soon as the war is over.'

She was suddenly bold. With her eyes on the beans, she asked him, 'Do you have a sweetheart there?'

'*Sì*. Before. Then I must go in the Army. When I come back? But she marry.' He shrugged and looked away, and Kate felt an odd shiver of relief.

'I'm glad you're here. Not in a POW camp, I mean.'

'Some cages have not the bars, *Signora*.'

They were silent for a moment.

'You want to go home,' she said, and felt an odd sadness come over her.

'*Sì*.'

'But Amiens is not so bad for you? Surely?'

'Amiens?' He looked into the air, to give the matter thought. 'Amiens, she is good.'

Kate smiled, relieved.

'And *Signora?* She is also good. Much good.' He grinned at her, teasing now.

Kate turned quickly away. Dangerous ground – dangerous for both of them.

~

Late that afternoon, Kate was in the kitchen finishing the potatoes when Meg appeared on Fiva, just before dusk. Canali was at the gate, on his way back to the single men's quarters. Kate washed her hands at the sink as Meg stood holding Fiva's reins, speaking to Canali. Kate frowned. Only when the POW headed off into the half-light did Meg loop Fiva's reins around the fence.

'You all right?' Kate said as Meg came in.

'I suppose.' Meg took a breath. 'I'm worried about Robbo. And I'm a goose.'

'Why? You want a cup of tea and a chinwag?'

'No thanks, to the tea. I just needed a ride, to stop worrying about Robbo. And you're my turnaround point.' Meg sat at the end of the kitchen table. 'But I am a goose. I was blabbering to Luca about Robbo. I'm worried you see, that, that, that Robbo's . . . Well, that he's dead and that we just don't know yet. It comes over me . . . that he's dead . . . and then I can't breathe.' Meg flashed a sad smile, the gap in her teeth showing.

Kate hugged her, then went outside with her. Meg pulled

158

herself up onto Fiva, who turned unprompted for home. As horse and rider disappeared down into the gully and the late-afternoon light, Kate heard the mournful braying of a hungry steer. She willed the date of the POW meeting to come quickly, so the captain would have to make good on his promise to buy the cattle.

CHAPTER 19

To the detriment of clip uniformity and so to the great displeasure of the woolgrower, it remains within the bounds of actuality that a black-woolled lamb may be born to a white ewe and white ram.

THE WOOLGROWER'S COMPANION, 1906

Kate was on wet knees scrubbing a mark off the kitchen floor when she heard the first truck. She looked up at the clock. Twenty past two. The graziers with their POWs were early. Her father had been in his office since lunch. She'd not even told him about the meeting – it was easiest, and he never emerged before dusk now.

Daisy came in from the verandah with the broom and, for some reason, let the gauze door bang behind her. 'Tindervale fellas are comin,' she said. It came out with a sigh.

Kate looked up from the wet floor. 'You all right, Dais?'

She paused before she spoke. 'Yeah, Missus.' Kate went back to scrubbing. Daisy was not given to grumbling, but she hadn't been herself of late. As the truck pulled up, Kate tiptoed across the wet floor and went out. Bill Riley had the Tindervale truck pulled up parallel to the fence, his two POWs sitting in the truck's tray. Kate hadn't seen him since she'd bought the grain at Babbin's. He beamed at her, his hat in his hands, freckles and sunspots peppering his scalp

160

under thinning fair hair. 'Afternoon, Mrs D. Where do you want us?'

'Mr Riley. The captain wants them down at the woolshed. You know the way?'

'That I do,' he said. 'And did you hear the Yanks and the Philippine fellas took Manila?'

'Yes? That's wonderful.'

'Gettin there, gettin there. All we need now is some rain, eh?'

They'd had nothing, and in a normal year the month would deliver a couple of inches.

'Ya father about?'

Kate shook her head, hoping he wouldn't emerge.

But behind her, the gauze door banged. Her father's voice boomed across the dead lawn. 'Bill, you old coot. How are ya?'

Kate was relieved to see her father was presentable.

'We're here for the meeting,' Riley said. 'The POW fellas with Captain Rook.'

Her father looked blank.

'Remember, Dad?' Kate said, swallowing. 'The captain asked if they could come here.'

'All of em?'

'Only for half an hour, he said.' Kate's voice faded.

'How ya been, Ralph?' Riley asked.

'Orright. Put your blokes on the lawn here, Bill,' her father said.

Kate opened her mouth in alarm.

Riley saw it. 'Woolshed's all right, Ralph. Boys'll be out of the way up there.'

'No, no. We'll have em here.'

Bill Riley smiled an apology at Kate and waved his men down out of the truck.

Harry appeared, as the two POWs sat on the dead lawn in the shade of the trees. 'What about the woolshed?' he asked Kate.

'Dad wants the POWs here. Can you run and tell your uncle?'

'Grimesy'll blow a gasket. He had the boys clean out the shed this mornin.' But Harry went off, ill-timing a kick at a black chook by the fence.

Her father and Bill Riley stood a bit inside the fence, chewing the cud about the war and the drought. Kate thanked her lucky stars it was Mr Riley who'd arrived first.

An Army staff car pulled up at the fence, Corporal Oil driving Captain Rook, with the little translator in behind.

'Mrs Dowd,' the captain said, climbing out of the car. He turned to Oil behind him. 'Corporal Boyle, you wanna start the roll call with those blokes?'

Oil sauntered across to the POWs on the dirt lawn, with a clipboard in hand.

The captain looked back at Kate, his ruddy face thoughtful under his slouch hat.

'Don't worry,' she said. 'I'll make myself scarce. So you can get on with it, with no ladies about. And thanks, Captain. For buying the cattle.'

'Don't mention it. To anyone, if you follow me.'

A second truck with POWs in the back came up out of the gully, and another one behind it. Her father went to the gate as the Amiens truck arrived from the woolshed. Bottinella dropped to the ground from the tray, smoothing his beard then feeling in his shirt pocket for cigarettes. Canali came next, then helped Harry down as Grimes and Ed got out of the cabin.

'Harry,' Kate called. 'You better come inside with me now.'

He took one pace back, his arms tight by his sides, and spun around like a soldier on parade, before he ran off, disappearing between the trucks. Kate shook her head. Damn that boy.

Inside, she went straight through the kitchen and into the laundry, where she found Daisy. The bucket sat upended, rinsed and draining on the laundry sink, with the mop already outside on the line. Daisy peered round the doorway to look through the kitchen windows at the POWs filling up the dead lawn. 'Lotta fellas here, Missus.'

'It was a mix-up. They're meant to be at the woolshed.'

'We gotta feed em?'

'No.'

'Lucky, eh? Big mob.'

Daisy went out the laundry door and, to Kate's surprise, sat down on the step to wait out the meeting.

There were dozens of POWs now, sitting, standing and smoking. They seemed barely changed from those men who had climbed off the train two months before, just better fed now, not camp skinny. Harry sat himself at the front of them, but Canali called for him to come back to him and Bottinella.

Captain Rook came up the verandah stairs and shot a look her way. Kate dived back into the laundry.

'Attention all.' The captain held a hand up but it had no effect. Canali put out an ear-splitting whistle and that quietened the POWs.

'All right, you blokes. You've probably heard it already, but we're down one POW in this district.'

He stopped and let the translator proceed. The man stumbled over some words. Then the captain went on slowly. 'Private Piero Salentino has been taken under escort back to Hay POW Camp, where he is to stand trial for fraternisation.'

As the translator proceeded, one word – *fraternizzazione* – jumped out at Kate. There were murmurs in the crowd of POWs, and for the first time their seriousness began to drop away.

'But, Captain,' a POW called out. 'She catch me.' He banged his index fingers together and the men around him laughed. Harry copied the gesture over and over, making Bottinella chuckle; in the laundry Kate frowned.

'I run but she so quick, Captain,' another called.

The captain wasn't having any of it. 'You will be charged – this is a criminal offence – if you fraternise. If convicted, Private Salentino goes to prison. He would serve out the years of his sentence in a military prison here in Australia. He will not be repatriated to Italy after the war until his sentence is completed.'

When the man had finished translating the last piece, the crowd was still. Kate was shocked – prison for that? With the lady willing? On the lawn to the right of Bottinella and Canali and Harry, a man got to his feet. It was the Riley POW, the older one. He was angry, his eyes narrow, and he spat his words out. 'You. You tell us this. Stop us at women. But Italy, she not fight you, not for two years.'

The POWs sitting on either side of him nodded, and then the man's voice got louder. He shook a fist at the captain and Oil and the translator on the steps. 'You keep us prisoners. Pay us shit. We are slaves. *Schiavi.*'

Schiavi. Schiavi. The chant went up, a few fists in the air, a few hands with cigarettes as well, like a mob at a fight. Bottinella and even Harry joined in. Kate got a look at Canali. He sat, silent, unmoved by the yelling.

'All right, all right,' the captain said. Kate's father went forwards from the sideline and put his hands above his head to stop the noise. She sucked in a breath, hoping he'd not get more involved. But the POWs stilled and her father stepped back as the captain spoke again.

'I know you blokes think you got it hard. Orright? But I'm just telling you the rules. When this war's over, you'll all go home. That's that.'

The man translated, and there was more chatter in the crowd. Rook put a hand in the air again. 'Look. That's it. To your transport now.'

Kate went onto the verandah and the captain walked

through the POWs, a mass of shifting men like sheep in yards. Her father stood at the gate, farewelling each. Kate was relieved. It was one of his good days. She went inside, quickly, before her father got back. She wanted to ring Addison, to arrange to see him, to try to extract any sort of promise that he'd help. An Army cheque for the cattle was coming, not that he knew that. In the meantime, she wanted to keep him on-side. She'd invite him to tea; he'd be out like a shot.

~

And he was. The following Saturday, in the middle of the afternoon, with her father safely asleep in his office, Kate sat on the verandah with the bank manager. 'More tea?'

Addison passed his cup and saucer to her. 'Thank you, Mrs Dowd. Or may I call you Kate?'

She concentrated on pouring the tea. When his cup was full, she set the teapot down on the small table between them and forced her mouth into a smile. 'Yes. Do. Call me Kate.' She could hear Daisy moving about in the kitchen, and she was glad Addison could too. He smiled and looked back out across the paddocks. 'An impressive vista, Kate.'

Vista?

'And the paths across the paddocks – sheep tracks – are most pronounced from up here. Like lines on one's palm.' Addison turned to her, proud of his simile. She didn't tell him the tracks were only visible in a drought.

'I thought about what you said, Mr Addison, when we met last month. You're right, it is hard to deal with things, with Jack away and with Dad sometimes not so well,' Kate ventured. 'So I'm grateful you suggested we chat, you know, about the place.'

'Anything I can do,' he said, his eyes on her, adding, 'Kate.'

He stood up and walked to the edge of the verandah, his back to her. It struck her that he was chicken-like in build, skinny and scrawny. He'd be a boiler if they had to eat him.

165

Vittorio Bottinella appeared on the track up from the crossing. He was pushing an old bicycle, its tyres flat and some spokes missing, one hand on the handlebars, a cigarette balanced between the fingers of the other. She wondered where he'd got the bike and where he planned to ride it. Officially, the POWs were not allowed more than a mile off the place, and then only on Sundays with a grazier escort. But that didn't worry Vittorio. He waved to them as he walked by, his beard split with a wide smile.

'Odd fellow, that one,' Addison said.

'Yes.' Ed called Vittorio *PBV*, for poor bloody Vittorio, because he was clapped out, happy as Larry one minute, down in the dumps the next, loony from too much war and too much time as a POW. And he was Vittorio now, not Bottinella, a part of things. Even Kate was calling him that.

'So. Mr Addison. Could you help? If I can get some money? I know everything has to be by the book, but what do you think?'

'I think you should be packing up to leave Amiens, Mrs Dowd, that's what I think.' He watched Vittorio wheel the bike, disappearing over the rise.

'But if I could somehow make a payment?'

'Where would you get this money?'

She shrugged. 'Just suppose. Would you help?'

He sighed and then smiled as if at a child. 'I would always try to help any customer, procedures permitting.'

'Thank you, Mr Addison. Thank you.'

'But truly, Mrs Dowd, I feel it is my place to tell you. My offer of assistance is academic, given how much you owe. You have to clear the overdraft, you see. Otherwise the bank will enforce eventually.'

'Still, I'm grateful, Mr Addison.'

He smiled slowly. 'Please. Call me Alwyn.'

CHAPTER 20

Like his more cautious handlers, a sheep will move towards an open area and can rarely be persuaded to enter a place from which there is no apparent escape.

THE WOOLGROWER'S COMPANION, 1906

Kate woke with a jolt in the night to a noise in her room. 'Dad?' she said.

She heard his breath, laboured, as if he were upset. A wooden joint creaked in her bedroom chair.

'You have a bad dream, Dad?' Her eyes grew accustomed to the darkness. He was sitting in the chair in his pyjamas, looking at his fists in his lap. She got out of bed and went to him, taking his hand. Above her, a breeze brushed the jacaranda tree against the corrugated iron roof like a broom.

'C'mon, Dad.' He rose and followed her to his room without any trouble, for which she was grateful. She tucked him in, kissed his stubbly cheek and returned to bed.

Within ten minutes, he was back, standing in her doorway. She got up again. 'Are you thirsty?' Silence.

She led him back to bed. 'Stay in bed, Dad,' she said, tired. 'Please?'

'Good night, daughter.'

Back in her own bed, Kate lay awake, listening for her

father's movement in the house. The minutes went by, and she heard only the soft breeze in the eucalypts round the house. As she tried to sleep, Canali crept into her thoughts. *Much* good, he'd said. '*Signora?* She is *much* good.' She laughed as she thought of his grin as he'd said that. And whenever they were working in the garden alone, she found her gaze drawn to him, and his would be on her. It was more than that. If they touched accidentally – as she helped him tie up a stake or shift a vine – that touch sent heat through her body.

Kate tried to push him out of her mind, and thought of the lecture Captain Rook had given the POWs. *Fraternizzazione.* She rolled over in bed and thought of Jack. But Jack could not help her family, and he'd been gone much longer than she'd known him. Her thoughts went back to Canali. Pulling the vine off the roof, digging dirt beds in the hard soil, gently tending a vine, he was always there, talking with her. Watching her. Kate smiled in the dark and felt herself falling asleep.

~

'Katie?'

She sat up, groggy. 'Dad. I'll take you back to bed.'

'Cuppa tea, Katie?'

'Now?'

'And a bikkie?'

He seemed almost himself, so she pulled on her dressing gown, and went into the kitchen, him trailing behind her like a child. She filled the kettle, put it on to boil and yawned widely.

'Tired?' he asked.

She looked at him and they laughed. 'You need to sleep, Dad. We muster tomorrow. Remember?'

He nodded. He'd taken it well when she'd finally told him she had sold the cattle to the Army. 'You ridin with em?'

'They're short-handed.' She didn't tell him Grimes was against it. Ed had persuaded him, just.

'You watch yourself, eh?'

'Ed's putting me at the back. The boys'll go after the breakaways.'

'Good enough.'

Kate poured boiling water onto fresh tea leaves in the pot. Sugar. He needed sugar. She put the bowl in front of him and offered him a biscuit. 'Anzac bikkie?' She held the open tin out.

'I lost somethin.'

The tin went on the table. 'Pardon?'

'The sapphire, y'see. I hid it t'keep it safe.' He stared into his tea.

Kate stopped, the mug at her lips. 'What did you say, Dad?'

'It was f'you, the sapphire.'

'From Mr McGintey?' He was hunched forwards, his hair mussed with sleep, his eyes red with sleeplessness. She willed him to be all right, just long enough to tell her.

'Better than cash in a bank, a sapphire is. For a lean time. Ya can hold this in ya hand.' He looked down at his palms.

'Did you hide it?'

He nodded. 'Keep it safe.'

'Do you remember where?'

He shook his head slowly.

'We have to find it, Dad. We have to. For the overdraft.'

He sat back, his head up now, and squinted at her in surprise. 'There's no overdraft.'

'You spent the overdraft on the sapphire, Dad. Truly.'

Squinting still, he shook his head at her, his neck going pink as he got angry. 'There's no overdraft,' he said again.

'Not now. There's almost none left. We're broke.'

'Bullshit.' He stood straight up, knocking over the mug of tea. 'Bullshit,' he said again. The tea spilled across the table, and steam flared from it as it leaked towards Kate and off the table in front of her father.

She grabbed a tea towel, mopped at the spilled tea, trying to dam the rest of the liquid on the table top. But as she leaned across the table, he did so too and with his face right next to hers he shouted, 'What *overdraft*?'

She gasped and pulled back, and he shouted again. 'I never used an overdraft in me life. As if I'd spend borrowed money on a bloody sapphire. Ridiculous!' He slammed the door after him.

Kate gripped her mug, hearing her own uneven breaths.

Later, when she was calmer, she got up, her thoughts all on her father. He was more and more forgetful. He *had* used the overdraft. Often, when he was starting out. Her parents had discussed it now and then. And she'd bet her last shilling that he'd used it to buy the sapphire, in his mixed-up way, even if he couldn't remember it now. She shook her head. She rinsed the cups, out of habit, and set them to dry, the clatter of the china against the metal drainer loud in the house.

In her room, knowing she had little hope of sleep, she took a brush to her knotty hair – so knotty, she was sick of it. As she tugged at the mess, she was just glad they would muster the cattle the next day, though stopping the bank was like holding back the tide.

CHAPTER 21

The noble beast grazes into the wind. A prudent woolgrower will
muster in the same direction for more than fair success.

THE WOOLGROWER'S COMPANION, 1906

In the gloom before daybreak, Kate made for the yards; the
only sounds were Gunner panting along beside her and the
call of a whip bird. She liked to be up early and out in the quiet
paddocks, but today she was too nervous about the muster.
She wanted to justify Ed's faith in having her ride with them.

Over the rise, she could see the horsemen already in the
yards: Ed, Grimes, Johnno, Spinks and Canali, all mounted,
towering above Vittorio on the ground. Damn, they were early.
She hurried to reach them, nodding a greeting as she took the
reins from Vittorio. A quick double-check of Ben's girth strap,
and then she pulled herself up while they waited in silence. Ed
coiled his stock whip and hooked it on his saddle.

'Orright, you blokes,' Ed said, settling himself into the saddle
on Dodd. 'This mob hasn't been mustered in a bit. Keep sharp,
eh? They'll be toey.'

'Toey?' Canali asked. Under him, Mustard moved sideways.
Canali settled him with some pressure from his knees. 'What
is toey?'

'Toey? Riled up, mate.'

171

Canali looked blank.

'Angry,' Kate said, quietly. Not exactly but that would do.

'Enough of the bloody nattering,' Grimes said from behind her and Kate flushed. Grimes might defer to Ed on cattle, but he didn't do so happily. And he certainly didn't want Kate there today.

'They'd smell us fore they see us, so we'll come in upwind of em. But no noise, eh? With the scrub on one side and the gully on the other, we gotta form em up into a mob quick, an get em moving towards the end of the paddock and the yards. Orright?'

In the silence that followed, Kate tried to ignore her nerves. She concentrated on the familiar warmth of Ben's flanks through her joddies.

'Spinks, Johnno: you take the fence line closest to the Box Ridge scrub. That's where most of em'll be. Canali, you're at the back of the mob, behind Spinks, to get any breakaways. Grimesy, you got the other flank, orright?'

The manager nodded.

'What do we want? Heifers?' Kate asked, and Grimes laughed.

'No, Mrs D. We take what's there, eh. You stay up behind Grimes and Canali. Every horse helps drive em. Be on ya toes, eh?'

'Toes, toey,' Canali repeated, and Kate wondered if he was teasing her.

'A handful willa gone wild. We gotta shoot em, the ones we can't get in.' Ed whistled high and hard and the dogs bounded off ahead of the horses.

The ride out was almost silent, apart from the occasional whistle from Ed. Despite her nerves, Kate could not help but feel euphoric. Amiens at first light was at its most beautiful, fog lining the creek beds like blankets yet to be thrown off and white dew softening the pasture that would be yellow again by mid-morning. But it wasn't only what she could see of these gentle hills: she was pleased to be working with the men. She just hoped she didn't make a mess of it.

Before the gate into Deadman's, Ed whistled the dogs in behind him and stood up in his stirrups. He ran his eyes back and forth across the paddock and then stopped, peering intently at one spot. Kate followed his line of sight. She could see only bush and scrub and black wattle trunks. No cattle.

Ed motioned the riders through the gate. Spinks and Johnno moved off to the right, Grimes to the left, and Canali stayed put; so did Kate. They moved forwards slowly, but Kate had no sight of the cattle and she was having trouble keeping Ben in line.

About a third of the way into the paddock, she saw a flash of movement on the left in the gully, and then it was gone. The elders among these cattle were wily and Kate didn't get clear sight of the herd until further up the paddock. Then, the mob must have smelt the riders behind them, because Kate heard cattle moving.

With only half a mile fence to fence, Kate saw her first animal. A young Hereford shot up out of the gully, dirt-brown with slashes of white on her face, chest and underbelly. She dived past Grimes to break back and escape the circle of riders. Grimes rode hard to turn her and she moved away, eyes wide, snorting in fear, back towards Spinks. Kate watched, awestruck, as Spinks and Ned moved as one, stepping sideways, blocking the Hereford from getting away. The heifer baulked, pulling back before lumbering up the paddock with the dogs at her heels. Kate watched her go, relieved. The heifer was big – Kate had forgotten, accustomed as she was to sheep – almost as tall as Ben, and with such weight and power.

But the heifer was not alone. Kate heard hoof beats that swelled to a force she felt in the ground, even on Ben. Instinctively she pulled him up as cattle burst out of the creek bed, jumping fallen trees, braying and galloping. Ed didn't hesitate. Cracking his whip, pushing Dodd alongside the leaders, he rounded them away from the scrub and forced them instead up the paddock. Spinks moved in tandem with Ed, driving the lines of stock, the kelpies working the mob, nipping at the heels to move them on.

Kate stayed in formation, relieved the men had the mob going north, towards the gate and the yards. A steer loomed out of the gully close by Canali and Mustard reared, almost unseating him. Kate gasped as Canali leaned into Mustard's back, gripping hard, and horse and rider came back to the ground as one. As the steer came towards Kate and Ben, Canali went after it, pulling Mustard around to block its path, but it kept on coming at her, not fifty yards out. Canali and Mustard got ahead of the steer again and wheeled to face it. This time the animal veered off the other side, and with a crash of timber reached the safety of the gully. A line of white sweat ran across Mustard's flank, and Canali moved his stock horse slowly back to position.

Sweat darkened his shirt, rings visible under his arms and down the middle of his back.

He turned, grinning at her. 'OK, *Signora*?'

Caught looking, she snapped her eyes away.

Ahead of them, the mob was moving, perhaps all of their four hundred cattle, a few bulls at the front, some bullocks, heifers, calves. A wave of dust above and following them, a mass of braying, lost calves and unhappy mothers. The riders and dogs moved behind them, waiting for a breakaway that might lead the others back.

Near the gate, Ed rode into the mob again, pushing the leader cattle through so the others would follow. A lone bullock broke back down the fence line and came on straight at Kate and Ben. Kate froze but Ben went forwards and blocked the bullock, turning it back toward the mob.

Ed nodded at her, and she leaned down to pat Ben's neck hard to thank him.

~

Dirty and thirsty after mustering, Kate walked across the dead lawn to the house, the last rays of the late-afternoon sun hot on her back. Her hands were reins-chafed and she was bottom-sore from the long day in the saddle, but she was glad she'd done it. Before the war, a girl would never have been allowed near a muster. It had been quite something, to see Johnno and Spinks in action on horseback.

On the verandah, her father was stretched out in a squatter's chair, one booted foot up, jutting out on its extension rest.

'Hullo, Dad,' she called but he said nothing. A rifle crack echoed across the house paddock, and her father got up, alarmed. He went to the edge of the verandah, looking out. 'What's that?'

'It's all right, Dad. It's just Ed. They're shooting the ones too wily to be mustered.'

'You muster today?'

'Yes. Remember, Dad? We're selling the cattle to the Army.'

At the second rifle crack, his fear shifted to annoyance. 'They bloody shootin em?'

'There were only a handful. Ed says they're wily from too long without a muster.'

He frowned. 'How many head they get in?'

'Right on the four hundred, Grimes reckons. Three pounds a head. That'll help. But it's a drop —' She stopped, not wanting to remind him of all the money they owed. 'We got the cattle into the yards for the night; watered them, quietened them down. We'll drive them in at first light tomorrow to the cattle train.' Kate sat herself on the verandah steps to pull off her riding boots.

'You ride with the boys, did ya?' he asked.

175

'Yes.'

His face clouded. 'Ya not to do it again. Ya hear me? Ya not workin in the paddocks with em.'

Kate opened her mouth but shut it when he went inside. Damn. Ed would have to do without her tomorrow, but after that with some luck her father might forget about this ban.

'Not garden today, *Signora*. Not light.' Canali was at the gate.

'You're right,' she said. 'Too late today. Tomorrow.'

'Tomorrow,' he repeated, leaning on the gate's cross-piece. 'You find her?'

'The sapphire? No, not yet.'

'I look too.'

'Thanks,' Kate said. 'A good muster today.'

Canali eyed the runner bean on the other side of the fence. He coiled a tendril back around its string trellis. 'These Johnno and Spinks, they ride the cows good.'

'Muster. Muster the cows.' She laughed. Kate knew the Aboriginal stockmen could ride, really ride. She hadn't realised Canali would muster so well too. It had been something to see, all right.

'You muster before, *Signora*?'

'No. Never.'

'Ah, you ride good, I see.' Canali winked.

Kate couldn't stifle a smile. 'I've always loved to ride. But my mother didn't approve of me working in the paddocks. Still, I liked the muster. Fast and exciting. And scary. The bee's knees, really.'

'What is bee's nose?' he asked, touching his own.

'Don't worry,' she said. 'It's not something you need to know.'

He nodded, pulling the gate shut behind him. 'Cheerio, *Signora*.'

The boys must have taught him that. 'Cheerio, Luca,' she called after him.

He stopped and turned back, a smile on his face at her use of his Christian name. They stood there, grinning at each other, until Luca's face clouded and he strode away without looking back.

~

Kate sat in Dr King's waiting room, trying to read the one *Women's Weekly*. The room was no-nonsense and dated now, reflecting the military training Dr King had had as a young medic in the First War. The crisp white walls were bare of pictures and the smell of Dettol and linseed oil hung about. The simple leather couch on which she sat was worn but polished. Perhaps as a token to patients' peace of mind, one potted plant sat in the corner, a spikey mother-in-law's tongue.

The other patient in the waiting room coughed raggedly. Kate had said hello when she arrived; it was Mrs Tuite, the mother of the Tuite boys and wife of the local undertaker and part-time roo shooter. She was as tiny as her boys were tall and lanky.

The faint noise of the ABC wireless played at the receptionist's desk.

'. . . But that isn't the fault of rationing. We can't . . .'

Kate knew the rationing spiel now by heart, she'd heard it so often. Her reverie was broken by that hacking cough. 'Sorry, dearie,' Mrs Tuite said, her bony hand over her mouth. She reached into her bag for a packet of cigarettes, lit one and drew deeply.

A weary young mother came into the waiting room with a baby in her arms. The child was one of Barrel's grandchildren – Barrel who operated the switchboard for the telephone exchange. The baby, six or seven months old, had an overlarge bonnet on. Kate smiled at the infant, but she looked back blankly.

Comparing her travails to a sick child or a terrible cough, Kate was starting to feel like a fraud. She wasn't sick, and she'd received the cheque from the Army for the cattle; that had made her feel better about everything. The Army Procurement people were efficient, all right; she got the money not long after Ed and Grimes delivered the cattle.

She'd give the cheque to Addison on 2 April, the first working day of the next month, as Emma had suggested. Just maybe, that might save them again from the bank for a bit.

'Mrs Dowd.' Dr King appeared at his surgery door and looked at her over his half glasses.

She followed him in.

'Now then, young Kate, what can I do for you? With Jack away, no point in worrying about a baby, you know.'

'Yes. I mean, no . . .'

For a doctor, he didn't listen much. It was a bit of a joke among the locals. You had to work hard to get a word in edgeways with Dr King. He was in his fifties, not much different from her father's age, and the only doctor in the town.

'I'm not here for that,' she said.

'No?' He sat back in his chair. 'How's your father, anyhow?'

'Actually, it's about Dad.'

'You hear the Americans have gone into Iwo Jima? That should cheer him up. But what is it? Headaches giving him curry again?'

For some ridiculous reason, tears came to her eyes. She tried to speak but was afraid she'd really cry.

The doctor reached into his pocket. He held a clean folded handkerchief out to her, smiling a little. 'Handkerchief, courtesy of my better half.'

She wiped her tears.

'So let's chat about what your father's doing. You say yes or no. How about that?'

Kate wiped her nose.

'How's he about the house? Is he forgetful? Losing things?'

'Yes. Sometimes.'

'Does he think you take his things? Hide them?'

She looked at him, amazed. 'Yes.'

'Does he get stuck on things? Keep on about them?'

'A bit.'

'How's his temperament now?'

'He still gets angry. Often now, very angry. Over little things.'

'Working in the paddocks?'

'Not really. He spends most of his time in the office.'

'Doing the books?'

She shook her head slowly. 'He's not paying the bills or anything.'

He frowned. 'But is he still managing the men, running the place and so on?'

'No.' Kate dropped her head and looked at her hands in her lap.

'Ah. But you've got a manager.' The doctor took his glasses off and rubbed the bridge of his nose with his fingers. 'The men like your father who served in the First War, they carry it with them. Some, the lucky ones, got more furlough, got some breaks from the front. But your father wasn't one of them. Oh, he was lucky all right: he didn't get hit. But that meant he never got pulled back from the front, not much anyhow. And living like that, under fire for years, seeing what they saw, doing what they had to do, does damage, I believe. Gives them migraines, flashbacks, mood swings, all the things we've seen over the years in your father.'

'But why's he getting worse?'

He frowned. 'I'll tell you now, there's other Bones'd disagree, but the original damage and their symptoms? I reckon that they age a man before his time, can make him soft in the head. Then you put another blow on top of that – your mother passing away – and that shock can trigger a downturn.'

179

Kate breathed in deeply. 'But he got better. A bit. Eventually. Not now, though. What can I do?'

He sighed. 'You need to look after him.'

'But you mean he won't get better this time?'

When the doctor shook his head slowly, tears came into Kate's eyes again. 'Never say never. But they don't tend to, once they've gone down that way. He's not physical, though, with you, is he? Violent?'

'Violent? No.'

'Good. War'll be over eventually. For now, keep him healthy. Daily Vegemite is what I'd suggest. Here, I'll write you a script so you can get an extra ration card for it.' He scribbled on his prescription notepad. 'But otherwise, grin and bear it is needed for now, I'm afraid, till Jack's home to help.'

Kate sat, the prescription in a limp hand. Home to help? Jack wouldn't be home for months. And even then he wanted them to move away, once the war was over.

Dr King made a note in the file on his desk before snapping it shut. 'Righto then, young Kate. Best of British to you and your father.'

~

On the trip back, and later at home as she swept and weeded and cooked, she thought about what Dr King had said. Her father would always be like this, maybe worse. That got to her, so she forced herself to do more jobs and to try to think about other things – rams and grain and joining and the drought, even.

But in the shower that early evening, she closed her eyes and cried.

Still crying, she turned off the shower and heard the pump cut out a second later. Towelling her clean hair dry, she made herself think about others who had it much worse, like Robbo and maybe even Jack. From a glance at the vanity mirror, her hair was a mess of knots. In her bedroom, she put the chair in front of the long mirror on her wardrobe, and sat down.

From the mirror, a serious young woman looked at Kate. She pulled her shoulders back and sat up straight, forced her expression to neutral, and started brushing at the ends of her hair. She held a clump below her shoulder and pulled the brush against its knotty end. Some of the knots gave way. She tried the knots closer to her scalp. They were worse.

In the mirror Daisy went by, carrying ironing to the linen cupboard. In a second, she returned. She stood behind the seated Kate, looked at her in their reflection and held out her hand for the brush.

Kate gave it up. 'It's a bird's nest.'

'Yeah; must be emu, eh.'

Kate smiled. Daisy worked her way around the ends of Kate's hair, brushing gently, her face in the mirror serious with concentration. She parted one of the matted locks and held it tight in a fist to brush at it, until the knots on the ends came loose.

'You're getting it,' Kate said in surprise.

Daisy nodded, and kept brushing. 'I fixed me mum's hair, eh.'

'My mother used to do mine, too.' Looking at Daisy in the mirror, Kate felt her loss, as deep as her own grief for her mother. Kate wanted to ask her if she got to say goodbye to her mum but she knew she couldn't. Daisy put the brush down and touched Kate's shoulder to show she was finished.

~

Sticking to Emma's instructions, Kate delivered the Army cheque for the cattle to the bank on the first Monday of the month. She was ready for the blinds rattling when Addison shut the door and she put the folded cheque on his empty desk. Her words came out in a rush. 'Mr Addison. Alwyn.' She swallowed. That was hard to say. 'Remember you promised you'd help? If I could get some money?'

He tapped his teeth with his letter opener and scrutinised her face.

'I got some money, you see.' She slid the folded cheque across the desk, trying hard not to be smug.

He didn't move to take it.

'It's from the cattle. I sold them.'

His mouth fell open, and he put the letter opener on the desk with a bang. 'Mrs Dowd,' he said, dropping the informality of his visit to Amiens, 'the stock are not yours to sell, not without my approval. The bank holds security over them. This . . . This is . . .' He stood up, agitated. 'My superiors will think that . . . that I . . . And . . . And you will have sold at a loss.'

'No, that's all right, Mr Addison. I got £1,200 for them – £3 a head.'

'Three pounds a head? You must be mistaken. Only the Army pays that sort of money, and then solely for big mobs. You have only three-hundred-odd.'

'Had: four hundred actually. And it *was* the Army; £1,200, Mr Addison. See?' She unfolded the cheque, and pushed it a little closer to him, wishing he'd take it, willing him to.

He opened his mouth again, then shut it. He sat himself down, put his elbows on the desk and rested his lips on his knuckles.

'Mrs Dowd. You have no head for business. It is a fact. And these latest shenanigans – selling stock under lien without even the courtesy of our approval – only convince me further of that.' He dropped his hands onto the table. 'I cannot be clearer; you still owe many, many times this. The overdraft has to be cleared. All the rest of it. Every penny.' He jabbed at the cheque without looking at it. 'I tell you, you must leave Amiens. You will not survive. Yes, you've bought another little bit of time today, and yes, very clever to pay this in the new quarter so we have to wait again to enforce.' He looked towards his closed door, and Kate knew he suspected Emma. 'But we will enforce. This is the *last* time you and I have this little chat, Mrs Dowd. Mark my words. Unless you pay back the rest of the overdraft in full, I am recommending that we enforce at the first available moment. And have you even established where all that overdraft money went?'

She couldn't tell him the truth; he'd send the bank in tomorrow. She shook her head.

'I see. Be gone by the end of the next quarter. We'll be in then.'

Kate worked that out in her head. 'So we have until the end of September?'

His eyes narrowed and he ran a skinny finger along the calendar on his wall. 'The twelfth of October, to be specific, Mrs Dowd. On or before. We *will* take possession then, at the very latest. You can set your clock by it.'

He stood up again, went to his door, and pulled it open with such force the blinds banged against the window frame. 'Miss Wright!' he yelled. 'Bank this cheque.'

'Goodbye, Mrs Dowd,' he said as she went out into the dim hush of the bank chamber. He shut the door hard behind her. She had another reprieve. She knew it would be her last; there was nothing left to sell.

CHAPTER 22

Woolgrowing husbandry might be said to be a study of time and patience, where the grower strives, year after year, to build his reputation and good name for fine wool.

THE WOOLGROWER'S COMPANION, 1906

Kate shivered when a cold breeze hit her joddied legs. Harry had left the kitchen door open as he came in after school. Daisy got him a bikkie and, with half an ear on his shenanigans, Kate left her sock-darning and got up and shut the door. It was late April and getting cooler with the autumn coming on. As she went back to darning her father's sock, she realised she was half settling into her new life. Most days Harry came to them after school. She did the pay every week and tried not to annoy Grimes. She worked in the garden with Luca; he was Luca to her now, not Canali. And she looked forward to those hours. That time alongside him was the best part of her day, and they talked about everything and nothing, about plants and sheep and Harry and even the war. With Luca, she could switch off for an hour or two from the worries of the farm and her father's illness. Kate had to watch her father like a hawk now. He was about less and less, spending much of the time in his room or in the office, sleeping. Only rarely did he work in the paddocks with the men now. At least that made it easier to keep him from getting upset in front of them.

She tugged on the wool thread to pull the stitch into line with its neighbour on the sock toe. The weeks were ticking by: March was gone, soon April would be May – and she could feel the October repossession lurking, like a snake you've seen in the garden but you can't kill. Every single day, she searched for the ruddy sapphire.

'En then e stabbed im in the guts!' Harry yelled, pushing an imaginary knife into an imaginary Minute Man next to Kate and her darning.

'Harry. Could we have another story? That's what, more than two months ago now?' Kate said, her eyes on her needle.

She rested the holey sock on her knee and ran through in her head all the searching she'd done in those weeks, worried that she was starting to cover old ground. She'd searched the bedrooms, the kitchen, the laundry, the bathroom and the office, as well as the dining room and the sitting room at the front. She found some odd things, like boxes of her old baby clothes. No sapphire. She'd been over the meat house, and she'd even searched the old outhouse.

'En Ed ripped the knife from is guts!' Harry pulled his knife arm back hard, bumping Daisy, who was coming in from the garden with a colander full of beans in her arms. The beans went all over the floor, and Daisy and Harry went down on their knees to pick them up.

'Dais, you drop em on purpose?' Harry asked.

She grinned and shook her head.

'She hates beans,' he explained.

Kate gasped. 'But you never said! And we've got a lot of beans out there.'

'It's good, Luca's garden, eh?' Daisy replied.

The new garden bed was bountiful, maybe because Luca had green fingers too. He was planting autumn crops now – spinach, cabbage and onion seeds in neat rows. Beans collected, Harry jumped to his feet and drove his imaginary knife into Daisy as the sheep.

'Truly, Harry. We're a bit sick of that story.'

'Dais doesn't mind it. Do ya, Dais? She likes t'hear about ole Ed. He's sweet on her.'

Daisy put the colander of beans in the sink, her back to Harry. He was right though; Ed hung around for a glimpse of Daisy whenever he came with Grimes to talk to Kate about the place. If Grimes was right and Ed had some Aboriginal blood, it made sense, really, although Daisy was far too young. It would be trouble for Ed, regardless. Daisy had seemed happier in the last few weeks too. Well, maybe not happier, just not so skinny. When she first came to them, Kate thought the girl would pine away to nothing.

'Ya know, Bert can fart when y'ask im,' Harry said.

'What?'

'Bert Patterson.' Harry got down on his hands and knees on the floor. 'E's gunna learn me. He does this, eh . . .' He rocked backwards and forwards, his face fixed in concentration.

'Harry. Get up this minute.'

But he kept trying, rocking and frowning.

'What about your lecturette on Anzac Day for tomorrow?' Kate looked up at the clock. 'The Prime Minister's speech will be on the wireless soon; you'd better shush and listen.' She had a quick search through the sewing box for the sapphire, which she did every time she darned anything, just in case.

'I don't want to do the ruddy lecturette.'

'Harry. No swearing,' Kate said. 'You have to do your home-work. And it should be easy. The Prime Minister is sure to talk all about it – this is his Anzac Day speech. Quick. Turn on the wireless.'

Harry stepped round Daisy and reached across to the wire-less set that took up the kitchen bench under the canister shelf.

After a few seconds there was a soft buzz, and then the voice of an announcer floated into the room.

'. . . *commemoration of Anzac Day tomorrow, the Prime Minister of Australia, the Right Honourable Mr John Curtin* . . .'

'You should take notes,' Kate said, picking up the sock again.

Daisy handed Harry's school case to him, and he extracted a chewed pencil and some grubby paper. He spun the pencil round on the top of his wrist, bringing it back to fall into his fingers after each revolution.

'. . . *spirit and sacrifice of our fighting men uphold the tradition of the Anzacs of the Great War. Our race is ennobled by their selfless devotion. Upon* —'

'Nobbled?' Harry asked. 'They nobbled the race? Like nobblin a horse in a race?'

'*En*nobled. It means "made noble". Shush and listen.'

Harry was doodling along the fold in his book.

'. . . *so that when peace comes, our race will be enriched.*'

Harry turned the wireless off. 'Not much chop, eh. You gotta help me. Spill y'guts. Who were them Anzacs? I thought they were bikkies. Speak slow, but.'

'Slow*ly*. Speak slow*ly*,' Kate said. 'And *those*. *Those* Anzacs. But yes, sort of. The biscuits were named in honour of the Anzacs. That's A–N–Z–A–C. That stands for Australian and New Zealand Army Corps. They were sent by the British in the First War to fight the Turks at a place called Gallipoli in the Dardanelles.'

'Where's that then? The Dardanelles?'

'It's in the south of Europe, just north of Africa.' Kate winced; she'd accidentally stuck a needle into her finger inside the sock.

At the sink, Daisy filled a small basin of water to rinse the beans.

'Who buggered it up?' Harry said.

'No swearing. It was nobody's fault. But the Anzacs landed in the wrong place. So the Turks were able to pick them off.'

'Struth. Landed off Aussie ships?'

Kate sometimes didn't know the answers to Harry's questions. But this one she did; Jack had told her. 'No. They landed from British ships.'

'Bloody Brits. Their stuff-up, then.'

'No swearing. And it was an accident.'

'Accident, my arse.'

'*No* swearing. Anyway, Anzac Day is the 25th of April. The date of the landing. The old soldiers march to commemorate it.'

'To celebrate losin?' Harry frowned.

'No. They celebrate the bravery of the men who fought on anyway, against all odds.'

'The boss marching, is e?'

'Not this year.' She suspected he'd not even realised it was coming up. Kate knotted the thread, then cut it close to the knot. Her father had been withdrawn, perking up, sadly, only when he was mad about something he'd lost or thought she'd hidden from him.

'I gotta march too. Tomorrow at dawn.'

'Really?'

'Yeah. Bomber's makin us, eh.'

'Well, I can see her point, with the war on. And all the returned soldiers march too.'

'Not the blackfellas,' Daisy said quietly, smoothing a fold into a tea towel from the washing.

'What?' Harry said.

'Them blackfella soldiers. They can't march, eh,' Daisy said.

'There's blackfella soldiers?' Harry asked, incredulous.

'Some, eh. Like me uncle. Gunner in the First War, that fella.' Daisy hurried a pair of dirty tea towels together and went out to the laundry.

'That's pretty rough. They fought but now they can't march,' Harry said.

Kate agreed with him but she kept quiet.

'I can write about that.' Harry twisted in his chair towards the laundry and yelled, 'Thanks, Dais!'

'Don't shout. And no, you can't,' Kate said.

'What?'

'You can't write about blackfellas. It just riles people up. Get on with something sensible.' Kate put the sock together with its hardier twin and tidied the needle and wool away into the sewing box.

Outside, she heard a rush of unhappy Italian. Vittorio, on about something.

Harry cocked his head to one side as he listened. 'You reckon them POWs are workin for nothin? That's what Vittorio tell me. Italy threw in the towel yonks ago, in '43, eh. So how can we keep em here? And pay em peanuts? He reckons the Poms and the Aussies jus makin em work. Reckons they could fight!'

Kate frowned. 'I don't know about that. There's lots of Germans still in Italy, as far as I know.' But it was a sleight of hand everywhere, keeping the POWs as prisoners, even on the Rural Employment Scheme. She guessed they – the Poms, the Aussies, the whole lot – had to have that POW labour, for the war effort. Heaven knew Amiens needed it.

The Italian voice got louder; she hoped it wasn't about the wages. Kate went to the door and followed the noise round the house. Vittorio was at the back fence with his new old bicycle, a cigarette in his lips, berating a hoeing Luca.

Out of the stream of words, she caught a phrase: '. . . *vecchia bicicletta* . . .'

'What's wrong with Vittorio?' Kate asked.

'*La bicicletta, Signora!* Grimes! No, no, no.' Vittorio waggled a finger from his free hand in front of Luca's long nose. 'Grimes!' he added. He blew a long, hard raspberry and drew on his cigarette.

Kate raised her eyebrows. 'What's Grimes done?'

Luca rolled his eyes. 'Not Grimes. Vittorio. He find the dead bicycle.'

'*Sì! Sì!*' Vittorio blew smoke into the air to empty his lungs. 'Dead. Buggered-up, *finito.*' He shook his head, frowning, and drew again on his cigarette.

'He fix her. Now Grimes say he must give,' Luca said.

'And Vittorio wants to keep the bike?'

'*Voglio tenere la bicicletta! Certo che voglio tenere la mia bella bicicletta. Ho lavorato duro per riparare la bicicletta. Grimes mi chiede di buttare la bicicletta nel fiume. Non lo farò! Giuro che non lo farò!*'

'He say: yes.'

'*Grimes è un bastardo.*' Vittorio slapped his right hand inside his left elbow then he pulled his left hand up. He got on the bike and rode off along the track to the single men's quarters, narrowly missing a chook.

'Can you tell Vittorio to keep the bike out of sight? I'll talk to Grimes.'

'*Sì, sì. Grazie, Signora. Grazie.* He love her, this bike.' He shrugged, smiling. Luca was grateful to her, and that made her happy.

CHAPTER 23

*One sheep will follow the next, and the next will follow him, and so
forth until eternity.*

THE WOOLGROWER'S COMPANION, 1906

'Mrs Dowd, could I come and see you and Mr Grimes? Late
today?'

Bomber, Harry's teacher.

'Of course. Is six all right?' Kate didn't ask on the party line
what it was about, but she quizzed Harry when he got home
half an hour later. 'What's happened at school?'

He shrugged. 'Dunno. Maybe I got a prize.'

'Maybe. And maybe not. You in trouble?'

He looked at his feet.

'You job someone? Punch one of the Mullens boys?'

'Nuh.'

'Did you punch Bert this time?'

'Nuh. We're mates now, eh.'

'Well? I don't think she's coming to talk about the drought.'
Kate wished she was; the month was almost gone and they'd
had just a half-inch of rain. They would get three times that in
April, outside of a drought.

'So? What is it then?'

'Bomber's dark about me report on bloody Anzac Day, eh.'

191

Kate stuck her head in the laundry. Empty; Dais was outside. She came back to Harry. 'What did you say?'

'I tole the truth, eh. Some of them darkies fought in the First War, but now they won't let em in the dawn march. A bit rough cos ya gotta get up at four, anyhow.'

Kate took a deep breath and shook her head. 'Did you say this out loud? In front of the class?'

He grinned, proud of himself.

Kate shook her head. 'Well, you're in for it now. And you better tell your uncle. All right? Mrs Pommer wants to see him too. Here at six.'

He nodded again, this time more slowly.

~

The headlights of Mrs Pommer's car appeared on the dot of six, flickering through the trees, up out of the crossing. There was no sign of Grimes. Kate wasn't surprised; he hadn't wanted Harry at the school in the first place. She just hoped he hadn't given Harry a thrashing for the lecturette.

Mrs Pommer got her formidable self out of her Humber and came across to the verandah. Even in the half-light, Kate knew Bomber's lips were pursed and she felt ten years old again, late for school on an uncooperative Ben.

They sat on the verandah, Mrs Pommer lowering herself into a chair.

'Should we wait, Mrs Dowd? For Harold's uncle?'

Kate had to think who Harold was. 'Let's go ahead. Mr Grimes is probably still out on the run.'

'I'll begin by saying that Harold is quite a clever boy. When he puts his mind to it, he can do well, surprisingly well, in maths and botany especially.'

'In botany?'

'Very good at his native plants, is Harold. Someone called Daisy taught him. A relative?'

'No,' was all Kate said.

'The point is, he can apply himself. He could even try for an apprenticeship in the railways if he works hard. But he's taken a wrong path. A dangerous path.'

Bomber reached into her handbag and handed Kate a grubby piece of paper. It had three scrawled lines on it.

No one knows but there was darkies in the Grate war who fort alot. But they cant march in Anzac day. I rekkon thats not fair dinkum. They shod march cos they fort.

'Harold has four years left at school, until he's fifteen. But he *must* follow the rules. Not write nonsense about the blacks.' Her task done, Bomber stood up. 'You will tell Mr Grimes?'

Kate nodded.

As she walked back to the car, Kate called after her. 'Watch out for roos. They're bad on the road out, after the grid.'

She wondered where this would all come out as the car's tail-lights dipped into the crossing. Grimes surprised her when he strode out of the dark and stopped on the dead lawn beneath her. Had he waited for Bomber to leave?

'I've got a bone to pick with you, Mrs D. Bottinella says ya told him he can keep that bloody bike.'

The bike? Not school? 'I told Vittorio I would talk to you about the bike, not that he could keep it. What do you think?'

'It's a bloody bad idea. He could do a runner.'

Kate frowned. Make off on a bike? With nineteen miles to the nearest real town, and four-hundred-odd to Sydney?

'Y'can't be tellin the men what they can and can't do. Got that?' He turned to go.

'Mrs Pommer was here, Mr Grimes. From the school.'

'I told Harry he's not goin to school. Enough's enough. He'll work here on Amiens with me now.'

Kate, open-mouthed, watched the blue of his shirt disappear into the gloom.

~

The following afternoon, Harry did not come to Kate, and as the hours passed she knew Grimes had done it, kept him home from school. When the truck passed by at about four, she went onto the verandah to check. Harry was there, all right, in the truck cab.

Grimes brought the truck to a stop, and Luca jumped to the ground to come into the garden. Harry didn't look at Kate, even when she came to the fence; he kept his eyes straight ahead as the truck moved off again.

Kate asked Luca, 'Did Harry go out with the men into the paddocks for the day?'

'*Sì*,' Luca said. 'Grimes say no school now. This is true?'

Kate shrugged, frowning.

'You tell professor? *Signora* Bomber?'

Kate laughed. 'It's Pommer, not Bomber. And no, not yet.'

'And your sapphire, *Signora*. You find her?'

Kate shook her head.

'Ah.'

They worked to extend the last garden bed closer to the back fence. Luca did the heavy work, driving a fork into what was left of the lawn at the edge of the bed, lifting chunks of earth and roots off onto a pile. He banged the fork's prongs flat against a round clump of soil, packed hard by the drought, broke it up and started again, driving the fork into the dead lawn edge. She caught herself staring. He was good to watch, his body almost black from the sun and sinewed from his work. A controlled power drove each stroke.

'*Grazie, Signora.*'

She looked away before his gaze could meet hers. 'What for?' she said, hitting a lump with her own fork. It shattered,

194

and she half-dragged, half-raked the loose soil across to the new bed.

'For this yarn today, for Harry, for his *bicicletta*. To Vittorio . . .'

Kate grinned at Luca saying 'yarn' for the first time and shrugged. 'Did Harry say anything today to you about school?'

'*Niente a nessuno*,' he said, hitting a clump of earth hard to break it up. 'He say nothing.'

Kate sighed. 'I read they caught Mussolini in the north. Are you glad?'

He snorted, an unhappy laugh. '*Sì, Signora*.'

'Why did you join up? To fight for him?'

'No, no.' He made a revolver with his index finger and thumb and held it to his head. 'I must go. You know?'

Kate shook her head. It was hard to imagine. 'Your village? Grosio. Is it small like Longhope?'

Luca shrugged. 'Small? *Sì*. But not like Longhope. *Grosio è bellissimo*.'

'Longhope's not beautiful?'

'No. She is ugly.' He said it without feeling; it was a fact.

Kate laughed. It was true; apart from the creek and the willows on it, there wasn't much that was pretty about Longhope.

'You miss home very much?'

'*Sì*.' He said it with feeling, a long sound, and then listed things on his fingers, the fork handle against his hip again. 'My father. This family.' He smiled suddenly, that half-grin. 'Food also. Taleggio. Is cheese. This wine, pasta.'

'Pasta. The stringy stuff Vittorio hangs on the fences to dry?'

'*Sì*.'

She pulled at a mat of grass roots and thought about these men so far from home. 'What's worst? About being here?'

He shrugged. 'My old work, maybe she go now. No more work.'

'You were a stable-hand at home?'

'*Sì*. With horses of Count. Many horses.'

'Were you a stockman? Mustering?'

Luca laughed. 'No, *Signora*. Lombardy, she is famous for the beautiful horses. For *Il Duce*, for kings.'

Kate was impressed. 'What did you do?'

'I work at *la scuderia*. The place for horse babies. They sell.'

'You like horses and that work?'

'I like work, *sì*. But free. Not a prisoner.' He broke open a clump of earth with the fork prongs. 'You know the horse work, the muster here?' He pronounced it 'm'star'. 'That – that is good work. For this I am a man. Not the prisoner.'

'But otherwise?'

'I am prisoner. This prison? No bars, *Signora*.' As he drove the fork prongs into the dry earth, she remembered he'd said this to her before.

'You want to go home.' Her heart fell, and she worried that she cared at all, and so much.

'*Sì*. The home.' He stopped, his hands resting on the fork handle in front of him. A shadow crossed his face and he looked sombre. 'What is left?'

Kate swallowed and spoke again. 'You know, after my mother died, it was difficult.' She made a fist inside her glove and brought it down on a clod of earth. 'But Dad needed me, needs me even more now. And it's good. To be needed by your family. You have that too.'

'*Sì*,' he said. It was muffled, as if he had wiped a hand across his nose. 'This brother …' Luca began, his voice soft.

Kate stood up. She took her glove off and put her hand on his on the top of the fork, his tanned knuckles warm and rough under her fingers. Eventually, he took a breath and exhaled slowly. 'My brother, he go. From August. Eight months now. Where he is?'

Kate left her fingers on his. Luca took her hand, squeezed

it, and put it back at her side. Again she felt that urge to hold him, pull him close to her. When he stepped away, she felt a surge of disappointment and relief.

He shook his head. 'You are my friend, *Signora*. More? Bad. Very bad. For you.'

'Bad for us,' Kate corrected and they stood for a long moment, looking at each other.

They went back to work, breaking earth until the sky over them turned orange and pink and was filled with the swooping dots of black bats.

In bed that night, Kate lay awake, listening to the sounds of the night all around her but thinking only of Luca, grateful and sad in equal measure for his strength of character.

~

The next evening Grimes turned up on time for another Bomber-commanded meeting. He walked across the flat as the headlights of her car came up out of the crossing. It occurred to Kate she'd best ask Daisy to warn her if her father emerged.

'Dais?' Kate called. When there was no reply, she went into the laundry and found her sitting down – Daisy, who couldn't be talked into a rest.

'Are you all right, Dais? Are you sick?'

The girl got to her feet. 'Nuh, Missus.' She sounded almost annoyed.

How odd. Kate felt a bit cross with Daisy. 'Can you let me know if you hear Dad coming out of the office? Bomber's coming.'

'Orright, Missus.'

Maybe she was just tired, not annoyed? Kate went back onto the verandah as Mrs Pommer came over from the gate. For a big lady, she moved fast and with purpose. As she settled into a cane chair, Grimes leaned himself against a verandah upright, his arms crossed over his chest.

197

'Harold must come to school, Mr Grimes,' Mrs Pommer said.

'No offence, Mrs P, but I don't take orders from you, not from no woman,' he said.

'It's the *law*.' Bomber's voice was strong, capable of carrying across a playground or a paddock.

'What you gunna do? Get Wingnut after me?' Grimes laughed, shaking his head. Bomber stood up so fast she startled Kate. She went right up to Grimes, and he dropped his arms to his sides, like a schoolboy in trouble.

'Now listen here, *Mister* Grimes.' Bomber poked him in the chest with a chubby finger. 'Constable Withers is *indeed* aware of my visit here tonight. And I *will* get him onto you if Harold is not at school bright and early tomorrow morning. Do *you* understand *me*?' She leaned into him.

For once, Grimes had no answer.

'Good evening, Mrs Dowd. Mr Grimes.' Bomber left, pounding across the dead lawn.

Grimes found his voice. 'Struth. The woman's a battle-axe.'

Kate took it to be a good sign that he hadn't just walked off.

'Maybe Harry could go to school for a few more days? Until Mrs P calms down,' she suggested. 'I could even take him in? We go to town tomorrow to cash the wages.'

Grimes just shook his head.

~

Kate kept an eye out early the next morning from the kitchen window.

'What you lookin for, Missus?' Daisy asked, a broom in her hands.

'Harry. I want to see if he goes to school,' Kate said, her eyes still. Daisy came to stand right beside her, and she was soft against Kate's bony hip. Daisy had gone womanly all of a sudden.

198

'Look. Good. There he is.' At the top of the rise was Harry heading off on Ben.

In town that morning, Kate went first to the bank, arriving as it opened. She could see Emma was in place, at her desk. Luckily, there was no sign of Addison.

The young teller smiled at her. He was one of the Wilson boys but everyone said he was clever, so he must be a ring-in.

'I'd like to cash this please. Our wages cheque,' she said as if to prove she wasn't frittering it away on dresses and the *Women's Weekly*. She was withdrawing a little extra too, to pay a bill. She was glad when the Wilson boy pushed the envelope of cash across to her under the grille.

As she left, Kate gave Emma a quick nod. No need to publicise they were friends.

She walked two doors down from the bank to Nettiford's, the haberdashery.

'Can I get you something, Mrs Dowd?' Irene Nettiford appraised Kate coolly, her palms on the counter, her long arms spread wide. Kate had not been in for months, too afraid to buy anything with money already overdue to them.

'I've come to settle our account,' she said.

The woman's face broke into a smile. 'I'll get Sid.'

Her husband appeared moments later, wiping scone from the corner of his mouth. He was as short and round as his wife was tall and thin.

'I hope cash is all right?' Kate said.

'Happy with anything, Mrs Dowd,' he replied, his eyes on her handbag.

'You have bonbons!' Three small boxes of Pascall fruit bonbons sat on the counter. Kate had not seen them since before the war. Her father had always bought a small box of them for her when she was small, on his weekly trip to town. She remembered, as a little girl, squealing with joy as he came up the homestead steps. While she searched through his pockets, he'd wriggle and squirm, denying he had any, until she found them.

She hesitated, knowing they'd be expensive, then reached for one box, and her rations cards.

'I'll pay for this now too.' She counted out the money. 'I'm sorry about it being late.'

'Paid now.' He smiled as he rang the money into the till. Kate left while the goodwill held and ignored the seersucker tablecloths in the window.

She was a bit along the street when someone called her from behind.

'Kate.' It was Elizabeth Fleming. 'So glad to catch you.'

'Hullo. Everything all right?'

'All well. John's busy, of course. But I wanted a word with you. To make sure you know. John says I shouldn't interfere, but I felt it my duty.'

'Know what?'

'They're all the same, you know. You mustn't feel bad about Daisy.'

'Daisy?'

'She's expecting, apparently.'

Kate's mouth fell open.

'You didn't know? My girl, Kay, heard it straight from her.'

'I suspected,' Kate fibbed.

'That's what I told John,' Elizabeth prattled on. 'Kate'd never keep the girl on the place if she knew, I said. But it's such a bore to have to train another one. She'll have to go back to the Home anyhow, till the baby's born and given up.'

'Yes,' Kate said, trying to take it in. 'Back to the Home.'

'Heaven only knows who the father is. I mean, she won't know, will she?'

It was almost certainly Ed. And if it were him, Kate would need to keep it quiet. She hated herself but she couldn't afford to lose him. What a galah he was. More than that, it was bloody unbelievable.

'Good luck with it all, Kate dear.' Elizabeth squeezed her arm. She pulled her cardigan tighter around her against the nip of the autumn breeze.

Kate watched her go, hoping it wasn't true. She already knew it would be hard to do her work and Daisy's. Would the Board even give her another girl, after this? Then she caught herself and began to think of poor Daisy, pregnant at fourteen. The baby would be taken from her for adoption. Kate had to talk to her.

CHAPTER 24

A prudent woolgrower guards against the least contamination of his clip and of all varieties, through urine stain, torn wool bales, errant bailing twine or even a tool, mislaid by a careless shed hand.

THE WOOLGROWER'S COMPANION, 1906

'You want more meat, Dad?' Kate asked, seeing his lunch plate empty. He shook his head. She'd eaten next to nothing, pre-occupied with thoughts of Daisy. 'Cup of tea?'

He frowned, shaking his head again. 'I'm looking for it, ya know.'

'What's that?'

'The sapphire.'

She put the plates down. 'You'll give it to me if you find it, won't you, Dad? You promise?'

He got up and left her for the office. She took a breath and went into the kitchen with the plates. Daisy was nowhere to be seen, though she had already made the tea, and the pot and cups sat on a tray on the table. Kate tidied up the lunch things, waiting for Daisy to reappear. Then she heard the laundry door go as Daisy came in from the clothes line.

'Can you pop in here, please?' Kate said, hating herself.

Daisy came round the corner of the laundry door, the sun-faded wicker washing basket in her hands, a mound of dry white

202

sheets and towels in it. She put the basket on the end of the kitchen table and reached for a towel to fold. Her hands were shaking.

Kate swallowed. 'Daisy. I must ask you about something, something serious. Are you expecting?'

'Spectin, Missus?' Daisy's hands stilled.

Kate's voice was soft. 'Are you having a baby?'

The girl's face crumpled, and her hands dropped to rest on the mound of washing, the towel still in her fingers.

'Was it Ed?'

Tears fell as Daisy shook her head. But Kate didn't believe her – it had to be Ed. He was the only one who was keen. She tried again. Maybe Daisy had been forced? Kate thought of the awful bruises.

'Was it a POW? Or one of the stockmen?'

Daisy kept her eyes still on the floor.

'Who was it, Daisy?'

She didn't look up.

'Please tell me.'

The girl's head shook, ever so slightly.

She was protecting Ed. Protecting him from being sacked. She inhaled deeply. 'You'll have to go back to the Home.'

The noise that came from Daisy was not a sob but a strangled cry. Kate looked away and forced herself on, trying hard not to show her sorrow for the girl. 'You need to pack your things, and I . . . I'll take you late this afternoon.'

Daisy nodded. She picked up the basket and went into the laundry. Kate could hear her shaking and folding the clean sheets, ready for ironing. Kate went to her room and closed the door. She sat on the floor and put her head in her hands.

~

That afternoon after school, Kate told Harry that Daisy was going back.

'Struth,' he said, his eyes wide. 'That's rough on Dais, eh.'

Kate put a glass of milk in front of him. At least her father wasn't being difficult about it. He'd said nothing when she'd told him.

'Look. Maybe once the baby is born, she can come back. Or even go back to her family. I don't know.' Either way, it would be without her baby. The Matron had said that much on the phone.

'Family? Matron tolda her family's all dead, eh.'

Kate knew from the Matron that Daisy had been taken from her family because her mother had had a sixth child, so the Matron's lie must have been to help Daisy start again completely. To cut the ties. She shook her head. 'Anyway, what's your homework? What reading do you have?'

'Bugger the homework.' He gave his school case a solid kick that sent it under the table into the next kitchen chair with a bang, got up and left. The fruit bonbons she hadn't even tried to give him, knowing he'd think it was a bribe.

A knock at the gauze door interrupted her train of thought. It was Ed, with his hat in big hands and a furrowed brow, looking out of place. He never came inside the fence.

'Can I've a word, Mrs D?' He glanced through the gauze door towards the laundry. Well might he look guilty.

'C'mon then.' Kate went out and walked back to the fence, to get out of earshot of the house. Ed followed.

'All right. What do you have to say for yourself?'

'Can ya let her stay, Mrs D? She's only a kid. A good kid.'

Kate was shocked. 'She must go, now she's in bother. You know very well the Welfare Board is strict about these things.'

He looked down at the hat in his hands. He was probably worried about his child. Bit late for that. Angry as she was with him, she respected Daisy's desire to protect him. He didn't deserve it. And Kate couldn't afford to lose him, either. 'Look, it's awful but there's no use crying over spilt milk.'

'Spilt milk? Mrs D, that's rough.'

'You've got some gall, Ed Storch. You're not a tenth of the person Daisy is. I don't want to hear about this again. You understand?' She left him, her plait thumping against her back as she walked.

~

Late that afternoon, Kate waited at the truck with Grimes. Gunner moved about their feet, not wanting to be left behind. When the dog jumped up, putting his paws on her skirt, she roused on him. 'Get down.'

'It's that bloody Canali, I tell ya,' Grimes muttered.

'She said it wasn't; she was clear as clear.'

'Ya can't trust the Abos.'

Puck barked from beyond the truck as Daisy came round the side of the house with Harry. He carried her small string bag that held all of her possessions: a comb, a tiny hand mirror Kate had given her, and the spoon she'd brought her back from Sydney.

Grimes frowned, unhappy with Harry. 'I'll git er into the tray.'

'Let's take the car. She can travel with us.'

Grimes looked at Kate as if she'd hit him. 'In the car?'

'She's expecting, Mr Grimes.'

'She's a bloody boong, is what she is. I'm not drivin an Abo about like Lady Muck.'

He was right. Eyebrows would be raised in town to see an Aboriginal – man or woman – in the car with them. If Grimes wasn't there, she'd have done it.

'All right then. In the tray.'

Gunner leapt all over Daisy when she came out of the gate, and she stopped. He put his paws up on her stomach. 'Gunner, ole fella,' she said as she rubbed his ears. The dog licked her hand, his ears down. Could he know? He dropped to the dirt and she squatted, rubbing his tummy, his tail flicking against the ground.

Harry stopped at the back of the tray, head down, his eyes and both hands on the handle of the string bag he carried for Daisy.

'See ya, Harry,' she said, and pinched his arm. He wouldn't look at her, and Kate suspected he was crying. Daisy climbed up into the tray, and Harry handed her the bag. He went off towards the grid, to Luca who was already there. Kate wondered where Vittorio was and hoped he wasn't the culprit. Ed was nowhere to be seen, either.

At the grid, Harry stood with Luca, waiting. As the truck passed, they waved, slowly. Kate looked in the side mirror and each kept a hand in the air until she could no longer see them in the vehicle's dust.

~

The Longhope Domestic Training Home for Aboriginal Girls was about two miles east of the town. It couldn't be seen from the main road. Then, once you turned off, it came into view. A long building, the old house might once have been grand. Now it needed a lick of paint. Its garden was gone, replaced with a cleared paddock and a dog-netting fence.

'Be hot with no bloody trees,' Grimes said as he turned the truck into the narrow track.

Kate had collected Daisy from the Home almost six months before, but she didn't remember it looking as desolate then. A deep verandah ran along the front of the house. That was empty too, bare of any furniture, and its two pairs of doors were closed, blinds drawn. For just a second in Kate's line of sight, a verandah pillar was caught between the doors, like a nose on a face, a face with its eyes shut tight.

Grimes paused the truck at the gate. It was manned by a rangy fellow sitting on a chair in the sun, hat propped over his eyes, arms folded on his chest. He got up and came across to the truck.

'Afternoon,' he said, lifting his hat, with an appraising smile for Kate.

'We come to see the matron,' Grimes said before Kate could speak. 'Bringin one of em back.'

'Ere? She's not gunna be pleased.' But he waved them on.

Grimes brought them to a stop in a gravel area at the front of the building.

Kate got out quickly and went round to the back of the truck. She stifled a gasp. Daisy was huddled in the very corner of the tray, her face hidden in her elbow.

'C'mon, Daisy. Let me help you down,' Kate said softly. She didn't want Grimes to see the child like this.

When Grimes's door slammed, Daisy found her bottle. She got to her feet, picked up her bag and climbed down out of the truck. On the ground, she took her eyes up from the dirt to look at Kate, who couldn't speak for fear of crying. Then Daisy straightened up and pulled back her shoulders, her face hardening with her stance.

A woman in a nurse's uniform appeared at the top of the verandah steps. Matron McAdams. She was short and Scottish, with a stiff smile and a brisk manner.

'Afternoon,' she said, in her soft brogue. 'Come inside for the paperwork, please, Mrs Dowd.'

Grimes stepped back to allow Kate to go before him up the stairs. The matron stared at Daisy. She must have sensed her resolve. 'Don't you look your betters in the eye, girl.'

Daisy turned away but didn't lower her eyes. Kate inhaled, shocked at what lay ahead for Daisy. And she had done it.

'Face the wall. And leave the bag for Mrs Dowd. You know you're allowed no personal effects.'

Daisy lowered the bag to the floor by Kate's feet and turned to the wall.

The room that served as the matron's office was small, with two visitors' chairs. Doors opened out onto the verandah and beyond that a flat area of cleared dirt.

'Sit, sit,' the matron commanded, smiling. 'Thank you for ringing ahead. Not all do, you know. They just drop them off as if we were the RSPCA,' she said as she sifted through the bundles of files on her desk. 'And I had no chance to tell you, Mrs Dowd. You were so quick when you rang. Straight to Armidale Girls' Home would have been best. Now the girl will be taken there first thing tomorrow.'

'Armidale Girls' Home? But that's a reform school, isn't it? For delinquents?'

'Yes. Black, white or brindle, that's where they go.'

'Daisy's not delinquent, Matron. She's expecting.'

'Well, that's the procedure when this happens.'

Kate had heard bad things of that Home, of heavy punishments. 'Do they keep them separate from the girls who are in there, you know, the ones in for reform?'

The matron shrugged. 'I don't know about that. Many of our girls find themselves there sooner or later.'

'Because they're expecting? Do many of your girls get pregnant?'

The matron nodded unhappily. Kate shook her head. She should have been more vigilant. There was little noise from elsewhere in the Home. Kate's eyes moved to the window and the dirt yard just outside. The high dog-netting fence separated the yard from what looked like a small cemetery, with twenty or so simple wooden crosses.

'I didn't know Longhope had another cemetery, Matron.' Kate realised once she'd spoken that it must be for the Aborigines. It had never occurred to her to think about where they were buried.

'Oh, that's for the Home,' the matron said, looking at the papers in front of her.

'But aren't there only children here?'

'Some of the littlies just seem to give up when they arrive. Even sleeping in a bed is a shock. They can't cope with the discipline, the routine. And the flu always takes a few. Not up to it. Sad, but there you are.' She shrugged.

Kate wished Daisy were further down the corridor so she couldn't hear this.

The matron sifted through a set of papers. 'Ah, here we have it.' She opened a file. 'But first things first. Is the father white? Single? He should be encouraged to consider marrying her. The intent is to get as many of these girls settled into white society as possible.'

'Daisy won't tell us who's responsible.'

The woman's face softened. 'Ah. That's a shame. Some of these girls are harder to help than others. But I see now why you'd want to get her off the place.'

Kate didn't understand. She said nothing, watching as the matron took a typed sheet of paper from the file, spun it around to put it in front of Kate and pointed to a dotted line at the bottom. 'If you can sign here, please, for the girl.'

'It's Daisy. Her name's Daisy, Matron.'

The woman leaned back from the desk and smiled sadly. 'I know her name, Mrs Dowd. I choose not to use it. This work – to break the natives' simple, stubborn nature – is not always easy. But perhaps her baby will have a chance in life, even if poor Daisy has squandered hers. The baby will be put up for adoption, if it's pale.'

Kate swallowed. She wondered about Daisy's family at Broken Hill, 750 miles to the west. They probably didn't even know where she was – and this woman had told Daisy her family were dead. What was Kate *doing*?

The matron nudged the paper across the desk to Kate. It was headed *Note to File: Return of Daisy Nunn*. The first paragraph read: *Reasons for return: refusal to work, lack of moral fibre/*

fornication. Absconding. Underneath, Kate's name was typed, with a line for her signature.

'Daisy never refused to work, Matron. And she never ran away. I wouldn't want the wrong things to go on her record.'

'Mrs Dowd, you bring me a girl in the family way. She can hardly work now.'

Kate opened her mouth but the matron held up her hand and spoke softly. 'We do not always succeed here at the Home. These native girls are amoral, not immoral. We face that burden in our teaching.'

Kate sat, pen still above the paper.

'Mrs Dowd?' The matron pushed the paper a little. 'Come along. These are the rules.' Kate put the pen onto the paper and forced her hand to sign.

'The AWB will probably let you have Daisy back, after the baby is born and adopted out.'

'The AWB? I thought it was called something else?'

'It was. It used to be the Aboriginal Protection Board. But a certain amount of rabble-rousing by the blacks in the cities about rights and whatnot meant the Board had to show they were doing something.' She rolled her eyes. 'So now it's the Aboriginal Welfare Board. Anyway, you can have this girl back in due course, or another would be available sooner. In a couple of months.'

Kate could not think of anyone else in Daisy's place. Still, she didn't want to have her near Ed again, either.

A bell rang and the matron stood. 'I must get on.'

'Until now, we've had no trouble with Daisy. Please, you'll take care of her, Matron? She's a good girl. Really.'

'I'm sure God will help her see the right path.'

Outside in the corridor, Daisy stood, as before, facing the wall, head up. Grimes didn't look at her as he went out, down the steps to the truck.

'Come along then, girl.' The matron walked away down the corridor.

Kate swallowed as Daisy pulled herself up to her full height and went after the matron.

'Daisy,' hissed Kate.

She stopped and glanced back.

'Your family. They're alive. You know that?'

Daisy nodded, once, and followed the matron along the corridor.

'Daisy,' Kate called again. But this time the girl did not look back, the soft *plip-plop* of her shoes receding with her. She turned the corner and was gone from sight, leaving Kate clutching the little string bag with shaking hands.

~

Kate returned to find Harry in the kitchen with her father, the boy sitting at the end of the table with a bikkie in his hand.

'Hullo,' she said, trying to sound normal. Harry got up, took his school case and left.

'Daisy get off orright?' her father asked, mouth full. He was leaning against the kitchen bench, in socked feet, munching an Anzac biscuit.

'It's awful, Dad. That place. And what's worse is that she's going on to the Armidale Home,' Kate said. 'She was something to see, though. Her head up.'

He started to laugh. 'Head up? Bear down, more like it.'

She frowned. He had such rough talk, nowadays. Her father shrugged. 'Well, maybe you should of done nothing. Just let em come for her.'

Kate shook her head. 'A girl who gets in the family way has to go back. It's part of the arrangement when they're given to you. The Board have a lot of rules. Administration. I suppose they have to have.'

But her father didn't hear; he had gone. Now the house was unusually quiet – no Daisy, no Harry – so Kate got up and went to her room. The truck was due soon, to collect her. With joining under way, the ewes and rams needed to be checked, and Kate was enlisted as another pair of eyes. Even a girl could do that. She would have been pleased to avoid it today. She didn't want to see anyone, certainly not Ed.

When the truck's horn sounded, she went outside. Luca and Vittorio stood in the back of the tray. They did not acknowledge her. She climbed into the cabin, pulling the heavy door closed after her, and Ed moved the truck slowly off. He said not a word throughout the drive to Riflebutt, registering his disapproval, which was pretty rich, but still a weight of guilt clung to Kate.

Ed braked to a stop at the Riflebutt trough, the big Southern Cross windmill above it clanking over the bleating of the ewes, pumping the water that brought the flocks back to these corners.

Out of the truck, Kate looked up at the turning blades. Right now, with her heart full of grief for Daisy, she found some relief in the sight, the windmill sail turning evenly in the light breeze, gunmetal blades against a bright blue sky. Her father said there'd been windmills for more than a thousand years.

'Orright,' Ed said to Kate and the two POWs, 'better have two of us in Bullant, and the other pair in Riflebutt. Ya know what ya lookin for. The rams won't stop to eat'n that makes em weak, so see they're orright. The ewes too'll be strugglin on this pasture. An them young rams might avoid the maidens. Got that?'

Luca nodded. Vittorio looked blank.

'Watch ya step round the rams, eh. They'll be workin so shouldn't mind ya.' Ed climbed through the fence into the Bullant paddock. Vittorio followed him, and Kate cursed under her breath. She'd have given anything to avoid watching sheep mating with Luca.

'See yez back here in half an hour,' Ed called as he moved off into the ewes.

Luca put a boot on the lower wires of the Riflebutt fence and pulled the top wire up to hold a gap open. '*Signora.*'

Kate climbed through, glancing at the muscles in his forearm, inches from her nose. She could smell him, that mix of sweat and soap. Even sad as she was, she liked it, his smells. Such a good sort, even with his *Signoras* and his bloody Eye-tie English. Kate suddenly thought of Daisy at the Home, and felt bad for thinking about Luca.

She moved away across the open ground towards the flock of ewes gathered in an arc from the water trough, and kept a wary eye out for rams. The smell of fresh dung was heavy in the air, despite the breeze. At least that got the lovely Luca smell out of her mind. She waded into the mass of ewes, moving through them, ewe to ewe, looking for any who limped or hobbled. They looked out of condition, their wool dull and dusty. Kate prayed the drought would break soon, to bring rain and then pasture. Engrossed as she was, though, whenever she paused she thought of Daisy.

Luca whistled, one sharp note, and pointed to the left. The young ram Basil was moving forwards into a hollow on the edge of the flock closely followed by a ewe. Kate went towards them, trying to get a look at the ewe's ear. The ram froze as the ewe sniffed his hindquarters, then he turned to do some sniffing of his own. The ewe stood still. From the ear notches they knew she was a maiden. Kate heard Luca behind her but still she watched the pair to see if Basil would do the job, or give up.

The ram scrambled to mount the ewe, and she bleated as he fell off.

'Try again,' Kate said softly. 'C'mon, Basil.'

The ram sniffed some more. Then he had another go, and Kate was pleased, both with the young ram, and because maybe this time the ewe might 'catch'. An empty ewe cost money.

Basil fell off again, and the ewe started to walk away, but the ram chased her, and mounted quickly as she moved along, his hind quarters in a two-legged walk.

Behind her, Luca laughed softly. Kate didn't acknowledge him. She *really* didn't want to talk about joining with him.

The ewe stopped and Basil stayed on. He'd done it. When Kate turned, Luca had gone, moved off to the far side of the flock. She knew that he disapproved of her taking Daisy back to the Home. Should she have waited for them to come for her? She'd been so sure it was the right thing to do, until she saw the Home and the matron again.

The drive back was also silent and Kate found little pleasure in the dusk sky, and none in the cirrus clouds streaked thin and high across the horizon. They pointed to fair weather, and she needed none of that.

She'd have preferred not to speak to Ed. She had to, though. 'I saw Basil have a go at a maiden. Three times. Kept at it but he got there.'

'She stand?' Ed asked.

'Yes. Didn't run.'

As the temperature dropped and the last of the light ebbed, Ed dropped her off at the homestead. She was left with the bats and the approaching cold, a quiet all around her.

Later that night – after they'd eaten, her father was in bed, and the kitchen was tidy – Kate felt the quiet again. She showered, even using extra-precious water to wash her hair, trying to make herself feel clean, feel better about Daisy. It didn't work. Still damp from her shower and shivering in the cold in her nightie, she sat on her bed to brush her knotted hair, thinking of the times Daisy had untangled the knots for her, the girl's hand gripping a clump of Kate's mouse-brown hair as she brushed the ends, protecting her from pain.

Kate looked at herself in the mirror, conscious that she was different now from a year or even six months before.

She brought her hand to her face, sun-beaten no matter how careful she was to wear a hat. Thinner too than before, her cheeks hollow, her jawline more pronounced. Bits of her long hair frizzed and clumped around her face, and grey-blue eyes blinked back at her above a serious set to her lips. Sad. She looked sad, and she felt it, a crushing weight of guilt.

She sat back and started on her hair as Daisy would have, beginning at the bottom, brushing the lowest knots out first, working her way up, but she couldn't get the ends undone. A windy trip to and from Longhope and then an afternoon in the paddocks had done it. She'd failed Daisy too, she knew that, both in taking her to the Home and in letting Ed get to her in the first place. Kate stopped and laid the brush in her lap.

She got up slowly. From her chest of drawers, she took out a pair of heavy black-handled scissors. Her hand shaking, she took hold of a clump of hair and she cut – cut in handfuls, first on the right side, then the left. She pulled at the few remaining locks below the nape of her neck and cut those off blind, with the scissors behind her head, letting the hair fall on the floor. Then she took up her hairbrush and pulled it hard through her short, short hair.

PART II

CHAPTER 25

Ewes accustomed to the sight of men on horseback will be less likely
to abandon a lamb after birth when a rider appears.

THE WOOLGROWER'S COMPANION, 1906

Kate never got used to Daisy's absence, even weeks after. As the weeks turned into months, as autumn slid into winter, she would look up, hopeful, as she caught sight of someone in the house, only to find it was her own reflection in a window, her unfamiliar self with short hair. She feared for Daisy too, and missed her terribly.

Harry made it clear where blame lay – he avoided Kate and the house entirely. In the cold July mornings, she might glimpse him as he went off towards Frenchman's Creek, but he never came near the homestead, even after school.

Ed avoided her too, which Kate found galling. Her father's headaches took a turn for the worse, and he was more and more uneven, not understanding her when she'd tried to tell him about VE Day and peace in Europe. Instead, he grumbled about her short hair each time he saw her, as if seeing it for the first time. At least she and Luca were on reasonable terms, sort of, although she knew he too disapproved of what she'd done. He'd said nothing directly. At first he asked every week or so if Kate had heard news about Daisy, but the matron had been more than discouraging, telling her it was none of her business, as these matters 'were best left to those who know how to handle these people'. Kate had felt the enormity of her error anew then, in sending Daisy back, in not watching over her.

As the winter dragged on, the war in the Pacific revealed new horrors; the terrible destruction of two Japanese cities by the Americans, unfathomable devastation that brought Japan's surrender at last. Relief though that surrender was, it worried Kate, for Jack would come home, and Luca would return to Italy. All through those difficult months, she found solace only in her work, and the company of Luca in the garden at the end of each day, tending the winter veggies. They stopped only for rain but there was little of that. Luca became her friend. Their talks, and even their silences, kept her sane, she was sure of it, as she struggled to deal with her father, her worry about Daisy and the bank, and her yearning for Harry's company.

It was not until early September, more than four long months after she'd taken Daisy back to the Home, months spent searching for the sapphire, that Harry finally relented and came to the homestead. He appeared one afternoon after school, standing in the kitchen doorway. He was bigger and taller but that spikey blond hair still stuck out at the back. It was in need of a cut. His shirt was untucked, and his school jumper had an unravelling hole in the elbow. Kate smiled at him, shy almost, after so many months.

'I'll get you some milk,' she said, fetching a glass. 'And a bikkie.'

'I hear Dais's pretty short on bikkies at that Home, eh.'

So Harry had not forgiven her. Not completely. Nor should he. He drank the milk in one go, and put the empty glass on the table.

'I come to tell ya. Grimesy wants a word. At the fence, eh.'

She followed Harry out across the dead lawn to Grimes. Gunner was with him, scratching an ear but he stopped when a willy wagtail landed a few feet away. The little black-and-white bird saw the dog and swooshed up into the scented gum.

'Afternoon,' Grimes said, taking his hat off. 'The old man doin the lambin with us this year?'

'I don't think so. He'll feed the poddy lambs with Vittorio.'

Grimes grunted, unsurprised. 'We be shorthanded.'

'I'll come,' Kate said, without thinking.

'It's hard yakka. Not for womenfolk.'

'But I did the muster all right. In the autumn. I can manage sheep. Let me try.'

He said nothing, looking at Gunner on the ground. Then he put his hat on.

'Please,' she said, her fingers seeking her now-absent plait.

'It's your bloody funeral, Mrs D.'

~

A week had passed since Harry had reappeared, and Grimes had agreed that Kate could help with lambing. As she spread the icing across her father's birthday cake, Harry's noisy one-sided chatter with her father in the background, it occurred to Kate that it seemed much longer. All she'd lived and breathed those past seven days was lambing, and her body ached from it.

She put the birthday cake on the kitchen table between Harry and her father, and got matches to light the candle. The wick burst into flame – a brief, bright flare – then gave off wandering black smoke, the candle slipping sideways in the still-wet vanilla icing. Kate nudged it upright again. With Daisy gone, and lambing on, Kate was frantic with work. She'd iced the cake only minutes before; there'd been no time to do it before she'd left early that morning to ride out to the ewes.

'Happy birthday, Dad,' she said.

'What's that, Janice?' Her father rubbed his chin, prickled with grey-and-black stubble.

'No, Dad. It's me. Kate.' He was doing that more and more. He was tired. They all were. With one hand cupped around the little flame, Kate nudged the cake in front of him, next to his mug of tea.

'Today's the 8th, Dad. The 8th of September. Your birthday.'

'The 8th?' He looked at the flame and rubbed his forehead.

'Is your head giving you trouble?'

He shrugged.

'Daisy's birthday's in September. She never knew the year, but,' Harry threw in. Kate gave him a look.

'Who?' Kate's father asked.

'Dais. That Armidale Home's a salt mine, I heard from Bert. His cousin was in there for a bit. And they're cooped up too. Locked inside. Dais hates that. Poor bloody Dais, eh?'

Kate exhaled, knowing Daisy must be quite far along. She just hoped she'd be all right: that they'd be all right, mother and baby.

Above them, a smattering of raindrops dashed the corrugated iron of the roof. Not enough.

'Come along, Dad,' Kate said as if she was speaking to Harry. 'Why don't you blow the candle out?'

Harry was up beside him in a flash, one hand on the table, the other on the back of her father's chair.

'Let him do it by himself,' she said.

Harry counted. 'One. Two.'

It was a ruse. On *two*, Harry jumped the gun and blew like a horse snorting. Her father had not tried anyway. Kate cut three pieces of cake. She leaned against the kitchen bench to eat hers.

Harry held out his plate for more as her father started to eat.

'That's it, though,' Kate said, giving Harry another piece. 'No more.'

'How old are ya, boss?' Harry said through his cake.

'As old as m'toes and a bit older than m'teeth.'

Harry stopped eating and looked at him.

'I'm fifty-five. Or fifty-six? What am I, Katie?'

'Fifty-six now. But it's rude to ask a person's age, Harry.'

Kate put her plate and fork in the basin inside the sink. Outside, Gunner barked. The mail truck.

'Ya can't be fifty-six,' Harry said. 'Grimesy's fifty-six, and you could be his dad.'

Her father didn't hear or didn't react. He chewed on, serious, with a mouth full of cake. Harry was right. Her father looked old, with his white-grey hair and sloped shoulders.

'Afternoon, all.' Mick Maguire filled the doorway, his arms around loaves of bread, the newspaper and the post.

'A letter from Jack, in there.' Mick set his load on the table and smoothed out the newspaper.

Kate grabbed Jack's letter, cut Mick a big slice of the sponge and put it on a plate in front of the spare chair at the table. Then she went to get her letter to Jack to give it to Maguire to post. Sometimes they'd cross, like today, but she felt it was better he get a letter than postpone to update it. Her letters all said the same thing now: her father was changeable, the drought continued, and she hadn't found the sapphire. She couldn't think of much else to write to him, not since he made clear he wouldn't fight for Amiens.

'They caught one of them POW buggers in Melbourne this week,' Maguire said when she returned, pointing to a column of print. 'On the run for three months, he was.'

Kate leaned over to read aloud. '*A German prisoner of war was recaptured in Elsternwick early on Saturday after an alert member of the public noticed a pastry chef with poor English in the bakery in Quinton Street. The man had claimed to be Finnish.*'

223

'Under their noses,' her father said.

'What's that, Dad?'

'It's why he lasted so long on the run.' He stood up. 'Anyway I'm gunna retire from the racket.'

'Wanna play draughts, boss?' Harry asked.

Kate's father shook his head as he left. 'Ya beat me now, Harry, every time. No fun in that.'

'I'm out this afternoon, Dad,' she called.

He didn't ask where she was going.

She opened Jack's letter, a single piece of paper the same size as the envelope.

Dear Kate

Nothing much to say here. I am still training the ruddy wheelbarrows. I hope to get back fighting ▆▆▆▆▆.

Shame about Amiens. We're moving when I'm discharged. Sooner if you have to. But you get out with your head up, with a bit of pride left.

Jack x

Ruddy Jack, same as before. She had her pride, but she cared much more about Amiens. And to save it, she had to hold off the bank.

CHAPTER 26

*Amongst all of cud-chewers, it is sheep who most store recollection of
a rough handling.*

THE WOOLGROWER'S COMPANION, 1906

Kate was in what had been Daisy's sleep-out and was now the
sewing room, mending a pair of her joddies. She sat with a rug
over her knees and her back to the rafts of weak late-spring
sun coming in the window, the sound of the usual Sunday
morning service filtering from the wireless in the kitchen.
Her father always had the wireless on, regardless of what was
playing.

She heard a horse and looked up. Someone was coming
hell-for-leather up the hill from the creek. An accident? Kate
dropped her mending and went out the door to the verandah.
She hoped it wasn't Luca.

'Kate! *Kate!*' she heard.

Meg. Kate went down the verandah steps and ran across the
dead lawn to the fence. 'What's wrong?'

Meg hurled herself off Fiva, and pulled the horse forwards
to the fence. 'It's Robbo,' she said, tooth gap flashing. 'The
Allies have liberated our POWs in Singapore.'

'Oh Meg.' Kate went out through the gate and hugged
her.

225

'I had to get out of the house. It's driving me crazy to sit at home and wait now. But I want to know, too. A nutter I am.'

'So no news yet? I mean —'

'If Robbo's still alive? For sure?' Meg shook her head and her face dropped. 'The Army fella says it'll be another week – the 15th September at the earliest – before we know.'

'You want a cup of tea?'

'Nuh. I want to get back in case we do hear.' She scrambled up onto the stump and from the stump onto Fiva, still breathing hard from the ride. With Meg mounted, Fiva turned in circles, wanting to be off again.

'You were right, you know,' Meg called. 'Sheilas have to be brave every bloody day. Men just need it in bursts, the bastards.'

'You think so?'

'By the way, Kate, you look buggered.'

'Thanks.' She laughed. 'I am. It's lambing. Or maybe I'm just getting old.'

'*You're only as old as the person you feel,*' Meg called. She turned Fiva away into the sun and was off, dust and dead grass in her wake. Kate went back to the sleep-out. She had never been much for praying until these last months. Now she said another silent prayer for Robbo and Daisy. Please let them be all right. Kate reckoned the baby must be due very soon, the next month probably, October.

She sat down again in the chill of the sleep-out. It was as cold as charity – heaven knows how Daisy had stood it. It was an hour before she was due in the yards at eleven, the late start out of respect for the sabbath. Pulling the rug up over her knees, she picked up her holey jodhpurs. The stitching had gone on the back seam. Kate sewed backwards and forwards across the seat with strong thread – linen – trying to reinforce them, but it looked like a long shot. A year earlier she'd have thrown them in the ragbag and ordered some more from Nettiford's, but not now. She had one other pair on their last legs too.

When a shadow crossed the windows, she looked up. It was her father on the verandah outside, wearing only what looked like his swimming trunks.

'Dad!' She dropped her mending again and went out through the doors after him. By the time she reached the edge of the verandah, he was shutting the gate. 'What are you doing?' she called.

He gave her a cheery wave. 'Swim,' he called back. 'Creek.' She jumped off the verandah and ran after him.

'Dad,' she said, breathless, when she caught up on the track. 'You can't swim. It's cold. And the creek's just mud now.' Her words tumbled out. When he ignored her, she took his arm gently. 'Please,' she pleaded.

'Cut it out.' He shook her off. Goose bumps covered his chest.

She took his arm again. 'Dad. Please, let me help you.'

He turned on her, grabbing her wrists so tightly the skin burned, pulling her into him. His face was close, his breath stale in her nostrils. 'You want to swim too?'

Afraid, Kate tried to step back. 'Dad. Please.'

'Please? Please?' He dragged her, gripping her right arm with his left. He moved so quickly she stumbled, but he held her up, pulling her along the track, pain shooting through her from his clamp-hold on her wrist.

'Dad. I'm begging you!' Kate was hysterical. She pushed at his hand on her wrist, trying to loosen it. When he wrenched her wrist up with his left hand and raised his right, she closed her eyes and steeled herself.

Please don't hit me.

The sound of a vehicle startled them. Kate opened her eyes to see the truck coming round the corner, Ed driving, Luca and Vittorio in the tray. Luca saw Kate and thumped hard on the cabin roof. With the truck still moving, he jumped to the ground, running as he touched down.

'Boss! *Signora!*' he yelled as he ran. Ed pulled the truck to a stop. Kate's father walked on again towards the creek, still pulling Kate with him.

Luca caught up, and he fell in with them as they walked. 'Boss,' he said, puffing. 'We need you help us today, boss.'

Kate's father ignored him. Luca skipped ahead on the track and turned to block the path so they had to stop. Her father grunted.

'We take boss,' Luca said with cheer to Kate. 'Ewe in Pot Creek bog. We get her with you, boss. Orright?'

Ed got to them then, and Luca nodded again. Kate's father said nothing, his eyes on the creek ahead of him.

'Boss come too,' Luca said to Ed.

'Is that right?' Ed said, his eyes on his boss's hand clamped on Kate. A red welt ran round just above his fingers where he'd shifted his grip on her wrist.

A gust caught them and Kate's father shivered.

'Boss put on the clothes,' Luca said to Kate.

On the ground inside the fence something moved. The bowerbird hopped towards the bower. Her father turned to watch but he didn't release Kate's wrist and, just as quickly, he lost interest in the bird and tightened his grip again. Kate tried to speak. Her throat was dry, as if she had a mouth full of dust. She swallowed and took a small step, leading her father with the heat of her gripped wrist. 'Come on, Dad. Back to the house.'

She held her breath. And then he moved with her.

'Pot Creek bog,' Luca said again, in step right behind them. Kate was never more glad of his voice.

At the gate, her father dropped Kate's wrist and went into the house. Ed left them and walked his uneven gait back to the truck. Kate rubbed her wrist, red and burning. 'Thank you,' she said to Luca, her voice still strangled. Luca looked at the welts and shrugged, sad.

228

In the kitchen, Kate held the back of the chair and took a breath. She jumped when her father reappeared, dressed for a day's work. He didn't look at her, just picked up his hat from the kitchen bench and went out.

Luca waited, his hands resting on the fence. They walked together to the truck and Luca closed the passenger door behind Kate's father, then pulled himself up into the tray. He waved at her.

It will be all right.

As the truck drove away, Kate sat down in one of the kitchen chairs, her heart alive in her chest. Her breath turned to hiccups, loud in the empty house. She felt her hands shaking in her lap and put them on the table to steady them. *He didn't hit me.*

She could make no sense of anything. Tea. She thought she should make tea. At the sink her hands spilled a cup of precious water. She put the spigot inside the kettle, a faint rattling of metal against metal, then got the thing onto the stove.

Back at the table, with the teapot and a cup in front of her, her eyes fell on the pattern in the pine surface. She followed the lines with a wet finger, a streak along the grain.

Peng meowed to be let in. Kate was confused until she looked at the clock. Just an hour since her father had walked past her on the verandah in his swimmers. She went to the sleep-out, and sat again under the blanket, her sewing in her lap. She stared at the useless jodhpurs in her hands, her eyes wet with persistent tears.

~

Kate was making lunch when she heard the truck. She went to the window to see her father climb out, then moved away so he did not see her watching. He didn't look at her when he came into the kitchen, just put his hat on the counter.

229

His grey hair was matted with sweat into a ring around his head.

'Did you get the ewe out of the bog?' Kate asked. Her voice shook.

'Yep,' her father said slowly. 'Lost the lamb, though.' He went to have a wash before lunch. From the sink, Kate saw Luca waiting by the gate, looking towards the house. Comforted, she half-raised a hand and he waited a bit, then was gone. She was a mess. Her father had thrown her thoughts about. Her father, her worries about the bank. Daisy. All of it.

At lunch, her father ate his cold mutton and mashed potatoes in silence, shaking heavy salt over his food. Kate made herself eat some too. At the end of the meal, he carried his own plate to the sink before he took himself off to the office.

She didn't leave the house. At four, she was washing spinach leaves when Luca came to the gate. He spoke to Gunner, squatting to pat him, then glanced at Kate, in the kitchen. *Well?* he asked.

She stilled her hands on the leaves and nodded at him. It was OK, sort of. He went to work in the garden, staying until well after dark. She knew he was still there because she could hear him talking to Gunner in Italian. At half six that evening, her father had not emerged from the office, so Kate tapped on the door.

'Time to eat, Dad.'

There was no response, so she tried again.

'Dad? Your meal's ready.'

'Orright,' she heard this time, and she went back to the kitchen to bang a few dishes onto the table, to make it clear she was serving. She heard the squeak of the bathroom tap and the splash of water in the basin.

When he sat down, he looked tired. The morning had knocked the stuffing out of him. Out of them both.

'Eat up, Dad. If we don't eat, I'll have to sell your ration coupons to Tony Biggs.' The local publican – and Jack's friend – had a name for dealing in ration cards on the quiet.

He frowned. Kate made no more small talk. She found her spinach tasteless. She'd keep it for the chooks anyway, to make their yolks a deeper yellow. At the end of the meal, her father took his own plate to the kitchen, this time against her protest. He surprised her again when he came and sat back down, resting his hands on the table in front of him.

'You feeling better?' she asked.

He frowned. Then he shook his head slowly, confounded. 'This morning. T'raise a hand t'you.'

'You didn't mean it, Dad.'

'Six of one and half dozen of the other. I did it.' He was bewildered.

Kate blinked back tears. 'Dr King. He's a returned service-man himself. Why not go and see him?'

He shook his head. 'Not for me, Katie.' Doctors were for the dead.

He stood slowly, without energy, and came to her. Awkwardly, he put his arms around her for an instant, then shuffled off to the office.

It was a hug. Kate was too astonished to do anything but close her open mouth.

CHAPTER 27

It may be safely said that a poor season (chiefly by drought) will give rise to a break in the wool.

THE WOOLGROWER'S COMPANION, 1906

'You all right, Dad?' Kate stopped folding the washing in the kitchen as he shuffled out the door onto the verandah. This was the first time her father had been outside in a full seven days, since it happened – the swimming business. And she'd not left the house much either.

Her father dropped into one of the wicker chairs. In the garden, Luca straightened up from between the rows and gave a half-wave to them.

From the kitchen, she called, 'You want a cup of tea, Dad?'

'What's that?'

'Tea?'

'Orright.'

He'd been no trouble that past week. Not himself, though. For the first time in her life, Kate saw him cautious, moving slowly, like a man recovering from a fall off a horse.

Harry appeared a few minutes later to rattle the biscuit tin. It gave her pleasure when he appeared, reminding her of all the times he'd absented himself. He took two bikkies and went onto the verandah.

'You should do your homework,' Kate said from the sink.

'You wanna game, boss?' Harry set up the pieces, scratching at the spikes of dirty blond hair.

Her father was looking at the horizon, his fingers interlaced in his lap. Kate put a mug of tea next to him and then brought the washing out to fold it on the verandah.

Harry opened. 'Your go, boss.'

Kate held up her remaining pair of jodhpurs. A split ran from the back of the waist to the crotch. 'Will you be all right by yourself, Dad? If I went into town with Grimes tomorrow for the weekly run? I have to buy joddies.'

Kate hugged the joddies against her chest, still warm from the line, and watched her father. He was thinking, rubbing his fingers along his forehead. Maybe he was all right now.

There was nothing for it. She'd get a lift to town with Grimes the next morning. They'd only be gone a couple of hours, and a quick dispatch of their chores while there. She'd avoid the bank, though. She had nothing for Addison and she knew he'd not ask Grimes about Amiens's affairs.

~

The next morning, in town, Grimes dropped her at Nettiford's while he went to cash the wages cheque. As Kate pushed on Nettiford's heavy door, she tried to put aside her usual worry that Addison would refuse to cash the cheque.

'What can I do you for?' Mrs Nettiford asked.

'I just need new joddies. Two pairs in fact.' One off, one on and one in the wash – only the third they couldn't afford.

'You got enough ration cards? They're expensive with all that thread in the material.'

'We've enough.' Kate hadn't bought any clothes for months, not since Addison had told her about the debts. She kept her eyes on the shelf as Mrs Nettiford sorted through the sizes, glad they had any stock at all. She grabbed one of those new seersucker tablecloths – no ironing – Elizabeth Fleming had mentioned.

'How're things out your way?'

'Dry,' Kate said.

'Well, now that the Japs have surrendered, we just need the drought to break.' Mrs Nettiford was keen to pass the time of day since the account was up to date.

Kate put the joddies and the tablecloth on the counter.

'You can put these on the account, ya know. If ya need to,' Mrs Nettiford said.

Kate paused, the purse in her hand. 'No. I'll give you cash now.' Who knew if the poor woman would get paid if Amiens was sold up.

Mrs Nettiford accepted Kate's money happily, the bell of the cash register drawer cheerful in the shop. She wrapped the joddies and the tablecloth in brown paper and string, handing the parcel over with a smile.

The parcel sat on Kate's lap in the truck and the time dragged as the miles went by on the way back to Amiens. Finally Grimes turned the truck off the main road. Yellowed-out pasture stretched away on either side of the track, with dirty sheep dotted across it, moving slowly, listless with hunger, their fleeces so heavy with dust there was little to pick them out from the ground on which they stood. As the truck passed a small group of sheep by the road, a sour smell filled Kate's nostrils, and she shuddered. It was the smell of drought, of decay and hunger, and it made her fearful.

As the truck came up out of the gully, Kate ran through the list of chores in her head: there was ironing to be done, some darning – her own socks now, not her father's – and sheets that had been out on the line for a day at least. And if her father was on the mend, she could get back out into the paddocks to help with the lambing.

~

Her list dropped out of her head as they approached the homestead. There was no sign of Gunner or Puck. No dogs, for country people miles from the nearest help, was a bad sign. Grimes pulled the truck up in the lee of the shed, out of sight of the house. No need to walk into a problem, better to come in quietly. 'I'll stop here, eh. See where those dogs have got to.'

He got out of the driver's door and retrieved the shotgun from under the seat. He cocked it open, slipped a cartridge into each barrel and snapped it shut. 'Stay in the truck,' he said.

He walked towards the back of the house with the shotgun resting on his hip, John Wayne style. Kate reminded herself to mention it to her father. It might make him laugh.

CHAPTER 28

It is best remembered that a starving sheep, doubtless like a man, will reach a point where no amount of pasture or feed can revive him and he fades away.

THE WOOLGROWER'S COMPANION, 1906

Grimes whistled to bring the dogs. A soft whine – Gunner – came back, not from the homestead but from the meat house, twenty feet away. Grimes changed direction and whistled again.

This time there was a short bark, then a low growl. That was Puck. What were they doing in the meat house? The door was ajar, although as he approached it, Grimes blocked much of Kate's view.

He brought the shotgun up to his chest and nosed the meat house door open with his foot.

'Jesus bloody Christ.' His voice brought Kate out of the vehicle. He emerged from the meat house as she got close. His shotgun was on the ground by the door.

'Don't go in here, Missus.' He stopped her forcibly, grabbing her arms, his face pale, his voice low.

'Don't,' he said again. 'Ya go to the house now. Ya hear?'

'No.' Her own hands shaking, she lifted his from her arms, and went past him into the meat house.

She sucked in air, involuntarily. Her father lay slumped on

his back where he had fallen, his head jammed up against the wall, a bloody mess on the cement floor and wall behind him, his revolver by his side. Gunner and Puck sat, forlorn, one either side of him.

Gunner came to Kate and sniffed her hand. She patted him out of habit, without looking. Above her father's body, blood and grey tissue were splattered across the wall at head height. He must have been standing when he pulled the trigger. Her father's face was intact, but his skin was grey and his eyes and mouth open. His moleskin trousers were clean too, his plaited leather belt and his beloved boots wrenchingly familiar. At his shoulders, blood seeped up from the floor, climbing the fibres of his shirt.

'Help me move him. Away from the wall,' Kate instructed. She didn't recognise her voice. She picked up one boot, the leather soft with polish, and waited for Grimes to take the other. But he stood, for once at a loss.

'Help. Help me,' she said again.

Together they pulled him by his boots towards the centre of the shed floor, his head leaving a bright red trail behind it, his arms out wide like a crucifix. Kate picked up his right arm, and gasped. His skin was warm to the touch. He could not have been dead long. She did not cry. Not yet. When she moved both arms to rest them by his body, the hands fell open awkwardly. She tried to put his hands right, but they wouldn't stay. Her heart pounded in her chest and she was breathing heavily, panicking at his hands and feet awry.

'I'll do this,' Grimes said. 'Go to the house.'

Kate shook her head. 'Want to,' she managed.

She looked at Grimes across her father's body and tried to slow her breathing to speak. 'Get a —' she stopped to breathe and tried again '— a . . . a sheet off the line.'

Grimes left, and she stood, not knowing where to look, not sure what to do. Gunner licked her hand again and lay back down beside Puck. She lowered herself onto the floor and sat cross-legged next to her father's chest. She held his hand in her own, accustomed now to its odd warmth.

When Grimes got back with the sheet, they draped it over her father's body, his boots extending from the end. Blood from the floor seeped upwards into the stark white.

'Ring the Tuites,' she said, and Grimes left again. The Tuites. She felt removed, as if she were asleep or dreaming. She could see things – her father's body, the dogs forlorn and silent next to him – but she could not understand them. She remembered feeling this same shock after her mother passed away. She took up her father's hand again. 'I'm sorry,' she said to him. Death swirled round her; both her parents were lost.

'*Signora.*' Luca stood in the doorway and his hands went to his mouth when he saw her father's body. He stepped forward and pulled the sheet, covering the boots and tucking in the corners. Then he held out his hands to help Kate up.

'Now you go, *Signora*,' he said. She rose clumsily, smoothing her skirt by habit when she stood. Blood had seeped into her corduroy skirt, and the damp material hung about her, blotted like butcher's paper. '*Signora*,' he said and touched her arm. 'Sorry,' he said, shaking his head. 'Sorry for your *papá*.' He wrapped his arms about her, and held her. She leaned into him, wanting his comfort. His smell filled her nostrils, dust and sweat and oil. A good smell. She buried her face into his neck and the tears came.

'Go,' Luca said again. She moved slowly, her limbs heavy.

'Tuite's —' Grimes stopped when he saw them, and Luca released her, holding her up as she staggered, her legs unsteady.

'Tuite's on his way,' Grimes said, looking not at Kate but at Luca.

Kate nodded, her cheeks now wet with tears. For the first time, she noticed blood on Grimes's blue shirt. Holding the doorframe for support, she went out into blurry sunlight.

~

She got herself back to the house by holding onto the fence. She went to her father's room, then to the office, half-searching for a note. But everything was as it should be, as if he'd gone across to the poddy lambs and he'd be back in a minute.

In the kitchen, she looked about in a haze. There was drying up on the sink drainer. She took up one of the plates and pulled open the kitchen cabinet to put it away. Instead, she knocked the plate against the counter, smashing it, pieces falling to the floor. A broken piece in her hand, Kate stood, staring at the others about her. She squatted, gathering pieces into her bloody lap, but when she got up, they fell across the floor, shattering anew.

This must be shock; she knew that. She dropped into a kitchen chair.

Brandy. Brandy was for shock. She got herself up again and went to the dining room, with one hand on the wall to steady her, and took the brandy bottle out of the sideboard.

She spilled the tea-coloured fluid into a glass, took a breath and drank it down, the taste harsh like disinfectant in her mouth. It burned her throat and she spluttered, coughing some of it into and out of her nose.

Gasping for breath, she willed herself to keep it down long enough to take the picture of her father's body and the bright red wall out of her head. She closed her eyes as her tears came.

Kate knew why he'd done it. He was afraid of harming her. With a deep moan, she lowered her head onto the table and began to wail like the Aboriginal women when they lost one of their own. Through her agony, she knew people would come soon: the Tuites, the police, the neighbours, the CWA ladies, all the silent workers, helpers. She didn't want them, not yet. She sat up and dragged a tea towel off the hook by the stove. Her elbows on the table, she crumpled it into a wad and pressed her face into it to muffle her lament.

~

When they came, she was asleep, her head on the table. She lifted her painful head and cleared her throat to get the bad taste out of her mouth. Her voice was gone. 'Coming,' she tried again, the words soft and dry in her mouth. The chair screeched back hard along the floor as she stood.

Wetting her face in the kitchen sink, she put the brandy bottle in the kitchen cupboard, inhaled and went out the door onto the verandah.

Two policemen stood on the lawn – Wingnut and a young one she didn't know.

'Can we come up, Mrs Dowd?' Wingnut asked, coming anyway. He was followed by the other one. The younger man didn't look at her, his eyes on her bloodied skirt.

'Sorry about ya father,' Wingnut said. He meant it. 'This here's Constable Hartwell. We'll do this quick as we can for yez. Orright?'

She nodded.

Wingnut flipped open a tiny notebook and took a pencil stub from its spiral. Kate reached out to a verandah upright to steady herself.

'Ya wanna take a load off?' He frowned at her over his notebook.

She lowered herself into one of the verandah chairs. Somewhere in the garden, a rainbow lorikeet shrieked. Daisy's lorikeets.

'Tuites are there now. With Old Grimesy,' Wingnut said.

She swallowed hard and willed herself not to cry. 'I drank some brandy,' she said.

'How much?' Wingnut asked.

'A glass.'

'Righty-ho.' He grinned and then thought better of it. 'Another half tonight going to bed, I reckon. Do ya good. Now, I gotta ask ya some things, orright, Mrs Dowd?' He licked his pencil lead, his eyes on his notebook. 'When did you last see your father alive?'

'This —' Kate tried, and this time some words came out. 'Today, early. About eight.' She stared at her hands in her lap, thinking of leaving him this morning. What had she said to him? She couldn't remember.

'Before yez went to town?'

'Yes.'

'And yez found im just after eleven?'

She nodded, brushing a fly away from her mouth.

'Any note?'

'What?'

'No . . . er, no note, or anything from him in the house?'

'No.'

'Insurance, Mrs Dowd?' Wingnut asked.

'What?'

'Did ya father have insurance?'

'You mean for the sheds? No. Doesn't – didn't – believe in it.'

'What about for himself? Life insurance?'

'No,' she snorted, as he would have done.

'Orright.' Wingnut snapped the notebook shut and looked meaningfully at his offsider. 'Accident probly. Cleaning his revolver. Whatcha reckon, Constable?'

Hartwell went pink, unaccustomed to the attention. It was Wingnut who should be blushing. Her father had been handling guns since he was a teenager. The idea of an accident was ludicrous. Kate knew what Wingnut was doing, leaving a door open, saving her father's reputation. She should be grateful but she didn't seem to care.

'We both know what happened, Constable. Do what you have to.'

'Condolences again, Mrs Dowd.' He held out his hand to Kate, and she stood, taking it in her own. Then the policeman's eyes went to their hands, hers covered in dry blood.

'I'll tell Dr King,' Wingnut said. 'Don't believe we'll need an inquest.'

She was grateful for that.

Ted Tuite, the undertaker, came across the lawn. 'Mrs Dowd,' he said, nodding a greeting. He spoke gently, as if she were ill. 'Sorry about your father. Can I send my wife out? She'll get the clothes for ya dad. Orright?'

'I can manage.'

He looked doubtful. 'Well, it's easier, that's all. For someone else to get em.'

'No. I'll be all right. I'll ask Grimes to bring them to you.'

But still he looked concerned. 'Funeral'll be Friday arvo, if that's orright. The reverend reckons e can do a two o'clock service.'

She felt dizzy, and sat down. 'At two? Yes. Good.' She got herself up and off to the kitchen door, where she turned and half-waved. Ted Tuite was watching her closely, so she went on into the kitchen.

Inside, she dropped into a chair and breathed deeply. She threw down the dregs of the brandy from the dirty glass. That made her feel better and worse. She had to fight not to cough.

Constable Hartwell's voice carried in from outside. 'Ruddy amazing. All that flesh, and his dogs didn't have a go at it.'

She let it pass. They would leave soon.

'Poor old bugger. It's the money, ya know. He owes a lotta money.'

There was no more talk. She heard a car door slam, engines firing. After a bit, she went onto the front verandah and watched them go, the police car travelling slowly, followed by the undertaker's with her father's body. She was glad her father would be buried on the place. He'd be home again soon.

CHAPTER 29

In the event that a lamb will not be delivered, it is the duty of the woolgrower to act promptly, to minimise the ewe's distress, and put her quickly from this world.

THE WOOLGROWER'S COMPANION, 1906

The gauze door banged at half-past three that afternoon, and Harry came into the kitchen. Kate had been waiting for him, and there he was, his shirt untucked, one sock up, and his school case partway on his back.

She sat at the kitchen table, her hands around a mug of cold tea. 'Harry,' she said, greeting him.

'Can I've some milk?'

She didn't move. She hoped Grimes had not told him about her father. Better that she did it.

'Please,' he added.

She got up, took his case and hung it by its strap behind the back door. 'Run along and wash your hands, first.' Her voice sounded unfamiliar, like overhearing a person in another room.

Harry washed his hands in the kitchen sink and then wiped them and his mouth on the tea towel. He dropped himself onto one of the kitchen chairs as she put a glass of milk in front of him and held out the open bikkie tin. 'Just one.'

His hand hovered while he identified the largest. Then she sat opposite him, putting the lid on the tin in front of her. He looked disappointed.

'You can have a second. But finish the one you have first.'

He banged his foot against the table leg. *Thump, thump, thump.*

'Don't bang.' She was surprised when he stopped. It didn't make it any easier to tell him, his being so good.

'Harry —'

'Ya pop's carked it,' he said matter-of-factly.

Kate nodded.

'Too bad.'

'Too bad,' she agreed. She swallowed hard.

'Who's gunna tell Dais?' he asked.

It hadn't occurred to Kate.

'But Rusty'll be orright now,' Harry said.

'Rusty?'

'Yeah. Your old man'll look after im.'

'He will. He'll look after him.' Kate heard herself exhale in the quiet kitchen and found herself pushing her nails into her palms to stop herself from crying.

~

Early the next morning, Kate stirred at first light, tired but relieved to give up the fakery of near-sleeplessness. She felt across the cold floor with her toes for her slippers, pulled on her dressing gown and went through the silent house to a dark kitchen. Still drowsy, she followed her routine: teapot onto the counter, tea leaves into the pot, two mugs from the cupboard. Then she put the second mug back. It occurred to her it was only Tuesday. The funeral, on Friday, seemed a very long way off.

At the kitchen table, she looked at the lone mug in front of her, waiting for its tea. A hairline crack ran from the lip to its base, and she thought of her father's habit of snapping a cracked plate in two.

The gauze door banged. It was Meg, in her riding gear. She came to Kate, knelt and wrapped her arms about her. She pulled a kitchen chair up to hold her again, and Kate cried into her friend's shoulder.

'Dad already sent a telegram to Jack for you. Yesterday.'

'Gosh.' Kate hadn't even thought of Jack. 'Thank you.'

'Dad says the Army won't let him come home for it, you know, for all the time it'll take to get here and back for the funeral.'

'Oh,' Kate said weakly, yet she felt relief. The last thing she wanted was to be someone's wife. She just wanted to grieve.

'Anyone else to tell? Apart from Jack?'

Kate shook her head again. 'Mum and Dad were onlys. Like me.' Maybe she was the last of the line.

'Cheer up. You're not dead yet,' Meg said, then put a hand to her mouth in alarm. 'Sorry. Trying to make you laugh.'

Kate turned the corners of her mouth up against their will. 'No worries. Any news of Robbo?'

'Well, they reckon he's alive.'

'Oh! Thank God!'

Meg hugged her again. 'Only just, but. We'll have to see what he looks like, poor bugger. Home in a couple of weeks.' She got herself some tea and they sat, silent in the still kitchen, her hand resting on Kate's wrist on the table. It was a relief to have Meg there, and not to have to say anything. In due course, Meg made more tea and refilled the bikkie tin with a batch she'd brought with her. 'From Mum,' she said. 'She'll be over too, of course.' She looked at her watch. 'You gunna be all right? Want me to come and stay?'

'No. But thanks. I'll be OK. Really.'

Meg hugged her again, her curls soft against Kate's face, before she went out. Later, Kate heard voices in the garden and went to the sink. Outside, Meg was with Luca, her head down. Luca. In the morning. He must have come to check on her. Meg wiped her nose on her sleeve, and Luca patted her arm. Even in the fog of her grief, Kate felt a lurch of jealousy, and then relief, as Meg climbed onto Fiva and moved off.

Kate sat in the silence of the house, sipping cold tea from the cracked mug. When she tried to eat some bread, it was tasteless in her mouth. She gave up, did the dishes and went to get dressed. She should go out lambing. Pathetically, she couldn't do that yet. She didn't think she could face the men, even Luca.

Mid-morning, she heard a car come up out of the gully. She put aside the list of local people she needed to notify of her father's death, and went to look at the unknown car. The driver parked a long way back from the fence. A townie, for sure. A little sparrow-like woman got out, much too small for the big car. It was Iris Tuite, wife of the undertaker. She flitted across the dead lawn to the house, and made no noise crossing the verandah either.

'Hullo, dearie. I've come, you know, to help.'

Mrs Tuite took the kettle to the sink to fill it. She smelled of cigarette smoke. 'Shall I choose his clothes, dearie?'

'No. I will.'

'Sure?'

'Sure.'

'Orright. I'll be right here if ya need a hand. Choose what he'd wear for a trip to town.'

She was glad in the end that Ted Tuite had sent his wife. That made Kate go to her father's room. She stopped outside, steeling herself to go in, then pushed open the door. She drew in a breath at the shock of her father's familiar smell.

Forcing herself to breathe, she got herself under control. Things her father would wear to town? It was good advice. She would like him to be buried looking respectable.

It took her a while. From the cupboard, she took her father's best white shirt and wool tie. She found her cheeks wet with tears.

She took his good jacket as well and a pair of moleskin trousers. She'd send some boot polish into town, too. He'd want them clean. Hanging the trousers, shirt and jacket on a coat hanger, she folded the tie into the outside coat pocket and carried everything to the kitchen.

Mrs Tuite was at the sink, drying up. The smell of scones had come from nowhere, too.

Kate hooked the hanger over the doorknob. 'All here. I'll just get some polish.' In the laundry, she shifted the rags off the tins of Kiwi. One was heavy in her hand. She sucked in a gasp as something small and round dropped out of the fabric and onto the floor.

'You orright, dearie?'

It was just a shoe brush, nothing more.

'Yes. I'm fine.' Kate put the brush back with the shoe-cleaning things and took a tin of polish into the kitchen.

Afterwards, Kate watched Mrs Tuite leave, cradling her father's clothes as if she carried a sleeping child. At the car, Mrs Tuite bent over to lay the clothes on the backseat, disappearing from view. She stayed there, out of sight, for a second. Then she came flitting back across the dead lawn to the house, a small piece of paper in her hand.

'It were in his inside pocket, dearie,' Mrs Tuite said, holding the paper, puffing slightly.

Kate smiled her thanks. The woman stayed, wanting her to look. So she opened the little bit of paper. *INVOICE – H.K.J. McGintey & Sons. Fine Jewellery and Chattels* ran in large letters across the top. Then Kate gasped. *Uncut yellow sapphire 30.24 carats. Price: £6,250*, it read, in Mr McGintey's spidery hand.

CHAPTER 30

Unlike his shepherds, a sheep will move more readily uphill than down.

THE WOOLGROWER'S COMPANION, 1906

'There's nothing else in the pockets, Mrs Tuite? Nothing at all?'

The woman shook her bird's head. 'You should look, too, dearie.'

She took Kate's arm and they went back to the car, Kate fighting an urge to run there. Mrs Tuite held up the jacket, and with shaking hands Kate rifled through the pockets. Then she went through the trouser pockets, turning the first inside out, the white cotton lining bright in the sunshine. She went over every inch of the coat and trousers twice. Nothing.

'Sorry, dearie,' Mrs Tuite said, and laid a featherweight hand across her shoulder. 'Might help to go to church in a while.'

'What?'

'You might want to go. Do you a power of good.' She gave a little wave and was gone.

Kate watched her go; her head was full of the missing sapphire, not church. Had her father taken the stone and receipt somewhere while wearing his jacket? Or was the receipt just in there from when he bought the stone in Sydney? She could not guess. Mr McGintey had said 'about £6,000' and he'd been right. If she could find it she could pay off the damn overdraft. Even in her grief, she cared about Amiens.

~

Late that Tuesday morning, Kate heard another car coming up out of the gully. It was Reverend Popliss. *Mr* Popliss, she recalled. He'd corrected her once. She went out to the fence, hoping to stop him from coming in, but he probably wanted a cup of tea after the nineteen-mile drive from town on a dirt road.

He wore his dog collar with a suit, yet looked unclothed without his long black robes. Squinting into the weak sun, he shook her hand over the fence. 'My condolences to you, Mrs Dowd. I'm sorry that your loved one has passed away.'

'My father,' she said, correcting him. He must have used the same phrase all the time. Raw, Kate tried not to dislike him for it.

'Yes. Now. The funeral arrangements. I'm sure you understand, I like to go over things with the family early.' He looked at the chairs on the verandah.

She ignored him. Grief had made her brave or rude, or both.

'Friday at two for the service. Mr Tuite tells me that suits you, which is marvellous.'

A marvellous time for a funeral. She hadn't thought of it like that.

'Mr Grimes, Ted Tuite, and his boys will be the bearers?'

'Yes.'

'Good. Yes.' He paused again and looked at the verandah. 'So, to the eulogy. You'll write something out for me?'

'For you?'

'As your husband won't be here, and with no other men in the family, I'll give the eulogy on your behalf.'

Ladies didn't speak in public. But her father had thought the reverend an idiot and it offended Kate that he would give the eulogy.

'Also, I'm afraid I must mention the charge for the service. It's a guinea. You'll not forget?'

Kate started to speak. He cut her off.

'But if it's a problem, Mrs Dowd, don't be concerned at all. All right?'

She was silenced by his unexpected kindness.

'I'll bring the money. But thank you.'

'All shipshape then. Until Friday.'

~

Not long after the minister had gone, she heard another car. It was Mrs Yorke, Meg's mother, come to see if she could help. Kate made more tea.

She followed the same pattern all that day Tuesday and Wednesday too, as callers arrived and went. Mrs Riley, Meg again, even Elizabeth Fleming. They came quietly, gently, bearing kind but unwanted cakes and scones and bikkies, each wanting to comfort. Their kindness overwhelmed her.

~

On Wednesday afternoon, in a lull, Kate made herself sit at her father's desk to write the eulogy, fighting back tears at the job ahead. She had to do it, but it was the first time she'd been in his office since . . . since it happened. The room was musty, the desk cluttered. To get some air through, she pushed open one of the verandah doors and propped it with the doorstop.

She had to get a grip. Carefully, she moved letters and bills aside. The desk in some sort of order, Kate tried to think how to start. It was not easy, the writing, knowing it would be Popeless who spoke these words. It made her angry to think of it. *Popeless be damned*, her father would have said. Then it

250

struck her. She *would* give her father's eulogy; she would. Her pique evaporated fast. How could she speak in front of all those people? She'd had the same fear at ten when she had to do a lecturette for school. She'd practised it over and over, to the wisterias, to the dogs and to her mum. Only she didn't have as much time to practise this, and she didn't have her mother to help. She wished her mother were alive. She felt a sudden anger then with both of her parents, leaving her so young and with such a mess of the money. She inhaled and picked up her pencil.

Ralph Francis Stimson was . . . Maybe she didn't even need to say that? Of course they'd know who he was. She rubbed that out. A big gust of wind hit the house, and the verandah door she'd opened blew shut with a bang. Kate got up and propped the door open again, and stopped to look out across Amiens. Her father must have stood here a thousand times surveying his land, this land that owned him. She didn't know how to do him justice.

She sat again at the desk for more than an hour, writing, rubbing out, writing again. Finally, she sat back, staring at the pieces of paper in her hand. It would have to do. With her hat in hand, she went into the garden to try out the speech on the jacaranda tree.

Under the jacaranda, a perfume hung about her, the soft scent of the wisteria blossom from the trellis, sprays of white flowers on one end, mauve at the other from the vines planted on either side. Kate had some listeners outside the fence, Gunner and Puck. Puck was patrolling, sniffing, exploring. Gunner lay on his side, soaking up the warmth of the spring sun. He moved to lie closer to Kate, and she read out what she'd written, trying hard to remember to be loud enough.

'Is it all right?' she asked, looking at the dog over the paper in her hands, but he ignored her. A bark floated in from some-where down the creek. Puck probably gone off after a rabbit or a snake. She wondered where Luca was. If she were honest with herself, she'd come outside partly in the hope of seeing him.

She read the eulogy aloud again, trying not to rush, trying to speak up, trying not to panic. Halfway through, a lorikeet shrieked above her. She'd prefer a couple of black cockatoos flying east towards the coast, but a lorikeet was better than nothing.

Kate went back inside. She folded the pages into four (to distinguish them from a letter) and placed them in the middle of her father's desk. For a flash, she thought she should not leave them in case he found them. Then her grief closed in around her again.

That night, she was sitting in the half-light of the dusk with a cup of tea in front of her and a piece of untouched toast. She had not been hungry since her father's death. Footsteps interrupted her and she looked up.

'*Signora.*'

Luca's frame filled the doorway and Kate smiled, despite herself. 'Everything all right?'

'*Sì, sì.*' Luca let himself in with one hand, a covered tin plate in the other, and flicked on a light.

Kate smelled something good, mutton-like. Luca lifted the top off the plate and a wisp of steam wound into the air from the food underneath. Pale-yellow strands lay coiled like smooth wool around the centre of the dish, with a dark-red sauce on top.

'From Vittorio. *Spaghetti alla Bolognese,*' Luca said.

Oh dear, Kate thought. She appreciated the gesture but couldn't face any real food. She looked at him.

Luca grinned. 'Is for you. For eat.' He put the plate in front of her and she sniffed it gingerly. It did smell good – very good, in fact. Meat and tomatoes and heaven knew what else. Luca rattled through the kitchen drawers until he found the cutlery and handed a fork to her. She sat, motionless, looking at the fork in her fingers.

Luca took it from her. 'Like this,' he said gently. He stood her fork, tines down, into the spaghetti and turned it, the pasta wrapping around like thread on a spool. Then he held the handle towards her. But when she took it from him, the pasta fell off, almost missing the plate. She tried herself to catch the pasta, turning the fork as Luca had done, but it would not stay.

He laughed.

'It's harder than it looks,' she protested.

Luca took the fork from her again, and twirled pasta quickly back onto it. This time when he held out the handle to her, he kept hold of the fork. With her fingers resting gently on his, he balanced the pasta and directed the fork towards her mouth.

'*Aprire*. Open, *Signora*,' he said.

With his eyes on hers, together they put the mouthful in, and then he pulled the fork out slowly from between her lips.

Conscious only of his closeness, Kate chewed carefully. She felt her eyes close as she savoured flavours she'd never tasted before. The pasta was thick and filling, the sauce savoury, the meat tender. She almost couldn't recognise it as mutton.

'*Spaghetti. Pasta.*' Luca watched her, pleased.

'It's good,' Kate said, surprised. 'It's very good. Peppery.'

'*Sì*,' he chuckled, 'but . . .' He took the hand towel from its hook and gently wiped away a spot of sauce from her cheek.

She was stunned. Luca reached down, squeezed her hand, and went out.

'*Buona notte, Signora*,' he called back, leaving her still in the kitchen, listening to his footfall across the lawn, willing him to return.

~

253

The next day, Thursday, Kate was relieved to see her latest caller off just before lunchtime. Mrs Nettiford had not stayed long, embarrassed to have come without an invitation. But Kate had thanked her warmly. Even in her fog, it meant something that people cared. Still, she willed the hours to pass, for the next day to arrive and for her dear father to be buried.

With Mrs Nettiford gone, Kate got her hat and gloves and went into the garden. The ends of her index fingers showed through the holes at the tips; still, the gloves worked well enough to protect the rest of her hand. Dropping her kneeling mat between the fence and the first bed, she wound a tomato vine tendril back around the trellis, and then started on the onion weed.

A few minutes later, Luca appeared at the gate and squatted to pat Gunner. Kate kept her head down.

'*Signora*,' Luca said, his hat off. He crouched beside her and she could smell him, soap and sump oil and sweat. She wanted him to hold her again, as he had in the meat house.

'OK?' he asked.

She swallowed and turned back to the onion weed. He retreated and they weeded in a silence broken only by the bleating of hungry sheep.

He startled her when he spoke. 'The wisteria – her flowers.' Luca pointed to the vine on the verandah trellis. 'You smell?' he asked, giving her his half-smile, revealing a chipped bottom tooth she'd not noticed before.

'In my village, it covers tree – *a* tree,' he corrected himself. 'Over all – a tree so big.' He pointed at the California pine stretching its thirty feet into the bright sky.

'*Glicine*,' he said. 'Her name.'

Kate closed her eyes for a second and breathed in the scent of the two wisteria vines. How had they both hung on despite the drought?

'March and April at Grosio – that spring – is beautiful.' He held his hands over his head and breathed in deeply. 'A hat of perfume.'

'My mother planted the vines,' Kate said. 'She loved the white one especially. She made me save the seeds every year.'

'And my brother. He, he like. He say like *neve*.' His face sombre, he fluttered his fingers down through the air, before turning back to his work.

'I found the receipt for the sapphire, you know, in Dad's coat.'

'You find her? This sapphire?'

'No, no. Just the receipt. The paper to show he bought it.'

'Ah.' He sounded disappointed.

Her thoughts went back to the eulogy. 'I want to speak at the church, Luca.'

'*Sì?*'

'But the minister – the priest – says I can't. He says it has to be a man.'

'Ah.'

'But there's no one else. And I want to speak about my father. What do you think?'

'No man to speak?' Luca shrugged. 'You speak.'

She felt comforted that he agreed. 'And it will help me, to have you there,' she said.

'*Sì*. And, *Signora*. I tell you,' Luca said. 'Your *papá*. He is —' He was struggling for the right words. 'He is brave.' He shook his head in disbelief. 'You understand?'

She nodded, slowly. He was brave. She turned back to her weeds but did not pretend to work, more tears on her face.

'*Signora*, the family is good.'

She looked at him quizzically.

'You have the husband. Good. It is good, this for you. This family.' He searched for the words. 'This is best. Best for you.'

He meant that she still had Jack but she felt no comfort

255

in that. Even though they were husband and wife, she didn't know Jack. And now there was Luca.

She looked down at the weed, already wilting in her fingers. 'Best?' she asked, her voice quiet. 'You think it's best for us?'

When he said nothing, she glanced up, shocked to see his face so drawn. '*Sì*. Best, *Signora*. For . . . for you.' His voice was strangled. He ran his fingers along her jawline to her chin and touched her lips, then took his hand away. She stared at him. When a vehicle came too fast over the crest of the hill, Kate sat back on her haunches to look. She could see it was a grey Humber. Tony Biggs? Why would he be out here? The vehicle disappeared into the gully. She heard it slow, then roar up the incline and over the rise. Jack.

CHAPTER 31

Whilst a woolgrower new to the work might well privately seek the counsel of one or more of his peers — and such growers are usually in no way backwards in the giving of their opinion — the buyer should first, and above all, before acquiring a stud ram, be secure of his own opinion, for it is he who must live with his selection.

THE WOOLGROWER'S COMPANION, 1906

Kate was sure it was Jack. Somehow he had managed to get home. A grand gesture. She felt a surge of dread. Abandoning her mat and the pile of weeds, she walked towards the house past Luca, who watched the approaching vehicle, hands on his hips.

'It's my husband,' she said as she went inside.

In the bathroom, Kate pushed the plug into the hole and ran a little brown creek water into the basin. She closed her eyes, splashed her face with the water and felt for the worn towel on the rack by the wall.

A car horn sounded outside, one short blast. She looked at her face in the mirror and pulled a hand through that short hair. She should tidy herself up for him, put on some lipstick and comb her hair, what was left of it. To hell with it. The gate clicked and she went to the kitchen. She didn't want Luca to see them meet. Kate brushed garden dirt off her new joddies.

Soil had smudged the knees so she tied an apron round her waist, hurrying, fumbling with the bow, to cover the dirt.

Jack took the kitchen steps one by one, rather than with his customary single stride, and stopped just inside, holding the gauze door behind him to prevent the bang. He was in uniform, his khaki slouch hat in one hand. It was many months since she'd seen him, and then only for a few hurried, awkward days. She'd forgotten how tall he was, a head taller than her, with the same solid build as Captain Rook, coiled energy under the khaki. He smiled at her with a closed mouth — she'd forgotten that too. Tanned, his face showed some fine lines now and his hair was very fair from the sun. He came round the table to her, kissing first her cheek, then her mouth. He pulled away and stared, touching the ends of her hair at her neck.

'I cut it.'

'You did,' he replied evenly. 'You did indeed.' He took a step back, still holding her hand and staring at her hair. 'You like it?'

'Yes,' she said, realising only then that she did.

His eyes moved down. 'Joddies?'

'I help in the paddocks now.'

'Ah,' he said, nodding slowly. 'And there's a bloody Eye-tie in the garden.'

'We're short-handed. They do a lot.'

He rolled his eyes, unconvinced.

'They let you come home,' she said.

'I told im it were just you left. My bloody CO musta took pity, for once. Took some doin t'get here, though.' He squeezed her hand. 'I'm sorry about your old man.'

Her eyes filled with tears — they were quick to do that now — so she turned away. 'Cup of tea?'

'Tea,' he said as if the idea was novel. 'Please.' He leaned against the kitchen counter, and spun his hat on his left hand. But it was a lumpy spin; that gammy hand now healed but not perfect.

She filled the kettle at the rainwater tap. 'Are you all right? I feel so lucky that they haven't posted you to the islands, lucky you're whole.'

'Whole?' He laughed. 'I suppose. Cooling me bloody heels like a big sook.'

'You still with the 9th?'

'Only on the books. I'm on transfer, though. Been training bloody wheelbarrows for too bloody long.'

The joke was old now. She smiled in commiseration.

Jack switched on the wireless. A dance tune filled the kitchen with brass and rhythm. The noise surprised Kate; she hadn't turned the wireless on since her father's death. Jack flicked it off. He sat down and stretched his legs under the kitchen table. Then he stared at her again. Kate grew embarrassed and she could feel her face flushing. She took the dented tea canister from the counter and paused, deciding between the silver teapot she used for visitors versus the everyday china. She chose the silver one. She put two of the good tea cups and saucers on the table next to Jack and poured the boiling water into the teapot. Jack leaned back and interlocked his fingers on his lap. 'Is it at St John's tomorrow?'

'Yes. Father Popliss.'

'He's still alive, the poor old bugger?'

Kate turned the teapot three times, counter clockwise, letting the tea leaves drift to the outside, then poured two cups, giving the second to Jack. He liked it strong. A silence settled between them. Kate sipped her tea. Jack's sat untouched, and Gunner whined outside.

'The wake at the Returned Servicemen's Club?'

'No. I'll have people back here afterwards,' she said. 'It's —'

'Cheaper.'

'Yes.' The kitchen clock ticked on. 'When do you think you might be home for good?'

'Who knows? Not soon. They reckon they'll need fresh

259

troops for a bit yet, for the mopping up, eh. We're gunna train em, like all the others.' He shrugged and looked about the kitchen. 'Daisy up the duff, is she?'

'It was Ed.'

He shrugged. 'They're all the same. You sent her back?'

'Yes. The baby will be raised in the Home. But if it's pale enough, it'll be adopted out. Poor Daisy. Poor baby. I wonder if I should have —'

'No. You did the right thing, sending her back. Give us a bad name otherwise. Mind you . . .' He stopped.

'A bad name's coming anyway? With what Dad did?'

He shrugged, looking embarrassed. 'Maybe. I have to tell you, I thought something was up when I was back here last time.' He turned the tea cup in the saucer in front of him but did not drink. 'I reckoned then that the old man had a kangaroo loose in the top paddock.'

Kate stared at him.

He looked away, chastened. 'Sorry. Bit rough round the edges, aren't I? Anyways, how'd he do it?'

Kate did not want to have the sight fill her head. 'He . . . he used his old revolver. It was in the meat house. I think he went in there to make the mess easier for us to clean up.'

Jack shook his head in admiration. 'Jeez, he was a tough old coot, wasn't he?'

She felt tears well again in her eyes. 'Now Amiens will be sold up.' Her voice cracked. She put one hand to her mouth, the other arm she wrapped about her waist.

'Yeah. What'd he do with the money?'

Her breathing was uneven and tears wet her cheeks. 'Dad borrowed a lot to buy Binchey's in '39, and he was doing all right, so far as I can tell. Then Mum died, and apparently he just stopped paying the interest.'

Jack looked down at his hands in his lap. 'You should be able to get out of that hole, eh?'

'Except that then he spent a whole lot, most of the overdraft, on that sapphire. And that's what's killing us.'

Jack exhaled. 'Why'd he buy it, ya reckon?'

'For me. For a rainy day, apparently. He didn't trust the bank with our cash.'

'But that was borrowed money he used, wasn't it?'

'He didn't realise that when he bought it. He wasn't . . . making sense.'

Jack shook his head in disbelief. 'So we're broke.'

'Yes. We're to be put off the place next month – the 12th October is when the bank says it'll come in.'

'You'll go before then, after the funeral. Before you're shoved.'

'But I still might find the sapphire.'

'In fourteen thousand acres? Needle in a haystack. The old man stitched us up, even if he never meant to, with the money and then doing himself in. Jesus.'

'Could you . . . Do you think . . . Could you ask your family to help?'

'I already told you no.'

'I know it's shameful to ask, but if it saves Amiens —'

'He won't do it, Kate. Orright.' His voice was angry. 'I spoke to my father. No bloody way.'

She swallowed.

'Look,' Jack started. 'The show's over. We've got to get you away, somewhere no one knows you. Or knew your father. New Guinea, maybe. Bougainville. They'll be after plantation managers soon, like I said.'

'What about Longhope? We could move into town.'

He laughed noiselessly. 'And never look anyone in the eye again, like that poor bloody Binchey fella?' He frowned. 'No. That's not for me. We're going. I've worked it out. You're to go to my oldies in Perth first. You can camp there for a bit.'

'Perth? That's two thousand miles away. And your parents have never met me.' Kate stared at him.

'Well, they will soon, eh.' Jack stood up, frowning, and placed his chair squarely under the kitchen table. 'The old man's brandy still in the sideboard?'

'I don't need it,' she said. 'Thanks.'

He laughed again, scratching the cleft of his chin. 'It's not for you, you numbat.'

'What? But it's two o'clock.' The words were out before she thought.

'It's two o'clock orright, and I'm getting a drink.'

CHAPTER 32

In rut, rams will fight others for dominance of the herd and privileges over ewes.

THE WOOLGROWER'S COMPANION, 1906

Kate sat unmoving at the kitchen table, her tea cold, her breath uneven. She could hear Jack rifling in the sideboard in the dining room. Movement in the garden caught her eye. Luca stood, a pair of clippers in hand, looking towards the kitchen. She turned away, confused, her head aching. She wanted to stop thinking, to get outside, to go to Luca, if only for a moment. The faint smell of cigarette smoke floated in. Jack always had a cigarette when he had a drink. One went with the other, he said. Her parents had never allowed smoking in the house.

Kate stood up and got down the wire egg basket from the top of the fridge. With the basket in one hand, the scrap bucket in the other, she walked through the garden and out the gate, eyes front, avoiding Luca's pale-eyed gaze. Bloody Jack. He was his same ramrod self. She remembered that now, that there was a steel to him. He was different, too, though. Maybe she was different. She felt her anger resurfacing at him telling her what to do.

When she came over the rise, the creek was less and less, a trench edged with myalls and red gums, a string of smaller and smaller water holes linked by the sandy bed. A white chook stopped and jerked a look at her as she passed. At the open gate, Kate checked that the snake waddy was in place and thought of her father. A habit he had taught her: keep your tools handy and maintained; you never know when you'll need them. She had her usual scan along the fence support for the sapphire too.

Greenwich the rooster came out to meet her, his gait officious, his eyes black under a dusty red comb. Kate put the egg basket on the ground and tipped the bucket of scraps out in front of him. He looked at her, then began picking his way through them.

As Kate went to the laying boxes, the clucking went up. Perhaps she'd unsettled them, so she called, 'Here, chookie, chookie, chookie.' In the first box, a black Napoleon hen sat on a bed of dirty hay, its wary eyes on her, its red comb set to one side. 'Chookie, chookie, chookie,' she sang again as she slid her hand under the hen to feel for eggs, its feathers soft and warm, the straw prickly underneath. The hen clucked, flapping her wings, and refused to move. Kate sang over and over as she groped about. Her fingers found the warmth of one egg. 'No babies for you, chookie. Not now,' Kate said, and felt sorry for the hen. She put the egg in the wire basket and slid her hand back in to check, just in case, for the sapphire. She moved on to the next laying box, but the clucking from the end of the chook run was even louder than before.

She had her hand on an egg under another ruffled hen when frantic screeches exploded. She stood straight up, egg in her palm, as a chook leapt past her towards the gate. Wary, Kate grabbed the basket and backed away. It had to be a snake or fox or goanna, with this sort of row. At the gate, she took the snake waddy and held it in front of her. Somewhere near the house, Gunner barked. The screeching continued and Kate took a step back. Then it came out of the second box in a blur, a black snake, six feet long or more, as thick as her wrist. It dropped, writhing towards the ground, coming for the gate, and her in front of it.

'Kate!' Jack's voice. 'Get out! Get out!' he called, and she backed away behind him, out of the gate as he snatched the waddy.

Puck bailed up the snake in the corner of the chook run and attacked, rushing it, trying to get his teeth into its backbone. Trapped, the snake rose up, surging forwards. Jack moved with Puck, each trying to get a clear strike, but the snake arched into the air and surged again, driving them back.

Kate heard banging in the dust. It was Luca on the outside, hitting the wooden corner post of the chook run with a lump of wood. The snake whipped about towards that noise, and Puck went in. He bit hard below the snake's head and held on, moving with the snake as it heaved its body about, trying to get a hold on the dog. Puck shook the snake viciously from side to side. As it weakened, Puck released his grip for a second and bit again, breaking its back. The snake thrashed, each time less than the last, as Puck held on.

His face set, Jack took to the snake, pounding and hitting it, again and again bringing the waddy down until its flesh began to break from its body.

'Jack! It's dead!' Kate shouted, but he went on. She came into the chook run behind him. 'Jack!'

He hit and hit. Pieces of snakeskin and blood sprayed over them. Jack landed a wayward blow on Puck, yet his expression didn't change. He kept on at what was left, hitting the rest of the body, his arm coming down over and over with vengeance in his posture, spits and scraps of snake splattering onto his shirt.

'Jack! Stop!' Kate shouted and took his arm. He slowed, breathing heavily. His arm dropped, still gripping the waddy, his eyes on the mess of snake in front of him. Expressionless, he went slowly to the open gate and returned the waddy to

265

its place on the fence, pieces of flayed snakeskin and flesh still sticking to the wire.

He walked by Kate and Luca, giving the Italian a hard look as he passed.

~

Luca helped Kate back to the house. She took in the comfort of him beside her, the feel of his arm under hers, his familiar smell.

She stopped short, his face inches from hers.

'All right?' he said, concerned. She withdrew her arm, her hands shaking, and looked about to be sure Jack had not seen them.

In the kitchen, Luca sat her down and laid his hand over her shaking fingers on the table. Then he left her, the gauze door banging behind him. Kate went to her room, still trembling. She had the oddest urge to crawl under the thin sheets of her bed, to hide like a child. Soon after, she heard the shower go on, then off again. A few minutes later there was a knock on her door.

'Kate?'

Jack came in, neat and tidy. She stood up. 'I'm going into town,' he said. 'I'll have some grub with Biggsy. Don't wait for me.'

From the window, Kate watched him drive off in Tony Biggs's Humber, going too fast.

~

Late that night, she woke to a noise in her room.

'Kate?' Jack's voice came thick out of the darkness. With a crash he knocked something over, and for a second she worried he'd wake her father. Boots squeaked on a floorboard, a belt buckle jangled and hit the floor. Then his fingers found her forehead. 'Gotcha.' He laughed, the bedsprings creaking

266

at the extra weight as he levered himself in beside her, naked, his skin cold against her warmth, the smell of stale beer and cigarettes about him. When he pushed his tongue into her ear, she moved her head away and felt him laughing into her hair. Rolling onto his back, he surprised her, pulling her on top of him. She lay on his chest, smooth and hard under her as he pushed open her legs. She didn't want him, with her grief so fresh, yet it was her duty. She moved to help but kneed him instead.

'Jesus,' he said, laughing again. 'Welcome home to you too.'

He kissed her, with his hand on a breast through her night-gown. 'Get it off,' he said, tugging at the material. She sat astride him and felt him harden. His fingers went to her bare nipple, squeezing it until she gasped. Pulling her to him, he pushed one leg between hers, took her in his arms and rolled her onto her back. His tongue sought hers, and he inched into her, gently at first, then harder. With each thrust, his breath filled her mouth, his smell of beer and cigarettes and sweat all around her. He came, clutching her neck, holding her down onto the bed, his shadow across the ceiling above her.

Lying still on top of her, his heart beat into her chest, his sweaty weight pinning her as he dripped from between her legs. Under him, she struggled to breathe and tried to move, to free her ribs.

With a sigh of exertion, he rolled off her onto his back, one arm across her belly. 'Bloody hell, Kate. I'm out of condition.'

It was the first time she'd heard him sound like himself. She pulled the sheet up over her breasts, and he laughed at her modesty and put his hands behind his head. Swivelling onto her side, she propped herself up on one arm to look at him.

'What's up? Spit it out,' he said.

'Are you . . . Are you all right?'

'Right as rain.' He shifted his eyes back to the ceiling. 'Never been better. You?'

'Same,' Kate said. A lie for a lie.

He hauled the covers up and over the two of them, and rolled onto his stomach, his face away from her. His breathing grew regular, his smooth back rising and falling under her fingertips.

But she was wide awake and she wasn't thinking about Jack. Her father. The snake, today. Luca. Her mind was overfull. She lay, listening to Jack's even breaths in the darkness, trying to empty her head. But Luca kept coming back into her mind, with his broad back and narrow hips, that nose and his pale eyes. He unsettled her. Bastard. The swearing, even in her head, didn't make her feel any better. She thought of him just over the hill, wondering if he lay awake as she did.

CHAPTER 33

*Whilst perhaps not so park-like as described by our first explorers,
much of Australia's plains country is nonetheless blessed with both
earth ripe for grazing stock and men determined to do it.*

THE WOOLGROWER'S COMPANION, 1906

The next day, the drive in from Amiens was fast and silent, Jack
still pre-occupied with a lingering hangover and Kate with her
thoughts of the funeral. Before she was ready, they'd reached
town. Along each side of the church, the wattle trees were in
bloom, fluffy yellow flowers on long sprays. Jack stopped the
truck in front, and she heard Grimes scramble out of the truck
tray. Jack stretched, putting one arm along the back of the seat
behind her. He didn't touch her and somehow she wished he
would.

'You orright?' he said. 'All be over soon enough.'

Grimes appeared at Kate's door and opened it for her, so he
could get in.

'We'll get over to Tuites now,' Jack said to her.

To help get her father's coffin. She knew. She felt the
morning sun on her face and was glad to be out in the spring
air. It would be warm today, for September, but the trees in the
Amiens garden would shade the mourners. Luca and Vittorio
were tidying it now and Ed would drive them in soon for the

service. She hoped the reverend would let the POWs into the church, but she had other things to worry about. Pick your battles, her father would have said.

She had always liked this church; it was so plain that it was pretty. Her mother's funeral had been there. 'She does the prayin for both of us,' her father used to say.

One of the last times Kate was there with her father, she was getting married. She'd stood on those steps in her mother's wedding dress, shaking at the prospect of having all the eyes in the church on her. 'Every girl is beautiful on her wedding day,' her mother had said. Kate was terrified anyway. Her father had misunderstood her fear. 'You're doin the right thing, Katie,' he'd said. 'A girl must have a family.'

She herself had no doubts. Kate had taken the arm her father offered to help her up the church steps. She'd been surprised again when he – a man embarrassed by any show of affection – had placed his hand over hers. He'd left it there all the way up the aisle too. In case she tried to do a runner? She smiled at the thought, then recalled the hug he'd given her the day before his death and she swallowed, so glad he'd done it.

The church interior was mostly cold and dark. The stained-glass windows filtered the sunshine into one tunnel of light, which fell just to the right of the altar. Kate wanted to fix it, to centre that bright blue circle.

'Kate, my dear.'

Reverend Popliss appeared, familiar in his long black robe. A leather belt round his middle disappeared beneath a slight paunch. Popeless and hopeless: her father had thought him both.

'Let's get started, shall we?' Popliss rested his hands together in front of him, long slender fingers interlaced. 'I like to run the family through things. It's quite straightforward.' The reverend turned and walked towards the altar. Kate had to move fast to keep up.

He veered off to the right towards a door at the end of the transept, and looked at his watch. 'Your father's coffin will be placed here in the apse.' He gestured with one of his hands at a long sturdy plinth in front of the altar. 'You'll be seated in the front pew there' – he walked and pointed – 'with Jack. Excellent that he's home. Mr Nettiford, one of our church aldermen, will sit with you in case there's anything you need. You know Mr Nettiford?'

She did and was glad she'd paid their account.

'Fortunately Mrs Binchey is back from Tamworth, so we'll have the organ.'

Kate inhaled. She wished it were anyone else.

'Now. The service. No communion, of course. You've chosen the hymns. "Oh God, Our Help" is nice but the 23rd Psalm is more appropriate.' He waved at the hymn board behind him, and sure enough the 23rd Psalm was already listed.

Kate opened her mouth, then shut it.

'I expect something of a turnout, even with all our boys away. People remember . . .' He swung round, his robe a sail-boat coming about. 'Now, the POWs: I won't have them, they're Catholics. I'm certain their pope doesn't allow that sort of thing anyway.'

'No?' Kate was disappointed. Her father strongly supported the POW Scheme; it was one of the last lucid decisions he made. She could hear her father's voice in her head: So what do we get for our guinea then?

Kate had no strength to argue. Luca and Vittorio would have to stay outside. Daisy would have been with them if she were there. Daisy. Dear Daisy. She hoped she was all right. It was hard to imagine the gangly girl big with pregnancy.

'A reminder about the eulogy. We try to keep them short and emphasise the departed's most admirable traits. You've told Jack? I'm glad he's home, for your sake of course, and that we're able to have a family member deliver it. Any questions?

No? Excellent. Quick cup of tea with Mrs Popliss, perhaps?' The reverend headed for the side door.

'I'd like to deliver the eulogy,' Kate said, weakly.

'I'm not sure that's a good idea.' His voice took on a stern edge. 'You feel composed now. Believe me, come the time, you'll be overcome. I know what's best.'

'Thank you. But I would like to do it.'

A sweat bead ran down his forehead from his hairline. Popliss came back to her and took her hands in his own spindly fingers. So close to him, she could smell that peculiar old-man smell. Her father had it as well – a mix of age and masculinity, the body winding down to stillness.

'I understand, Kate, dear, that you were very close to your father. Still, I can't allow you to do this.' He patted her caged hands.

The church door banged.

'Jack,' the reverend said with relief. 'My condolences. You'll do the eulogy of course?'

Jack's face did not change, and he turned his khaki slouch hat round in his hands as he stood in the aisle.

'Good. Good. I'll leave you two to have some time to yourselves. You're welcome to that cup of tea, if you hurry. The Tuites should be here' – he checked his watch – 'shortly.'

'They're outside,' Jack said.

His head down, the minister left, and the cool silence of the church was between them.

'I'm glad you're here,' Kate said, and stretched up to kiss Jack's cheek. 'For this, and for the wake.'

'No worries. Oh, and Biggsy'll bring a keg out. It's orright. It's a gift. Most unlike im, I said.' Jack grinned absent-mindedly, glancing round the church.

'I want to do the eulogy.'

'Yeah?' He raised his eyebrows. 'Bit of a turn-up for the books, a sheila doing it.'

'I think I can, though. I'll be all right.'

'Yeah, well, give em what for. No bloody apologies, orright? And nothing about your father's screw loose, either. Let's get out of here with our heads high.'

Kate said nothing.

'If it turns out you can't talk then I can say a few words.' He turned. 'I better give the Tuites a hand.' The door banged after him.

Kate went to her pew and sat to open her handbag and unfold her handwritten pages. She began reading out loud, softly, starting at random in the middle. '*Some of you knew and . . .*' Her voice faltered as it hit her that she must stand and speak in front of people.

She forced herself to breathe slowly, slowly. She thought of her childhood and of her father, of the thrill of a special treat, an early-morning ride with him. She closed her eyes to see the dawn sun, a red sliver on the horizon as the day overtook the night, the horses, anxious to be off, stamping under their tightened girth straps, their breath clear in the morning cold. Noise in the church brought her back. She could hear people arriving, filling the pews behind her. Not just people; Jack. He and the Tuites set her father's coffin in front of the altar. Her eyes rested on the coffin, the eulogy limp in her hands. Mr Nettiford nodded at her gently as he sat next to her. Kate wondered if his wife were at the back. Jack sat on her other side, squeezing her hand briefly.

'The first hymn is the 23rd Psalm,' Popliss intoned. The organ swelled to life and the congregation stood with the noise of people, shuffling, clearing throats.

As she stood, she glanced towards the back. The church was full, with so many people her father had known.

'*The Lord's my shepherd . . .*'

Kate could hear her father. More bloody sheep.

The service proceeded, and she tried to concentrate on the

273

reverend's words. But as Popliss said pretty much the same thing at every church service, she could not take them in. She looked at the coffin behind the minister. With knots in the wood grain, it was plain, perfect for her father. On top was a wreath of flowers Meg's mother had made: a circle of eucalypts and red flares of bottlebrush. She saw Reverend Popliss catch Jack's eye. The eulogy was approaching. Kate hoped she would be able to speak.

'Let us pray.' Stillness descended. 'Merciful God. We submit Mr Ralph Stimson, our friend, our neighbour, a member of our flock, to your safekeeping. Let us learn from his time with us of the nature of your wisdom through his good works in the district.'

It occurred to Kate, a little late, that perhaps the reverend's usual funeral service might not be suitable. Good works? Her father had never believed in charity. God helps those who help themselves.

'Let us hear a few words about our friend.' Popliss nodded at Jack, who just leaned back in the pew and crossed his arms. He was not going anywhere. But neither was Kate. She could not get up.

Popliss looked a little alarmed, if only for a moment. 'Let me speak to you about our friend Ralph Stimson. A gentleman, his word was his bond.' There was some shuffling in the congregation, and Kate stiffened. There were people sitting behind her for whom Ralph Stimson's word was not his bond; they were owed money.

Kate managed to get up though her hands were shaking. 'Reverend Popeless,' she croaked. Damn. Popliss, not Popeless.

'A man for whom his family —' the minister continued.

'Reverend Popliss.' Kate took the one short step up to the altar, careful in her unfamiliar heels, and the reverend stopped, his lips pursed. Kate turned to face the mourners. With all the pews filled, men stood along the walls and behind the last row.

People were staring. She mustn't cry. Kate opened her mouth to speak, yet no words came.

Meg caught her eye and gave her a quick grin, her gap showing, with a gentle, curious look: Go on, then.

Kate inhaled, and the sound broadcast her fear across the church. Her eyes went to a stripe of colour behind the last row of pews, to Luca and Vittorio in their plum POW uniforms. They stood against the wall between Captain Rook and Corporal Oil. Even Harry had come. Next to Grimes, he fidgeted, scratching a scab on his knee.

Pale eyes found her. Luca. His presence gave her strength. Kate swallowed and unfolded her pages.

'My father —' Her voice was soft, lost in the church full of people.

'Speak up,' Jack said conversationally, as if it were just the two of them in the church.

'My father,' she said again. 'He came to the district as a young man, a soldier settler. He worked hard. He loved his land and he took care of it. He was proud of Amiens and its wool. There was a time when he could tell you the clip for every property between here and Tamworth for this year and the year before and the year before that.

'That . . . that was before he was sick. He was sick for a while. His wounds from the First War gave more and more trouble as he got older. Some of you – many of you – knew or guessed and you helped us in these last years and months, and even now, in all sorts of ways. I didn't thank you. I was, I was too proud to say he was sick, but I am grateful for every kindness and understanding. I'm sorry for the way he was sometimes and I want to thank you now, thank you for your help.'

Kate dropped her hand with the pages by her side, and her eyes followed it down. In the silent church she went back to her pew to sit between Jack and Mr Nettiford. Jack frowned.

'All rise.' The reverend's tone was thick with disapproval too. 'Please join me now in the Lord's Prayer.' The congregation stood promptly, relieved it was over. Jack, Grimes, Ted Tuite and his son Kevin moved forwards to lift the coffin onto their shoulders. The reverend followed the pallbearers, the long fingers of his hands intertwined in front of his paunch. He motioned to Mr Nettiford as he passed, and the little round church elder stood, offering Kate his arm. The aisle was much longer than she remembered, a sea of faces on both sides. She dared not look people in the eye, in case she cried.

On the steps outside, Kate loosened her arm from Mr Nettiford's and watched, in a fog, as the pallbearers moved the coffin into the back of the Tuites' ute and tied it down. Ted Tuite and Kevin rocked the coffin gently, making sure it was secure.

~

The trip through town was mercifully slow, Jack driving the truck behind the Tuites' ute and then the funeral procession making its way behind them to Amiens.

Jack glanced across at her and shook his head. 'What happened to no apologies, like I said?'

Kate looked down at her hands, and inhaled, too tired to explain. 'Sorry,' she said. Jack was an odd mix. Their name was important to him and he was proud of Amiens. But he didn't see that to the good families her father would always be a soldier settler. Even Jack himself was a ring-in. He'd only been in the district five minutes. And he caroused with the likes of Tony Biggs, a publican, someone the good families would never have anything to do with.

'And them bloody Eye-ties in the congregation? I was surprised you didn't get Johnno and Spinks and all the blacks in there too, eh? Jesus, Kate. Lucky we're bloody getting out of town.' Jack shook his head again, frowning. They stayed in that unhappy silence.

It was the Amiens dogs that woke her, barking as they ran about the truck. Kate sat up and Jack pulled the truck to a stop by the house gate. As she reached for her car door, it swung open. Luca. He smiled at her, and she drank him in, so glad he was with her. Jack muttered something, shaking his head.

'Can you show people the track to the cemetery?' Kate asked Luca, wanting to get him away from Jack. She realised she was protective. 'Run on ahead?'

'Aw, he can run orright. Eye-ties are bloody good at running.'

His face set, head back, Luca stopped and turned to Jack. But he'd slammed the truck door and was gone. The first of the mourners' cars and trucks came up out of the gully and Kate searched to find the gumption to welcome them.

~

Only Kate, Jack and Reverend Popliss fitted inside the little cemetery. The mourners fanned out beyond the iron fence, where the pasture had been mowed. The smell of cut grass in her nostrils, Kate glanced at the visitors. Perhaps much is forgiven in death, she thought, looking at Mr Babbin, the stock and station agent. But Mr Babbin was a businessman. He'd still want to be paid.

She stood back, watching the men lay the coffin next to her mother's grave.

'Move closer, dear,' Reverend Popliss instructed and Kate did as she was told, stepping forwards to stand by Jack, only a foot or so from the edge. She couldn't look down into that hole, keeping her eyes instead on the coffin.

A gust stroked her back, and she hoped there might be a few drops in the scuddy clouds. She even thought she could smell rain, which would be a proper send-off for her father. Her dear father. The men lowered the coffin into the ground. It would take some time for the earth to do its work, to rot the box and have it collapse about him and embrace his remains. He loved that country. From there, you could see most of Amiens, its paddocks all the way to the State Forest and Mount Perseverance. He'd always be there. Even if she lost the place.

She felt Jack touch her arm.

'The dirt. He needs a bit of dirt,' Jack said softly. Kate stepped round the hole to take up a handful from the pile by the grave, throwing it in towards the side, not wanting it to land on the coffin itself. Some raindrops spattered the mourners, but only for a second. Kate stepped back and Jack offered her his arm again. The Tuites would begin the long task of enclosing her father's body in the earth.

CHAPTER 34

A flock is averse to movement towards dogs or men, so judicious attention to placement of hands will greatly benefit the prudent woolgrower.

THE WOOLGROWER'S COMPANION, 1906

After the burial, the mourners spread into the homestead garden and Kate went towards the house. The food – scones, pikelets, sponges and sandwiches – was laid out on tables on the verandah. Vittorio had been up at first light, making the sandwiches at the quarters on the quiet. He'd made the scones, too, with Daisy's recipe. Daisy's mother's recipe, she corrected herself with a pang. Vittorio was off now with the other POWs, out by the trucks. Kate had help, though, with the tea things, volunteered by the Yorkes, and some other ladies. She heard voices in the kitchen as she went up the verandah steps.

'John can't see how she can carry on now,' Elizabeth Fleming was saying.

'None of our damn —' Meg stopped when she saw Kate through the gauze. 'Hullo, Kate darling. I was just telling Elizabeth . . .' She paused, her face set. The other woman froze, eyes wide, and Mary Yorke, washing up at the sink, paused too.

'I was just telling Elizabeth we should get you a cup of tea. Yes?'

Kate shook her head, grateful to Meg for sticking up for her.

'Afternoon, Mrs D.' Tony Biggs banged on the gauze door, a cigarette in his lips. He didn't take it out to speak. 'Where'd you want the keg?'

'Could you ask Jack?'

He grinned. 'I reckon between us we'll know where to put some beer.'

Mary and Meg replaced Biggs at the door, carrying plates of patty cakes. Meg looked at Kate intently, perhaps afraid she might cry. But it was odd: close as Kate was to crying, she couldn't, not really, not yet. She hoped she didn't see Luca for a bit. She might cry then.

By the middle of the afternoon, the wake was going well, as if it mattered. Her father didn't give two hoots for this sort of thing. They're just here for the keg, he'd have said.

With Meg and Mary in the kitchen, Kate took a plate of Vittorio's sandwiches to the garden. As luck would have it, Mr Addison had just arrived and was walking across the lawn alone. She intercepted him. She had to; she might not get another chance. 'Curried egg? Peppery though. It has shallots in it.' She didn't tell him who'd made the sandwiches.

Addison took one. 'I'm sorry about your father.'

'Thank you, Alwyn. I'm so grateful for your help. The district is lucky to have you.'

'I do what I can,' he said, uncomfortable.

'It's a difficult time.' She reached out to rest her spare hand on his arm, forcing herself to make it stay there. 'But we shear in late November and the wool cheque will come in December.'

'What's that?' He seemed surprised.

Kate hated it, but made herself leave her hand on his arm. It felt bony through the shirt cloth. 'If you . . . If the bank could hold off until then. I mean hold off until December . . .'

He took her hand in his, to any onlooker simply a kindly bank manager consoling a grieving customer. But then he put his other hand on top of hers, capturing her fingers within his, and she felt the pressure of his fingers stroking her palm, cold on her skin. His voice was low. 'I *can* help you, you know, Kate. If you'd allow me.'

Involuntarily, she snatched her hand away, horror on her face.

He flushed red, and flicked his eyes about to see if anyone had witnessed his humiliation. When he spoke, it was with such intensity, she was afraid. 'You will regret that,' he said.

'No, no. I didn't mean . . . But I know what Dad spent the money on . . . the overdraft money.' The words tumbled out, disjointed, overwrought, as she tried to regain his trust. 'I've found a receipt . . . for a sapphire my father bought. I'm – I'm sure I'll find the stone itself soon too. It's very valuable. It's —'

'Forget it, *Mrs* Dowd, I shall do you no more favours.' They were interrupted by the Rileys, Bill trailing his wife. The big woman took a sandwich from Kate, and smiled at their frozen faces. 'Do you think there might be some rain in that?' She looked towards a small bank of cloud on the horizon to the west. 'Let's hope so,' she said, answering her own question. 'Some other good news instead. You know we're sponsoring our POW, Giacomo, Mr Addison? To come back, after the war. He'll work for us for two years, but we hope he'll stay for good. He's like family, now. Will yours come back, Kate?'

Kate's head was pounding from Addison's venom, and she knew Luca would never return to Australia. She left the Rileys with Addison and went to Captain Rook and Corporal Oil on the far side of the lawn.

'Mrs Dowd, the POWs are off soon,' the captain said. 'Being repatriated. Not the one serving time for fraternisation, of course, but all the rest. You'll hear officially, shortly.'

It took Kate a second to realise that her mouth was open. She closed it, and felt her pulse banging in her head. Luca. She would lose Luca. What could she do to stop it? She caught herself. This was ridiculous, crazy thinking. Still, she wanted him to stay.

'October. The 15th for this district, they reckon,' he said.

She left Oil and went back to the kitchen, confused by her fear of losing Luca.

'Hullo.'

Kate looked up, startled from her thoughts.

Emma Wright, alone in the kitchen, was drying up. 'Meg says she'll take that tray out to the Italians.' She pointed with the tea towel at a small tray of buttered scones.

'I'll go. Thanks for coming today, Emma. And, well.' She looked out through the gauze door towards Addison, still with the Rileys on the lawn. 'Thanks for everything.'

'No worries. But I need to speak to you on the quiet about the will. Your father's will.'

Kate shook her head. 'I'm stupid. I hadn't even thought about a will.'

'We have it at the bank.'

'Does everything go to Jack and me?'

'No,' Emma said. 'Your dad must have done it not long before you got married. He was clever. Joint tenants for everything.'

'What does that mean?'

'It means you owned the lot as soon as your dad died.'

'You mean now?'

'Right now. No need for paper or forms or transfers.'

Kate heaved a sigh of relief. At least Jack wasn't an owner with her, yet. 'But that really means I own a whole lot of mortgage?'

Emma smiled. 'Yes. And you know what? The galah Addison's locked the drawer, the one with the Amiens file in it, so I can't see it now. And I see he's mad as a hornet with you today, looking daggers across the lawn. What happened when you talked to him?'

'He stroked my hand. So I flicked him off, like it was a spider.'

'Ooof,' Emma said. She set a dried cup down on the table and picked up the next from the sink. 'So it'll be the 12th of October for sure, if not sooner. Don't go away, will you?'

'What do you mean?'

'If you leave the district, even for a few days, he'll enforce – take possession – before the notices. He'll argue you've abandoned Amiens. So be sure you're out and about in plain sight. No hiding away either.'

Kate smiled sadly. 'Dad used to say that was the best place to hide. In plain sight.'

'Well, no hiding now. We want to see lots of you – but not with me! Addison doesn't want me talking to you. I'm sorry.'

'Don't be. You're a treasure, you are.'

'Just be prepared. You'll get a special notice now – notice of default proceedings and so on. It'll come in the post. And then there'll be another one. Addison will deliver that one in person with Wingnut as bailiff.'

Kate exhaled. 'I'd better get these scones to the Italians.' She shut the mortgage out of her head, locked it away, just as Addison had done with the file drawer. There was only so much she could cope with that day. Then she pushed the gauze door open with her back and manoeuvred the tray of scones around it to go out towards the POWs. She could see Harry was with them. Luca was yarning with the Riley POW, his mate Giacomo. Both northerners, apparently.

Luca walked to the fence to swing the gate open for her, nodding in greeting at her. She smiled her thanks, glad just to be near him and that he'd been at the funeral when she spoke. She took the tray on to the three POWs, all smoking, by the trucks.

Vittorio let out a masculine laugh, the kind that only comes at the end of a dirty joke. Kate frowned. Harry was hearing whatever that was. He came to her and snatched a scone.

'*Thank you*,' Kate said for him. She held out the plate of scones to the POWs.

'*Condoglianze a lei, Signora*,' Vittorio said, taking a scone with one hand. 'Sorry for you.'

'Thank you,' Kate said and looked away. Off beyond the meat shed, a dog barked. It sounded like Puck, unhappy to be tied up.

Giacomo took a scone and held it up to Kate. '*Grazie, Signora*.'

'*Prego*,' she said.

'*Prego? Signora! Prego? Brava!*' Vittorio applauded, smiling round the cigarette held in his lips. Kate was glad he seemed on the up-and-up. He might already know. 'Have you heard? You're to leave, start the journey home,' she said to the POWs, her eyes on Luca.

But it was Giacomo who replied. 'Me, I come back, Missus.' He grinned proudly. 'Mrs Riley she do for this. *Sì*. I work then. Here.' He pointed to the ground.

'We all need the hands, that's for sure.'

'They come back? These boys, eh?' Giacomo grinned, slapping Luca hard on the back.

Both Luca and Vittorio shook their heads, Vittorio with a stream of Italian which Kate took from the tone to mean that he would rather burn in hell. Kate avoided Luca's eye and went back to the house, trying not to think of the three weeks she had left with him. And that assumed the bank had not forced her off Amiens even before then.

~

By five o'clock that evening, all the visitors were gone and Ed had long since chivvied Luca and Vittorio back to the paddocks for lambing. Kate had changed and was in the vegetable garden, more to occupy herself than anything, waiting for Jack. As she weeded, the men's voices floated down from the verandah. Only Tony Biggs remained. Untroubled that Jack had so little time left at home, he had taken up residence in one of the squatter's chairs on the front verandah. Jack was in the other. Kate could see their legs and booted feet extended on the long footrests, and the smell of their cigarettes carried to her from time to time.

She worked her way along the trellis of beans, trying not to resent Tony Biggs, but failing, and hoped she couldn't be seen by the men. Be seen, Emma said. Hide, said her head. Plain sight, said her father. It all jumbled together in a whirl of grief and weariness. And there was no Luca today in the garden – out of respect for her grief, no doubt. It was probably just as well; he and Jack were combustible.

A movement just outside the garden fence caught her eye. It was the bowerbird, active now that the sun was low. He picked along, a small pebble in his beak. As he turned, the sun caught the stone and reflected with a glint.

Kate jumped into the garden bed so fast she frightened the bird. It fluttered into the air and hopped away as she fell on her knees by the bower. Oblivious to spiders and snakes, Kate rifled through the jumble of pebbles, rocks, shells and bits of glass.

She stopped, very still, then leaned forwards, brushing dirt and dead leaves away from a creamy stone in the middle of the bower. She picked it up, her eyes fixed on it: a rounded yellowish stone, like a piece of glass smoothed by the sea. She gasped as the sun lit it up, even through the dirt and dust.

'You orright, Kate? You in the garden?' Jack's voice came down from the verandah.

'Yes,' she said, but her voice was strangled. 'Yes,' she called, more clearly. Breathless, she ran from the trees to Jack and Biggs on the verandah.

Biggs nodded at Kate and climbed out of the squatter's chair. 'Goin to splash me boots,' he said.

'Jack —' Kate started.

'The man's as rough as bags,' Jack said, smiling. He headed into the kitchen, and Kate followed. Automatically, she set about the very last of the cleaning up, feeling the sapphire pressing into her from her pocket. She had to tell him about the stone.

'Jack . . .'

'You ready to hit the frog and toad, mate?' Biggs's voice from the verandah. 'I'll get the empty into the truck.'

'You orright by yourself with that keg?' Jack replied.

'You're pullin my leg. I carry empty bloody kegs every day of the week, mate.'

She had not realised Jack was leaving with Biggs. He would not spend his last night with her.

Jack headed to their bedroom. 'What'd you say, Kate?' he called.

'I . . .' she said, but to an empty kitchen. A few minutes later he was back with his Army duffel bag. He set the bag next to the door and smiled lazily at her. He'd had a few. She told herself she didn't care.

'Jack —'

'Don't worry about taking me into town. You're not much of a driver; we both know that. Biggsy said he'd give me a lift to the station first thing tomorrow. We're gunna get on the grog tonight.'

Now Kate was mad. 'Good old Biggsy.'

'Settle down. It's not his fault you're in this mess.' There was silence in the kitchen. 'Anyhow, I forgot t'ask. Is your old man's will sorted out?'

'What? Yes. Emma told me today. The bank has it.'

'All to you? Or to us both? That'd save us the trouble of a transfer, if he did.'

Kate was suddenly grateful to her father. 'Everything went to me. Joint tenants, or something, so it was automatic, apparently, when he died.'

He frowned. 'I suppose there's no point in getting it transferred to me if we're losing the lot anyhow. Can't wait to see the back of the place, now.'

It occurred to her that Jack wanted to go, wanted to leave the district at any cost. She put her hand in her pocket and touched the stone. 'But what if I . . . ? What if I found the sapphire?' she said.

'You won't. And I'd keep it quiet if you did. It'd set us up nicely somewhere else. We're not stayin here now. That's for sure.'

Kate took her hand out of her pocket. 'I don't want to leave, Jack.'

'Bloody hell, Kate. Not again. You've got no flaming choice.' He shook his head and glanced again out through the gauze of the kitchen door towards Biggsy's truck. 'Look, I don't want to have a blue with you. Not now.' He came to her and enfolded her in his arms.

'We'll be orright,' he whispered into her hair. 'The next few weeks'll be rough, but you go off to my family in Perth before the bank comes in. Ruddy creditors'll leave you alone there.'

She opened her mouth to object. He kissed her instead and she kissed him back, angry and sad, ashamed of him and of herself. He kissed her forehead and she felt the cleft of his chin against her.

He pulled away and squatted by his duffel bag to extract an envelope. 'Here's some cash for the train ticket and the address of my folks in Perth. Then I'll send for you, once I'm settled up north. Won't be for a bit, mind. They say I'm gunna be training troops till the cows come home, for the occupation.' He held out the envelope to her. When she wouldn't take it, he dropped it on the table between them.

287

'Hooroo, Kate.' He hoisted the bag onto his shoulder and went out. The gauze door banged behind him.

~

That night Kate slept fitfully, waking to check the sapphire, which she'd tucked into her pillowcase. When she woke at about two in the morning, she could not go back to sleep, and she lay, clutching the stone. The smell of Jack in her bed – his sweat and their lovemaking – made it worse.

She pushed the blankets back, swung her legs over the side of her bed, put her feet on the cold floor and into her slippers. She set the stone on her dressing table, took her pillow for comfort and, hugging it in her arms, looked through the French windows. A half-moon seeped from the bank of clouds that had come in from the west, and threw a weak light across Amiens. She could make out the spikes of the myalls along the creek bed, the hills beyond and even some dots of sheep, bright on grey hills. And the moon itself, just a sliver, shone from within the travelling clouds. This was a beautiful night for her father to be on the hillside. She might save Amiens now that she had the stone. She wished he'd known. Might she have saved him? If she'd found the sapphire sooner? She wanted to think so, but in her heart, she knew.

She went back to bed but still she couldn't sleep, conscious of being by herself, no father, no Daisy, no Jack. The house seemed very big, and her thoughts went to Luca, not half a mile away, taking in the same air, under the same sky. She wondered if he were sleeping and smiled at the thought of him. The sapphire kept creeping back into her head, that and the two long days before she could try to give Addison the stone.

CHAPTER 35

Come lambing, the prudent woolgrower, when alerted, provides an especially close attention to a ewe in difficulty.

THE WOOLGROWER'S COMPANION, 1906

The next morning, Kate was glad of the kookaburras in the trees around the homestead. Conscious of the quiet of the house all around her, she bustled about the kitchen making tea. A movement in the garden caught her eye. She went to the door, and smiled at Luca, legs astride, bent from his waist to pull at the weeds at the foot of the bean trellis. She could tell him about the sapphire.

'It's Saturday,' she called out. He was often only in the garden during the week.

He straightened up. '*Sì.* Orright, *Signora?*'

That's why he was there. To see how she was. She felt a rush of gratitude as he bent back to his work.

'Yes. I'm all right. Really. Tea?' she said.

He waggled his head, the way he did when he was thinking. '*Sì, sì.*'

She took two mugs out. Above her, that kookaburra was at it again with its long, demented call from the eucalypt tree.

'She laugh,' Luca said, taking his tea from her. 'Crazy laugh.'

'They always sound drunk or mad to me.'

Luca startled her by copying the call. With quick stac-cato yelps he sang along with the bird. 'Ooh-ooh-ooh-ooh. Aah-aah-aah-aah.'

Kate laughed and it felt odd. She hadn't laughed since her father died. The bird's call went on. Luca tried again, only louder, his voice deeper and slower. This time, the bird fell silent.

'She's listening,' Kate teased him. 'She's keen on you.'

Luca smiled at her. 'Maybe,' he said and Kate looked away, feeling her face grow hot. She sipped her tea.

'I found it,' she said. 'The sapphire.'

'No. This is true?' He looked at her intently.

'Yesterday. It was in the bower, the bird's bower.'

'Aaaah.' He nodded, smiling. 'This is good place for hide. Now you sell her?'

'I'll give it to Addison on Monday.'

'This is very good, *Signora*. Much, much good for you.'

~

Monday morning, at nine o'clock sharp, Kate sat herself in the office and set the sapphire on the empty desk in front of her. She picked up the telephone and Barrel put her through to the bank.

Emma answered.

'Emma! It's Kate. Kate Dowd. I want to make an appoint-ment to see Mr Addison today. About it. I have it. I found it,' she said, hoping Emma would understand.

But there was a pause.

'Emma?'

'I'm here. Can you hold on a second?'

Kate heard muffled voices, and then a man's voice – Addison? – saying no, absolutely not. Then there was silence. Kate inhaled. He must still be mad about the wake. Damn.

'Mrs Dowd?' Emma said.

Mrs Dowd? 'Yes?'

'I'm sorry but Mr Addison is booked up.'

'It doesn't *have* to be today. Tomorrow's fine.'

'No, well, you see . . . It's all this week, actually.' Emma's voice sounded odd.

'He's away?'

'Er . . . not exactly.'

Kate was quiet for a moment. Was he refusing to see her?

'Next week?'

'I don't believe so. I'm sorry. I must go now, Mrs Dowd. Good day.'

Addison must have been standing over her. Kate put the receiver back in its cradle. Bugger and damn, as her father would have said.

She didn't give up. Late that day, she rang the bank again.

'They won't answer now, dearie,' Barrel said down the line. 'They're balancing their books for the week.' She should know. Barrel had been a Wilson before she was married and one of her nephews worked for Addison.

'Can we try? Please?'

The number rang on.

'I told you, dearie.' Kate could sense Barrel's pursed lips.

Finally, someone picked up the call. 'Yes?' Addison's voice was clear on the line. 'The bank is closed. Who is this?'

'It's me, Mr Addison. Kate Dowd. I've found the sapphire.' Party line, or no party line, she had to tell him, stop him serving his notices to take Amiens.

'The bank is closed, Mrs Dowd. Good day.'

'But . . . I have it.'

'The bank only accepts cash.'

'Oh. But —'

'Good day, Mrs Dowd.'

'Wait! I . . . I could go to Sydney and sell it for you.'

'To Sydney?'

'I can. I will. The Wednesday train?' It was the first one.

291

There was another pause.

'Best of luck in Sydney, Mrs Dowd. Good day.' He hung up.

Kate stared at the telephone. Had he forgiven her? He must have; he'd wished her luck, for heaven's sake. So he would hold off serving his dratted notices. She would sell the sapphire in Sydney and then the noose round her neck would be loosened.

~

As it turned out, there were no seats left on the Wednesday train: it was 'reduced carriages' schedule that day. Kate almost cried. She had to be content with booking for the Saturday train. With lambing on, at least the days went by quickly. It wasn't until Thursday afternoon, as Kate walked towards the homestead tired and dirty from lambing, that she started to think seriously about her Sydney trip. It occurred to her, even weary as she was, she was almost happy. She'd found the sapphire, it seemed that Addison would hold off on his bank notices while she went to Sydney to sell it, and today only the lambs and one ewe had died on her, the ewe messily.

Kate loved newborn lambs. They were wet and slimy and covered in gunk, but a good clean from the rasp of the ewe's tongue, and then they were struggling to their feet. They'd feed and feed, and bleat and bleat. She loved it when they'd start to play, gambolling, ridiculous leaps and jumps and hops, with sheer pleasure to be alive. Her father had loved lambs too, chuckling at their gymnastics. Thinking of her father brought back a rush of grief.

At the homestead steps, she took her boots off and carried them in her hands, taking the rest of her filthy self along the verandah towards the bathroom for a wash. When she came round the corner, Mick Maguire was standing by the back door, his arms full with bread, mail and the paper. It was mail day. She was losing all track of time.

'I take it that's not your blood, Mrs D?'

Kate looked down at her clothes. What was not muddy was dark red with drying blood, from her coat to her trousers. Only her socks were clean.

'No.' She managed a smile. 'Not mine.'

He followed her into the kitchen and she washed up as best she could in the laundry.

Peng stood up from her position on the kitchen chair, her head poking above the table. Maguire stroked her. 'You're a sook, old Peng,' he said, then turned to Kate.

'I got a coupla letters for your Eye-tie fellas. Captain Rook asked me to give em to yez.' He pushed two letters across the table, again stampless with just the Red Cross emblem like a postmark.

He cleared his throat and put another envelope on the table in front of her. The return address said *Rural State Bank of New South Wales, 202 Elizabeth Street, Sydney, New South Wales*. 'Special delivery for ya. Ya gotta sign near *Receipt*, eh.' Maguire jabbed at the spot on the page.

She couldn't understand. Addison had as good as blessed her trip to Sydney. Why would he serve the notices?

'Ya gotta sign, eh,' Maguire said again, clearing his throat.

There was nothing for it. She signed, slowly, carefully, willing her hand not to shake. Maguire folded the signed paper and put it in his shirt pocket. He gathered his things and left. No yarning today.

A breeze rattled through the Californian pine. Kate shivered. She was watching his truck drive away when Harry appeared.

He slung his school case on the floor. 'Can I've a scone?'

'School all right?'

'Yeah. S'orright,' he said with a mouthful. 'They're not as good, ya know.'

'What?'

'Your scones are orright but Daisy's are better. She's a good cooker. She's workin in the kitchens at the Home now, is what I hear. And about to pop, too, eh.'

'Harry. Don't say that,' Kate chided. She felt the weight of her guilt. Poor Daisy. On her feet all day in a hot kitchen? With the baby due?

'What's that then?' Harry asked, nudging the bank letter. Kate exhaled, and used a bread knife to open the envelope, careful not to tear the heavy page inside.

It was headed *NOTICE OF DEMAND AND DEFAULT*.

CHAPTER 36

Mother Earth seems curiously predisposed against the lamb. Maternal desertion, the elements and predators all work to snuff the life from a newborn lamb ere it has begun.

THE WOOLGROWER'S COMPANION, 1906

Kate read it, trying to make sense of the words. There was *overdue mortgage interest*, and that was almost exactly £1,000, and a number for the *cancelled overdraft*. The *total due and payable*, they gave as £6,052. Bloody hell. It was still a big figure to see typed on the page, but it made sense, if she took the cattle money into account. The last bits were very clear: *failure to pay within seven days* and *if unpaid, enforcement proceedings to be brought with a view to obtaining possession on or before 12 October 1945.*

On or before. Two weeks and one day. Jesus. Why was Addison doing this? When he knew she'd found the sapphire.

She was interrupted by the sound of a car. It came, its lights on in the approaching dusk. Emma. Thank goodness: she might know something.

'I'm so sorry,' Emma called as she crossed the dead lawn. 'I didn't want to use the party line.'

'No, no, thank you. But what's he doing? I spoke to Addison on Monday and he as good as told me to go to Sydney to sell the sapphire, you see. I thought he had to have cash. That's

295

what I don't understand. If he agreed on Monday, why serve the notices on me today?'

'Did he really agree?' Emma asked. 'Or did he just say nothing?'

Kate thought back. 'You're right.'

'He wants you away. If you'd gone to Sydney, it'd be easier for him.'

Kate gasped. 'He lied to me.'

'Good as, yes. He'll come in then, y'see. As soon as you go away. He'll claim you've "abandoned" the property so the bank's security is at risk. *Assets in jeopardy* bucket.'

'The man's a snake!' Kate spat out the word.

Emma smiled and squeezed Kate's arm. 'Don't go to Sydney, whatever you do.'

'What will I do?'

'You'll think of something,' Emma said, but her words sounded hollow.

As the red tail-lights of Emma's car dipped into the gully, Luca appeared at the gate.

'All right, *Signora*?' he said as Kate came down the verandah steps.

'Not really. That was Emma from the bank. Addison wants me off the place in Sydney so he can come in. Put locks on the gates.' Kate sat down on the steps. 'He won't accept the sapphire itself, so I have to get to Sydney to sell it, but I can't leave Amiens or Addison will pounce.'

'You must buy her in Sydney?'

'Sell, yes. I have to sell it in Sydney. The sapphire buyers here know I'm in trouble. They'd give me nothing for it. And it's so big, I doubt they'd have the money anyway.'

Luca moved along the garden beds, pulling out weeds, entwining tendrils back into the trellis. 'Meg can do her, no? She go to Sydney for her brother. He come there soon.'

'Meg's going to Sydney? How do you know?'

'She say me.'

The low hum of cicadas was the only sound in the dusk sky, and Kate felt a familiar pang of hurt. She was too tired to give herself a lecture on how inappropriate it was for her, a married lady, to be jealous of a POW's feeling for a single girl. Even if it wasn't right that they should be flirting in the first place. Still, it ate at her, that Luca might be keen on Meg.

'Meg, she buy for you,' Luca said again. His tone implied he'd solved the problem.

'Sell,' Kate said, eventually. 'Sell, not buy.'

'Sell, *si*,' Luca said.

~

Early on Saturday morning, Kate walked wearily across the frost-white ground of the early morning, towards the men in the yards. All available hands were lambing.

Even in her weariness, Kate was thinking about the bank. Meg was taking the sapphire with her to Sydney on the train today, and, just as Luca had said, she'd be back on Wednesday with a cheque for Kate. Kate would take the money straight to the bank, well before Addison was officially due to come in on 12 October. She had taken every precaution, even asking Meg to have Mr McGintey make the cheque out to the bank, which would save weeks. Now she just had to wait. In the waiting, though, her grief had found her again. The rhythm of work had helped her through the first days after the funeral, but now she was tired first thing, even when she woke. She had one big task ahead, though. She'd ask Mr Grimes to meet her on Monday morning at the homestead. She had to tell him to follow *her* orders now that her father was gone. She knew he would not take it well, and that worried her.

She climbed through the rails at the yards and said a quiet general 'good morning'. Ed, Grimes and Johnno were already mounted. Luca and Spinks were still mucking around with girth straps and Harry was scrambling onto Mustard.

Vittorio held Ben's reins and she took them from him, leaned against Ben's neck and yawned, looking out at the red arc of sun in the east and the pale sky. She tightened the girth strap tight, bringing an unhappy snort from Ben, hauled herself up on him, and followed Luca out of yards, into the line of riders moving slowly across the paddock. She pulled her jacket more closely around her to ward off the chill. And her loss. She might forget her grief for a few seconds or a minute, now and then, but it always came back.

She watched Luca ride. You could tell if a horse was unwilling, if they didn't like the rider, or was just bad tempered, but not these two. Luca rode easily, moving comfortably. In her tiredness, Kate's eyes rested on his behind in the saddle. A very nice bum, Meg would have observed. Bloody Meg.

He turned in his saddle and gave her his half-grin. She looked away, cross with herself for being caught. How did he know? She was too weary even to be sensible.

She had never known this sort of tiredness. Her back ached from lambing, from pushing against the ewe's rump, pulling on the lamb's legs. The smell of the afterbirth clung to her clothes, no matter how she washed them. Funny old Jack, he didn't like stock work. 'Give me a machine over an animal any day,' he'd say, although not in her father's hearing. Perhaps he'd come to decide he wanted his own land, not work like a navvy on someone else's. Maybe that was even part of her appeal to him. She felt a pang. She and Jack — what would become of them?

'You take Harry, orright?' Ed said and Kate nodded, pulled back to the present. Ben turned off towards Riflebutt. He knew where to go, and Harry on Mustard capered around them. Even with school five days a week, he was full of beans. Grimes headed off away from her to the north. Kate had done nothing about speaking with him, about him taking his orders from her. She couldn't face that conversation just yet.

She and Harry started into Riflebutt, moving down the fence line.

'What's that then?' Harry pointed to a long row of rocks. The line turned and came back on itself, a flat-topped oval, extending into the paddock. He dismounted where the line of rocks went through the fence. With his reins in one hand, he pulled at a rock with the other, shifting it backwards and forwards to free it.

'Don't touch it!' Kate warned.

He stopped, surprised. 'Why not?'

'It's a Bora ring.'

'A bore? For water?'

'No. It's the Aborigines. They built it, brought all the rocks here.'

'What for?'

Kate shrugged. 'I don't know. Corroborees and things, I suppose.'

'Them dances?'

'Yes.'

'So why can't I move em?'

'It's bad luck, Dad reckons. Reckoned.'

Harry straightened up, running his eyes round the Bora ring. 'Why'd they leave, ya reckon? The Abos?'

'I don't think they ever stayed long in one place.'

'What about them rocks, then? If they never stayed put? Johnno and Spinksy reckon their mob've been here forever. Grew maize before the war'n everything.'

Harry could be very annoying, like a dog with a hold on a goanna's tail.

They spread out then, to either side of the paddock. A few minutes after they'd split, Harry cooeed to get her attention. He stood up in his stirrups and pointed. At first, Kate couldn't see anything. His energetic jabbing kept her looking. About a hundred yards ahead on the ground was a ewe, lying still, so dusty she was hard to tell from the ground and the grass around her.

Kate and Harry dismounted about thirty feet out, and left the horses. Kate looked meaningfully at Mustard, hoping she'd be a good influence on the wayward Ben, stop him straying too far.

As they approached the ewe, a crow hopped away, and Kate was concerned at what Harry might see.

'You should go back.'

'Nuh,' he said, matter of fact. It occurred to her she had no authority with this boy. Why then did she think she could manage his uncle?

'Well, stay away from her rear end. You hold her steady.'

For once he did as he was told. Harry in place, Kate shooed a second persistent crow away. Just the lamb's head – no hooves – stuck out from the ewe, its eye sockets empty, flies crawling about the dried blood. Maybe the lamb had been dead before the crows picked its eyes out, but she doubted it.

Kate moved back to squat beside the ewe's muzzle, and held her hand in front of its nostrils against the ground. A faint trickle of air passed across her fingertips. Damn. The ewe, at least, was still alive. Then she went back to her rear end, hoping the sightless lamb was dead. She cleared away some of the birth sac that clung to its head, and tried not to look where its eyes should have been. She put her fingers on its tiny pink nostrils. Nothing. Good. She felt a weight lift off her. How odd to be pleased by death.

'You all right?' she said to Harry.

He shrugged. She walked back to the horses, took off her coat and tied it on firmly then pulled her lambing kit from the saddlebag: the hessian bag, some fat and a bit of rag. As she came back, she rolled up her right sleeve, and applied the fat.

She squatted at the back of the ewe, balancing herself with her left hand on its rump and working her fingers into the ewe, behind the protruding head. She gasped in shock when the lamb shuddered under her fingers; it was alive. Harry came round quickly and then kneeled down, his mouth open, transfixed.

'Go and get Ed.'

He stood up slowly, still staring at its empty eye sockets.

'You wanted to come,' she said and immediately felt guilty. He stepped backwards, almost falling over a tussock of knotgrass.

'You're a big help, you know,' she said, cross with the ewe and the lamb and with him and with herself. 'Now go and get Ed for me. Quick sticks.'

He went off to catch Mustard.

'Careful. All right?' she called after him. He didn't seem to hear, off at a trot then a canter. She was glad Mustard was sure-footed as well as sensible to make up for Harry's riding.

Kate started anew, gently working her hand into the ewe's uterus, her fingers around and behind the lamb. She tried to push the lamb back so that she might get its legs out in front of the head but on one go it was clear that would never work. There had been no contraction while she'd been there. She looked at her watch, ten past nine. The men might collect at the homestead at about ten for a cup of tea and Harry would get Ed to come to her. She hoped they'd be with her well before that.

She tried again, this time pulling on the lamb to bring it out, feet back or no feet back. It didn't move. She stopped for a bit and sat by the ewe's head, stroking her muzzle. Kate could still feel a faint breath from her nostrils.

With more fat smeared onto her right arm, Kate tried yet again and was rewarded with a contraction that gripped her arm. 'Good on you. Push!'

She stayed where she was for five minutes, then ten, without another contraction. She looked at her watch. Almost ten. Someone must come soon. She hoped it would not be Grimes.

She had her hand in again, behind the shoulder blades, when she saw a horse approaching. Ed. Thank God.

'When did she last have a contraction, do ya know?' he said when he'd dismounted, moving about her, checking the lamb first and then the ewe.

'About a half hour ago.' Kate checked her watch again. 'Closer to forty minutes, actually.'

'Before that?' He held his fingers under her nostrils and moved quickly to feel for a pulse on the lamb's neck.

'That was the only one I felt.'

He checked each of the animals again and stood, his big hands on his hips. 'They're cactus, Mrs D.'

'What do you mean?'

'Dead.'

'Both of them?' Her voice cracked.

He nodded. 'Sometimes ya just gotta give up.'

She shook her head and began to cry, too tired even to be ashamed.

Ed looked back towards the house paddocks. 'Ya better go back for a cup a tea, eh.'

When she didn't get up, he went to the horses and led both mounts in. He held out Ben's reins to Kate until she took them but she stayed sitting on the ground.

'Kate.'

He'd not used her Christian name since she got married.

'I've gotta get down to the lease. You'll be all right.' And then he was gone.

She cried, the weak sun on her back. A pair of black cockatoos wheeled their awkward flight across the southern edge of the paddock and her tears began again. Maybe Ed was right about giving up. She began to sob, too, not bothering to quiet her crying, so far from anyone who would hear.

She wept for her father's death, for his illness, for Amiens, for the drought, for her absent Jack, and for damn Luca and his crush on Meg. She wept for herself, alone in a thirsty paddock with a dead ewe and a dead lamb.

Kate sat in the paddock until her crying stopped and her sense came back. She felt piss-poor, lily-livered. Jack had lots of names for the weak-willed. She wiped her nose on her sleeve and got to her feet, one leg numb from the cold. Ben was not far off. She hugged his neck hard and they went back to work.

CHAPTER 37

It is in the blackest of times that the prudent woolgrower should adhere to his daily schedule, and with ruthless dedication. Toil succours the heart, as bread nourishes the body.

THE WOOLGROWER'S COMPANION, 1906

When she got up early on Monday morning to get ready to see Grimes, Kate was still embarrassed about crying in front of Ed. He would say nothing, though.

As she made tea, she tried to enjoy the dawn chorus of birdcalls, but she kept coming back to the time she had left. Eleven days until 12 October. She was glad she'd eked out what little there was left of the overdraft, making it last for the men's wages, paying cash for the few parts they needed from Babbin's and some other essentials.

She prepared the tea things for Grimes's visit, then leaned against the kitchen counter and drank the dregs of her break-fast tea.

'Hullo?' Grimes's voice carried into the kitchen and his bulk filled the upper frame of the gauze door.

'Oh. Come in, Mr Grimes,' Kate said. 'Would you like to sit down? I've made some tea.' As she'd expected, his eyebrows went up in surprise at the offer. Grimes remained standing, his hat in his hands, so she poured and then held the cup of tea out to him. He frowned as he sat.

She came straight to it. 'Now that Dad has passed away, we'll need to sort out a new way to manage the place, to make the day-to-day decisions and so on.'

'Decisions?' His eyebrows knitted, the grey hairs almost joining in the middle of his forehead.

'About Amiens. We can talk each day at dusk. When you come in from the paddocks. If I'm not out with you. About my plans.'

'Your plans,' Grimes said flatly.

'Yes. So, for example, Mr Finnegan and his shearers will be here soon, in late November, for the shearing. We've got to get the shed and the yards ready before then. On those days when I'm not out on the run, if you could please come here daily at dusk? We can talk about that sort of thing.' She didn't say that the bank might sell them up before then.

'You think ya gunna run the place.'

'With your help, yes.'

She saw an expression come over his face she'd not seen before. Pity.

'Look, Jack'll look after yez.' He got to his feet and picked up his hat.

It hit Kate that Grimes *knew* and he was doing her a favour already, staying until the bank came.

But Amiens was hers, even if only for another eleven days. She had to run it. 'Will I see you at dusk then? Is that all right?'

He jammed his hat on. 'Yeah, right,' he snorted.

~

Grimes didn't appear that Monday afternoon, and Kate wasn't surprised. When she saw him at the yards early on Tuesday, he did not meet her eye and she was too chicken to raise it with him in front of the men. She'd lost the round, she knew that, too pre-occupied now with the sapphire and Addison to pursue it. And it was a big loss.

On Wednesday, Kate didn't go out lambing with the men, waiting at the homestead, hoping that Meg would find a way on the day of her return from Sydney to come over to Amiens. But she had still not appeared when Luca came in from the paddocks.

They worked silently in the garden, she and Luca. Her impatience grew, and spilled over into snapping weed roots, breaking runner bean stems; she was cross with herself and Meg. Luca worked on, leaving her to her thoughts.

It was not until close to five that Meg appeared. 'Yoo-hoo!' Her voice carried across the flat.

Luca straightened up and smoothed his hair with his hand. Kate frowned. She really couldn't have them carrying on at Amiens. They had enough black marks in the district. That thought made her feel better. This concerned respectability, not her feelings for Luca.

'Hullo, hullo!' Meg said as she flicked herself backwards off Fiva, her fair curls flying. 'I have it! The cheque,' she called, looping the reins round the top fence rail.

'Thank heavens!' Kate said, although her voice sounded odd. She went over, pulling off her garden gloves as she walked.

Meg withdrew an envelope from her jacket pocket and smoothed it out against the fence rail before handing it to her with pride. 'Sorry I couldn't get it to you earlier. Mum had Elizabeth Fleming out for afternoon tea.'

Kate silently cursed Elizabeth as she opened the envelope. She held the cheque in front of her so they could all see, Luca looking over one shoulder and Meg the other.

'Six thousand pounds. See?' Meg said, leaning over her to point. 'That should stop old Addison!'

Kate turned around, so Luca and Meg were obliged to part. 'Thanks, Meg. Really.'

'That's all right. When will you take it to the bank?'

'Tomorrow. First thing. Thanks again.' Kate retrieved her gardening gloves, and pulled them on.

Meg looked from Kate to Luca in embarrassment. 'I'd better let you get on, then. But Robbo's orright.'

Kate hadn't even asked. 'Of course! How is he?'

'A skeleton. Really. But he's alive.'

Kate squeezed the girl's arm. 'He'll get stronger and stronger.'

'Yeah. He is, I reckon. Squabblin with Dad already. They still don't get on. I reckon Robbo'll be off when he's well. Anyway, good luck with the bank.' She untied Fiva's reins and mounted, pulling the horse round as she did. Kate could not watch Luca farewell the girl. She left them and went inside.

~

At just before nine o'clock on the next morning, Kate stood on the stone steps in Longhope, waiting for a bank johnny to unlock the door when they opened for business. In her hand was the cheque from Mr McGintey. She looked along the street to where she'd parked the car and observed she'd not done a very good job. Its bonnet was jutting out into the road. But she'd not wanted to distract Grimes from lambing nor tell him why she urgently needed to come into town, so she'd driven herself. She'd managed it, although she'd had to pull over four times to let people overtake her.

The jangle of keys and the heavy click of the door lock got her attention. The man on duty fiddled with his tie as he held the door for her. For once, Kate was not so intimidated by the quiet hush of the bank chamber. She had the cheque. She went straight to Emma, surprised at her reaction, for the girl's eyes were wide behind her glasses. 'Mrs Dowd.'

Kate grinned. 'Is he in?' She had the cheque in her hand.

'Yes. No. I'll see,' Emma said, unhappily.

'Miss Wright . . .' Addison appeared round the corner of his office door. He stopped short as soon as he saw Kate.

'Mr Addison! Good morning. I've come to make a deposit.'

With a bang, he shut himself back in his office, pulling the door so hard Kate could hear the blinds rattling inside. She looked at Emma in astonishment.

'Is everything all right?' Kate asked. 'Can I see him?'

Emma shook her head. 'No. He's given instructions that if you came in, he would not . . .' She trailed off.

Kate stared at her. 'He won't see me?'

'I'll try,' Emma said, getting up quickly. She tapped very softly on the door but there was no answer. She tapped again and went in, closing the door behind her. But she was out again just as quickly.

'Mr Addison is tied up,' she said, looking wretched.

'Can you give him this, anyway? Even if he won't see me?' Kate pushed the cheque across the desk.

She exhaled. 'I'm sorry, Kate. He says only he's authorised to accept deposits. He says I can't.'

Kate gasped. 'But I'm a customer.'

Emma squirmed. 'He . . .'

'What about a teller?' she said, picking up the cheque.

Emma leaned out to catch Kate's arm. She whispered, 'He called us all together. Not half an hour ago, before the bank opened. Said anyone who accepted a deposit from you would be sacked.'

Kate gasped. She looked across at the four tellers. To a man, their eyes were on her.

'I'm so sorry.' Emma's words followed Kate across the silent chamber.

CHAPTER 38

A prudent woolgrower shall disallow exceeding commotion or move-
ment, whether in mustering or in the yards themselves, and counsel
his hands to move soberly amongst his flock.

THE WOOLGROWER'S COMPANION, 1906

Outside the bank, Kate got herself into the car. She was
trembling, her breathing shallow and her heart drubbing in
her chest. She would lose Amiens. She concentrated on her
breaths, and tried to make them deeper and longer. She had to
get on. Home. She must go home.

She started through Ed's checklist, but her hand shook on
the gear stick. A look in the mirrors, then she put her foot on
the clutch, and turned the key in the ignition. The car started,
and the loud noise gave her a jolt. She put it into gear and
let out the clutch. The engine roared but the car didn't move.
Why not?

Into gear. Release clutch.

She had a sudden terror that she'd have to ask for help, and
all of Longhope would know she couldn't cope.

Handbrake!

She released the brake and the car shot onto the road.

~

Her drive home was slow and again she had to pull off the single lane of bitumen three times to let other vehicles overtake. Addison's rejection weighed on her. For one of the first times since she'd learned about the debt on Amiens, she had no plan.

Late that morning, as she walked from the car to the homestead, she felt a sense of relief to be home, taking comfort from the familiarity of the garden, the rattle of the breeze through the trees, the screech of Daisy's lorikeets, but she felt a keen sense, too, that Addison would take it all from her. There was no one about. The men were already out in the paddocks and it was too late to get Vittorio to catch a horse for her.

She turned to her chores, washing the floors, but found it difficult to concentrate. She mopped, restless, wishing the afternoon would pass so Luca would come to the garden. Her thoughts kept going back to the bank. Addison was crazy. Stopping her from depositing the cheque in Longhope?

That was it! He had stopped her *in Longhope*. But Addison only controlled the bank in this district. She had to go beyond, to a branch that didn't report to him. So to Armidale – Armidale was big. And far. Four hours' drive, more for Kate. She'd not get there today before the bank closed at three. She'd go early tomorrow.

She was pouring water from the mop bucket across the verandah when she heard a car. They must have a visitor. Up out of the crossing, came a police car, and another. Addison. He would try to seize Amiens now. She took the bucket inside, forcing herself to be calm.

The noise of a car door shutting filtered in. She pulled the cheque from its hiding place in her wardrobe and went back to the kitchen. She straightened herself up as she'd seen Daisy do at the Home, and went out onto the verandah.

Wingnut stood with Addison just in front of the steps on the dead lawn. The police car, empty, was parked next to Addison's

Hudson. And behind the two, mercifully, the Amiens truck was coming to a stop, with Ed and Luca aboard. Luca would give her courage.

Kate went to the top of the steps, staying on the verandah, above the men. 'Afternoon, Sergeant. Mr Addison.'

'Mrs Dowd.' Wingnut touched the brim of his police hat with his fingers, his big ears hidden inside the band. He frowned as he unfolded a letter. 'I, ah, I gotta do this, see, Mrs D.' He threw a look at Addison, who stood straight, hands clasped behind his back, a small leather briefcase at his feet on the dead lawn. Wingnut exhaled and read, '*Are you Mrs Katherine Louise Dowd, individual and director of Amiens Pastoral Company?*'

'Yes.' Her voice was barely audible.

'*I am authorised in my capacity as Sheriff of Longhope*' – he threw another unhappy look at Addison – '*to serve upon you this court order to quit and vacate the property known as Amiens, in the District of Longhope, New South Wales. You have here*' – he stumbled over the wording – '*hereto failed to pay and are also . . . here*— *hereby directed to pay the amount of* —' he paused '*the amount of £6,052 . . . to the Rural Bank of New South Wales of 202 Elizabeth Street, Sydney. You have failed to tender payment or other security acceptable to the bank* —'

'But I have the overdraft money. More than £6,000. I found the sapphire,' Kate said. 'And I sold it.' She took the cheque from her pocket, and held it out to them.

Wingnut's eyes locked onto the cheque. He gave a low whistle. 'Ya better have a gander at that, mate.'

'Serve the court order, Sergeant,' Addison said.

Kate went down the steps. 'Dad bought a sapphire for me in Sydney. Years ago. It was thirty carats. I just sold it and now I have the money for the bank.' She held out the cheque, though her fingers shook. 'And shearing's in a month. There'll be the wool cheque for you then too.'

'Get on with it,' Addison snapped at the policeman.

'Well, now, we gotta do things by the book. The lady's *"tendered payment"*, I reckon. With this?'

'No she hasn't. It's not payment.' Addison tugged at his moustache with his fingers. He still didn't look at Kate.

'Cheque's even made out to ya bank, Adders,' Wingnut said mildly. Kate blessed her foresight in getting Meg to have Mr McGintey do that.

'I'm telling you to get *on* with it,' Addison said. 'The secured assets are in jeopardy.'

'The secured assets are in . . . ?' Wingnut said. He looked about, as if this jeopardy might reveal itself.

'Go ahead, man!'

The policeman pulled off his hat, freeing his ears. They stood out now, like unfolded butterfly wings. 'Well, the Sheriff's Office can't be lockin people out of their homes if the paperwork's not in order. I can only see a cheque, m'self. Nothin else. So I betta have that from you in writin, eh? If y'gunna say no t'the cheque, I mean.'

'Look,' Addison said, annoyed now. 'Sergeant. You . . . If you must . . . I'll hand-write you a notice now.' He squatted beside his briefcase and started to flick through it, looking for paper.

The policeman watched him, and spoke slowly. ''Cept I can't take anythin handwritten. Not for the bank.'

'Of course you can. You know me.'

Wingnut shook his head. 'Sorry, mate. I need a proper letter on the bank's notepaper. Gotta be by the book.' He folded the notice and held it out to the bank manager.

Addison glared at him.

'Y'better take that cheque, too, eh.'

Addison's face flushed with anger. 'I will not be told what to do by a *policeman*!'

'Orright, mate, orright. Only, lady's got a cheque, see. Got

312

your name on it. And she owes ya money. So if ya don't take it, I reckon your bank's not gunna be too happy.'

Still Addison would not accept the cheque.

'And if ya don't take the cheque, you'll need to get another order from the Court too, mebbe? Magistrate's in town first Friday of the month, I reckon. November now, eh? Just before shearin. An I'll come along. Let the magistrate know what I seen.'

Kate held her breath. Addison's face was puce. He snatched the court order from the policeman, and then the cheque from Kate's hand. He turned on his heel for the gate, ignoring Ed and Luca.

They watched the car roar down the track into the crossing.

'He'd best slow down there . . .' Wingnut said, then winced as the car's transmission bottomed on the rocks, '. . . else ya rip the guts out of it, eh.' He scratched his ear again, and levered it back inside his hat.

'Thank you.' It was all Kate could get out.

'No worries, Mrs D,' he said.

'Can you . . . Can you stay for a cup of tea?'

'Nuh. Thanks but I gotta get goin.' He went towards the fence and his vehicle. 'Afternoon, gents,' he said to Luca and Ed as he passed. 'Good luck, eh, Mrs D,' he called back.

It was over. Wingnut had stopped Addison, and Kate said many more silent thank yous to the policeman as his vehicle disappeared into the gully in a cloud of dust.

CHAPTER 39

It appears great pain in lambing may inhibit mothering instinct, at least for a time. Men of science have established a correlation of sorts between the length and difficulty of the birth, and the time a ewe will lie prone thereafter.

THE WOOLGROWER'S COMPANION, 1906

A currawong called out from the California pine, startling Kate. She had not dreamed it. Amiens was saved. With Ed and Luca still in front of her, Kate dropped herself onto the verandah steps, feeling the warmth of the stone through her joddies.

'Mrs D?' Ed said.

'What?' Kate was distracted, still taking in that Addison had been routed.

'Can I've a word?' Ed pulled his hat off his head and looked at it. 'I . . . Ah . . .'

Kate came out of her daze. Please, please let Ed not be leaving. 'What's wrong?' she asked.

'It's Daisy, Mrs D.'

There was a pause as Kate took that in. 'Daisy?' she said. 'Has she had her baby?'

'Nuh. But she run away, see, from that bugger of a Home in Armidale.'

'How do you know?'

Ed frowned, uncomfortable. 'She's here.'

'On Amiens? Right now?'

'Yeah,' he said. 'She walked from town.'

'She walked? It's nineteen miles. Is she all right?'

'Yeah. She wants to hide the baby, see. Otherwise, they'll take it for adoption. An she wants to have it on country. That's blackfella talk for the right land. That's Amiens.'

'On country? Isn't that Broken Hill then, where she's from?'

'She'd never get there. She's due in a coupla weeks.'

'Where is she?'

'Down near the Abo camp.'

'With Johnno and Spinks?'

He laughed. 'No. Only women allowed for the birthin.'

Kate inhaled. 'We're lucky Wingnut didn't know she was here – but the police'll catch her, you know. Eventually.'

'Yeah. Probly. Can she stay, but?'

Kate weighed this in her mind. If Daisy was caught on Amiens, the locals would be convinced Kate was as loony as her father, or that she'd gone native. But with his death, many probably thought that anyway. Kate bitterly regretted sending Daisy back to that Home. And for now, Amiens was safe from the bank.

'She can stay,' she said. 'Of course.'

Ed nodded, relieved. She understood his surprise. She wouldn't have said yes six months earlier, but things were different now. 'Do you think she'd be willing to talk to me? I'd like to see how she is.'

Ed shook his head. 'Aw, I'd let it go for now, eh, Mrs D.'

'Does she need anything? Has she got enough food?'

'Johnno's keepin damper up to her. She's gettin bush tucker too.'

'I'll get you a loaf of bread for her, and some jam and bikkies. But be careful, won't you? Grimes'll dob her in to the

315

police if he gets wind of this. And how will she have the baby? Who'll help her?'

'The Auntys from the Mission'll come. Aunty Nance and so on.'

'She's not really Daisy's aunt, though? She can't be.'

'The old girls? They're all called Aunty, the whole lot of em. Aunty Nance is orright – I hear them women stick together, eh. Aunty Nance is one of em who does the birthin, and Dais seen a few bein born, too. Growin up.'

Heavens. Imagine a child seeing a baby come into the world. Kate knew nothing about birth apart from what she had learned in lambing. All this information rolled round in her head. Daisy was lucky she had Ed. 'You're right to help her.'

'Yeah. Ta, Mrs D.'

Kate stood on the verandah and watched the truck trundle away. From the passenger seat, Luca gave her a lazy wave, with a broad smile of something. Of what? Then it struck her. Pride. Luca was proud of her.

~

Early the next morning, as Kate headed for the chooks, she saw someone moving along the creek bed. In among the myalls and the red gums, just before the ground fell away behind into the sandy dirt of the dry bed, was Daisy, standing, holding a stout walking pole, watching her. She had her future before her, Kate's mother would have said, her belly round and high.

Kate gave a sort of half-wave across the hundred yards that separated them. Daisy was still, watching. She must have been heading to get an egg too. Now she probably wouldn't, not with Kate there. So Kate would be quick, she decided. She walked on to the chooks, checked for the waddy on her way in, then did the rounds. She got three eggs, the last just laid, warm in her hand. Coming out of the run, she looked at the spot where she'd seen Daisy at the edge of the creek. The girl was gone.

'Here, Missus,' a voice said, and Kate turned.

Daisy was sitting on a dead tree trunk, on its side in among the fallen trees between the creek and the chook run. She got to her feet, putting her weight on the pole for support. Kate went to her. Overhead, a family of galahs shrieked, chiacking from one tree to the next, filling the silence.

'You all right, Daisy?'

'Yeah, Missus.'

She was different from the girl Kate had last seen five months before. Big with the baby, of course, and wary of Kate. That was fair enough.

'You should stay. To have the baby,' Kate said.

'Yeah.'

She held out the eggs. 'Please. You have them.'

Daisy looked at her, her face unreadable. She didn't take the eggs. Kate swallowed. She leaned down and placed the eggs, one by one, in the dead grass at the edge of the track. 'They're for you. Please.' She walked away and left the girl, afraid to look back, but with every step she felt an almost physical pain. She knew now she cared so much for Daisy, and felt for her, for the hand she had been dealt. If Kate could undo the months since the young girl had arrived, she would.

CHAPTER 40

A sheep separated from its flock will panic, for it thrives, not unlike its human shepherds, only in the safety and comfort of the herd.

THE WOOLGROWER'S COMPANION, 1906

In the two days after Addison was seen off, and Daisy had arrived, Kate felt off kilter. Perhaps it was natural, she told herself as she went about her work. All those months with the fear of the bank taking Amiens? Now that her fear was gone, there would be some shock, surely, some adjustment. And there was Daisy. Ed seemed unworried by the impending birth. Kate was not.

The second afternoon, when she went into the garden, she didn't have the patience for light work. Instead, she had a go at the yellow trumpet vine that was now, despite the drought, spreading tentacles along the pipe that connected the roof to the tank. She took the ladder to the tank stand, dragging it round from the lean-to and across the dead lawn, propping it against the tank, shifting its feet about until it felt stable against the curve of the corrugated iron.

The ladder stayed put on the tank as she climbed, one careful rung at a time. From the top, she could see over the shrubs running along the fence line. On the other side, only forty feet away or so, the truck was pulled up in front of the shed, with its bonnet up, hiding Grimes's head as he worked, the sound of metal on metal. The heavy shed hose snaked out from the building, across the track, filling the trough for the bigger poddy lambs.

Kate got to work, clipping and pulling, pruning in an arc from her perch. When Luca came in through the gate, she waved at him from above.

'All right, *Signora*?' He put a hand on the ladder to steady it. 'I get clippers.' He glanced at the ladder and then disappeared briefly.

'Down now, *Signora*?' He waved his clippers up at her; he wanted to switch places.

'I'm almost finished. And it's pretty stable.'

He frowned and stayed put, clipping, always within an arm's length of the ladder. She went back to her work but out of the corner of her eye she saw a bicycle come up out of the gully. Vittorio. He rode across the house paddock up towards the shed, where Grimes was working on the truck. He had a bag hung from each of the bike's handlebars, and he cycled along the track, one hand holding a cigarette, the other steering.

'It'll be done soon,' Kate said to Luca at her feet. 'I tell you, really, you don't have to stay near the ladder.' But he did, and Kate went back to her cutting.

A noise made her look up. Now just past the truck, Vittorio had blown a raspberry at Grimes, loud and long.

Grimes swore at him and the sound carried into the garden.

'What do this?' Luca asked. The tankstand blocked his view. From atop the ladder Kate could see everything.

'Vittorio —' she started to explain, glancing down. But the dogs barked beyond the shed and there was another shout. Suddenly, Vittorio and his bike were on the ground at Grimes's feet, the heavy hose out of the trough, water running across the ground.

Vittorio got out from under the bike, wet patches on his trousers, brushing the dirt off his bag.

'C'mon, ya little dago,' Kate heard Grimes say. He dropped the hammer and, fists up, waved the POW to fight. 'Ya blew off at me, you pansy?' When Vittorio didn't move, Grimes gave him a shove and he stumbled backwards, still clutching his bag.

Gunner arrived, barking, confused.

'You'd better go over, Luca,' Kate said, and he went.

'What's in the bloody bag?' Grimes yelled. He grabbed at it with his left hand, and threw a punch with his right, landing it on Vittorio's chest.

'Stop it!' Kate shouted. Grimes didn't turn.

He threw another punch and Vittorio fell backwards onto the bike. Kate came down the ladder, jumping from the last rungs, and ran for the gate, throwing her clippers onto the lawn. When she came round the shrubs, Luca held his clippers in front of him like a knife. Behind him, Vittorio was on all fours, a cut bleeding above his eye. Luca and Grimes circled.

'Stop!' Kate yelled.

Grimes picked up his hammer and threw it hand to hand, his face red. 'You got your eyes on some skirt, you little wanker Canali? Wanna do time like that other bastard?'

Luca moved with him, ready, wary, the veins in his arms bulging as he gripped the open clippers in his hand. Grimes lunged at him with the hammer, but Luca swerved and got behind him, grabbing him round the neck with one arm, holding the clipper blades to his chest with the other. Grimes dropped the hammer but pulled at Luca's wrist, wrenching it off his chest. Grimes punched, fast and hard, up and over his shoulder at Luca's nose, and the clippers fell away. Free of Luca's lock, Grimes grabbed for a fistful of shirt and held on, landing another punch, but the shirt ripped, freeing Luca, revealing the deep scars across his chest. The two men circled again, and Grimes lunged another punch at the POW.

'Stop!' Kate yelled at them. 'Stop this now!' She grabbed the running hose, put a finger over it to increase the pressure and came at Grimes from the side, pushing the wide stream in his mouth.

He stepped back spluttering, turning from her, his shirt wet and filthy with dust.

'You will stop this, I tell you!' Her voice was low with anger.

Coughing, Grimes looked at her with contempt. 'Or what, Mrs D? Or bloody *what*?'

Luca, breathing hard, picked up the clippers. Ready.

Grimes spat. 'I quit, anyhow. I've had it.' He stalked away, shaking his head.

Kate was shaking. If Grimes quit, dear God, what would become of Harry?

~

As the last of the sun lit the horizon, the truck came to a slow stop at the homestead. Kate, in the veggie garden, could see the moving outlines of Johnno and Spinks in the truck tray as Ed limped over to her at the fence.

'Grimes quit?' Ed asked.

'Yes.' Kate looked at her fingers through the holes at the tips of the worn-out gloves. 'This afternoon. He won't be talked out of it.' She'd gone to the cottage to try. 'They go first thing tomorrow. You'll need to take them into town, if that's all right.' It occurred to her that with the bank closed on a Sunday, she'd have to use the five pounds they kept in the storeroom for emergencies to give Grimes what she owed him. Jack would have tried not to pay him but that wasn't right.

'Where's Harry?' Ed asked.

'I'm not sure. He took off, Luca said.' Kate didn't tell Ed that Luca had gone to find Harry, hoping to convince the boy to stay on Amiens, but Harry had already shot through somewhere. His uncle would never allow him to stay anyhow. 'What do you think Grimes'll do?'

'I dunno,' Ed said. 'No shortage o' work. There's a drove due in a coupla days from Canning Downs.'

'Droving? How could he take a child droving?'

'Bin done before. Harry's pretty handy round stock now, too.'

Kate pulled her gloves off. If they went droving, Harry would have to give up school. 'How's Daisy?' she asked.

'Orright. She reckons it's close, now.'

'Has she got help?'

'Aunty Nance comin tomorrow mornin.'

'Good. Good luck,' she said. If she were about to give birth without midwife or family around, Kate would be terrified. 'And I'm here too,' she added, wondering what help she'd be.

~

Kate got up early on the Sunday morning, just before five, thinking of Daisy, aware of each hour. She took a moment to stand at the kitchen door, her hands cradling a mug of hot tea, to listen to the sounds of the morning. She looked out across the Amiens garden, the house paddock, on to the crossing and the hills on the horizon, and felt a deep sadness at Harry's departure in a matter of hours.

Later, as Kate was preparing Grimes's last pay packet at the kitchen table, Ed tapped at the door, his hat in his big hands. He looked worried.

'You all right?' Kate asked.

'Daisy started at four o'clock this mornin.'

'Is the Aunty there yet?'

'Due this mornin too.'

'Where's Daisy?'

'Near the camp.'

'Can I go down? Would she have me?'

'Don't rightly know,' Ed said. 'Luca'll stay, within earshot. Least till Aunty Nance gets here.'

'I'm here if you need me. Ask her?'

Kate watched him walk back across the lawn and said a silent prayer for a safe delivery of the baby. She wondered – too late to ask – why it was Luca, not Ed, standing by?

~

An hour or so later, the truck, with Ed driving, stopped at the house gate. A few pieces of furniture stuck up from the truck tray, tied in for the trip to town. Harry sat in the front between Ed and Grimes. Kate hoped she'd get to say goodbye.

Grimes came up the verandah stairs, a lit pipe in his mouth; he no longer worked for her and could smoke where he liked. He counted his pay carefully, put the cash in the breast pocket of his shirt then signed the ledger. Taking a long drag on his pipe, he blew the smoke away from her. 'You shouldn't be ashamed, you know, Mrs D. About the bank and all that.'

So he had known about the debt. She kept her eyes on the ledger.

Then his voice was softer. 'It's not a job for a girl, runnin a place. You're a worker, orright, but you'll never do it.'

'We'll see.'

'I liked your old man, ya know. Bloody shame for ya when he started to lose his marbles.'

Kate looked up.

'I seen how he was. But I stuck it out for him. Now he's gone. No offence, but I'm not working for a girl.'

Kate didn't trust herself to say anything else. She stood up but Grimes wasn't finished. He took a puff on his pipe. 'I reckon Daisy's round here too, eh? I hear she's missin.'

'I haven't seen Daisy since you and I left her at the Home,' Kate said.

'Bloody Abos, eh? Remember Ed's Abo, too. He'll go

walkabout, f'sure. So if you reckon he's gunna stick around . . .'
Grimes shook his head.

Kate told herself he was trying to help her. 'Where will you go with Harry?'

'Now that's my business.' He put his hat on. 'Good luck to ya, Mrs D.' He walked back to the truck.

Kate followed him out to the fence. Harry sat in the truck cab next to Ed, with his eyes down.

'Goodbye, Harry,' Kate called. 'Good luck. Don't forget us, will you?'

He snuck a glance at her and wiped his nose on his sleeve. She tried not to cry herself; it would make it harder for him. Yet when the truck moved off towards the crossing, she couldn't hold her tears. After driving over the grid, the truck stopped and Grimes got out to tighten the tie-downs on their sticks of furniture.

With Grimes in the tray, Harry jumped down from the cabin and ran full pelt up the hill towards her. She came out of the gate and he grabbed her, more a tackle than a hug, his spikey hair prickling her chin. She held him tight until he pulled away and ran back to the truck.

CHAPTER 41

A 'new chum' woolgrower, standing as he does before an abyss of knowledge, may feel keenly the complexity of his vocation.

THE WOOLGROWER'S COMPANION, 1906

After lunch, with Harry's absence weighing on her, Kate spotted Vittorio on his way to the poddy lambs and she called for him to come.

The cut above his eye was a line of dried blood. He had a plaster on it, the edge of it caught up in the top of his beard sideburn.

'Is Aunty Nance there now? With Daisy?' she asked.

Vittorio frowned and looked off towards the shed and the pen.

'You know, Aunty Nance and so on? Are they here?'

'Aunty Nance,' he said, scratching his beard. '*Sì.*'

Kate was relieved. A little. 'So is the baby born? *Bambino?*' She rocked her arms, miming for him.

'*Sì, bene,*' Vittorio said, nodding.

'There's a baby?' Kate said, grabbing his wrist. 'Really? When?'

'No, no. *Nessun bambino.*' Vittorio rolled his eyes as if she were an idiot.

Kate gave up and abandoned him to the lambs. It was almost two o'clock, and Daisy had been in labour for ten hours. Kate knew little about babies, but ten hours was much too long for a ewe.

Luca did not turn up to garden, and Kate worried alone in the veggie beds, more and more concerned as the day stretched into the late afternoon. She hoped he was near Daisy and Ed, ready to do what he could. When she heard a vehicle just before five, she threw her gloves onto the lawn and ran for the gate.

The truck was pulled up at an odd angle to the shed, engine idling. It was Luca. He jumped down, leaving the cabin door open. '*Signora! Andiamo! Aunty Nance non è qui.*'

He was distracted. These were Italian words.

'Aunty Nance?' she said.

'She is no here! You come now!' He gestured for her to go with him.

Kate ran into the house, threw the kettle on and scrubbed her hands hard and fast with soap and hot water. She grabbed the basket she'd prepared early that morning, just in case: clean rag and a towel, a water bag, some bikkies, and now a Thermos of that warmish water. She delivered her basket and her father's tarp into the hands of Luca, and ran back into the kitchen.

'*Signora, rapidamente!*'

This time, she grabbed some dripping, mutton fat, from the kerosene fridge, hoping, dear God, she would not have to use the lubricant. Kate ran out with the mutton fat in her arms, and scrambled up into the cab.

Luca moved the truck off, as she pulled the cabin door shut. 'Is Daisy all right?'

But he said nothing, his concentration on the darkening track. The engine pitch climbed and Luca shifted up.

'Is the baby born?'

'No.' He would not look at her.

'Daisy has trouble?' Kate pressed. 'With the baby?'

Luca nodded. '*Sì.*'

Kate could say nothing. But she was fearful. How could she help?

As they approached the camp, Kate saw Johnno and Spinks squatting by the fire in front of the hut, the flames throwing red shadows across their shirts. Johnno gave a gentle wave at the truck, but Luca drove on.

'Stop,' Kate said, pointing. 'There's the camp.'

'No, no.' Luca hunched forwards, hands gripping the steering wheel.

Where was he going? There was nothing along this road for a mile or more. With no warning, Luca braked hard and put his arm in front of Kate to stop her from hitting the dash. He switched off the engine and jumped out, leaving his door open. He grabbed the tarp and jogged towards the creek. '*Presto!*' he called, and disappeared down between the black wattles. Worried she'd lose him, Kate followed in the dim light.

Down in the creek bed it was darker still, a canopy of wattles overhead. She found Luca and Vittorio. 'Where's Daisy?' she asked. Luca pointed beyond a fallen trunk. Daisy was squatting in the sand, hunched up against the tree, her huge belly in front of her, the dress tight around it, a small campfire just beyond.

'Where's Aunty Nance and the others?'

Ed frowned. 'We run into three Auntys on the way t'town t'day, me and Grimes, just inside the Amiens fence line. Grimes told em he'd call the cops if they didn't go back into town with us.'

Jesus. Ruddy Grimes. 'So where are they now?'

'Aunty Nance – she's one of em – woulden give in. She musta dropped off the truck, cos when we got t'town, we still had two but she were gone. I reckon she must be comin overland through the back paddocks, but she shoulda bin here now, eh? I'm gunna get a horse up into that country. Tracks are too rough for the truck.'

'Maybe send Spinks and Johnno? But first can you help me move Daisy to the camp or the house?'

'She won't go. She wants the baby birthed outside, on country like she was.'

'You sure?'

'Bloody sure.'

'But will Daisy even want me then?'

'She was askin for ya.'

Kate said nothing for a bit, silenced by Daisy's forgiveness. 'I can leave when the Auntys get here.'

'Aw, I reckon they'll want ya there, eh.'

She swallowed. That'd be the easy bit for Kate, after the Aboriginal midwives got there – for now she was on her own. 'Find Aunty Nance. Please.'

'Too right, Mrs D.'

Ed warned the POWs, 'You blokes make yourselves scarce too, eh.' He walked back along the creek bed. Vittorio followed at a clip, needing no encouragement to leave.

Luca must have seen her fear. 'I am here. Up. Behind.' He pointed to the top of the bank where the roots of the eucalypt spiked into the darkening sky. Then he ran his fingers along her jawline to her chin and touched her lips, just as he had done that day in the garden, before her father's funeral. '*Buona fortuna*,' he said.

Shocked again by the feeling of his fingers on her lips, Kate watched him walk away. With her basket, she went to the far side of the creek bed, and climbed through the branches of the dead tree. Daisy was still on her haunches, head back, eyes closed, her face washed out with pain.

'Daisy, it's me,' she said. Kate pushed a curl of her hair, matted with sweat and dust, gently behind her ear. The girl rolled her head over but didn't open her eyes. Kate poured a little water from the water bag onto a clean rag and wiped her forehead. 'Can you hear me?'

The girl's eyelids fluttered. She could not focus. When Kate took up Daisy's hand, she whimpered at the touch, then she grunted, sucking in a breath as a contraction started. She yelled something Kate didn't understand, and gripped her hand as the contraction went on. When it started to subside, Daisy panted with relief.

'You want some water, Daisy?' Kate got the bag and held it to her lips while she sipped a little, still puffing. Water spilled across her chin and down her front, yet she didn't notice. What should Kate check? Daisy was breathing all right. What was next? Birth sac. Holding the girl's hand in one of her own, she used the other to feel around on the ground, patting the dirt under Daisy's haunches. Dust and dry sand met her fingertips. 'Daisy,' she said as she mopped the girl's forehead gently, 'did you lose your water?'

The girl opened her eyes and gazed at her blankly.

'Did your water come?'

She dropped her head back. 'No water, Missus.' Then she pulled her head up, looking straight at Kate. 'You reckon e's orright, me baby?'

'For sure.' Kate squeezed the girl's hand and smiled. 'Right as rain. Just got to get himself born.'

Daisy inhaled sharply and gripped Kate's hand as another contraction came on. She yelled and panted through it, her knuckles white on Kate's, relaxing only when the pain ebbed. Kate looked at her watch again. Where was Ed?

CHAPTER 42

*Blood will tell. The progeny of even the boldest ram will disappoint if
he is put to ewes of poor fleece weight or low muscling.*

THE WOOLGROWER'S COMPANION, 1906

Kate glanced up into the gums on the bank but could not see
Luca, so she sat, holding the girl's hand, feeling worse than
useless. 'What can I do? Please tell me.'

Daisy dropped her head back and stretched her neck from
side to side. Kate shifted behind her, and leaned in to stroke
the girl's shoulders. There were no more contractions.

'Dais, I'm going to have a look. Underneath. All right?'

She didn't respond. Kate tried her best, but all she could see
in the fading light was the mass of black hair between Daisy's
legs. She wished the contractions would keep coming.

Daisy shivered, a shake that went across her body in the
failing light. Heat: Kate could do something about that. She
pulled one of the smaller branches of the dead tree and dragged
it to the fire. She watched, worried about the thirsty trees on
the creek beds catching.

'Missus.'

'Yes?' Kate came back from the fire and took Daisy's hand
again. The girl's breathing was more regular.

They sat for a few minutes in silence, Daisy looking with

blank eyes at the fire. Then she spoke. 'Ya mum alwus come, eh, for the bornins. Ya mum, an the Auntys.'

Kate nodded, not trusting herself to speak. She was glad that Luca was off in the trees. She felt stronger, knowing he was out there.

'An you come, eh, Missus?'

She nodded again and squeezed the girl's hand.

Daisy half-smiled and closed her eyes. Night approached. Kate did what she could. She wiped Daisy's forehead and gave her sips of water and rubbed her neck and back.

At last, lights from a vehicle snaked into the black sky. Kate heard Luca moving through the scrub towards the truck. The lights stopped still and Kate heard voices. Moments later, she could make out Luca and Vittorio in the creek bed and a little figure following behind.

As Aunty Nance came into the firelight, Kate could see her more clearly. An Aboriginal woman with white-grey hair, and a gait as quick as Luca's, she was short – no more than five feet – with stick arms and legs. She had a long string dilly bag on her back with a big coolamon in it, the flat of that shallow dish against her spine. She took the bag off, dropping it in the sand. Smiling at Kate, Aunty Nance moved by her to Daisy, clucking her tongue as she ran her hands over Daisy's face, under her nose, down her neck and over her belly. Then she stood and flailed her arms at the men, scowling, waving them away, and they disappeared into the darkness along the creek bed.

'Dais. Dais, littlie, y'orright, eh?'

Daisy opened her eyes and smiled at the woman, relief flooding her face.

Aunty Nance turned to Kate. 'Up now, girl.' She motioned Kate to help her get Daisy on her feet and together they did, one on either side. Daisy groaned in pain at the movement.

'To the house?' Kate asked.

The old woman shook her head. 'Birthin tree, Missus.' She patted the thick trunk of the tree. 'We stop ere, eh. Bornin here. On country.' She tightened her grip on Daisy's waist. 'Walk, daughter. Walk, eh.'

Daisy hung between them, staggering at first, more carried than walking. Then she put weight on each foot, more aware of where she was, every few steps followed by rest. She was lucid now, and calm. They kept up the routine for thirty minutes: a few minutes' walking, a few minutes' rest. Still there were no contractions.

'You got tucker, Missus?' Daisy asked. Kate rifled in her basket and brought out the brown paper bag of Anzac biscuits. Daisy chewed a little then drew in a breath. Aunty Nance clucked, pleased, yet Daisy swallowed a cry.

The old lady prompted, 'Sing out, daughter. All ya air.' So Daisy did then, yelling for her baby and for herself. When they next got her up, Aunty Nance coaxed the girl to put her hands on the thick branch above them, and she hung from it, her huge belly before her.

'Up, up, littlie,' Aunty Nance said and when Daisy stood, water glistened down the girl's leg.

The woman pulled Daisy down into a squat and had Kate kneel in front of her and take her arms, closing her fingers round the girl's elbows. Daisy leaned a little forwards, her eyes and weight on Kate for support, as Aunty Nance clucked and cajoled.

'Push em, Daisy! Don't stop!' Aunty Nance said and Daisy wailed with effort.

'Agin, eh. Push liddle bit!' Aunty Nance coaxed and the girl yelled, Kate knowing the fire of the pain as Daisy's grip tightened on her hands. At the end of the fourth hour, Kate sensed a change in Aunty Nance, an excitement. With one last groan, Daisy clamped hard on Kate's arms and clenched her teeth, pushing, a sheen of sweat shiny across her face. Daisy yelled with relief, panting and there was a short wet sound as she pushed the baby free into Aunty Nance's waiting arms.

Aunty Nance motioned with her head for Kate to lower Daisy onto the ground, while she looked hard at the baby, clucking. Even as Kate worried it was dead a tiny wail emerged, growing stronger. Aunty Nance smiled broadly and she gave the baby, a girl, to Daisy. She lay back, panting, the mewling baby pale in her arms, flickering wet in the firelight.

Aunty Nance rattled about in her dilly bag and produced a piece of sharpened rock, and cut the umbilical cord. She used the same blade to cut Daisy's dress, two vertical slits in the bodice, then levered each of the breasts through. She massaged the nipples, large and dark, until clear fluid came. Then she motioned to Kate to take the baby from Daisy.

Kate cradled the tiny wet thing, wanting to warm it against the night air. She ran her fingers over its body and to its tiny perfect feet, the soles paler still. Kate had never seen a real newborn. It was much paler than Daisy, but then Daisy was only part Aboriginal, and Ed even less. With Daisy moved nearer the fire, the old woman took the baby from Kate, placing her back in Daisy's arms, and coaxing the baby to take her mother's nipple.

Kate sat on the sand by the fire, a few feet from them, awash with relief. The baby was born and Daisy was all right. Daisy had done it the way she herself was born, on country.

As she watched them in the peace of their sleep, Kate wondered what would become of Daisy and her baby. She got up to find another branch to put on the fire. As she pulled it into the coals, a gust rattled the canopy of leaves above her and Kate looked up at a thousand stars planted across the blackness, each perfect and in its rightful place. She felt a sudden phys-ical longing for that rightness, to be like Daisy, connected to the land and the generations before her. She stood and made a tiny wave with her hand – I'm going – but Aunty Nance motioned her over. Smiling, she took Kate's hands and placed them on the baby. The infant's skin was warm and damp to her touch.

Kate stroked the tiny thing, patted Daisy's arm and then gathered her things. As she came over the top of the bank, she heard a voice a few feet ahead of her. She could see little, her eyes used to the light of the fire.

'*Signora.*'

Luca. He'd been waiting. His hand found hers. 'OK?' he asked.

She swallowed to speak. 'It's a girl.'

'*Molto bene.* Very good.' She could see enough now – the truck was ahead of them – but still Luca didn't let go. He stopped next to the truck and looked at her, turning her arm over in his hand. He ran his fingers from the inside of her elbow to her palm. Then he squeezed her hand and let it go.

After a pause, Kate was able to speak. 'Where's Ed?' She had to tell him he had a daughter.

'To the town.'

Of course, his baby is born, and he disappears, Kate thought. 'Vittorio?'

'He sleep.' He took her round. Vittorio lay in the back in the truck tray. Luca waggled one of the sleeping man's boots.

Vittorio stirred and pushed himself up onto his elbows to look at them blearily. '*Bambino?*'

'*Sì, bambino,*' Kate said.

'*Una bambina,*' Luca corrected her. 'Girl.'

Vittorio laughed and began to chatter. '*Una bambina. Daisy ha una bellissima bambina.*'

Luca fired up the truck engine, the noise loud in the stillness of the night. He moved the truck off slowly, driving up past the camp towards the single men's quarters and the homestead. Driving at night was like diving into an inkwell, her father had said. She felt entirely at peace with Luca in the darkness.

'All right, Daisy?' he asked.

'I think so.'

He stopped outside the single men's quarters to drop Vittorio. Kate was grateful Luca would take her home alone. 'Can you warn him? He can't tell anyone about the baby. The police will take it if they find out.'

'*Non dire a nessuno di questo bambina,*' Luca said out of the truck window to Vittorio. '*Se lo scoprono i poliziotti prendono la bambina.*'

'*Sì, sì.*' Vittorio disappeared with a yawn into the quarters.

Luca put the vehicle into gear again. 'Police take the babies?'

'The baby might be in danger.'

'Daisy is danger?' He looked incredulous.

Kate shrugged. 'That's what they think.'

'The Romani,' Luca said. 'In *Italia*, they do with the Gypsies. Take children. Me? I think babies, they stay better, you know?'

Kate looked down at her hands, ashamed. She agreed. No one else seemed to.

Luca pulled the truck up to a stop by the homestead gate. When he switched off the engine, she felt her stomach jump. They sat in silence for a time. Kate was conscious of her hand on the bench seat between them. She wanted him to move his hand to hers.

A spate of raindrops pinged the truck cabin roof. 'I'd best go in,' she said. She wanted him to come with her. Still, she said nothing, just pushed open the truck door and climbed down. She walked to the house, neither hurrying nor dawdling, hoping. There was no sound behind her. Inside, she stood against the closed door with her hand on the doorknob, and waited, listening.

CHAPTER 43

The measure of a good woolgrower may best be found in the character of his flock, in the strength of line.

THE WOOLGROWER'S COMPANION, 1906

The next morning when Kate woke, her body ached as if she'd been lambing. She opened her eyes, surprised by the amount of light in her room, and sat up.

Her head was fuzzy with tiredness. She'd had trouble getting to sleep, her thoughts full of Luca. She'd waited for him in the dark of the kitchen until finally she'd heard the truck's ignition. She wondered how Daisy was, and her beautiful baby.

Mid-morning, she saw the Amiens truck trundle by, empty but for Ed at the wheel. She ran into the garden and flagged him down, to congratulate him.

She went out the gate and looked up at him in the driver's seat, as he leaned on the window, the engine idling.

'You should be so proud, Ed! Of your baby.'

Ed's surprise shook Kate.

'You didn't know?'

He looked perplexed.

'She's beautiful. And Daisy was tough as nails.'

Ed swallowed hard. He turned the ignition off, and opened the truck door to climb down next to her.

'I think we better go in, Mrs D,' he said.

'What?'

He went ahead, and she could not understand it. Was he mad? Going into the homestead? But she followed into the kitchen.

'What's all this, Ed? Babies are born every day. You'll be all right.'

He seemed to have something unpalatable to say. He inhaled and looked at his boots. 'It's not mine, Mrs D, that baby.'

'What?' The kitchen grew small. Ed shook his head, pulled out a chair and motioned her to sit. He cleared his throat. 'The baby's not my kin. It's yours.'

Kate felt a physical pain in her chest. Somewhere off by the shed, a dog barked, and she heard her own shallow breaths, loud in the kitchen.

'You people got any grog in the place?' he said.

Grog. Always grog. Kate looked towards the dining room. Ed was soon back with her father's brandy. He took the tea cup off the sink, poured and pushed the cup across the table towards her. 'Drink it.'

She reached for the cup with shaking hands.

'C'mon. One go.'

She gulped, trying to swallow it like cod liver oil, and got half of it down but coughed, the spirit burning her throat.

'Did. Does Jack —?' she managed to say.

'Jack?' Ed said, shocked. 'It weren't Jack. It were ya father.'

Kate gasped, staring; she could not believe him.

Ed shook his head, frowning. 'Why'd ya think Aunty Nance 'n' Dais let yez down there, eh? Like it or not, that baby's y'sister.'

He poured her another tot of the brandy, put the bottle on the metal of the kitchen sink and left her.

~

Hardly was he gone, that Kate got angry. She threw the brandy into the sink. Why would he say such a terrible thing? Ed was lying. He had to be. Her father would never do that. Have relations with an Aboriginal girl? *Rape* her? Ed must be mad. Kate gulped in a cry.

Her father? It was true he'd been less and less himself, especially towards the end. But this? Bastard. How dare Ed? After all her father had done for him . . .

She thought of the times she'd seen her father and Daisy together. There weren't so many that she remembered: Daisy had made herself scarce when Kate's father was around. She seemed almost . . . afraid of him. Kate gasped. The bruises. The bruises on Kate's arms. And on Daisy's.

No, Kate could not believe her father capable of it. Daisy was afraid of her father, yes, nothing more – she was afraid of a lot of people, men in particular. Daisy was shy, that was it. But then . . . Kate thought of her father's odd comment that morning in the kitchen, the day after the POWs arrived. He'd been encouraging Daisy to eat more. What had he said? A man likes something to hold on to. Kate drew her breath in. He couldn't have meant . . . He *couldn't*.

Kate stared unseeing into space. Daisy was only fourteen, a child. She thought of her after Kate's Sydney trip, Daisy sitting at the kitchen table, weeping silently, refusing to tell Kate what had happened, her wrists a map of bruises. Kate hid her face in her hands. Jesus.

She sat for a long time, unable to take it in. Her father had raped Daisy. Raped her. She closed her eyes, trying to block out the image of his attack, or attacks, on poor Daisy. She got up, and looked about blankly. She put the kettle on the stove. Had he always done this? Was Daisy one of many? God almighty. A sound penetrated the fog of Kate's head. A noise. A whistle. It was the kettle, the kettle boiling. She lifted it off, making tea she would not taste, even if she could bring herself to drink it. Now, this baby. Her father's child, evidence of his violence, embodiment of it. Her mother's heart would have broken.

Nonetheless, this baby was Kate's sister. She put her head in her hands again. How she'd wished for a little sister or brother when she was small. And now she had a sister. A black sister. Kate shook her head. And what about the Board? The Aboriginal Welfare Board was strict; half-caste children, especially fair babies like this one, were put up for adoption to be raised as whites, far away from the mothers. At least on Amiens, Daisy and the baby could hide for a few days or weeks until perhaps they could go to Daisy's family out west. Now their safety mattered even more. God forbid that Daisy thought Kate knew. Kate hoped they were all right, mother and baby, and she wanted to see them both. But she must let Daisy decide if she wanted that. Kate would talk to Ed.

~

Late that day, Kate was relieved to see Luca come in through the gate to work in the garden. She'd been waiting for him, wanting to talk. But oddly, now that he was there, she was at a loss as to where to begin. She shovelled out a garden bed border instead, with intensity.

Luca watched her for a bit then he spoke. '*Signora*?' he asked softly. 'What is this?'

'This? The garden bed.'

'No. Your trouble. What is this?'

'Luca. I can't tell you. Really. There's too much.'

'*Signora*, say me. You say me everything. We have this time.'

As he gently dug in front of her, she spoke, putting into words things she'd never dreamed she'd need to say. That she was so very ashamed of her father, and of what he'd done to Daisy. That she feared what might happen to Daisy and the baby. Kate's sister. That she still worried for Amiens, for the men who worked on it. Even if they managed to make it pay, the drought might break them yet.

Luca listened, digging. She knew he would not understand it all. But he seemed to know it helped to unburden herself to him. He gave her solace.

'Thank you,' she said. 'For listening.'

Luca straightened up, and leaned across to pat her hand. She felt the warmth of his touch.

'*Non è un problema, Signora,*' he said. The Amiens truck appeared, coming round from the men's quarters. Ed braked to a stop, got himself down from the cabin and limped across to them. 'Afternoon,' he said, leaning his big arms on the top rail of the fence.

'Aunty Nance still there?' Kate asked.

'I'll givera lift into town tonight, eh.'

Kate brushed the dirt off her holey gloves. 'Can you get her some rations too, as a thank you?'

'Orright.'

'Where's Daisy?' Kate said, not game enough yet to ask to see them.

'She's still down the creek.'

'She's not going to try for Broken Hill yet, is she? To get back to her family?'

'Nuh. The cops'd pick her up on the way for sure.'

Kate was conscious of Luca behind her. 'Do you think . . . do you think she might stay on Amiens? If I asked? I mean, for now.'

Ed nodded slowly. 'She'll wanna hear it straight from you, eh, Mrs D.'

'All right. What about the manager's cottage? That's empty. It's still got a bit of our furniture, though – there's enough there for her to be comfortable.'

'You two betta talk first, eh.'

'What's the baby's name?' Kate asked.

'Dunno. I'll bring em here.'

'Ed,' she called after him. 'I . . . I'm sorry,' she said. 'I thought . . .'

He shook his head, dismissive. 'Ya reckon I done it, Mrs D? Why ya think that, eh?'

She had no reply. She knew she'd misjudged Ed, just as she'd misjudged Luca, months before.

~

At dusk, as the swallows and bats swooped in the half-light, Ed returned in the truck with Daisy and the baby. Kate took a deep breath and went to the fence. Luca took the baby from Daisy like a man handling china; his face was alight with pleasure, and Kate felt a pang of sadness to see it. He held out the baby over the fence to Kate but she shook her head. She couldn't hold this child, not yet, not with the images of Daisy and her father that she could not get out of her mind.

Luca cuddled the child once more but the move had startled the baby, and her eyes grew large. For a second, to Kate's shock, the baby had a fleeting look of her own father. His eyes? Something.

The baby whimpered. '*Bambina*,' Luca cooed to her, '*bella bambina*.' He put his hand above the palm of the baby, and smiled when two tiny fingers closed around his. Kate blanched, forcing another image of her father with Daisy out of her head.

Daisy came to them and took the baby but the whimpering went on. Ed and Luca retreated to the far side of the truck. The breeze ruffled Daisy's hair. Kate remembered pushing a curl away behind an ear, down the creek when she was in labour. Now the girl looked intermittently exhausted, afraid and angry, her full breasts pressing against her shift dress. It was not even a year before that Daisy had arrived on Amiens, aged fourteen. Now she was a mother, a child–mother, and that by rape.

She rocked the whimpering baby, her eyes watchful. Kate knew Daisy didn't want to be beholden to her, and, in some way, Kate didn't want them on Amiens, a living reminder of her father's violence.

Her eyes still on Kate, Daisy clucked at the baby, yet the whimpering went on. 'You gunna tek her, Missus? Grow her?' she asked.

Her words startled Kate and she froze. She knew what that meant, knew what it must cost Daisy to say it.

'S'orright, Missus,' Daisy said, her eyes narrow, fearful.

Kate dropped her head, feeling the weight of her own failings. Daisy, at fifteen, was brave enough to give her baby to Kate to save her from being adopted. But Kate herself could not decide. She did not know if she had the courage to take on this child, to raise a half-caste when no one did such things. And then she caught herself. Child? Half-caste? Whatever she called her, this baby was her sister.

'You gunna, Missus? You gunna tek her?'

'I'm so sorry.' Kate swallowed, ashamed. 'I don't know.' She looked at the baby. 'Will you – can you – can you stay here on Amiens? For now?'

Daisy didn't move, not a yes or a no, just a sway to quieten the baby.

'What's her name?' Kate asked.

'Pearl, Missus,' Daisy said. 'If ya like.'

Kate smiled. 'Pearl is lovely. Perfect for her,' she said.

Daisy nodded.

'Ed could take you and Pearl to the manager's cottage for a few days. If you wanted.'

Daisy was still, her face wary. Kate guessed she might have preferred to be with her, in the homestead, for company and for familiarity. While Kate could not bring herself to do that, not yet, she didn't want Daisy to go. And the girl had guts. She just might set off for Broken Hill, no matter the risks.

'Please stay. Please.'

Pearl decided it for them. She started to cry again, and she would not be placated this time. Daisy went to the truck where Ed was waiting.

Luca came inside the fence and stood with Kate to watch the truck go off towards the manager's cottage. 'Good,' he said to Kate. 'This is good.' Back to work, he picked up his hoe, swinging it in an easy arc in the air, stopping only to wipe sweat from the bridge of his nose.

'It's only for now,' Kate warned. It would not be long before someone got wind that Daisy and the baby were there. And then the police would come, the baby would be adopted out, and the Aboriginal Welfare Board would place Daisy on another property, far away, indentured again. God almighty. Kate could not bear to think of it, just as she could not see how to stop it.

CHAPTER 44

The prudent woolgrower is heedful of an animal's prime wool-producing ages, for upon reaching four years, a sheep's fleece grows dryer and coarser. For a black sheep, the fleece grows paler with the years as well, not unlike the mane of an aging shepherd.

THE WOOLGROWER'S COMPANION, 1906

Early the following morning, Kate sat eating her toast in the kitchen, with Peng on the chair next to her. A kookaburra launched into a laugh and Peng looked up. But Kate was thinking about Harry, wondering where he was, hoping he was all right. Her thoughts were interrupted by a baby's cry carrying in from outside. Pearl.

When Daisy came into the kitchen, with Pearl in her arms, she looked exhausted.

'Dais, you're not thinking of working? You mustn't,' Kate said, getting up. She was thrilled to see them, yet worried about the unhappy baby, and more worried about Daisy.

'Orright, Missus,' Daisy said, forlorn, rocking Pearl as she stood.

'You should rest,' Kate tried again but Daisy didn't leave and Pearl's wails grew louder, stopping only when her mouth tried to suck.

'She not drinking?' Kate asked.

344

'No, Missus,' Daisy said, close to tears.

'Maybe you can stay for a bit, eh? Dais?'

Relief flooded the girl's face.

'I'll get you some tea. Sit down and rest.'

Daisy looked alarmed. Still Kate pressed her to sit, with Pearl, crying, in her arms. Peng disappeared into the hall, her ears flat with unhappiness at the noise.

Kate poured tea for the girl. 'Here you go. Now, I'll leave you in peace so you can feed her, Daisy.'

She went into the laundry, embarrassed to even be mentioning the feeding. Kate folded washing, and worried as the baby's broken crying went on. From what she could guess, Pearl wanted to suckle, but couldn't and then she'd cry, frustrated, hungry and tired. Kate stood in the laundry with a clean tea towel unfolded in her hand, feeling her ignorance afresh. She knew nothing about babies, but she didn't want to intrude, either. Daisy's bosoms would be bare, for heaven's sake. Then she heard Daisy crying and Kate found her gumption.

'Can I come in, Daisy?'

'Yeah, Missus,' came the weary reply.

Daisy's hooded eyes and drawn face made Kate forget her embarrassment. Pearl was unable to feed, her tiny mouth stretched wide, arms flailing. She couldn't stay latched on, her mouth grappling with the nipple, missing it again and again. As Pearl shrieked in frustration, Daisy switched her about, trying one side after the other. Wincing with the pain, she massaged each engorged breast and milk leaked down her front. Kate wanted to offer to hold Pearl. Try as she might, she just couldn't. A horrible mix of guilt and shame stopped her from touching the baby.

Still Pearl would not suckle. Kate knew she couldn't go to anyone for help, for fear it would get back to Wingnut that Daisy was on Amiens. Kate got clean tea towels and some water and made fresh tea. She did what she could, feeling her uselessness more keenly as the hours passed. By late morning, when Pearl still couldn't suckle, Kate grew fearful, as worried as Daisy beside her. How could they solve this? *The Pastoralist* wouldn't help, but the *Women's Weekly* might.

Kate listened for the Amiens truck until she heard its slow rumble. 'I'm going to try to get a magazine, Daisy. To see what we can do.'

Daisy hardly heard her.

Outside on the lawn, Kate waved madly at the truck, so wildly Ed jumped from the cabin, followed closely by Luca. 'You got a snake, Mrs D?'

She smiled ruefully. 'No, no. Pearl won't feed. Aunty Nance has gone, hasn't she?'

'Yeah. I give her a lift in last night. The little bugger was doin what it should yesterday. What happened, eh?'

'I don't know. But I've got an idea. Can you get me the box of Mum's *Women's Weekly* magazines from the shed? There might be some tips in that.'

'Ya reckon? She'll get the hang of it soon, eh?' But Ed went off in the direction of the shed anyway.

'Not the worry, *Signora*,' Luca said, following Ed. 'Many babies in the world.'

Why was it always men, Kate wondered, who knew everything, even about newborns they'd not borne? She watched Luca walk towards the shed. When she found her eyes on his bottom, she had some stern words for herself. In no time, the two men were back, Luca carrying a box of her mother's old magazines. Ed had two beer bottles in one hand and a small box in the other.

'I don't think beer is going to help, Ed,' Kate said as she took the carton from Luca.

Ed grinned. 'No, Mrs D. They're empties. To feed the littlie. Look.' He held out the box and it was full of rubber teats. 'They're poddy lamb teats. That might work, eh?'

'Yes.' Kate almost hugged him, and took the bottles and the small box.

'We'll keep an eye on yez today. Drive by the house as we're comin an goin. If ya need anything. Orright?'

Kate nodded, so grateful for their help.

Luca smiled at her. 'Many babies, *Signora*.'

Back inside, Kate showed the bottles and the teats to Daisy. 'Not a bad idea of Ed's?' she said to Daisy. The girl was too tired to reply.

Kate boiled the teats to sterilise them. 'I can put water in the bottle, Daisy. But that's not food . . .'

'Bidda sugar, Missus. Mebbe,' Daisy said, over Pearl's crying.

Kate boiled some water, dissolved some sugar in it, and fanned it to cool. She poured the solution into the beer bottle, fixed the poddy lamb teat on the top and handed it to Daisy.

Daisy put the bottle teat gently into Pearl's wailing mouth. Pearl's eyes widened as she latched on and sucked at the boiled sugar water from the beer bottle. The bottle gave them blessed silence for a bit, but they both knew it wouldn't satisfy her for long.

When the bottle was finished, Pearl slept, exhausted from hungry crying. Daisy closed her hooded eyes. Kate was pleased, hoping Daisy might get a little rest.

At the kitchen table opposite, Kate quietly turned the pages of the *Women's Weekly*, copy after copy. Then she found an article headed *Guidance for New Mothers*, about feeding.

To avoid spoiling, ensure firmness when dealing with the newborn. Kate rolled her eyes.

Adhere rigorously to a strict feeding timetable. She laughed. But it was the last sentence that caught her eye. *Cabbage leaves may sometimes assist the mother of an uncooperative newborn.*

Cabbage. Kate got up as quietly as she could and went out into the garden. As she walked along the veggie rows, the family of lorikeets tree-hopped and screeched. Kate scowled at them. They'd better not wake Daisy or the baby . . .

But soon Pearl was awake. She needed changing and Daisy did that in the laundry. She was coaxing a crying Pearl to take more sugar water. The baby was tired of it; she was still hungry, and she grew more and more unsettled. Daisy had a towel over her breasts for modesty but it soon fell off, and Kate gave it back to her.

'Don't worry,' she heard herself saying. 'As long as you don't mind.'

Fretful and hungry, Pearl would not suckle or even take any sugar water. And the *Women's Weekly* article was so coy, it was impossible for Kate to know what to do with the damn cabbage. Desperate, she par-boiled a little of it with butter and salt, willing it to cook faster as Pearl hiccupped angry wails.

When it was done, Daisy swallowed some mouthfuls, feeding herself with one hand, rocking the shrieking Pearl with the other. Daisy put the cabbage aside and gave all her attention again to Pearl, trying to keep her tiny mouth on the nipple.

A few drops of milk found their way onto Pearl's tongue and, with the next attempt, she opened her mouth very wide and latched on, so fast and hard that Daisy gasped, 'Missus!'

Pearl pulled away again, wailing, but her mother coaxed her back on and this time she stayed, her mouth sucking and pushing like a poddy lamb on a bottle. Pearl batted her mother's bosom with tiny hands as she sucked. Daisy's eyes widened and she looked across the table in a glorious silence.

'You've got it,' Kate marvelled.

'S'orright, Missus.' Daisy smiled but she didn't take her eyes from the small thing chomping away at her breast. She inhaled deeply. Kate was grateful this had happened on Amiens, that Daisy had been able to settle Pearl down and get her feeding there. What had Luca said? We have this time. She was grateful for it. It struck her that in all the time she'd been worried about Pearl, she'd not thought of her father, and what he'd done.

And she'd not thought either about Wingnut. She shivered. He must find out eventually, and come for Daisy and Pearl. What could she do?

CHAPTER 45

A new lamb may show vigour, if attended to in a timely fashion by the ewe. But the vigilant grazier watches carefully. A lamb grows apace weak as well as strong.

THE WOOLGROWER'S COMPANION, 1906

Kate learned that a few hours are a long time in a baby's life. A change was wrought in Pearl; the baby ate and slept and ate and slept, and grew stronger and stronger. Daisy managed to sleep a little when the baby did, and looked all the better for it.

Then, late in the day, Vittorio appeared at the homestead carrying what looked like a modified fruit crate. On the verandah, he set the thing down in front of Kate and Daisy, who had Pearl in her arms. The wood had been sanded and the open-top box attached firmly to two long arcs of carved wood made from barrel hoops. He beamed, leaned down, and with a flourish set the thing rocking.

'It's a cradle,' Kate said. Daisy was thrilled, and it went into the corner of the kitchen.

'Beautiful, no?' Vittorio said. He ran a finger along the rocker, pointing out the row of tiny birds on the wing carved into the wood. 'Luca,' he said, admiringly.

Kate thought of the little carved dog that Harry had appeared with, after Rusty died. It must have been Luca.

350

She looked out across Amiens, wondering where Harry was, hoping he was all right.

~

The next morning, Kate was up early, had eaten, prepared some more cabbage and cleaned the kitchen, all before Daisy was due with Pearl, in case they'd had a bad night. This time, though, it was Daisy's singing that carried across the flat, not Pearl's wail. It occurred to Kate that she had never heard Daisy sing before.

'You slept a bit?' Kate asked, when Daisy appeared at the kitchen door with the baby swaddled to her back.

'Yeah, Missus.' Daisy smiled – she looked almost rested.

'Are you sure she's safe in that thing?' Kate asked. Daisy had Pearl wrapped inside a wooden coolamon fastened to her back with a shawl.

'Yeah, Missus. Me nana carried Mum that way too. Mum too. S'orright, eh.'

'Now, nothing strenuous, will you? Just look after Pearl and yourself,' Kate said. But she knew that was like telling Daisy not to breathe. She sat at the end of the kitchen table and spread the Amiens bills in front of her. She might have Addison off her back for now, but she still had to make Amiens pay.

Daisy got to work sweeping and mopping around Kate. The baby seemed quite happy on her back and was soon asleep. Kate kept on with her bills. A few minutes later, out of the corner of her eye, Kate saw Peng sniffing at Pearl's empty cradle. The cat's haunches wiggled as she lined up to jump in.

'Peng, no,' Kate called but it was too late. The cat was in and out immediately when the rocker tipped with her weight. Peng scuttled from the kitchen.

A wail came from Pearl and Daisy chatted to the baby. 'Now, tiddlie, ya not gunna whinge, are ya? Eh?' But the baby continued to cry, and Daisy untied the shawl that held the coolamon to her back and jiggled Pearl on her hip instead. 'See? Y'orright, eh, tiddlie?'

Pearl didn't let up. 'Sorry, Missus,' Daisy said over the wails.

'Does she want a feed?' Kate still hadn't been able to hold the baby, not once, not since she'd found out about her father. This sin was hers, and she felt a crushing shame.

'Nuh, she jus cranky. I bin busy this arvo. Probly wants a cuddle, eh.'

Kate was glad for Daisy that things were better, and that Daisy was almost chatty. She had seen the day before just how hard it was. Pearl fussed when she went to sleep, and Daisy would fret, struggling as she learned to mother her baby.

Daisy put the chops on a plate and slipped it into the warming oven. Then she laid Pearl, still grumbling, in the cradle and rocked her gently. Pearl quieted and put her fist in her mouth. 'Right as rain, eh? Aren't ya?' Daisy smiled at the baby. 'I'm gunna get the washin, Missus. Might be we get little bit rain tonight, eh.'

Kate rested her eyes on the bills. The Nettiford's account was up-to-date so she put that in one pile. Babbin's was not. She still owed him for the bales and baling twine from the previous year's shearing. She drew in a breath. Next to her, Pearl grumbled, and Kate rocked the cradle.

Shearing would be upon them soon, and Kate would need the shearers' wages, the bales, twine, and fencing wire. Pearl was whimpering, and Kate began rocking again. Then the baby started to cry. Kate exhaled. 'Pearl, you're grumbling, aren't you, wombat?' When she squatted down next to the cradle, Pearl quietened, diverted for a moment, looking up with her mother's deep-brown eyes. Kate smiled at her and was rewarded with a yawn. But the yawn set off a wail, first a little one, then bigger with each baby breath.

'How can that noise come from something so tiny? Hey?' Kate said, hoping Daisy would come in soon from the washing line.

Pearl took a breath and gave an almighty bellow. Kate hesitated, then reached out and picked up the baby. She nursed her in her arms, but Pearl squirmed, and Kate remembered the baby didn't like to be on her back. So she lifted her, held her against her neck, the smell of milk and baby filling her nostrils. Pearl quietened for a second, the change mollifying her.

Then she started to wail again. 'There, there, there,' Kate said, her voice soft but an octave up. Pearl still wailed, so she walked about the kitchen. 'Look? Here's the stove. And the kero fridge. And here's the gauze door. And outside, there's old Gunner at the fence. See?'

The dog moved, though, heading off towards the shed. Kate wondered if there was a drop of rain about, as Daisy had guessed. Pearl relaxed against her, warm and soft, and Kate remembered the baby when she was born, in the glow of the fire in the creek bed. Then Kate heard the rain, one drop, then another and another ping against the tin roof.

'Rain, Pearl. You heard that?' Kate carried the baby outside towards the clothes line, where Daisy was rapidly pulling the washing off.

'Rain, Dais!' Kate yelled, pleased, as the drops gathered force.

'Yeah, Missus.' The girl's face broke into a broad smile, and Kate retreated back to the safety of the house as it started to come down, her hand above Pearl's head to protect her from the drops.

'Mebbe letta feel it, eh, Missus?' Daisy dropped the basket of dry washing just inside the laundry door, came back to Kate, and took the baby in her arms. 'Rain, littlie. Rain.'

The women laughed as the baby's face clouded, her eyes blinking wildly, taking in the strange drops that fell on her. It was gone as soon as it started. Still, there was enough for Kate to wipe a raindrop from Pearl's forehead. We have this time, Kate thought.

~

Late that same afternoon, Kate would much rather have been out in the garden, but she had to write to Jack; she'd put it off long enough. Daisy came in from the laundry with a basket of fresh washing, two-day-old Pearl snug on her back.

'Orright, Missus?'

'Yep. Pearl asleep?'

Daisy grinned, shook her head, and turned her back to show the baby. Kate smiled at Pearl as the baby sucked on her fingers, her dark eyes serious.

'Is she hungry?'

'Soon, Missus. But she sing out then, eh.'

Kate made herself go back to her letter-writing. It had taken her long enough to even put pen to paper. It was six days since Wingnut had stopped Addison from seizing Amiens. Every day since, she'd intended to write to Jack, to tell him Amiens was safe. But every night, as she got into bed, she realised she had not. She'd heard nothing from Jack since her father's funeral. They were like bad neighbours, both looking the other way but joined all along their boundary.

She read over what she'd written.

Dear Jack

I hope you're well. I have news here. The best of it is that I found the sapphire. Meg sold it in Sydney and I gave the money in to Addison, paying off the overdraft, with a little to spare. And we've had some rain, bits here and there, enough to make me hopeful.

I work out on the run with the men every day. Grimes has left. I hear he plans to join the next drove coming through.

That made Kate think of Harry. She worried for him, and pushed herself to read on.

The Italians will be shipped out soon, in less than a week. There are more and more returned servicemen home now, discharged, so I'll be able to find people to work the place with Ed and me and Johnno and Spinks, perhaps even Robbo Yorke, if he doesn't want to work for his father. And of course you'll be discharged eventually too, once they have enough men trained for the occupation of Japan.

She didn't write that she'd found the sapphire when he was home, that day at the end of the wake. And she didn't write that she was hiding Daisy and Pearl on Amiens. Both would make him mad. With Daisy and Pearl, Kate told herself it was in case the letter went astray and someone found out they were on Amiens. But, in truth, Kate had decided not to tell him. He would tell her, *instruct* her, to give them up, and she knew now she could not. If he made her choose, he would regret it.

So far they'd managed to keep it quiet about Daisy and Pearl. But for how long? Her fool's paradise must come to an end. The Italians would leave in just five days. Shearing was a matter of weeks away. And Jack would come home. Her guess was he'd still want her to sell up so they could be gone. He just didn't want to stay in the district, not after her father's disgrace. And he didn't even know about Pearl.

Kate put the letter back on the table, thinking. If she accepted Pearl into the family, she'd destroy what little respectability was left in the Amiens name. With a sickening feeling, it occurred to Kate that Jack could refuse to return to Amiens if she allowed Pearl to stay, that he might even divorce her. Her face burned to think of it. Whether because of Pearl or a divorce, Kate would be ostracised. There'd be no prospect of remarriage, and no children.

She heard the gate go again. Luca, there to work. She scribbled *Regards, Kate*, on the bottom of the letter and began to put it into the envelope, but changed her mind. *Regards* would send Jack off, even if nothing else did. She rubbed out *Regards* and wrote *Love*. Then she licked the envelope so fast she cut her tongue, sealed it and put it on the counter with the others for Mick Maguire on Saturday.

She got her gloves and went into the garden, bats in the sky above her. Luca was already at work, extending the bean trellis, his face serious, looping string from one upright to the next to take the beans as they pushed upwards.

She smiled at him, struggling to accept that he would be gone in days. 'Where's Vittorio? Cooking?'

'*Sì*.'

Vittorio had taken to cooking for the place in the evenings, since her father's death and it was a help, all round, now that Daisy was busy with Pearl. Luca delivered the meals, one to Daisy at the manager's cottage and one to Kate.

Luca glanced across at the clothes line. Daisy was hanging out washing, hauling white sheets up onto the line, talking all the while to Pearl on her back.

'What you do, *Signora*? They take them? The policeman?' Luca knotted a piece of rope close to an upright and cut the ends short with his clippers.

'Sooner or later.' Kate got down on the kneeler and reached for the base of some Mayne's curse. 'Word'll get out eventually.'

He unravelled more string from the roll at his feet. 'Then you tell no,' he said.

When Kate laughed, it came out a gulp. 'It doesn't work like that. It's not my choice.'

He shrugged. She could not just keep Daisy and Pearl; the law favoured the Aboriginal Welfare Board. Even so, she felt responsible and she hated her father for that.

'*Una bambina minuscola*,' Luca said. He was looping the string around the upright and tying it off at intervals of six inches or so. 'You help. *Sì?*'

Kate shook her head. It was impossible. 'Pearl is a quarter-caste, so she will be put up for adoption. I'd have to adopt her myself. Even then the Board might not let Daisy stay here. Chances are they'd move her far away and she'd never see Pearl again.'

Luca said nothing, just tied off the string at the top of the next upright.

'And I've never heard of anyone who did this,' Kate said. Apart from the McGees, and no one would have anything to do with them.

'No black *bambini* with the white *papá*?' Luca laughed.

'Not that.' That was not what she meant, and he knew it.

'Fight one war. Then more,' Luca said.

'You mean fight one battle at a time?'

'*Sì*.'

She could not see a solution, and it made her sick to her stomach. She couldn't think about it. 'I need to ask you about something else,' she said eventually.

'*Sì?*'

She pulled at the roots of a weed that had embedded itself next to the base of a bean stalk. 'We . . . We can sponsor you.'

'Sponse?'

'Sponsor. You and Vittorio, help you to come back to Australia after the war.' It was madness – Jack would not agree. Still, she had to offer, to do the right thing. Her father would expect that of her. Doing the right thing, and her father; the two were at odds now, and she felt sad. 'But if you wanted to come back, you could, you know.' She rattled on, trying to read him.

He began to shake his head. '*Grazie, Signora.*'

She felt a weed stalk break off in her fingers.

'*Grazie.*' He gave her his sad half-smile. 'What I want?' He

357

shrugged. 'What I want, she is not for me. I must to *Italia*. For *miso papá*.'

She looked down at the weed in her hands, bright green, soon dead, cut from its root.

'*Hai capito, Signora?*'

She couldn't speak. Instead, she tried to savour the warmth of the late-spring sun on her back, with the soft sounds of Luca's clipping just beyond her.

They saw it at the same time; the police car, a blip in the distance as it navigated the crossing. An Army staff car followed.

Daisy dropped the pegs from her hands and made for the arbour, the sheet abandoned in the dirt.

'No, no, Daisy! Go inside!' Kate yelled. Pearl started to cry, jostled on her mother's back.

'To the storeroom. Quick. Shut the door!' Kate hoped the stores, the sacks of flour and grain, might muffle any crying. With Daisy and Pearl inside, Kate turned to watch the vehicles coming towards the homestead.

CHAPTER 46

A grazier's son should be taught at the knee that a single well-trained dog can herd as many as eighty unwilling sheep. For therein lies a lesson in character-building as to what the boy might one day accomplish among his fellow men.

THE WOOLGROWER'S COMPANION, 1906

The vehicles approached the homestead slowly. Wingnut, it seemed, was in no hurry. Kate wondered at the Army car. The sound of the engines brought Ed into the garden from the shed.

Kate was surprised to see Grimes with the policeman. Wingnut came in through the gate, followed by Captain Rook and Oil, the corporal. Grimes went to the fence, lit pipe clenched in his teeth, he and Luca eyeing each other across the top rail.

The captain nodded a greeting at Kate, all business, and that put her on guard.

'Afternoon, Mrs D.' Wingnut inhaled; it was almost a sigh. He pulled a notebook from his pocket. Behind them, Grimes leaned his palms on the top rail of the fence like he owned the place.

'Righty-ho. Mrs D, do you know a' – Wingnut looked at his book – 'Daisy Nunn, lately of the Longhope Domestic Training Home for Aboriginal Girls?'

'She was our domestic.'

'Daisy has been missing since' – Wingnut looked at his note-book again – 'the 14th of September. It has been alleged' – the sergeant glanced at Grimes – 'that you or others on Amiens are shelterin Daisy Nunn, and a half-caste baby, offspring of said Daisy Nunn.' He stopped there. 'Well, Mrs D?'

Kate was stone-faced. Wingnut glanced at Luca and Ed, as unreadable as Kate.

'Look. We all know ya got Daisy and ya got the baby. You wanna save us a lotta trouble and get the girl and the tiddlie out here now, eh?'

Still Kate said nothing.

Wingnut frowned. 'She wuz seen, Mrs D. I don't wanna have to haul the girl out. You don't want that neither, do yez?'

Kate shook her head.

'Orright then. You get her, eh.'

Kate went into the house, her head down. Behind her, she could hear Grimes to Wingnut. 'The girl'll do a runner, I tell ya.'

Inside, Kate tapped on the storeroom door. 'Daisy, Wingnut knows you're here. We have to come out.' They had become a 'we'.

The door opened and Daisy stood there, her mouth trembling, Pearl's hand pulling at her mother's face, patting her fingers on her lips.

'I'm so sorry,' Kate said. Daisy tightened her grip on Pearl then, her back grew straighter, she held herself taller, and her face was set, impassive. Pearl sensed her mother's fear and began to cry a little.

They went down the steps together, Kate and Daisy, Pearl whimpering in her mother's arms.

Wingnut nodded unhappily. 'Orright. Captain? Ya wanna do the honours with the Eye-tie?'

Captain Rook nodded. He looked around, his weathered face serious. 'Luca Canali,' he said, motioning for the POW.

Kate went still. Luca banged his gardening gloves hard on the top rail of the fence. Grimes had to step out of the dust, and he chomped down on his pipe, watching the POW with narrow eyes.

Luca came over to the captain and to Wingnut.

The captain spoke. 'Luca Canali, it is alleged that you have fraternised —'

Pearl's whimper turned to a cry, and Rook had to speak up.

'— that you have fraternised, on one or more occasions, with an Aboriginal girl, Daisy Nunn —'

Kate gasped.

'— which Daisy Nunn was not at that time and remains not of age.'

'No, no.' Luca shook his head in disbelief.

He stepped back but Oil blocked him, at the same time retrieving a pair of handcuffs from his pocket. 'You're not going anywhere, mate.'

Pearl cried louder.

'Daisy,' the captain said to the girl, speaking over the crying baby, 'is this the man?'

It was as if Daisy chose not to hear. She stood, immobile, her face unreadable, Pearl screaming in her arms, Ed behind them.

'It were im, orright,' Grimes said from the fence.

Kate tried to speak but could not.

Oil got a handcuff onto Luca's left wrist. As he tried with the other, the Italian shoved him back and held his clenched fist up, out of reach.

Oil yelled, 'Jeez. Give it up or I'll job ya.'

Kate tried again to speak, over Pearl's cries and her own fear. 'It's not,' she said, her voice caught in her throat.

Luca leaned in to Oil, his nose inches from the corporal's own. 'I tell nothing. *Mate.*'

'Wingnut,' Kate called, finding her voice.

'Mrs Dowd,' Wingnut said wearily. 'What can I do for you?'

'You must ask Daisy who fathered the child.'

'Oh I *must*, must I? Orright, Mrs D. Orright. Daisy, who was it? This fella here?' He poked Luca's chest.

At first, it was hard for Kate to tell if Daisy's head was moving but then she was sure. Daisy shook her head.

'No. You see?' Kate said to the sergeant.

'That's bull,' Grimes said from the fence. 'Mrs D's carryin on with the Eye-tie herself.'

Kate gasped. 'You should be ashamed, Keith Grimes.'

With that, Grimes came in the gate to Daisy, his pipe clenched in his mouth. The baby shrieked, sensing her mother's terror. Grimes grabbed Daisy's shoulder and shook her. 'Tell the bloody truth. It were Canali, weren't it? Eh? Weren't it?'

Ed swung, landing a punch hard on Grimes's jaw, and the older man went down, his pipe knocked from his mouth.

'Jesus. You bloody idiots. Cut it out, you hear me?' Wingnut yelled. But Ed aimed a boot at Grimes, down on all fours on the dead lawn, and Wingnut pulled him away by his shirt.

Grimes got up slowly, wiping blood from his mouth. 'She's a bloody liar, they all are, the whole flamin lot of em.'

'You can't take Daisy,' Kate said to Wingnut.

The policeman turned back. He took his hat off and ran a hand through his short hair, his big ears free in the sunlight. 'Look, Mrs D, let's get this clear. Ya not bloody telling me what I can and can't do. Orright?'

'Ask her who fathered the child,' Kate said. 'Ask her. You have to.'

'Orright. Orright. For Christ's sake, orright. Who fathered the bloody kid?' Wingnut yelled at Daisy.

The baby bellowed now, an open mouth of screams, and Daisy clutched Pearl to her chest, shaking with fear. Still she didn't speak.

'Please tell him, Daisy,' Kate said over the baby's yells. 'Please.'

'C'mon, Dais,' Ed said to her. 'Tell im.'

Daisy turned to Wingnut, her eyes down. 'The boss,' she said, her words almost lost in Pearl's screams.

'What?' Wingnut said. 'What you say, girl?'

'The boss.'

'She's lyin,' Wingnut said to Kate.

Kate shook her head, her heart heavy. Pearl wailed.

'Shut the kid up, will ya!' Wingnut yelled at Daisy. The girl pressed the baby into the crook of her neck, muffling the cries only a little.

Wingnut turned back to Kate. 'She's lyin,' he said again.

Kate shook her head slowly. 'It's true. She's my father's child.'

The sergeant came over to Kate and took her by the arm. He dropped his voice. 'Are ya bloody off ya rocker? Whatever your reasons are, eh, Mrs D?'

She knew what he meant. But it didn't matter. For Kate thought she would weep, she was so ashamed of what her father had done. And now, she was ashamed of herself, not sure if she did this for Daisy, for Pearl or for Luca.

'What about Jack? Does he know ya doing this?' Wingnut asked.

Kate shook her head.

'Jesus,' the sergeant said, incredulous. He leaned in and dropped his voice still lower. 'I'm going to ask you one more time and I want ya to wait and think *very* hard before ya reply. You understand me, Mrs D? I'm giving you a second chance, orright? You'll bloody thank me for this one day.'

A gust blew through the garden, and Kate went cold.

'Tell me – *please* – that you don't know who did this to Daisy,' Wingnut said, his eyes narrow.

A weariness came over Kate, so much so she realised she was watching a bank of clouds coming in from the west, not thinking at all. She swallowed and made herself speak. 'My father, Ralph Stimson, fathered Daisy's child. I'm claiming the child as a relative. They will not go to the Home.'

'It's your bloody funeral, Mrs D.' Wingnut shook his head, disappointed in her. Then he turned and yelled, 'Oil. The girl stays. Let the bastard Eye-tie go too.'

'You're off the hook, mate,' Oil said, releasing the handcuff in an easy movement. Luca stepped back, rubbing his wrist.

Wingnut exchanged a look with the captain. 'Righty-bloody-ho,' he said as he marched off, still shaking his head, towards the police vehicle, Grimes beside him, berating him as they walked, gesturing, his dead pipe in his hand.

'Mrs Dowd.' Captain Rook sighed deeply, shaking his head. 'A reminder that the POWs are off on the 15th. Five days away.' He headed for the staff car. 'Good luck, Mrs Dowd.' He looked almost sad.

She knew what he meant. The town would never forgive her.

CHAPTER 47

The prudent woolgrower ensures well before shearing that all gate-ways, yards and the woolshed itself are cleared of wire, twine and other miscellany.

THE WOOLGROWER'S COMPANION, 1906

That night, after Daisy had taken Pearl to their cottage and Kate had finished another Vittorio-prepared meal, she was surprised by a soft tap on the back door. It was Ed, his hat in his hands, worry across his face. Behind him, the long shadows of late afternoon streaked the dead lawn.

'You all right?' she asked.

'Maguire's bin out. Brung me a telegram.'

Kate was surprised. Maguire must have come in the back way as she hadn't seen the truck. But she suspected he was embarrassed about having to serve the bank notices.

'What's wrong?'

'Me dad's had an accident on the bullock wagon.'

'Is he all right?'

'Well, he's still alive, eh, but he lost a leg. We bloody jinxed on the leg front, eh?'

'What happened?'

'Bloody dray rolled back. They was settlin in a new lead bullock.'

'You must go.'

'I reckon. I can get the mail truck to Glen Innes tonight. Then I'll hitch if there's no train. Should get home by late tomorrow mebbe.'

'You go. You must.'

'Sorry, Mrs D. It's a bad time with shearin comin up. But I talked t'Johnno and Spinks, eh. They'll go ahead, gettin ready. They'll stick to the back paddocks, check the fences and the gates for gaps and wire. I'll tell Luca and Vittorio to do the ones between here and the dam, and get Vittorio to walk the woolshed yards, pick up any wire, throw any big rocks, ya know. The usual. Rocks'll find their way into the tracks from stock and even the truck, eh.'

She knew. 'Don't worry, Ed.'

'Can you tell Dais, eh? That I hadda go?'

Ed limped back across the lawn.

~

The next day was full. With Ed gone, all other hands – Kate, Luca, Vittorio, Johnno and Spinks – worked to prepare the yards and the woolshed for the coming shearing.

The real heat of summer was a way off yet. Still, it was hot and dusty work in the yards. The five of them formed a line, in what Kate's father would have called an emu parade, moving forwards, eyes on the ground, looking for bits of fencing wire, or bolts or even rocks that might injure a sheep, or tempt it to eat what it should not.

Kate liked the work, and Luca was never far away. He always managed to be near her, or near-ish enough, for a chat now and then. When she finished for the day, she gave him a smile, conscious that in four days, he'd be gone.

'I come to the garden, *Signora*. Say good night to her.'

Kate smiled. Luca loved his garden, and she loved to work with him in it. She would miss him very much.

Daisy was standing on the homestead verandah, Pearl in her arms, when Kate came in the gate. Kate felt the unaccustomed jolt of pleasure to see them there, and to see Daisy content. She was a good mum.

'Miss Meg's ere, eh, Missus,' Daisy said, as she left for the night.

Inside, Kate greeted a downcast Meg.

'I saw Daisy. Is it true? About ...?' Meg asked, avoiding Kate's eyes.

Kate let that lie. 'You want to sit? Cup of tea?'

Meg shook her head. 'I can only stay a minute.'

'Do your parents know you're here?'

Meg shook her head again, her curls moving. She had tears in her eyes and she suddenly looked very young. 'They say I can't come over now, because of ...' She shrugged.

Kate turned away, furious. The Yorkes were as close to family as she had. 'You don't have to do everything they say.'

Meg looked at her in astonishment. 'Yes I do. For now, anyhow. But I wanted to tell you to your face, you know?' she said. 'It'll blow over, one way or another.'

'Maybe.' Kate didn't think so. She felt a sadness at losing the Yorkes, and a crushing disappointment in Meg.

'I know you don't believe me but we'll be all right, one day. I'm just sorry for now.'

Impassive, Kate let herself be hugged. Anger blocked any tears of her own.

'I'll say goodbye to Luca, too.' Meg went out the door. Kate couldn't watch her leave.

With a bowl of apricots near the sink, she took a paring knife out of the drawer and began to halve them and take out the stones. But she looked up when she heard Fiva snort. Meg must not yet have gone. Sure enough, Fiva was tied up by the mounting stump. And Meg and Luca were by the fence, close together. Kissing.

Kate looked again. They were kissing, Meg folded in

towards Luca, her head arched up, her eyes closed, his lips on hers. Kate dropped the knife with a clatter on the tin of the sink. Meg pulled away and went off towards Fiva without looking back, her head down.

Luca looked at the house and saw Kate at the kitchen window. As he shook his head, she turned away from the sink, still shocked. She couldn't understand it. She shifted the apricots to the table and forced herself to keep going. Bloody Luca. But she had no right to be angry for herself – she was a married woman. There was nothing for her and Luca. But even still, Kate got more and more upset as she worked on the apricots. She felt wronged. Luca cared for Meg? When he and Kate were so close? He should be ashamed. Men.

Kate got madder and madder. She wanted to give Luca a piece of her mind. How dare he lead Meg on like that? And her, for that matter. She looked out into the dusk. He was gone from the garden. Of course. Coward.

Daisy came in with the empty scraps bucket from the chooks, Pearl happy on her back.

Kate pulled her apron off and hurled it onto the table.

'You orright, Missus?' Daisy looked at her.

'Yes, yes,' Kate said. 'I, I forgot to tell Vittorio and Luca something. I'll be back in a bit.'

The gauze door banged behind her. She headed to the single men's quarters, seething.

At the quarters, a light was on in the kitchen. She rapped hard on the verandah door.

'*Sì?*' Vittorio appeared in a makeshift apron made of an old flour bag, tied at his waist with twine, a spoon in his hand. '*Signora.*'

'Where is Luca?'

'Luca, *sì*. Luca,' he said, nodding.

'Where is he?' She opened her palms in a shrug, to make him understand.

'Ah, *sì*. The water, *Signora*.'

'At the creek? He's at the creek?'

'No, no, *Signora*. Beeg leg, *sì*. Beeg leg.'

Kate looked down. Big leg? Whose big leg?

Vittorio mimed swimming. 'Big lek.'

'The dam? He's at the dam?'

'*Sì*. Dam.' Vittorio clapped his hands together, still holding the spoon. Kate went straight to the shed. She'd be darned if she was walking all the way to the dam. She climbed into the truck and in her head she went through the checklist Ed had taught her. Gears in neutral. Hand brake off. Adjust mirrors. Foot on the clutch. Ignition.

The engine roared to life and she reversed, lurching a little with the sensitive clutch. She could not ding the truck, that was for sure, no matter how cross she was. She got the truck turned around and directed down the hill towards the crossing. It rattled under her as she shifted gears.

Daisy, with Pearl on her back, stood on the verandah, watching, her face worried. Kate focused on the track in front in the fading light. Why would Luca go to the dam? To *swim*? That'd be a fine thing. She was still mad when she stopped the truck below the dam wall. She was careful to leave it in gear and to pull the brake on.

When she got to the top of the wall, Luca was in the water, and he seemed surprised to see her. He was standing with just his head, his neck, and the tops of his brown shoulders out of the water. She went towards him, stopping only when the dirt turned to mud. 'I need to speak to you,' she said.

His pale-green eyes looked perplexed.

'Now. Please come now.' She motioned again and gritted her teeth. Men, bloody *men*. Still he didn't move; he looked alarmed.

'Now!'

'*Signora*. I sorry.' Luca lifted his hands out of the water in a shrug, as if there was nothing he could do.

Kate was too angry to wait. 'You have led Meg on. That is cruel and unkind. She is very young.' She realised she was shaking a finger at him. 'Cowardly!' she yelled across the water, the same pink as the sky. 'You are ashamed, and so you should be. Not even to come out of the water.'

'*Signora*,' he said and stood up a little, the welts of his scars visible across the definition of his chest.

But she would not be distracted. 'Well?'

He pointed at her feet. She looked down and could see nothing. He pointed again, and this time she turned. His clothes – all of his clothes – were folded over the bicycle, which lay on the ground at the start of the dam wall. Her mouth dropped open. He had nothing on. He shrugged again, embarrassed. 'Please.'

She went straight back the way she had come, fast. Behind her, she could hear him splashing, leaving the water, and she waited on the far side of the truck, trying not to think about him unclothed.

'*Signora*.' His voice was soft as he came round the corner of the truck, his trousers damp on him, an old towel round his neck. He pushed down his wet hair with one hand.

'You have been unkind. Meg feels for you. You should never have led her on.'

'No, no, *Signora*.' He waggled his hands in front of him.

'*Sì, sì*,' Kate replied. 'You and Meg.' She brought her fingers together.

He shook his head. 'But, *Signora*. Meg, *she* kiss.'

'Yes. I saw. You should be ashamed.'

'*She* kiss *me, Signora*.' He pointed at an imaginary Meg and then back at himself.

It hit Kate why Luca had looked so stunned when she accused him. Meg had thrown herself on him, not the reverse.

She'd done it again, misjudged someone. She sat back onto the running board of the truck.

'Meg is young,' Luca said, and shrugged. He came and sat beside Kate, his arm warm and damp against hers. 'You is angry of this, *Signora*,' Luca said, happy.

She looked away, mortified now by her anger. 'I'm sorry.' She got up and turned to pull at the truck door handle. But he moved, too, putting his arm across her, holding the door shut. She could see droplets clinging to the hairs on his arm, and she felt the warmth of his breath against her neck and her ear, the soft smell of dam water about them.

He tightened a wet arm around her, pulled her to him and kissed her, and she him. He pressed into her, his mouth on hers. At her back, the truck door was still warm from the sun, and at her front, Luca grew against her. He took a breath. 'I kiss *you*, *Signora*,' he said. 'Not Meg.' Eventually he stopped, with small kisses on her cheeks and eyebrows and her chin.

'I'm so sorry,' Kate started. 'I'm married. I should not —'

He stopped her with another kiss then pulled away. 'I do not the plan today, *Signora*. You know?'

'I know.' She hadn't planned it either.

'But I think much. I am good of this.' He smiled again.

'Me too.'

He laughed loudly, the first time she had heard him really laugh.

'Now you go,' he said, and he stepped back to open the cab door for her. She climbed in but sat on the edge of the truck seat and he looked up at her, his arms and fingers against her legs, the warmth of them penetrating through her skirt, as if it were normal. She smiled down at him again and he patted her leg to turn it frontwards, into the driver's position. He swung the door gently closed, then stood on the ground with his hands on his hips, looking up at her like a man who'd done something he was proud of. She grinned at him, fond even of his pride.

'You'll go back to the quarters now?' she asked, through the window.

'I wait a little, *Signora*,' he said. 'Not a bicycle for me now.' He laughed again.

She smiled, embarrassed. With her hands on the steering wheel, she tried to think about driving. Eventually, she got the truck into gear, and released the clutch. It lurched off.

On the track, she glanced back at Luca in the mirror until he faded in the dusk. She drove on, savouring him. The headlights punched into the darkness, showing her what she could not see before. Madness, glorious madness.

CHAPTER 48

Perhaps not unlike the weaker among their shepherds, when faced with danger each sheep acts for himself alone, driving into the heart of the herd until the danger has passed.

THE WOOLGROWER'S COMPANION, 1906

Daisy was still waiting on the verandah when Kate walked across from the shed, after her careful parking of the truck.

'We goin now, Missus.'

Kate brushed her fingers against the baby's cheek. 'I hope you both sleep well.'

With a fleeting smile, Daisy headed off with Pearl to the manager's cottage for the night. Kate knew that they should be at the homestead, but she still wasn't ready to do that, not yet.

Tonight, especially, Kate wanted to be left alone. Luca would deliver her dinner, as usual, in an hour or so. She wanted time to think about what had happened with him at the dam. And about what might happen tonight.

She ran a bath and dropped her clothes on the floor. In the warm water of the tub, she wriggled up and down like a platypus in a creek, covering herself in the scant water. The enamel mug her father had kept in the bathroom for ladling was still there, and she poured mugfuls of water over her shoulders. Dipping and pouring, dipping and pouring, a ritual cleansing of her pain and her anxiety. She took a mug, full to the brim, and tipped it back over her hair. Setting the mug aside, she lathered in the precious little that remained of her real shampoo. Then she lay back in the tub, closed her eyes and let the water run into her ears, cutting off the sound. All she could hear was her heart, loud in her ears, earnest and insistent in the water silence.

Kate sat up, reached for a towel and wrapped it around her head. In front of her dressing table mirror, she combed her hair, trying to smooth it, but it would not be tamed. She got dressed, foreswearing her jodhpurs for a real dress. It was red with thin shoulder straps and a gathered skirt, a frock she'd not worn since before her mother died, when she was courting.

She closed her eyes as memories of Jack pushed their way into her head. Enough. She would get on. She would go out and get some flowers for the table. She hoped Luca might stay to eat with her. Even thinking it surprised her. Brazen, her mother would have said. Kate had never understood what that meant until now. She got out her good shoes but realised it would be madness to walk in them around the garden at dusk in snake season. So she put her boots on instead, with socks. She looked down. Luca would laugh if he saw her.

In the kitchen, Peng meowed at her. 'Wish me luck,' Kate said but the cat shut her eyes and yawned widely. Kate went into the garden with her mother's secateurs and cut two fronds from the red bottlebrush near the bowerbird's nest. Her mother loved to know the proper names – this was *Callistemon* – but they didn't matter to Kate. She was at the kitchen steps, the fronds in her hand, when Luca appeared at the gate, neat comb furrows in his still-wet hair. He held a covered saucepan in one hand and an old beer bottle, with a cork in it, in the other. Kate went over to get the gate for him.

He looked at her boots. 'Beautiful, *Signora.*'

She laughed. He took in her dress and smiled again. 'Beautiful.' He was so serious this time, she blushed.

In the kitchen, he sat the saucepan on the table, next to the bottlebrush blossoms.

Kate took the cover off, and the rich smell of tomatoes and onions and mutton filled the kitchen.

Luca leaned down to stroke Peng. '*Come stai, gatta?*'

Kate didn't even ask if Luca might stay, just split the pasta between two plates, with more on one than the other, and put them on the table. When he sat, she felt a surge of ridiculous pleasure. She'd never really seen him sitting before. Back straight, legs crossed under the chair, he still looked ready to move. '*Signora?*'

'Kate.'

'Kate. I give this,' he said, looking at the bottle.

'Beer?'

He grinned, shaking his head. 'Wine from the apricot.'

'Is it good?'

'No.' Luca answered so fast that Kate laughed. 'But we drink her anyway. In Italy, you drink all the family. Together. For *aperitivo*.'

She got some scotch glasses from the sideboard in the dining room. They were dusty, so she washed and dried them up, then put them in front of Luca. There was an awkwardness between them. He poured a small amount of the honey-coloured liquid into one glass and more into the second.

'Big,' he warned, giving the smaller glass to her.

'Strong?'

'*Sì*. Strong.'

She held up her glass, smiling at him. 'Cheers,' she said.

'*Salute*.'

Kate coughed as the alcohol burned her throat: rough but sweet. Luca got her a glass of water.

'OK?' he said from behind her chair. She nodded, tears in

375

her eyes. He patted her back and she was conscious of his hand on her, of his body behind her. He always smelled so good, that mixture of soap and sweat.

He sat quickly, awkward again. Kate picked up her fork and motioned for him to eat too. She took a mouthful of the sauce, warm and rich in her mouth. They ate on in silence. In the garden, a lone kookaburra threw out a long laughing call.

Kate cleared their plates, the clatter of cutlery into the sink loud in the silent kitchen. Unsure what to do and anxious to do something, she ran water into the basin. But she'd turned the taps on so fast that a stream splashed up and over her front. Her senses heightened, she felt conscious of Luca behind her, that his eyes must be on her. She stood up straight and then felt like a dolt. He must have seen that. She took a tea towel and dried up the first plate, still warm from the water, trying all the while not to look at him, yet sneaking glances all the same. When Luca finished the last of his wine, he brought his glass over to the sink. Her heart fell. He was going. But he surprised her when he took the tea towel from her and held her hands in his, against him. She could feel the contour of his chest, his skin warm under her fingers, her hands, pale and bare, covered in his. He leaned forwards, his eyes on hers, to kiss her, gently at first, then hard. As she kissed him, he pulled her to him, one arm around her waist, the other at her neck and in her hair. She wanted him more than she'd ever wanted Jack.

Eventually, he pulled away a little, nibbling her lip to tease her. She took his hand and led him to her room.

~

Lovemaking had always seemed to Kate an odd term for such a frenzied physical act. But as Luca moved slowly, slipping the white strap off, kissing her bare shoulder, kissing her mouth

376

tenderly, purposefully, she wondered if perhaps she was beginning to understand. When she stood, wearing nothing but her boots, he looked down at them.

'For the snakes,' Kate said.

He laughed, then kissed her hard. She sat on the bed and he knelt at her feet, tugging her boots off. He came to her again and ran his fingers over her face, down her breasts to her stomach. She drew in a breath in surprise as his hands moved over her, into the space between her legs. There was a gentleness to Luca, a joy to his kisses, a pleasure in her she had never felt before. She reached out, tentatively, to unbutton his shirt. She had a moment: a sudden horror or even hope that she might get pregnant. Just as quickly the worry was gone. She had never managed it with Jack. She gave herself back to the tight, purposeful embrace of Luca.

Tesoro, he said over and over between kisses. *Tesoro*. Kate ran her fingers across the purple welts of the scars on his chest. He smiled at her. He made her wait, kissing her mouth, her neck, her breasts until she spoke.

'Please,' she said. When he did enter her, her body clutched to his. But still he moved carefully, a man who'd thought of this too much to waste it.

He moved into her and with her, again and again, until a feeling came over her that filled her senses. She cried out his name in surprise and Luca opened his eyes in mock horror, putting a finger to his lips. Then he kissed her open mouth. She felt him grin against her cheek and she moved again. 'Cut it out,' she whispered, laughing. 'You're cruel.'

'*Sì*,' he said, thrusting into her harder and faster and she kissed him back, her tongue pushing into his mouth, seeking his. He groaned as he came, and then he was still, not breathing, as he filled her.

Slowly, he started to breathe again and he took his weight from her, the dark of his skin broken with sweat. He lay with his nose against her cheek. Peng startled them when she yowled from inches away, atop the bedroom chair.

'He like to watch?' Luca said.

'She. It's a she.'

'*She* like to watch.' He raised his eyebrows. 'Strange land.'

With his fingers he traced the line from the top of Kate's forehead to her chin and then kissed her.

'This face,' he said. 'You. You are my bee's knees.' Then he looked sad and kissed her again, hard, desperately, before wrapping her into his arms for them to sleep.

Late that night, a bang woke her, like the slam of a car door. She sat straight up, afraid that it might be a visitor, putting Luca in danger if they were caught. But Luca, dressing, reached out to hold her arm.

'Is it a car?' she asked in a whisper, afraid.

He shook his head. There was another bang, and a pine cone skittered down the slope of the tin roof and off into the garden.

'Ah.' Kate exhaled in relief.

Luca went back to dressing, preparing to leave so he would not be caught with her in the house in the morning. 'Please don't go yet,' she whispered into the dark. He came back to bed, but not, at first, to sleep.

Early the next morning, in the pre-dawn, Kate woke, alone. She thought first of the day. Today was Friday. And Luca would leave on Monday.

The kookaburras outside cackled their long chorus, and she hoped the lone bird from the night before had found its mate.

CHAPTER 49

The 'new chum' woolgrower should be alert to actions which precede joining, such as kicking, pushing and pawing.

THE WOOLGROWER'S COMPANION, 1906

At breakfast, Kate avoided Daisy's eyes, but the girl gave no sign she knew anything. The *plip-plop* of her shoes around the kitchen was a comfort in its familiarity. Kate relaxed into her cup of tea.

'You out in the run today, Missus?' Daisy asked, looking out of the kitchen window.

Kate was wise enough to say nothing. She went to stand by Daisy at the sink to see. Luca led two horses, Ben and Dodd, saddled, bags and all, from the yards towards the homestead, Gunner bounding about, happy with the promise of a day out. Kate spoke slowly. 'Ed wants us to check the woolshed paddocks and the fences to the dam. The boys are down in the back paddocks, checking the fences there, and Vittorio's going to work on the woolshed fences, too.' It was only half a lie. Fornication is what the matron would call it. And for it, Kate had shipped Daisy back to the Home, thinking the girl had embraced her lover as willingly as Kate embraced Luca. She swallowed, ashamed.

'Ed orright, was he? Bout his dad?'

'I think so. He's a tough nut, Ed.'

When Daisy looked down, Kate realised how much safer she must feel with Ed on Amiens. Instinctively, she put her fingers on Daisy's. 'He'll be back before you know it.'

The girl nodded, her face drawn. 'I'm gunna get yez tucker, Missus,' she said, and withdrew her hand.

'Thank you. For . . . Thanks.'

From the fence, Luca waved his felt hat – her father's hat – at Kate, and tied up the horses. The weight of her conversation with Daisy heavy on her, Kate went out to the fence. She did a double take at Luca in her father's hat. It suited him. Then he smiled at her in a way she wished he could do all her life.

'Kate,' he said. 'You sleep good?'

She laughed. 'You?'

He shook his head and shrugged.

'Are we riding?'

'*Sì*. We check fences.'

'Not with the truck?'

He shook his head slowly. 'I like the ride. You also, I think.'

She never rode just for fun, not since she was little.

'So we work and we ride.' Gunner sidled up to Luca for a pat. 'Daisy is making us lunch.'

He grinned again. Kate hoped Daisy wasn't looking. She must guess. She probably had anyway.

'You bring this food,' he said. 'So we go.' He leaned down to pull on Gunner's ears.

In the kitchen, Kate saw that Daisy had produced an instant lunch – what were probably mutton sandwiches in grease-proof paper, some Anzac bikkies and a Thermos of tea – and she was packing the things into a canvas rucksack. 'Hold on, Missus.' Daisy handed Kate's best garden hat to her, the one with the red bow at the band.

Kate took the hat and went out. She couldn't look Daisy in the eye.

~

There was something luxurious about riding for pleasure, even with the after-ache of her lovemaking. After the gate into Riflebutt, Luca stayed on the ground, leading Dodd, walking the fence line, looking for gaps. Kate walked with him, leading Ben behind her, Gunner running arcs, off after a rabbit or a wallaby.

Luca spotted a gap in the fence and handed Dodd's reins to Kate. From his saddlebag, he took a pair of pliers and a tight roll of wire and squatted to repair the hole.

'You talk nothing today?' he said and glanced up.

She shook her head and smiled. She was happy not to talk, just to be with him with the day ahead of them. Luca stood and reached out for her hand. What she wanted was for Luca to kiss her, but if they started that, no work would be done. Perhaps he knew it, too. So they walked the fence line instead, hand in hand under a bright blue sky over dust-yellow pasture, with a cockatoo screeching a call from the scrub.

When he stopped to look at another gap, she plucked up the courage to speak, to his back, broad under the purple of his POW shirt.

'I am sorry,' she said. Behind her, Ben pushed at her arm with his nose, his white whiskers prickly on her elbow.

'You say what?' His eyes on the fence upright, he threaded wire backwards and forwards across the gap to plug it.

'I feel guilty. Bad for you. I am. I am married.'

He stopped pulling at the wire in the gap and looked at her, rolling his eyes. 'Sì. Married. Sì. Stick too. We each is stick.'

'Stuck?'

'Sì. Stuck.' He grinned. 'Soon I go back to Italia. I stay there. I must. For this family. And in Italia, I have no land. Nothing for you. Not this.' He waved an arm across the paddock in front of them. He shrugged and looked down. 'So. No plan for this, you or me. But? But we are here. These days. Just these days. You know?'

She nodded slowly. She did know. Ed would not be back for three days. There would be no visitors, as Amiens was now akin to a leper colony. For the first and only time, she was glad the locals would steer clear. She and Luca could be themselves and have each other, if just for three days, until he had to leave. What had he said that day in the garden? We have this time.

At lunch, they took the horses up to the bluff at the end of Riflebutt, to a eucalypt up-ended in a blow, its dappled white trunk stretching for thirty feet or more along the ground. It still grew, even with half of its roots exposed, the branches adjusting, pushing skywards.

Kate and Luca sat on the smoothness of the trunk, the lunch set between them, Gunner patrolling round their feet for a scrap. 'What will it be like, do you think?' Kate asked as she took the sandwich Luca offered her. 'At home.'

He shook his head. 'She is bad, *Italia*. No food, work.'

'What will you do?'

'My letters, they say *il conte*, the boss, he come back now to Villa Visconti.'

'Was it bombed? The villa?'

'*Sì*. But he grow her back, they tell.'

'And your job in the stables?'

'I hope. But this job? All jobs?' He shrugged.

She busied herself pouring tea, but thinking of the thirties, not ten years back, remembering the men who walked from property to property, looking for work in return for food. Dodd snorted, tied up off by the exposed roots at the end of the trunk.

'This is bad time for her, for *Italia*. Perhaps like the First War? Then *Italia* fight, but after? At Versailles? She is forgotten. She get nothing. The peoples, they remember and *Il Duce*, Mussolini, he comes up for their pride. So. Maybe it happen again, you know? Hungry people? Crazy people.' He frowned.

'Will you be all right?'

'*Sì*. But now? I am soldier. I have seen war, things. Changes. When I go home? The same, same as before. But not me, I am not same.'

Kate smiled. She was not the same either.

'And my brother is . . .' He dropped his head now. 'Gone. He is died.'

'Did you hear from home? A letter?'

'*Sì*. They say this before. A long time. Now I believe also.' He exhaled, a sigh of weary acceptance.

Kate reached out and put her fingers on his arm. He took her hand.

'I'm sorry,' she said.

He said nothing, his eyes full. They sat like that for a long time, her fingers intertwined with his. A hot breeze gusted through the clump of eucalypts behind them. Luca looked off down the hill where a herd of kangaroos grazed, assessing them. When he spoke, his voice was uneven. 'You shoot for eat?'

'The roos? Not unless you have to. Mum swore they're full of worms.'

'Soldiers eat all things.'

'Did you like being a soldier?'

'No, no. But I must.'

'Now it's over.'

He shrugged. 'The war, I carry there.' He tapped his head. 'Your *papá* also, perhaps.'

'Taking care of the family will help, I think. So will your work. I know it's not the same, but that helps me, makes me happy. Looking after Dad and Harry when they were here. Daisy and Pearl now. And Amiens.'

'*Sì*?' he said, his face clouded with thought. '*Sì*.' He looked out again at the paddocks. The buck bounded off and the kangaroo herd followed. 'They like the cats?'

Kate was puzzled for a second. 'You mean, can roos be pets?'

'*Sì.*'

'No. They're a menace, you know. They eat the new grass shoots that we want for the stock.'

'But they here first,' Luca said.

She smiled. 'I suppose so.' Luca surprised her when he leaned in to kiss her. He kissed her so hard they overbalanced off the tree trunk, laughing as they fell apart. 'I think we must work again, no?' he said, helping her up.

She nodded, sad the day was slipping away. That the days were slipping away. They had just three days left before the train would take Luca, early on Monday.

She packed up the lunch things, careful to pour the dregs of her tea on a deserving clump of parched buffel grass. Luca put his hat on the ground, open side up, and poured some water into the crown for the waiting Gunner, who lapped.

'We go. Now you need the men for this muster? For this shearing?'

'I will ask Robbo, Meg's brother,' Kate said.

'But he work for the father, no?'

'They don't get on, and he wants to go. If he's leaving the district, he may as well stop off here first, at least for the shearing.'

'The family?'

'They won't approve.'

'But you like this family.'

'Very much. They're like my own. And before, I wouldn't have done it. But now I'm a pariah anyway, we need the hands, and I know he wants to get away from his father. Anyway, if he stays in the district, Mr Yorke will thank me in the long run.' Or hell might freeze over.

He laughed in admiration. 'Much brave, Kate.'

They walked on along the fence line and finished the paddock a little before four. Kate was sorry. She didn't want to go home, even to work in the garden with him. Luca helped her mount. Ben moved off as she sat, keen to get home. 'Now, a suh-preez,' Luca said.

Only when he turned an unwilling Dodd off the track at Bullant, towards the dam, did she guess.

'We swim?'

'Perhaps.'

'But we don't have cozzies. You know, the right clothes.'

Luca clapped an open palm against his forehead, as if this was news to him. When she blushed, he leaned across from his saddle and squeezed her arm. 'Is OK,' he said.

At the dam, she made him stay with the horses so he wouldn't see her go in.

'Ugh,' he said, shrugging. 'So we go back then. I only come to see.'

She laughed at him. 'Turn away. Go on. Promise.'

She didn't know why she was shy after their night together, but she was. She had never swum naked, not alone and certainly not with anyone, not even Meg. With Luca safely between Dodd and Ben, Kate went in, the water on her ankles cool and brown. The feeling of her nakedness was delicious. She was up to her knees when there was a low wolf whistle.

'You lied,' she yelled, and dived. Behind her, Luca cheered as her bare bottom went under the water.

Kate swam towards the middle of the dam, and with each movement through the water, a delicious freedom engulfed her. No clothes, no hat, no cozzie, nothing but the empty sky above her, and this alluring water all about her, cold against her bare body. She was startled from her reverie when Luca stepped out from behind the horses and she laughed out loud. He was covering himself with his hat – her father's hat.

'You laugh at this man. Not well.' He turned his back to her, and she laughed even harder. His bottom was white, a perfect white patch from his hips to his knees, where his shorts stopped and started.

He growled again as he backed in, tossing the hat away out. She was laughing so hard she got a mouthful of dam water, spluttering and coughing it out.

'Ugh? Ugh? So it is,' he said as he approached her. She coughed on, for he didn't swim so much as walk. He reached her, still walking, and took her in his arms.

She caressed him and her fingers felt the ridge of scars on his back. She wanted to ask him about them. At the same time, she didn't want to remind him. She moved her hand away, further up his back, and he kissed her again.

~

The next day, they did the same, riding out to the run together, working, talking. There was no sign of Johnno or Spinks or Vittorio, all working on fences far from the homestead, and that gave Kate and Luca time alone. They were at the gate between Riflebutt and Bullant, clearing the rocks from the gateway, the horses behind them, Gunner running loops about, when Luca spoke of Daisy.

'Is good. Amiens is good for Daisy and Pearl,' he said.

'I worry for them, you know. For us.'

Luca shrugged. He was hurling any biggish rocks out of the gateway, anything that might slow the mob or trip an animal up.

'You have it,' he said, waving a hand at the horizon, without even looking. 'Amiens, she give —' He stopped, searching for the word. Finally, he clenched his fist and held it up to her. 'She give this. *Potenza*.'

'Potency? Strength? Power? Power.'

'*Sì*.'

'But I don't know how I'd manage it. How will Pearl be taught, grow up . . . ?' Kate trailed off.

He nudged a rock with his boot, then picked it up. 'You have afraid, *Signora*,' he said, hurling the rock over the fence, out of the yards.

'Yes.' She looked down at her feet and crossed her arms. 'It's Jack. He'll never stand for it, me having Pearl and Daisy here. He . . . he might leave me. Divorce me. Because of the scandal.'

'Perhaps he go. But the *bambina* is the family. You family.'

She picked up a big pebble near her feet. It was flat and round, smooth in her palm and warm from the sun. 'You're right,' she said.

'*Sì*. Right, me. All the times. Please remember.'

She laughed, reminded of Meg's guess − that Luca's sisters had made him more broad-minded than most men. They walked the horses on to the next gate. 'But what will people say? Everyone. The Flemings? Reverend Popliss?'

'Ugh,' he groaned. 'Australia, she is big. Look.' He shook his head at the paddock in front of him, flat dusty pasture as far as the eye could see. 'And she is old and new. All is possible here. Your father, he made Amiens. Made her. No father or family or land before. This he do, your father? Never in *Italia*. Never.'

'He's the exception, you know. Most of the soldier settlers failed.'

'Not him.'

Kate squinted at a pair of birds flying low off to the west. Damn.

'I think he knew. Dad, I mean. I think he knew when he got here, when he got off that train with all the other settlers after the war, that they couldn't make a go of it.'

She'd never admitted this to anyone, not even her mother. 'There'd been naysayers from the start, about the soldier settler scheme.'

'Nay . . . ?'

'People who said it wouldn't work. And Dad believed this. He knew it was impossible for most.'

'Why this?'

'The blocks were too small. No one could make them pay. So he worked out he just needed to outlast his neighbours.'

Luca looked confused.

'He watched, worked hard and waited for his neighbours to fail, to get into trouble. He made trouble for them, too, with the dam.'

'He stop the water.'

'Yes. Then when they did get short of money, when they were very poor, he'd buy their place for next to nothing. For little money. To get more land. They'd sell to him, hate him for it, but sell anyway.'

Luca hurled another rock into the paddock.

'You never do that, you see. In the bush. You help your neighbour because one day they'll help you.' She shook her head, ashamed.

'This is him, not you. You say me it's well to forget. Eh?' Luca turned to look at her, his hands on his hips. 'Well to forget.'

'Yes.'

'I am right. All the times. You forget already?'

She laughed.

'And I wish for the city, me. Before. To make something. But now?' He shrugged and sighed, a sound rare from him. 'Now I must stay Grosio, my town. Not me for the city.'

'Really? But you love the country and horses?'

'Few moneys in country, you know? No moneys for land.'

They turned back towards the homestead, Gunner about their feet, Kate guilty but pleased at the luxury of another meal ahead with Luca, and another night.

~

The final days came and went all too quickly. Kate and Luca worked and rode and swam and made love and talked of everything and nothing. She slept little, Luca bringing her dinner and staying, only departing when the kookaburras started up at dawn. Kate had never been happier or sadder. She lived a life different from her own. But as their last day together passed, they spoke less and less, and they parted silently, when Luca left her at the homestead gate just before lunch. Kate had preparations to make. She'd invited Luca and Vittorio for a farewell afternoon tea with her and Daisy. Ed was not back until early the following morning but there was nothing left to be done.

Now that the day of the afternoon tea had arrived, though, Kate half-regretted organising it. It meant one missed afternoon with Luca alone, his last afternoon. But Vittorio, for one, was excited about the event. He'd hung around the homestead kitchen, badgering Daisy for some sort of special cake tin. In the end, after offering him everything they had, she let him go through the kitchen cupboards. He'd emerged with a shout of joy, holding a metal milk billy, five inches high and five across. Kate and Daisy exchanged glances. He was as mad as a hatter.

Kate laid a white linen cloth on the table on the verandah, picked some flowers from the garden and put them in a little vase on it. She and Daisy had whipped up pikelets, and a sponge and scones, and they all looked rather lovely laid out on the table. But it was Vittorio who claimed the cook's prize. He came over the rise, proudly bearing something covered on a tray, like a magician. He bounded up the verandah stairs, followed with a little less enthusiasm by Luca.

'Eh? Eh?' Vittorio said, laying the tray carefully on the end of the table on the verandah.

Luca collected Pearl from the cradle inside and returned. But Vittorio would not uncover the thing until Daisy joined them from the kitchen. Finally, he pulled the tea towel off, shouting, '*Panettone! Panettone!*'

His audience clapped, to his great pleasure.

It was the oddest thing Kate had seen: a tall, narrow cake, Alice in Wonderland-like in its proportions. She just hoped he hadn't put pepper in it. And how he'd managed to get it to rise, she couldn't imagine. But it was delicious. 'Christ mass,' Vittorio explained to Kate. 'For the Christ mass.'

'Christmas,' Luca corrected. 'We eat her for the Christmas.'

Kate smiled at him. It was so good, so natural to have them all with her, Daisy, Pearl, Vittorio. And Luca. She tried not to imagine how different her life would be in just twenty-four hours. And she pushed that thought out of her head and watched Vittorio's explanation for Daisy, with actions, on how to cook the tall cake. And so the afternoon passed, and for once Kate did not lament the bright blue sky, enjoying the heat and hoping it might bring some rain.

But her sadness came on in earnest that night. She and Luca ate their evening meal together in silence. Vittorio's peppery pasta was as delicious as usual but Kate had little appetite. Partway through, Luca reached out for her hand across the table and held it. She hung her head, and tears ran down her nose into her pasta. He got up and came round to her, to lean over her from behind, and buried his face in her hair and her neck. He stopped still, then straightened up as drops of rain spat onto the tin roof above them. Kate held her breath as the patter turned to a drumbeat. Then it started to pour, really pour. And it carried on, the first solid rain in years.

They went onto the verandah to see it. It was now so heavy that the gully was just visible through the sheets of rain as they watched it. Luca took her hand again. 'Thank God,' she said, grateful for good rain at last, half thinking it might be so heavy the road would be cut off and Luca would be with her another day, or days. But she knew that was just wishful thinking.

Back inside, with the comfort of rain on the roof, she gave him a present. It was about the size of a cigarette box, and she'd wrapped it in brown paper. He looked stricken; he had nothing for her. She just smiled. 'Open it,' she said.

He shook the small packet and it rattled. With the string

and paper off, it was a flat tobacco tin, filled with fat, black seeds. He knew what they were: seeds for the white wisteria.

'For your brother. To remember him.'

'*Sì. Glicine*,' he said, reaching to kiss her.

They went to bed that night under the glorious pounding of rain on the roof. Luca held her for the longest time, lying still, his arms around her, the only movement the gentle rhythm of the rise and fall of his chest as he breathed, in the quenching embrace of rain all around the homestead. When they made love, it was almost more than she could bear, his kisses across her fingers, her arms, her shoulders, a farewell.

She awoke just before dawn. The rain had stopped and even the kookaburras were songless as she lay alone in the quiet house. Her life stretched out, silent and uncertain, in front of her.

CHAPTER 50

The woolgrower's target shall be the good thriving of his flock and its pastures, and so of himself and those whose livelihoods depend upon his enterprise.

THE WOOLGROWER'S COMPANION, 1906

Just after seven that morning, the dogs started up as the truck arrived. Kate and Daisy, with Pearl swaddled to her back, went from the kitchen to the verandah and down onto the lawn, still damp from the shower the night before.

Ed covered the ground from the truck to the fence with his odd limp, his eyes on Daisy.

'How's your father?' Kate asked.

'He'll live. Be a peg leg, but he'll live.' He shrugged wearily. 'I'll drive the Eye-ties in, y'know, Mrs D, to the train.'

'It's all right. I can make it. You stay with Daisy.' She wanted every last minute with Luca. Also, the gossip about her father would be all around the district now, and she didn't want Ed to have to deal with it. It was her family's mud.

'When ya back, Mrs D, I'll come and have that yarn about findin some blokes for the muster.'

'Good. I'm going to talk to Robbo Yorke, too,' she said.

If there was a reaction from Ed, he covered it fast. Kate

enticing Robbo away from his family to work for her was incendiary, given the family's refusal to see her.

'Best I ride over and see Robbo, eh? Rather than y'self?' Ed suggested.

'That'd be good,' she said. They needed to find the men as soon as possible.

For the farewell, Johnno and then Spinks climbed down from the truck tray. They were dressed for a work day, ten-gallon hats in place. Vittorio came down next, all spruced up for the occasion. His faded, plum-coloured uniform was pressed and starched and creased. He'd borrowed the iron.

'You look spic-and-span,' Kate said. Vittorio must have understood because he smiled proudly. He'd even trimmed his beard for the occasion; it was close to his chin now, and from side on, he seemed grown-up, regal, like King George himself. Luca stood on the edge of the tray and then leaned forwards, to half fall, half jump to the dirt. He looked so good to her. He stood with his hands on his hips, avoiding her eyes. Kate did the same, fearful that the charge between the two of them must be plain as day to all. There was an awkward moment until Pearl started to grumble on her mother's back. Daisy rocked her back into silence.

'We got yez a pressie, eh,' Ed said. He took two parcels and two brown paper bags from the truck seat and gave one of each to Vittorio and Luca.

'*Grazie*,' Vittorio said, grinning. He tugged at the string until Ed limped forwards and cut it with his knife. He did the same for Luca's parcel. From within the brown paper came a whip for each, made of kangaroo skin, plaited and bound up, neat and rolled for the trip.

'*Bellissima*,' Vittorio said and then he began to cry noise-lessly, tears rolling down his cheeks.

'*Grazie*,' Luca said, looking at each present in turn. '*Grazie, Signora*,' he said to her. Vittorio fished about in the brown paper bag and pulled out a felt hat. He put it on and looked just like the stockmen around him. Luca put his on as well, and they stood together under their hats, smiling. Vittorio's seemed too big for him. Luca looked like he'd worn one all his life. Handsome, he was, even with his chipped tooth smile.

'Ya better get goin, eh,' Ed said. 'Train's in ninety minutes, and you got the drive.' Luca nodded slowly, looking around him, at the homestead, the avenue of trees, the yards and the meat house, taking it in. Ed reached out to shake Luca's hand. But the Italian leaned in, putting him into a bear hug, thumping him on the back.

'Jeez, mate.' Ed laughed, wriggling out. Still grinning, he was more gracious with Vittorio and ready for a hug. Kate felt a sudden pang for Harry, sad that he could not be here to see them off.

'Good luck then, you blokes.' Ed gave a kind of half-wave, half-salute as they climbed in. Vittorio had the good sense to ride in the tray, leaving the cabin for Luca and Kate.

Out on the main road, Luca shifted up into fourth gear. He reached across the bench seat for her hand, and held it. Kate kept her eyes straight ahead, fearful she would cry if she looked at him. Then he touched her cheek with his fingers. When she turned to him, his fingers went to her lips.

'Lipstick. For you,' she said.

'*Grazie.*' He smiled.

Outside, the myalls and eucalypts shone in the morning light. The miles rushed by, Kate's life with them.

~

At the station, a perfect sky, empty of everything but smoke from the waiting train, sheltered the chaos of noise and movement on the ground. Kate pushed her fingernails into her palms, steeling herself for Luca's departure, and climbed down from the truck cabin. POWs, their graziers, the graziers' wives and children, all milled about beside the waiting train. At the heart of the crowd, by the end platform of the passenger wagon, stood Captain Rook and Corporal Oil, signing POWs in.

Vittorio passed their sacks and bags from the truck tray down to Luca. They had the bags they'd arrived with, plus a duffel bag each, and Luca had a small wooden crate as well. Kate knew what the bags contained: all the clothing castoffs they'd been able to muster (including the last of her father's things) and in Luca's crate, wood – red gum carved and to be carved.

So much had changed. The POWs themselves seemed well, not the watchful men of skin and bone who'd climbed down off the train ten months before. Some were jubilant; today they embraced their freedom, anxious to start their long journey home. Others were quiet, aware of the great losses they must face upon their return.

The graziers were different, too, and many wives had come along, with children in tow, the families who were sad to be losing these men they'd grown fond of. Kate kept close to Luca, unwilling to leave the shelter of the truck. Some of the wives – most – would shun her after all the goings-on at Amiens. With a pang, Kate missed Meg, her fun and nonsense.

One thing was the same, though, as when the POWs arrived: two black cockatoos sat on a high branch of the dead pepperina tree.

As they made their way through the crowd, Vittorio bounded ahead, and Kate and Luca followed. They were obliged to stop every few feet for Vittorio or Luca to be greeted with a *ciao* from a fellow POW, to shake a hand or receive an embrace. When the three walked near Frank Jamieson, his pipe, unlit as always, in his mouth, Kate went to the *Tablelands Clarion* editor. She'd not seen him since she'd heard the news that his son had died in Singapore.

'Mr Jamieson,' she said. 'I'm sorry. About Doug.'

'Thank you.' He nodded at her and his eyes grew wet. She remembered that herself, that a tiny kindness would undo her, undam the careful containment of her grief. She touched his arm and moved on. When Luca nodded at the man, Jamieson looked straight through him.

Kate saw Elizabeth Fleming, with her husband and their Italians. 'Hullo,' she called automatically, smiling. Elizabeth didn't turn towards her. Kate thought she hadn't heard so she went over then realised, too late, that Elizabeth had heard her all right.

'Hullo, Kate,' she said, embarrassed and distant. This time, it was Kate who turned away. Behind her she heard Elizabeth's husband, John. 'In the manager's cottage? The half-caste baby and the girl, too?'

It struck Kate that Meg would find her blunder and Elizabeth's failed slight funny. She had a hunch that she and Meg would be mates again soon enough. The girl was right – wise to let things settle down before any flouting of her parents' ban on Amiens visits, and Kate felt a rush of gratitude for her friend.

Vittorio clenched her in a quick and fierce hug. '*Grazie, Signora. Grazie,*' he said and bounced off towards the train. He threw his bags onto the carriage and scrambled up after them. Within a minute, he'd reappeared, sticking his head out of the window. '*Arrivederci, Signora,*' he called.

Then she lost Luca in the crowd, until he appeared beside Vittorio in the carriage.

Kate tried not to be gutted. Mrs Riley came over to speak to Kate, her husband looming behind. The big woman looked down at her curiously. 'You all right, dear?'

'Yes. Thank you. Thank you.' Kate smiled gratefully.

'You people get any rain yesterday, dear?'

'A bit.'

'Us too. Thirty points or so. Are you working today?' Mrs Riley, dressed for town in hat and gloves, looked at Kate's jodhpurs. Her Italians were already on the train, Giacomo still as cheerful as the other was sullen. 'Such good boys. And we'll bring them back. You sponsoring yours?'

'No. Vittorio doesn't want to, and Luca has family to look after.'

'Ah. Luca's the nice young man, isn't he? Giacomo speaks highly of him.'

'Yes. Very nice,' Kate said but couldn't look at Mrs Riley.

From the train, Oil waved his clipboard above his head to get attention. 'All aboard,' he called. Kate jumped when the engineer released a long loud blast of the train whistle, a column of black smoke and steam shot into the perfect sky. She willed Luca to come off again to say goodbye.

And then he was beside her. He offered her his hand. Kate took it, feeling the warmth of his palm, the comfort of it. When she let him go, he held on for a second longer, his pale eyes on her face, and he smiled, his sad half-smile. He picked up her hand again and squeezed it. Beyond them, Mrs Riley blew her nose into her hanky.

'Good bye, *tesoro*,' Luca whispered. 'Much luck. Much luck, unless . . .' He shrugged.

'And to you,' Kate tried to say, yet the words would not come. Luca followed the last of the POWs up onto the train. She held onto the picture of him in her head, his eyes and his face. The train began to move, and POWs hung out of the windows, skylarking, yelling, cheering, hooting and crying. Kate caught sight of Vittorio, waving both arms out of the window, and Luca, behind him, still, his gaze on her.

Next to Kate, Mrs Riley was crying wetly as the train pulled away. Kate hoped her own tears went unnoticed. The train picked up speed, pounding, drumming, pulsing away, and grief took hold of her.

'Such good boys. Like our own children, not that we were

blessed with littlies. Who'd have thought it, eh?' Mrs Riley blew her nose again. Her pressed hanky had a border of tiny robins inside a crocheted edge. 'So sad to have them go. But we must go ourselves now. Goodbye, dear.' She kissed Kate. Then she added fiercely, looking about as the crowd dispersed, 'Pay people no mind, you hear me? There'll be something else to talk about tomorrow.'

Kate reached up to hug her back. She watched the Rileys go then she stood for a long time as the station emptied and the train became a smoky dot on the horizon. Her limbs were heavy as she walked back to the truck. The quiet emptiness at the station engulfed her, the stillness of the barren plain and the empty sky. From the dead tree above her, the two black cockatoos lifted off and she watched them as she walked. They banked together, languid in the air. Then she stopped. They flew due east, straight on, as if the Dividing Range was all they had in mind – the Range and then the shelter of the coast before a big wet.

'I seen em too, eh,' said a voice behind her.

Kate turned, incredulous. 'Harry!' she yelled, and ran to him.

'Aw, bloody hell,' he said, struggling out of her arms.

'No swearing.'

His spikey blond hair needed a wash and a cut. He was wearing a shirt she recognised from before. It hadn't seen an iron in a while, but at least it looked clean. And he seemed a good inch taller; it could just be the hair. 'Where's your uncle?'

'Moree, by now, eh. We got on the train here at five this morning, the train to Mullenvale and on to Moree. But I jumped off about a quarter of a mile out.' He grinned widely, proud as punch.

'Does he know you're all right?'

'Dunno. He shook his fist at me.'

'Will he come back for you, do you think?'

'Nuh. I bin givin im curry. He's had a gutful, I reckon.'

'So what will you do? Can you come home with me?'

Harry squinted, frowning. As if considering his options, he rolled his whole head to look from one end of the empty station clearing to the other. 'I reckon you'll do,' he said.

Kate smiled. They got into the truck and Kate reached for the ignition. Then she stopped.

'I can drive, eh,' Harry said. 'Ed learned me.'

'I'm sure you can.' She shifted the big bench seat forwards, Harry shuffling up to help her. She thought of Luca's legs that had stretched there just where she sat not an hour before. She took a breath, adjusted the rear-view mirror and the mirror on her side and ran through Ed's checklist in her head. Then she put the clutch pedal down and rattled the gearstick.

'She's in neutral,' Harry explained.

'Just checking.' Kate fired the ignition.

'An I were goin to school. In Longhope, eh.'

'So I hear.'

'Bloody Grimesy were dark about it, but.'

'No swearing.' Kate checked her mirrors, put the truck into gear and released the clutch. They lurched forwards, and Harry rolled his eyes.

'I'll go back t'Bomber now. T'school at Frenchmans.'

Kate glanced across at him then got her eyes swiftly back on the road. Harry had it all worked out.

'Daisy's orright? And Ben?' he asked.

'Yes. Daisy's staying. With the baby.'

'The bub come? Jeez, eh. That'll sort er out.'

Kate drove, wincing with each crunch of the gears, and Harry chattered. She listened. In her bones she felt it, a physical pain, the distance growing between her and the train bearing Luca away. A gulf widening, a moment passing. Her time with Luca had changed her, she knew that now, and helped her see what she had to do for Daisy and Pearl, to help them and to protect Amiens for them, even from Jack. As Luca said: fight one war, then more.

AUTHOR'S NOTE

Apart from obvious historical events, this is fiction. The idea for the story came to me out of the experiences of my grandmother, Gladys Wyndham Mueller-Chateau, 1906–2009. While it is not her story, it was inspired by her. She spent much of her life on her family's sheep property in northern New South Wales, including throughout the Second World War, when Italian prisoners of war were assigned there. My grandmother's recollections of life on the land, of the impact of the war and the drought on the district, the circumstances of the Aboriginal people and the strict social codes in place in her girlhood, evoked a sometimes wonderful, sometimes terrible place, which I wanted to capture on the page. Some of the material covered in the book is confronting. For authenticity, I have been obliged to use terms which are offensive, like 'Abos' or 'Aborigines', rather than 'the Aboriginal people'.

For more information about the novel please go to joyrhoades.com and thewoolgrowerscompanion.com

ATTRIBUTIONS

Fairfax Syndication and Trove

The newspaper article entitled *Aborigines Moving Camp* is based on a *Sydney Morning Herald* article of 30 November 1935 of the same name, sourced from Trove: 1935 'ABORIGINES', *The Sydney Morning Herald* (NSW: 1842–1954), 30 November, p. 17, at http://nla.gov.au/nla.news-article17218540.

John Curtin Prime Ministerial Library

The Anzac Day broadcast is modelled on the speech by the Prime Minister Mr John Curtin of 25 April 1945, available via the John Curtin Prime Ministerial Library. Records of the Australian Broadcasting Corporation. Anzac Day messages, 25 April 1945. JCPML00408/15.

National Archives

The rationing broadcast is modelled on 'A short talk by the Rationing Commission presented to the Workers of Australia', available at publication at http://www.ww2australia.gov.au/allin/livingwar.html and the National Archives.

The Woolgrower's Companion, 1906 does not exist, apart from in my imagination.

ACKNOWLEDGEMENTS

In accordance with Aboriginal custom and protocol, I pay respect to the Elders and descendants both past and present who are custodians of the Australian lands on which I have lived and worked.

I acknowledge all those who were so willing to share their knowledge and thoughts, the academics and other experts, family and friends. I am intensely grateful. Any errors are mine. My heartfelt thanks to advisors John Hall, Gian Luca Manca, Stephen O'Mally and Peter Stanley, and to Paola Barrachi, David Crean, Sandra McEwen, Melanie Oppenheimer, Gaetano Rando and Simon Ville.

I am deeply indebted to those who spoke to me about the history of the Aboriginal people. I salute Aunty Kerry Reed-Gilbert, a woman of the Wiradjuri Nation, from whom I have learnt so much, and thank her from the bottom of my heart for her cultural guidance, her gentle suggestions and her keen eye. My profound thanks also to Catherine Faulkner, a woman of the Anaiwan Nation, for her expert guidance on birthing practices, and for her help in ensuring respect for traditional knowledge and cultural practices. My thanks also to Cleonie Quayle, a Maljangapa woman of the Pooncarie Paakantj nation, and to Lorina Barker, a descendant of the Wangkumara and Muruwari people of Bourke, Weilmoringle and Brewarrina in north-western New South Wales. My sincere thanks also to Heather Goodall, and especially to Diana Eades and Victoria Haskins for their invaluable advice.

My grateful thanks to Jeffery Renard Allen, and also to Alexandra Shelley for her encouragement and guidance during the development of the book – a terrific cheerleader – and to my wonderful editors Beverley Cousins, Clara Farmer and Catherine Hill. Thanks also to my agent, the indefatigable Stephanie Koven, and to literary assistant Jessica Mileo.

Last but most of all, I thank my family for their love and humour through all of the pages.

RECIPES

Kate spends a good deal of happy time in the kitchen, and that sprang from wonderful childhood memories I have of the country women who filled their kitchens with scones and tea, with people, and laughter, and still do so now, all across the bush. A mainstay is the *Country Women's Association Cookbook*, which I use too. I was lucky enough to recently find a copy of the 1941 edition, and it's a trove of good sense and good food. The scone recipes, set out below, are much as Kate and Daisy would have made them.

While the CWA is most famous for the legendary cooking skills of their members, they also do so much to help country communities in remote and not-so-remote Australia.

I'm also attaching some much-loved recipes from my family's collection – Anzac biscuits, a boiled-fruit cake, Orange Delicious and a wonderful sponge. I hope you enjoy them very much. I was raised on them!

SWEET SCONES
1lb flour, 1 cup milk, 2 tablespoons cream, 2 tablespoons sugar, 2 teaspoons cream of tartar, 1 teaspoon soda, ¼ teaspoon salt, 1 cup sultanas or cut-up dates.

Beat cream and sugar until light, add milk and stir well, then flour, rising and fruit. Roll out, cut into scones and bake in a hot oven for 8–10 minutes. Brush a little milk over before baking.

CREAM SCONES

2 cups plain flour, 2 large teaspoons baking powder, 2 dessertspoons sugar, salt, ½ cup cream, 1 egg, milk.

Sift dry ingredients, add the sugar, mix into a soft dough with egg, cream, and milk if necessary. Turn on to floured board. Knead. Roll out. Cut into squares with a sharp knife. Place on greased tin, glaze with egg-glazing. Bake in hot oven for 12–15 minutes. Turn on to cake cooler. Serve hot with butter.

PRIZE-WINNING SCONES

1lb flour, 2ozs icing sugar, 2ozs butter, 1½ cups milk, ½ teaspoon salt, 1oz cream of tartar, ½ oz bicarbonate of soda, 1 egg if liked.

Sift dry ingredients three times, then mix with milk and egg. Bake in a fairly hot oven. The mixture should be handled as lightly as possible and patted into shape with the hands. Then cut into shapes as desired and brushed over with a little milk. Bake on a hot floured tray until a rich golden brown.

RECIPES FROM MY FAMILY

BOILED FRUIT CAKE

Put into saucepan 1 cup sugar; 400g raisins/dried fruit; 240g margarine; 1 teaspoon bicarbonate of soda; 1 teaspoon spice; ½ cup cold water; ½ cup brandy or port.

Bring to boil and cool.

When cool add 2 cups self-raising flour, then 2 well-beaten eggs, and some vanilla essence.

Bake in greased tin about 1¼ hours at 190°C. Cool in this tin.

ANZAC BISCUITS

Put 125g margarine or butter and 1 tablespoon honey in saucepan and melt.

Put into basin ¾ cup sugar; 1 level cup plain flour; 1 cup rolled oats; a pinch of salt; ¾ cup coconut.

Add 1 teaspoon soda to 2 tablespoons boiling water and then add this to the margarine and syrup mixture.

Add this to the dry ingredients, mix well, drop in small spoonfuls onto a greased tray. Cook at 180°C for 8–10 minutes. If too stiff add a little water as they are nice a bit thin.

MAVIS'S SPONGE CAKE

4 eggs, separated; a pinch of salt; 1 small cup caster sugar; ¾ cup plain flour; 2 heaped teaspoons cornflour; 1 level teaspoon baking powder; 1 dessertspoon butter; 2 tablespoons milk; 2 tablespoons boiling water.

Beat egg whites until very stiff, with a pinch of salt. Add sugar slowly. Add beaten egg yolks – beat in together.

Sift flour, cornflour and baking powder together. Add to the egg whites etc., and fold in very gently. Put butter, milk, and boiling water in saucepan and bring to boil.

Make hole at side of mixture and pour boiled mixture in, folding gently. Then pour mixture into 2 greased and floured sponge tins. Bake for 20 minutes in 225°C oven.

ORANGE DELICIOUS

Peel and segment 3 oranges, place them in the bottom of a greased pudding dish. Cream 60g butter with ¾ cup caster sugar and the grated rind of an orange. Add 2 beaten egg yolks, then ½ cup self-raising flour and the juice of 1 lemon. Beat the egg whites until stiff.

Add ¾ cup orange juice and ¾ cup milk.

Fold in the egg whites, ⅓ at a time. Pour over orange segments and cook for 30–40 minutes at 180°C.

BOOK CLUB QUESTIONS

1. The novel opens as the graziers, along with Kate, the only woman, await the arrival of the prisoners of war. Why do you think the author chose to begin in this way?

2. Landscape plays a big part in the book, and we see Kate's love of her environment, albeit a brutal and inhospitable one. How do you think landscape shapes Kate's character? Do we also see its impact on Daisy? Harry? Luca?

3. Kate finds her strengths over time but is flawed too, failing to see things and sometimes assuming the worst of people. Did her flaws help you to sympathise with her? Make her more believable?

4. Ralph suffers from shellshock, or post-traumatic stress disorder in today's terminology. The local doctor is ahead of his time in recognising the long-term nature of the condition. What did you think of his suggestions to Kate for dealing with her father's condition?

5. Jack loses control and continues to beat the snake long after it is dead. What parallels with Ralph's condition might the author be drawing with this image?

6. Because of the race and class constraints of the time, Kate and Daisy never reach a real friendship, but can only develop a regard and respect for each other. Can you imagine how their relationship might unfold today?

7. Dirt is a perennial image in the novel: the dry earth of the dead lawn and paddocks; the dirt of the veggie garden; the dirt covering Ralph's coffin. What do you think the author's intentions might be in using such imagery?

8. Did you enjoy the quotes from the fictionalised Victorian wool-growing guide at the start of each chapter? How did they help you understand the story?

9. The novel contains a number of secrets and surprises. Which were most important to your enjoyment?

10. Kate reaches out to Luca for her own fleeting happiness near the end of the novel, yet it is left unclear as to whether Jack will return, and how Kate will respond to him if he does. What do you think might happen?

11. Why are the relationships between the women – Kate and Daisy, and Kate and Meg – important to the success of the story?

12. The author grew up in a small town in Australia, which she has said is a lot like Longhope. Did you find the town and its characters believable?

13. The novel closes at the railway station, where it also opened. Why do you think the author chose to do this? What are the most striking contrasts between these two scenes?